TREASURE HUNT 1904

DEBRA KORNFIELD

Jill, I hope
you enjoy the
story! ♡ Debbie

BOOK TWO OF THE CALLY AND CHARLIE SERIES

Author: Debra Kornfield
Treasure Hunt 1904 by Debra Kornfield
ISBN:
1. Fiction/Historical/General
2. Fiction/World Literature/Ireland/19th Century

Published by EA Books Publishing, a division of
Living Parables of Central Florida, Inc. a 501c3
EABooksPublishing.com

Cover image by Joel Griswell
Cover design by Robin Black
Interior format by Ardythe Kolb

ISBN: 978-1-955309-12-7

For Marsha and Vance
who helped me research
and drove me to see the Oregon Trail
across southern Idaho and all the way to Oregon City.
I hope you enjoy the way this story turned out!

For William Malcomson VI (Will)
and the other living descendants of Uncle William
(with my apologies).

And for Curtis W. Johnson
and the other living descendants of the Stricker family
and the Friends of Stricker.
Thank you for your support of this book.
I hope many people will want to visit the Stricker Homesite.

CONTENTS

The Malcomson Family in this book

Historical/*Fictional*/***Main characters***

Uncle William (William Malcomson I) 1813–1892, younger brother of Joseph

Peter Malcomson 1838–1900, fictional son of Joseph, deceased husband of ***Cathleen****, Waterford*

Peter and ***Cathleen****'s* children:

Daniel and Meghan, Belfast, Ireland

Margaret and Percy, Waterford, Ireland

Thomas *and* ***Cora****, Kansas City, USA; their children:* ***Shane, Shauna, Josie***

*Charles (****Charlie****), Waterford, Ireland when he's not on tour in Europe or America*

*Callandra (****Cally****); her daughter* ***Felicity****, Kansas City; both adopted by Thomas and Cora*

Peter's cousin ***Nathanael*** *and* ***Sarah****, New York City; their daughter Matilda, her daughter Lizzy*

Nathanael's brother Silas and Priscilla; his mother Charlotte; Dublin, Ireland.

Pronunciation Guide

Aisling: *ash-ling*
Caoimhe: *kee-va*
Killeagh: *cilla*
Laoise: *lee-sha*
Roisin: *ro-sheen*
Youghal: *yoo-gull*

Note: Maps and additional historical information and photos can be found on HorseThief1898.blog.

TREASURE HUNT 1904

PROLOGUE

Boise City, Idaho, Monday May 9, 1892

CREAKY-VOICED WILLIAM MALCOMSON, 77, chairman of the Limerick Steamship Company, missing for almost two years from his estate in Clonmel, County Tipperary, Ireland, sat in the opulent office of Mr. Hosea Eastman, director of Boise City National Bank, confessing his sins.

"I suppose we all thought, because of my eldest brother Joseph's force of personality, that he would live forever, Mr. Eastman. He had always been the leader, both in the family and in business." William folded his hands together to control their trembling and continued.

"Upon Joseph's sudden demise at age sixty, we discovered he had left no plan of succession for Malcomson Brothers, then one of the most prosperous shipping and trading companies in the world. Chaos ensued. None of my other three elder brothers—happy with their own slices of the commercial pie—wanted the responsibility of managing the whole company. Thus, it fell to me."

Mr. Eastman shifted in his seat and took a drink of water.

"My decisions sabotaged enough of Joseph's carefully built enterprises to take his empire to bankruptcy. I now see my fault in this. But the family's hostility made me bitterly angry. I—"

Mr. Eastman interrupted. "Mr. Malcomson, I fail to see the relevance of what you are telling me. What is it, exactly, you wish me to do for you?"

"Oh, it's all relevant. In fact, you should be taking notes. What I am about to request of you relates to the whole Malcomson family. It's best you know the background."

Mr. Eastman dipped his pen in the ink and scrawled a couple of phrases, then looked at William, eyebrows raised.

"I've recognized of late an element of revenge in the catastrophic decisions I made for Malcomson Brothers. In our father's eyes, Joseph could do no wrong, you see. I, on the other hand, could never please him."

"Him your father or him your brother?"

"I was referring to our father, David Malcomson. But now that you mention it, I could never please my brother Joseph either. He made decisions over my head even in my areas of responsibility in the company."

William shifted his gaze from Mr. Eastman to the carpet.

"Mr. Malcomson?"

"I just realized ..." William's voice was barely audible.

"Sir?"

William looked up and cleared his throat. "I just realized why I tried to rob Joseph's youngest son, Peter. How self-centered I have been, all my life! The robbery was conceived out of envy. Peter to Joseph was like Benjamin to the biblical Joseph, you see. My brother gave Peter Mayfield House—"

Mr. Eastman raised a hand. "Relevance, please, sir. I have yet to understand where all this is leading."

"Yes, well, settle in, Mr. Eastman. One Malcomson or another may appear before you in this office one day, and it's best you know where they fit in our family drama."

"If you say so."

"I do. I am about to ask you and your bank to take on an unusual responsibility. It will be profitable for you, I promise. May I continue?"

"Yes, sir. I have exactly one hour to spend with you. Then I have another appointment. We're twenty minutes into your time."

William coughed and took a drink of water. "I'll try to summarize, but everything I am telling you matters."

"I am taking notes, sir."

"As I was trying to explain, during my time in Idaho, with the help of several of your citizens, I have reconsidered many of my life choices. Thus, I have created a sort of treasure hunt for a member of the Malcomson family to follow. Whichever one of them may be foolish or courageous enough to take it on."

"A treasure hunt, sir?"

"Yes. It follows the old Oregon Trail. I was fascinated to learn that thousands of people left their homes and faced unbelievable hardships to embrace new lives in this foreign place. The treasure hunt will begin here in Boise City, with you or with your successor should you no longer be in charge. I have created an account with your bank. You may invest the money as you wish until a Malcomson shows up for the treasure hunt."

"When might that happen, Mr. Malcomson? And what do you expect of me or my successor?" Mr. Eastman dipped his pen into the ink and waited.

"I am about to sail for Ireland. I will instruct my lawyer in Waterford to contact you upon my death. Five years from that date, he will send a letter to my son William, inviting him to embark on my treasure hunt if he wishes to recover some of the money I took from Limerick Steamship Company when I left Ireland without notice two years ago."

"Is your son likely to accept this invitation?" asked Mr. Eastman.

"If William and his sons refuse the offer, he is to pass the invitation to my son Joseph and his sons. If they refuse, it goes to my oldest living brother, John—"

William pulled a sheet of paper from his case. "Here. I've written out the line of succession. My brother Joshua is dead. John and Rebecca have no children. Robert—"

"I can read it for myself. You omit your brother Joseph. Had he no sons?"

"I am no longer on speaking terms with Joseph's sons, David, George Pim, and Frederick. If they or any other person appears claiming to be my relative but is not on this list, you will know he is an opportunist."

"The list contains only male names."

"True. Women's husbands are responsible for their welfare. I apply this to my daughters and their husbands. As you see, they are not on the list." William stretched and settled back in his chair.

"Yet your own wife will not benefit from this treasure hunt?" asked Mr. Eastman.

"Ah. I see the irony. My true wife, Elizabeth, mother of my children, died in 1860. My present wife possesses her own fortune. Our marriage has not been altogether congenial. It's no secret I married her for her money. I only discovered after the fact her father's devious arrangements to protect his patrimony from me. She was his only child, you see—"

"I see. So, upon your death, your Waterford lawyer will advise me or my successor of the fact, and five years later will begin circulating an invitation to your treasure hunt through this line of succession, until someone accepts it. At that point—"

"At that point, Mr. Eastman, this Malcomson, whoever he is, must travel to Boise City to request from you the first clue."

"And this may happen any time after five years have passed following your future death. And until then I or my successor may invest a sum of money you have deposited with the bank."

"That is correct." William sat back and crossed his arms.

“Idaho is an ocean and a continent away from Ireland. Have you considered the possibility, sir, that none of your family members will accept your invitation? What happens in that case?”

“If no Malcomson from my list has shown up here within fifteen years of the date of my death—ten years from the issuance of the invitation—you or your successor must hire someone to pursue the treasure hunt, and any treasure thus acquired will belong to the bank.”

“Fifteen years is a long time,” observed the banker.

“I have my reasons, Mr. Eastman.”

“I see. What I must do now, Mr. Malcomson, is consult my bank’s lawyer and have him write up your proposal for your signature and mine. How long will you be in Boise City before returning to Ireland?”

“I must catch the train day after tomorrow to reach New York City in time for my ship.”

Mr. Eastman stood. “Then we have a narrow window in which to accomplish this. I will meet with my lawyer yet today. Please make an appointment to approve and sign his document tomorrow afternoon.”

“Yes, sir. Now I would like to tell you about each person on my treasure hunt list of succession so when someone shows up, you will know who you are dealing with. My son—"

“I have another appointment now, sir. Write down any information you wish me to know and bring it with you to our meeting tomorrow. I bid you good day, sir.” Mr. Eastman walked to the door and held it open.

“But I must leave the first clue with you.”

“Please bring it and anything else you wish me to have or to know, in writing, to our meeting tomorrow. Good day, sir.”

I will lead her into the desert
and speak tenderly to her there.
I will transform the Valley of Trouble
into a gateway of hope.
Hosea 2:14–15

CHAPTER 1

HORSE THIEF

Kansas City, Saturday, April 16, 1904

CALLY GLANCED OUT THE WINDOW as she carried a pan of hot rolls to the breakfast table. "It's a beautiful day for a picnic," she said. "Look at that gorgeous sunrise!"

"Come with us!" said Charlie.

Three children chorused, "Yes, come, Aunt Cally!"

"Please, Mummy," said Felicity Rose.

Cally looked at Cora, then back to her daughter. "We plan to cut out you three girls' summer dresses today."

"But we can join you at the park when we finish. Josie, you must finish your oatmeal if you want one of Auntie Cally's cinnamon buns," said Cora.

Josie pouted, but she put a bite of oatmeal in her mouth.

"What's the news this morning, Thomas?" Cora asked her husband.

"The St. Louis World's Fair is about to open. Reminds me of the Chicago World's Fair."

"Morning sickness," said Cora. "That's the main thing I remember about Chicago."

"What's morning sickness?" asked Josie.

"It's how many women feel during the first months of pregnancy," said Thomas, turning a page of the *Kansas City Star*. "Mummy was pregnant when we went to the Chicago World's Fair, but we didn't know she would have twins."

"That's us!" Shane and Shauna said at the same time.

"Yes! How can you two be ten years old already? Unbelievable." Thomas looked at them over his spectacles.

"I'm almost seven!" Josie banged her spoon. "But Felicity is only five."

"You got it." Thomas turned another page of the newspaper and gasped. "Cally! What in the world?"

Cally, Cora, and Charlie jumped from their places at the breakfast table and crowded around Thomas. Giant black letters spelled WANTED: HORSE THIEF. An almost-perfect drawing of Cally's face, complete with a curl escaped from her hat, took up the rest of the page.

"Oh no, Cally," cried Cora.

Charlie caught Cally as she collapsed. Felicity jumped from her seat and ran to her mother.

"Why does Aunt Cally look all white?" Josie asked, her brow puckered. Felicity burst into tears.

Cally sat up. "I'm all right. Just surprised."

Cora brought Cally a glass of water. Charlie returned her to her chair.

Hugging Felicity, Cally repeated, "I'm all right, sweetheart."

"Aunt Cally is turning pink again," observed Josie.

"What is this about, Daddy?" asked Shane.

"The story is on the next page," Thomas said. "If you all sit still and quiet, I'll read it."

Cally pulled Felicity onto her lap. Charlie and Cora returned to their places.

"Everyone ready? Here we go," said Thomas. *"Our readers*

doubtless remember the sensational story from six years ago when a brazen lad made off with the renowned mare Felicity. Her owner, Mr. Anthony Finelli, dressed only in his nightwear and boots, gave chase bareback on another of his horses. Unaccustomed to riding without a saddle, he fell off and broke his leg, so the thief escaped. 'God himself passed judgment,' it was said later, for the thief returned to Kansas City in a coffin, accompanying famous Felicity, none the worse for the experience. The thief was buried in the New Santa Fe cemetery."

"We went to the cemetery and Mummy told me the story," said Felicity. "She named me Felicity to remember the beautiful horse."

"That's right," said Cally. "Shall we listen to the rest?"

Felicity nodded and Thomas continued.

"A letter from the esteemed Dr. George A. Tann accompanied the horse and the coffin. In his letter, Dr. Tann described finding the thief and the horse by the side of the road near Olathe, the lad unconscious with typhoid fever. Mr. Finelli sent the good doctor reward money for returning his beloved racehorse.

"Well. For months now, Mr. Abernathy Graham, custodian of the New Santa Fe cemetery, has been agitating for permission to dig up the coffin. He claims—no, he swears under oath—to have seen the horse thief visit the grave. Not a ghost. The thief, he insists, was not a boy, but a young woman, alive and well.

"'Could she not be a relative—perhaps a sister—perhaps even a twin?' the court asked Mr. Graham. 'The only way we'll find out is to open that coffin,' the cemetery guardian insisted. 'I tell you, Felicity's thief is alive. It ain't right.'

"That must be the man Felicity and I saw at the cemetery," said Cally.

"He was raking leaves," said Felicity.

Thomas lowered the paper, then raised it again.

"Mr. Graham returned to court with the same petition week after

week. Finally, the Honorable Judge Jones heaved a sigh and granted his request, on condition the local precinct captain accompany Mr. Graham in the exhumation.

"To the astonishment of all in attendance but Mr. Graham, who couldn't stop laughing, the coffin contained naught but stones cushioned by an old blanket. 'I'm going to find that woman and claim the reward money!' he shouted. 'She's the thief, I know it!'"

Cally gasped and put her hand to her mouth. Cora pushed back her chair, but Cally shook her head. "Go on, Thomas."

"The police, of course, interrogated the esteemed Dr. Tann, who though retired, still serves Montgomery County and the Oklahoma Indian Territory in an unofficial capacity. He explained that upon discovering the typhoid-stricken lad was in fact female, and pregnant, he found himself in a quandary. By law, of course, a horse thief must be fined and imprisoned. Often enough, vigilante justice leans toward lynching and hanging. But when well enough to speak, the girl explained she had simply 'borrowed' the horse and had left a note for the owner stating her intent to return Felicity as soon as possible."

"Didn't Felicity's owner find my note?" asked Cally.

"Perhaps we'll find out," said Thomas. *"After much hemming and hawing, Mr. Finelli admitted to finding this note, but only after horse thief reward flyers had been distributed far and wide. The girl, according to Dr. Tann an immigrant from Ireland, apparently didn't know the penalty hereabouts for 'borrowing' a horse."*

Shane started to speak, but Thomas said, "Let me finish reading, son, and then we can discuss this."

"Yes, Daddy," said Shane.

"What would you do in such a case?' Dr. Tann asked his interrogators. 'The options open to this girl, living the rest of her life as an outlaw fleeing execution, or imprisonment, seemed unconscionable to me. Both options implicated a second life, the girl's innocent unborn

child. In my letter I stated that 'he' did not survive—indeed, the boy Calvin perished, since from that time on the girl assumed her God-given gender. I appeal to the compassion I know resides in the hearts of our citizens. The mare Felicity was returned, as her borrower had promised. 'I would never steal anything,' she told me, and I believe her. She borrowed the horse under extreme duress and has lived as an upright, contributing citizen ever since.'"

Cally opened her mouth and closed it again. She shifted Felicity on her lap.

"'What about the reward money? Surely in this circumstance it was inappropriate for you to receive it, Dr. Tann,' came the challenge. 'I fully agree with you,' he replied. 'I set aside the money, asking God for clarity about what to do with it. I will gladly return it to Mr. Finelli. However, I believe Mr. Finelli's chief concern was the return of Felicity unharmed. He didn't care whether the thief was found alive or dead. Since he knows his horse was only 'borrowed,' I propose he use the money for some charitable purpose.'"

"Makes sense to me," said Charlie.

"So, dear readers. The entire matter might have been resolved there and then, had Mr. Finelli agreed with Dr. Tann. Instead, he has chosen to concur with Mr. Graham's conviction that the law is the law, a theft occurred, and the thief has not been punished. He offers the reward money anew to anyone who apprehends the thief. Mr. Graham believes the drawing on the reward poster well represents the woman he saw, along with a young girl, visiting the horse thief's grave."

Cally buried her face in Felicity's hair.

"Judge Jones exhorted Mr. Finelli to drop his suit, but as the law is indeed the law, and Mr. Finelli's desire for what he calls justice has been strengthened by the enthusiasm of Mr. Graham, the claim proceeds. Mr. Finelli has also sued Dr. Tann for fraud due to his letter about the thief's supposed death and the contents of the coffin."

"But—" said Charlie, jumping from his chair.

"One more paragraph," said Thomas. "*This reporter and the* Kansas City Star *wish to register our outrage at Mr. Graham and Mr. Finelli's actions and our sincere hope that the young woman who borrowed Felicity and the doctor who saved her life may yet escape this travesty of 'justice.' We invite our readers to express their sentiments*."

"Mummy, are you in trouble?" asked Felicity Rose.

Cally, white and trembling, wrapped her arms more tightly around Felicity. She glanced quickly around the table seeking an answer to her daughter's question. Thomas intervened.

"We don't really know yet, Felicity. But I promise you, we will do all we can to keep your mummy safe."

Charlie stood. "Who wants to help me prepare our picnic?"

"I'll help," said Cora. "It's good of you to do this with the children, Charlie."

Cally watched the children run to the kitchen with Charlie and Cora, then buried her face in her hands. *What should I do? How terrible that Dr. Tann is suffering a lawsuit because of me.* Tears fell on Cora's linen tablecloth.

Thomas touched her shoulder and Cally jumped. "I'm sorry, I didn't mean to startle you, Cally. Please tell me what you're thinking."

"I must leave your home, before you suffer too, like Dr. Tann." *I should have known better than to begin believing life could be good for me. Thomas and Cora have been so kind. I stopped watching for the trouble I always cause the people I love.*

Cally noticed Thomas watching her and gave herself a shake. "I'm sorry, Thomas. What did you say?"

"I said the reason you should probably leave is for your own protection, Cally. Kansas City is not such a large town that you won't be traced to our house, rather quickly I suspect. The Anti-Horse Thief Association sometimes takes the law into its own hands if they don't believe the legal penalties are severe enough. We must move you somewhere else. Today, if possible."

"What is the law? What could happen to me?" asked Cally, her voice trembling.

"Legally, I don't think you can be shot or hanged. But horse theft is a felony. I believe a horse thief must pay a fine double the value of the horse, and prison can be up to ten years, again depending on the value of the horse. I'll ask my attorney to be sure. In times past, the thief was also whipped. I don't believe that is done anymore, but it's still legal. Every so often there's an article in the paper demanding reform of our laws, either making them more severe, which is the Anti-Horse Theft Association's position, or aligning them with actual practice, which would eliminate the flogging penalty."

"But I could go to prison?"

"Vigilante justice would be worse than that. We need to send you away until this calms down." Thomas repeated.

"Will Felicity go with me?" asked Cally.

"Let's consider options. We need a place far enough away that this local *kerfuffle* won't be news there. What about your friends the Anthonys?"

"Both Miss Anthony and Aunt Mary are in Berlin at a women's suffrage conference." Cally thought for a moment. "Do you think your father's cousins in New York City might take us in? It's been a long time, but they were so kind to me and Teddy when we first came to America."

"That's a capital idea! The train to New York leaves at 2:00. I'll send Cousin Nathanael a telegram."

"You've memorized all the trains' itineraries."

"Of course! It's my job," said Thomas. "You don't happen to remember Nathanael's address, do you?"

"I'll never forget that address. It's 353 East 53rd Street," said Cally.

"Max can send the telegram after he takes he picnickers to the park. Hang on while I get paper and a pencil... How does this sound: 'Cousin Nathanael, my adopted sister Cally and her daughter Felicity need a place of refuge for a time. I am writing a letter to send with them. My brother Charlie will accompany them on the train from Kansas City. They will depart KC at 2:00 p.m. today and arrive NYC Monday afternoon at 4:00. Gratefully, Thomas Malcomson.'"

"Charlie might go with us?"

"Well, he doesn't know it yet. Let's ask him. Charlie!"

"You called me, Thomas?"

"When is your next concert?"

"I'm taking a week off, since Cora invited me for my birthday," said Charlie.

"Where do you go after that?"

"Three concerts in New York City, then—"

"Perfect! See, Cally? Sometimes things work out," said Thomas.

"What are you two scheming?" Charlie asked.

"I think Cally and Felicity should go to Cousin Nathanael in New York City until this horse thief commotion settles down."

"Ah. And you want me to accompany them on the train. Eh?"

"Yes. We'll miss the time with you, Charlie, but I think Cally must leave Kansas City today, before nosy people track her to our house. And she'll feel safer if you're with her."

"Brilliant. I suppose you already know the next departure to New York City, train man."

"Two o'clock. Your picnic will have to end earlier than you planned, piano man."

"I understand," said Charlie.

"You haven't even unpacked, have you, since you arrived late last night, and we had an early breakfast." said Thomas.

Cally's breath came out in a whoosh. "Thank you, Charlie. Running away will be so much easier for Felicity and me with your company."

"I'm glad to do it, Cally. Max is ready with the carriage. Will you explain the plan to Felicity?"

Cora poked her head around the dining room door. "Oh, there you are, Charlie. Are you ready to go?"

"Listen in to what Cally explains to Felicity, Cora," said Thomas.

As the carriage pulled away, Cora said, "I know what you should wear on the train, Cally: my mourning dress from Thomas and Charlie's father's funeral four years ago. It has a veil, so it will be a good disguise. Come try it on, then I'll help you pack."

"After that let's cut out the dresses, Cora. I'll have hours and hours to sew on the train."

ଓଃ

"Stop fiddling with the veil, Cally," Cora instructed as the family waited on the platform at the train station. "I know you're not used to wearing one, but you must pretend you are. You look like a lovely lady in mourning."

"I am mourning, Cora. I'm mourning the loss of the wonderful home you have provided for me and for Felicity. And I'm mourning the trouble that may come to you through all this."

"Nonsense. Thomas reacted so quickly I don't believe anyone will trace the horse thief to us. Focus on making this a delightful adventure for Felicity. Won't it be fun to introduce her to Nathanael and Sarah? The kindest people in the world, so I've heard."

"I do look forward to seeing them again. How long has it been—almost thirteen years? Their children must be grown!"

"Write and tell me all about them. And we'll let you know what happens here. I have faith in the people of Kansas City. They aren't cruel, most of them. I'm proud of the *Star* taking your side against that Mr. Graham. I don't think Mr. Finelli would have pushed the suit if it weren't for that man's insistence. I'm sure he's after the reward money."

"I hope you're right about Kansas City people!"

"Of course I am, sis. Oh, there's the train. Don't worry, Cally. Someday we'll look back at all this and laugh."

"I hope you're right," Cally said again. "Goodbye, dear Cora. Goodbye, Thomas. Goodbye, Shane, Shauna, Josie. I hope we'll see you again soon!"

CHAPTER 2

RUNNING AGAIN

[Note: Laoise is pronounced *lee-sha.*]

Train to New York City, Saturday, April 16

CALLY SQUINTED AT THE FARMLANDS AND FORESTS rushing past. *Cora's veil makes everything look foggy.* She shifted Felicity's head in her lap. *Running again. It's been almost thirteen years since Teddy and I ran away from Cathleen and Captain Malcomson. More than six since I ran away from Jeb. I rode the train on this very same route the other direction, to Kansas City, thanks to the kindness of those Quaker farmers. I was so sick I don't remember much. Someone—my seat mate I think—stole my money.*

Cally's eyes widened, and she put her hand to her mouth. *If my money hadn't been stolen, I'd have taken the train from Kansas City directly to Oklahoma. I would never have met Felicity the horse, and I wouldn't be in the trouble I'm in now. But I also wouldn't have met Dr. Tann, or Cora, or the Williams family. Without Dr. Tann's help, I might never have found Teddy. My whole life took a different direction because that thief stole my money. I never realized this.*

Careful not to disturb Felicity, Cally reached in her bag for the *Star* article Thomas had torn out for her. *Now that I think about it, the old man at the cemetery—he must be Mr. Graham—did look at us strangely as we left.* She stared at the image of herself in the paper, so amazingly her, drawn from an old man's memory.

Why do I always bring trouble to the people I love? Will someone trace me to Thomas and Cora? Will Dr. Tann and his family pay an even higher price for helping me? Maybe I shouldn't go to Nathanael and Sarah's house. What trouble will I bring to them?

Fighting tears, Cally tucked the article back in her bag, sensing Charlie's eyes on her from the seat opposite. He closed his book and whispered, "Cally, are you all right?"

Cally sniffed and nodded.

"I'd like to talk, but I'm afraid of waking Felicity," Charlie whispered. "Would you mind if I go to the dining car to work? We can talk later, maybe after Felicity is tucked into her berth."

Cally nodded again. She breathed deeply and set her face into a pleasant expression behind the veil as she watched Charlie lurch down the aisle with his black bag. *That's the same bag Cathleen's cousin Johnny teased him about in Albany, all those years ago. I could get Charlie a new case for his birthday. This one's gotten scruffy.*

Cally imagined Charlie spreading piano scores across the dining car table, and the furrow of concentration that would appear on his forehead as he quickly notated the music with his pencil. *I've seen him do this every time he visits Thomas and Cora. I never have learned what his markings mean. I love being Charlie's sister, now that Thomas has worked out his sibling adoption of me. I still don't know how Thomas managed that with no identity papers for me.*

Taking a small round mirror from the pocket of Cora's mourning dress, Cally studied the effect of the veil. *I don't think anyone can recognize me, especially since this hat covers my hair. Cora has good taste even in mourning attire. I love all these ruffles! It's been four years since she wore this dress, after Captain Malcomson died.*

Felicity shifted in Cally's lap.

Hmm, maybe I can take a wee nap too. I'm exhausted.

ↀ

The St. Louis train station was almost empty. "Run around while you can, Felicity," Cally told her daughter. "We'll soon get back on the train. It's way past your bedtime. I'll settle you for sleep once the train starts moving again."

"I'm going to catch you, Pipsqueak!" said Charlie. She darted away, squealing.

ↀ

"How do you know these things, Charlie? Like the history of St. Louis you told Felicity?"

"I travel a lot, Cally. It amuses me to learn about the places where I play, including most of the cities on this route. My head is full of useless cultural and historical trivia."

"Great uncle material."

Charlie laughed. "It is that. I can always pull out something to intrigue the young ones."

Cally hesitated, then said, "I've been wanting to ask you, Charlie—it must be lonely traveling by yourself all the time. Have you thought of getting married and having children yourself? You're so good with them, just like you were with me when I was a little girl. You always seemed so old and smart and kind."

Charlie laughed. "Four and a half years age difference doesn't seem like much anymore. Let's see. I'm turning twenty-five next week, so that means you'll be twenty-one in October."

"So, about my question..." persisted Cally.

Charlie sobered. "I don't think I'll ever marry, Cally. How could I ask a wife to put up with the kind of life I lead?"

"Marry a musician! Let her play at your concerts!"

For a moment, Charlie couldn't breathe. *Laoise. What dreams I once had.* He forced a smile. "There's a thought. What about you, Cally? Have you met anyone interesting?"

"Whoa, not so fast, Charlie. I saw you react when I said you should marry a musician."

Charlie took a deep breath. "Well ... I'm not sure I want to talk about it. I never have."

"I would like to know, big brother, if you're willing to tell me."

"All right ... but this goes nowhere else. Promise?"

"Promise. I'm good at keeping secrets."

"I know you are." Charlie took another deep breath. "When I studied music in Dublin, I met a beautiful violinist named Laoise. We became friends. I haven't seen her since we graduated. Now, though ..."

"What? Tell me!"

"Well, the New York Philharmonic has envisioned an Irish Classics concert and invited both me and Laoise to play. They scheduled a meeting with us June third to plan the concert."

"So you'll see Laoise again!"

"Yes. I'm equal parts terrified and excited. I've tracked her career, but I know nothing about her personal life. For all I know, she may be married."

"Oh, Charlie. How exciting! I can't wait to find out what happens!"

"She's probably forgotten me. But it will be delightful to see her again. She's gentle, but she turns to fire when she plays her violin."

"Tell me more about her. What does she look like?"

"She's small and slender, with dark hair. Sapphire eyes. She used to ask me for help with music theory. I never quite understood why she found it challenging, since she's an intelligent girl."

Cally grinned. "I bet she just pretended to need your help because she liked you."

"You think so? Your turn, Cally. Have you met anyone interesting?"

"No. Not a chance. Who would marry me, a single mother?"

"The right person, that's who. One who sees your beauty, your kindness, your care for others, your plucky spirit."

"That's the nicest thing anyone has ever said to me!"

"It's all true, Cally. I think you sell yourself short."

"I'm blushing. Despite your kind words, I haven't met anyone interesting, nor tried to."

"What do you want to do then, once Felicity doesn't need you so much?"

"I've been puzzling over that question. Thomas and Cora have been so kind, and I like to believe I've been helpful with their children and home, as a small return for their generosity to me. But it would be nice to earn money somehow, so Felicity and I can take care of ourselves and Shauna can have her own room."

"What do you mean?"

"Shauna would love to have her own quiet space, separate from Josie's constant chatter and energy. Whenever I figure out my life and we move out, Shauna's dream can come true."

"I think the girls balance each other. But what do you dream of, Cally?" *I've never told anyone my dreams are tied to a girl whose heart I broke so badly there's no going back. I'm not ready to say this even to Cally. What if I never find my way through the darkness that has clouded my soul since—* Charlie gave himself a shake and tried to focus on what Cally was saying.

"For a long time, I wanted to be a doctor. With a child to care for, that doesn't seem practical. I love reading, so I've thought about writing books. But I don't know whether I can earn my living that way. Maybe I can become a nurse and write books on the side. What about you? It seems like you're living your dream. But there's sadness in you, Charlie. Is it because of your father's death?"

"You're perceptive, Cally. I don't think many people notice that about me. I try to project confidence and joy."

"You do that very well. But sometimes when you think no one is watching, a shadow comes over your face."

"Perhaps I am a bit lonely, traveling constantly with no home base since Father died and we lost Mayfield. Losing him so young is part of it, and I worry about my mother."

"That is so understandable, Charlie. I know how it feels not to have a home. Miss Anthony and Aunt Mary became a sort of anchor for me during my years on the Erie Canal. I can't say Cap's barge felt much like home."

"I have three anchors of that kind: Thomas and Cora in Kansas City, Nathanael and Sarah in New York City, and Margaret in Waterford, especially with my mother there. But none of the three, as you say, feels like my own place. I miss Mayfield."

"Thank you for telling me what you have, Charlie."

"Thank you for caring and listening. But enough serious talk for tonight. Would you like to learn a game? I played a card game called Vint in St. Petersburg last year. It's meant for four players, but we could each play two hands. Thomas and Cora have taught you bridge, right? So, in Vint the ace is high..."

A few minutes later, a young man across the aisle cleared his throat. "Excuse me. We are Jack and Annie. We've been listening and think we understand the rules of the game you're playing. Could we join you? It may be more fun with four players."

Charlie looked at Cally and she lifted her shoulders slightly. *They boarded the train in St. Louis, so I doubt they know anything about the horse thief.* "Why not?" she said. *I wonder how much of our earlier conversation they heard. Oh well. We'll never see each other again. They don't know who we are.*

Their new acquaintances charmed them, and the game was fun. Cally laughed at an amusing story they told. *Maybe I'll be able to sleep after all. Too bad they'll be leaving us in Pittsburgh.*

After a trip to the water closet, Annie slipped Cally a folded note. Cally tucked it in her pocket. Before settling into her berth, she read, "I too have suffered a great loss, Cally. I'm glad you have your gentle brother and your sweet daughter to shelter your heart as you heal. I will pray for you. I always say this before I go to sleep: 'In peace I will lie down and sleep, for you alone, O Lord, will keep me safe.' With love from your new friend, Annie"

"It's Aisling's prayer," Cally whispered, tears filling her eyes. *Annie doesn't know this mourning dress is a disguise. But it's true, I have suffered great losses, the greatest of them my Da. This return to Cousin Nathanael and Sarah's house touches that deep grief in me.*

"Uncle Charlie! Where are we now?"

"Good morning to you too, Pipsqueak. We just arrived in Indianapolis. Before you ask, I'll tell you. This city was named Indiana because it was designed and built to be the capital of the state of Indiana, and polis means "city" in Greek."

"Indiana like the Indians Uncle Teddy lives with?"

"Yes, but not the Oneida. Mostly Potawatomi, Shawnee, Kickapoo, Delaware, and Chippewa. Most of them have moved to Oklahoma Territory, though."

"Maybe Uncle Teddy knows them."

"Yes, maybe so. Some people call Indianapolis the 'Crossroads of America' because so many railroads and highways pass through it. The station we're pulling into is famous because instead of each railroad company having its own station like in other cities, Indianapolis has one station serving all the railroads. It's fancy. Would you like to see it while your mummy rests?"

"Thanks, Charlie. I heard the porter say we'll have half an hour here," said Cally. She waved to them out her window, then took out pen and ink to write a letter to her brother.

Dear Teddy,

I'm so glad Felicity and I could visit you for your birthday and your marriage. It's been a whole month since then, and I miss you. I'm proud of you, Teddy. You are a kind young man, like River Runner. I'm glad he is there to be your friend. Starlight is as lovely as her name, like the starry skies over Killeagh. I'm glad she speaks enough English to communicate with us.

Felicity and I are on a train traveling east to visit Nathanael and Sarah Malcomson. It's been almost thirteen years since they gave us refuge after Da died. Remember Cousin Nathanael running to hug us when we finally got back to East 53rd St. after Roisin and Malachy kidnapped us? You were only a year older than Felicity is now when we escaped and made that long journey back. It's hard to imagine we could have done that.

It will be good to see Nathanael and Sarah, though returning there makes me sad again about losing Da. Their children must be so old by now. I'll mail this letter to you from their home. I'm not sure how long we'll be there. I'll let you know when we return to Kansas City.

I love you, *a stór.*

Cally

"How many more stops will we make, Uncle Charlie?"

"Hmm. Next is Columbus, Ohio. Then Pittsburgh, Harrisburg, and Philadelphia. All of those are in the state of Pennsylvania. And the next one after that is New York City, our destination. We'll sleep on the train again tonight, but tomorrow night we'll sleep warm and comfy in Cousin Nathanael's house."

"This is a very long trip."

You have no idea, my precious child. Try riding an ailing mule from

Rochester, New York to Hershey, Pennsylvania and then fighting typhoid fever on the train to Kansas City. That's *a long trip. I feel flooded with memories... Da's death. Roisin and Malachy kidnapping Teddy and me. Paddy and the gang in Albany. Cap and all those years on the Erie Canal. Then Jeb. Most of this I haven't told anyone, not even Cora.*

Cally pulled a jar of water from their lunch basket. "Sweet Felicity, you're talking Uncle Charlie's ear off. Shall I read you a story, so he can work? Auntie Cora sent a book along for you. It's called *The Tale of Squirrel Nutkin,* by Beatrix Potter. She remembered you like *The Tale of Peter Rabbit."*

"I miss Aunt Cora." Felicity burst into tears. "And—and Uncle Thomas, and Shauna and Shane. I e—even miss Josie. Wh—why do we have to go so far away? When can we go home?" She buried her face in her mother's lap.

Charlie, part way down the aisle toward the dining car, hurried back in alarm. Cally put her finger to her lips and shook her head, whispering "She'll be all right. We'll look for you at lunch time." Charlie frowned, but slowly turned to make his way through the crowded car and the double doors connecting to the diner.

"It's hard, and confusing, isn't it, sweetheart? But I believe everything will work out fine. When you're ready, I'll read you the story."

Before Felicity lifted her head and blew her nose, Cally had time to wipe her own eyes under the black veil that had begun to feel unduly confining.

In the mountains between Pittsburgh and Harrisburg, the train had to stop for a few hours while repairs were made to the track. The conductor explained that passengers could stay on the train or explore the lovely, forested terrain surrounding them. Spring was arriving in the Laurel Highlands. The trio of travelers exclaimed over every new-to-them species of wildflower, creamy trillium carpeting the forest as far as they could see, and the thousands of tightly furled buds of philodendron.

"Imagine what it will be like when all these flowers bloom, Felicity!" said Cally.

"Can I pick this pink flower, Mummy? It has three leaves and three petals."

"That's a more unusual color of trillium than the white ones. You could pick it, I suppose. If you do, though, it will die. If you treasure it alive in your mind, you can revisit your memory and admire its beauty whenever you like."

Baby leaves seemed to open on the trees as they walked. Too soon, jumping over a small stream, they heard the toot of the train calling them back to their journey.

Kansas City, April 18

"Cora, look at this!" exclaimed Thomas, sorting through the day's mail.

"If it's the flood of responses to Cally's story in the *Star*, I've already read through them, Thomas," said Cora. "Overwhelmingly favorable toward Cally, don't you think?"

"Yes! Perhaps she'll be able to come home soon! But look at this missive from Ireland. Quite peculiar. I'll have to add a page to the letter I'm sending Cally and Charlie with the packet of horse thief newspaper clippings."

CHAPTER 3

MEMORIES

New York City, Monday afternoon, April 18

"HOLD MY HAND, FELICITY," said Cally.

Charlie scanned the train station as they deboarded in New York City. "I don't see anyone from Nathanael's household. I'll hire a carriage. Porter! Please help us with our baggage."

"I'm so glad you're with us, Charlie," said Cally.

An hour later, descending from the carriage in front of Nathanael and Sarah's house, Cally stopped, her hand to her mouth.

"Are you all right, Mummy?" Felicity's brow furrowed.

"Yes, sweetheart. This place holds many memories for me. Someday I'll tell you. Oh, there's Cousin Sarah! Sarah, how wonderful to see you again, after so many years! This is my daughter, Felicity Rose."

"Dear Cally. Felicity Rose, tis lovely to meet thee. Charlie, can I help with thy bags? Nathanael has had a fall, I'm sorry to say. Come in—he is anxious to greet thee all," said Sarah.

Nathanael sat on the sofa, one bandage-wrapped leg resting on a hassock. "Come in, come in. What joy to see thee, dear Cally! And this must be thy Felicity. We welcome thee, lassie. Charlie, dear lad. Thee are rich in nieces and nephews, nine now if my count is correct."

Charlie set down the luggage he carried and counted on his fingers.

"Daniel's two . . . Margaret's three . . . Thomas's three . . . and Felicity. Exactly right, Nathanael!"

"Go freshen up from thy long journey, dear ones. We will catch up at supper in—how soon, Sarah?"

"Twenty minutes, if that suits thee, husband. Allow me to show thee thy bedroom, Cally and Felicity." Sarah moved toward the stairs.

"I have a letter from Thomas explaining our situation, Nathanael." Charlie pulled the envelope from his case, then hefted Cally's bags. "I'll follow you ladies upstairs. Shall I sleep in Ben and Jimmy's room as usual, Sarah?"

"Yes, Charlie. Cally, thee slept in Matilda and Florry's room once before, when thee was not much older than Felicity. Almost thirteen years ago."

"I remember your kindness, Sarah. It meant so much to me after Da's death."

"Hast lost another precious one, then?" asked Sarah.

Cally frowned, then it came to her. "Oh! This dress!" Cally held Felicity's hand as they followed Sarah down the upstairs hallway. "Cora wore this dress after Captain Malcomson died. She thought it a good disguise when I suddenly had to leave Kansas City."

"Indeed, I am concerned to know what situation hath required thee to seek refuge in our home, Cally. Here we are. I believe thee and Felicity will be comfortable. Please come down for supper when thee are ready."

"Thank you, Sarah. Thanks for helping with our bags, Charlie." Cally surveyed the sunny, cheerful room, memories washing over her.

"Mummy?"

"I'm sorry, Felicity. Let me help you wash and change."

"I read Thomas's letter, and have told Sarah the gist of it," Nathanael commented as they gathered for supper. "We will be glad to know more when the time is right. It's impossible to imagine you as a thief of anything, Cally, much less of a horse."

"May I ask you first about your children? They must be all grown up." Cally settled Felicity in a chair beside her own.

"They are, yes. Matilda married a young man named Devin. They have three children. Their second daughter, we think, might be a welcome playmate for Felicity. Lizzy is five, as are thee, are thee not, lassie?" Nathanael shifted his ailing leg to a more comfortable position on an extra chair.

Sarah continued, "Matilda's family lives nearby, so we see them often. Lizzy's older sister is Lydia, and her young brother is Luke. We've taken the liberty of inviting them for supper Wednesday evening so Felicity and Lizzy can get acquainted. Would that please thee, Cally?"

"Of course! Thank you! And Tobias?"

"Toby, as he now prefers, is traveling with his Uncle Silas in South Carolina," said Nathanael. "Silas has been asked again to lecture on the true meaning of emancipation. We are distressed at the unjust laws so many states have passed to limit the freedoms of our darker-skinned brothers and sisters."

"Oh yes!" said Charlie. "Thomas mentioned he was glad Toby could go with Cousin Silas, since he is unable to do so this year. I would love to hear more about that. Sarah, may I have another serving of your delicious casserole?"

"As much as thee like, Charlie. Tis always a pleasure to see thee eat."

"I don't often have the opportunity to enjoy home cooking when I'm touring, Sarah. Your hospitality whenever I have concerts in New York City is a gift." Charlie turned to Nathanael as Sarah disappeared into the kitchen. "I know Florry and Ben have graduated from Oakwood. Thanks to Nathanael and Sarah, Cally, Oakwood School has invited me to play for their commencement exercises in May. It's in Poughkeepsie, not far from here."

"Yes, and Jimmy started sixth grade at Oakwood last year," said Nathanael. "Our youngest, old enough to study away from home! Florry and Ben are spending a year with the Quaker community in Dublin, living with thy cousin Priscilla and thy grandmother Charlotte, as thee once did, Charlie."

"I'm sure they are missing Silas."

"Yes, but they understand the importance of the work he is doing."

"And I imagine you are still busy printing materials for them to distribute," said Charlie.

"Yes, that work occupies a great deal of my time." Nathanel laughed. "Sarah is operating the printing press while I am laid up with this leg injury. She is a woman of many talents."

"What motivated Florry and Ben to go to Ireland?" asked Charlie.

"Florry told us she wanted to understand the Irish part of her, and Ben offered to accompany her. They plan to visit thy brother Daniel and his family in Belfast next month."

"Oh, I wish I could join them," Charlie said.

"So, only the two of us are at home now," said Sarah, setting a basket of hot biscuits on the table. "I ask God every day what he wants to do with this house, too big for just Nathanael and me and the printing press. Thee are welcome here, Cally and Felicity, for as long as thee wish to stay."

"I think Felicity is asleep," Cally said, entering the living room.

Sarah offered Cally a cup of tea as she settled beside Charlie on the sofa.

"Thirteen years is a long time, Cally. Please share with us anything thee wish to tell us of thy journey since leaving us," said Nathanael.

Tears sprang to Cally's eyes. "Being here again has brought it all back. Da's death. Roisin and Malachy kidnapping us..."

"I'll never forget the precious moment of thy return." Nathanael wiped his own eyes.

"We did not understand why thee did not go back to thy loving relatives in Ireland, Cally. Can thee tell us?" Sarah asked gently.

Cally glanced at Charlie. "I have not told anyone about that, not even Cora."

"Perhaps the time is not yet right. Be at peace, Cally."

"Thank you, Sarah. Well, Teddy and I stayed in Albany for a time, with a gang of street boys led by an Irish lad named Patrick. Paddy, we called him. He was good to us," said Cally.

"Thee were the only lassie in a gang of lads?" asked Nathanael.

"Yes, in a way. Paddy cut my hair and gave me boy clothes to wear and called me Calvin. But after a few weeks, his friend Cap took us to work as hoggees on the Erie Canal."

"I don't know that word, hoggee," Sarah said.

"Hoggees care for the mules or horses, and ride or walk with them as they pull the barges," Cally explained. "Cap's barge floated from Albany to Buffalo and back again, over and over until the canal froze in the winter. Mostly he carried produce from the farms to Albany, and manufactured products to Buffalo. Most barges had already lost their business to the trains, but Cap was determined to hold on to the way of life he loved."

"I see. Were thee and Teddy with Cap a long time?"

"Seven years. Well, I was. Along the way we met River Runner again—remember, the kind man who took us in his canoe all those miles down the river to Yonkers on our way back from Sleepy Hollow? When he was eleven, Teddy decided he was tired of being a hoggee and went to live with River Runner's people, the Oneida. He took our dog Cash with him."

"That must have been hard for thee," said Nathanael.

"It broke my heart. I missed both Teddy and Cash. I still do. But the

Anthony sisters helped me."

"The Anthony sisters?" Sarah asked.

"Yes. Miss Susan B. Anthony and her sister Aunt Mary, in Rochester. They grew up Quakers, like you. Every winter when the canal froze, they took us in. They fed us, which Teddy liked, and schooled us, which I liked. Each Christmas they gave us new clothes. They loaned us books even when we went back to Cap in the springtime. When the barge stopped in Rochester, we traded them for new books. Teddy and I read to each other and to the mules while we walked. And the Anthonys checked up on Cap."

"Oh?"

"Aunt Mary called Cap an alcoholic. She told him to throw away his bottles, but he never did. Finally, he died, frozen in the canal. It was sad, but by then he was only existing, not living. A man named Abner in Rochester cared for his mules. I visited them every day."

"Were thee staying with the Anthonys when Cap died?" Sarah asked.

"Yes. That was my last winter with them."

"What made thee decide to leave Rochester?" Nathanael asked.

Cally looked down, tears springing to her eyes. "I haven't told anyone about that," she whispered.

Charlie tucked a handkerchief into Cally's hand and put his arm around her shoulder. "But you wanted to find Teddy in Oklahoma Territory, right?"

Cally blew her nose and looked at Charlie gratefully. "Yes. River Runner sent a message that the Oneida had traveled south, and Teddy with them. I wanted to find him, but I had no idea where in Oklahoma Territory he might be. Kind Dr. Tann located him and took me there."

"That must have been a wonderful reunion!" Sarah said.

Cally frowned. "Yes. But Teddy thought I wanted to take him away. He is happy with the Oneida. He adopted their culture and speaks their language. Felicity and I attended his marriage to a lovely Oneida lassie named Starlight on his birthday a few weeks ago. We visit whenever we can. He won't come to Kansas City."

"Let me think. Teddy hath just turned—nineteen, is that right?" Sarah asked.

"Yes. He's a man. He hasn't needed me for a long time."

"How did you find Thomas and Cora, Cally? They weren't in Oklahoma Territory, were they?" Nathanael asked.

"Oh no. On my way to Oklahoma, I got sick with typhoid fever. I fainted and fell off the horse I was riding. Dr. Tann—the man who helped me find Teddy—found me unconscious beside the road. Cora came along in a carriage and took me to the home of Dr. Tann's friends, the Williams family. I don't remember any of that. Cora heard me speak Irish in my fever and kept in touch with Mrs. Williams to know how I fared. Eventually, she invited me to live with her family to help care for her three children." Cally paused to take a sip of now-cold tea.

"And Thomas decided to adopt you as his sister, which makes you my sister, too, and Felicity my niece! One of the best decisions Thomas ever made!" Charlie's eyes twinkled at Cally, and she smiled in return.

"Thomas and Cora have been very kind," said Cally. "We've lived with them for almost six years. It has been wonderful for Felicity to grow up with three cousins."

Charlie yawned and stood. "Well, I don't know about Cally, but I'm tired. I've arranged to spend the day tomorrow practicing at the Presbyterian church. I will say good night."

Cally rose with him. "It is lovely to be with you once again, Nathanael and Sarah. Thank you for taking us in. I'm ready for bed too."

"My bed at present is this couch, since I can't make it up the stairs with this injured leg," Nathanael said. "Allow me to say a prayer for us all. *In peace I will lie down and sleep, for ye alone, O Lord, will keep me safe.* Give peace to each one of us, Lord God."

Aisling's prayer again! But it doesn't work. My nightmares don't feel the least bit safe.

"Thank you, Cousin Nathanael," Cally said. "Good night."

"Good night, dear Cally. We are honored thee hath come to us again."

ଓଃ

Cally's nightmare was the worst she had experienced in months. Jeb's leering face loomed every direction she turned. And when she ran, an old man with a rake leaped at her, cackling, while a faery shouted "It's mine! Mine! Yer treasure is mine!"

Cally didn't know she was screaming until she heard, "Mummy, Mummy, wake up! Please wake up!" Felicity shook her, sobbing. Candles flamed as Charlie and Sarah converged on her bedroom. Sarah gathered her in as she had done so many years ago when Cousin Roisin threatened. Charlie lifted Felicity and carried her out of the room and down the stairs to the rocking chair, crooning softly. Nathanael's voice rose from downstairs, in prayer for her.

"Would thee like to tell me?" Sarah asked, as the trembling of Cally's body eased.

"Je—Jeb was after me. And the cemetery man too." Cally dissolved into sobs.

"Jeb?"

"Felicity's fa—father. Ple—please don't tell her."

"I won't, dear heart."

"I—I don't want to talk about it."

"I understand, Cally. May I sing to thee?"

Sometime later, Charlie appeared at the door of the bedroom with Felicity fast asleep in his arms. Sarah rose to make room for her on the bed. Charlie kissed Felicity's forehead and whispered, "I'm across the hall if you need me, Cally. Think about happy times."

"Dost think thee can sleep now, Cally?" asked Sarah.

Cally nodded and watched the two candles disappear. But she didn't fall asleep again until the sun rose, brightening the curtains in her room. Hours later, she woke to the sound of Felicity laughing downstairs.

Wednesday evening, April 20

Lizzy and Felicity stared at each other across the table. Lizzy made a funny face and Felicity giggled.

"Do thee two wish to be excused?" asked Nathanael.

"Yes, please, Grandpa. Can we play on the back porch?"

Cally jerked. *Not alone on the back porch.*

Sarah glanced at her and said smoothly, "It will be dark soon. Thee can play in my sewing room if thee promise not to touch anything, Lizzy."

"Except the clothespins, right, Grandma? We can play with those?"

"Yes, thee may, Lizzy. Shall I call thee for dessert?"

"Oh yes please!"

"Grandma makes the best desserts," Lizzy informed Felicity as they ran out of the room.

"Well, I think that is going well," Nathanael said.

"Felicity doesn't have friends, except for her cousins," observed Cally. This will be a new experience for her."

"A happy one, I hope," said Matilda. "Lizzy is high-spirited, but she has a loving heart. I believe they will enjoy one another."

"You're much too serious and grown-up to play with clothespins, though, aren't you, Lydia?" Charlie smiled and Lydia blushed. "You'll be eight soon, isn't that right? I remember when I was eight. My favorite thing in the whole world was my horse, Midnight, but I was too frightened to ride her by myself until later. Then my parents gave me an Irish setter I named Rosy. Do you have any pets?"

"Big doggie Caspar," said Luke, waving his hands. "Lydia wee doggie Melchior. Lizzy doggie Balthazar."

"We gave the children puppies for Christmas," explained Matilda's husband Devin. "We had been talking about the three magi, so the children decided to name their dogs after them. Never mind that the puppy Balthazar is female."

Everyone laughed.

"Perhaps we should have dessert, Mama, so we can take our three home to bed," suggested Matilda.

"Certainly, daughter. Will thee call Lizzy and Felicity, Lydia?"

Cally stood to help Matilda clear the table. "I'm surprised," she said as they stacked the dishes in the kitchen. "You aren't wearing Quaker clothing, and you don't speak like your parents do."

Matilda laughed. "Yes, my generation has largely abandoned the old Quaker ways. We're just as committed to Quaker principles, but we express it differently. We value simplicity instead of plainness. I can explain more another time if you like. Are thee ready, Mummy?"

"Cally, would thee like to carry the cake? I'll just finish lighting the candles."

"Candles?" Cally did a quick count. "Twenty-five ... Oh! Charlie! I completely forgot! Oh my. Thank you, Sarah, for your thoughtfulness."

"Happy birthday to you ..." the women sang as they entered the dining room.

Charlie stood and bowed. "A quarter of a century! I'm getting old!"

"We're honored to celebrate thy birthday with thee, Charlie," said Nathanael. "Make a wish!"

"Mmm, delicious! I love thy spice cake, Mummy-in-law," said Devin.

Lizzy jumped from her seat and ran to her father's side. "Can Felicity sleep over tonight, Daddy? Can she? Can she? Please?"

"Ask Mummy, Lizzy. And then you must ask Auntie Cally."

Matilda whispered to Cally, "May she call you Auntie? Since she calls your brother Uncle Charlie?"

"Of course," Cally whispered back as the two girls, eyes shining, turned to her.

"Let me talk to Felicity for just a moment, Lizzy. She's never been away from me overnight. I need to be sure she feels ready to do this. Come with me to the kitchen, Felicity."

"I want to go, Mummy."

"Do you? It's perfectly all right for you to say no, or to say maybe another time."

"But I don't want Lizzy not to like me, Mummy."

"Lizzy will be fine either way. And she'll still like you and want to play with you."

"Promise?"

"Promise."

Felicity sat with her brow furrowed, intense concentration on her face.

"Mummy, I'm worried about leaving you alone. You get scared during the night. I think you need me with you."

Tears rushed to Cally's eyes. "Oh, sweetheart. It's all right. I'll be fine if you go with Lizzy."

"Promise?"

"Promise."

Felicity leaped from the stool and ran into the dining room. "I can go, Lizzy! What should I take? I never did this before."

"Just your nightie, and clothes for tomorrow," said Matilda.

"I'll be right back."

Felicity pounded upstairs, Cally trailing after. *How long has Felicity felt she must take care of me, instead of the other way around? I wish I could stop having nightmares!*

"Oh, what did you say, Felicity? Yes, that's a fine bag for packing your things."

“I’ll see you tomorrow, Mummy!” Felicity hurried down the stairs, with Cally once again trailing after.

How can I stop her from growing up so fast?

“Charlie, thee hath a fat letter from Kansas City,” said Sarah a few days later. Charlie shook raindrops from his summer coat and accepted the package.

“Oh my. Is Cally around? This is something she’ll want to see.”

“Good news, I hope. Yes, Cally is on the back porch reading to Felicity. Apparently, they both love the rain.”

“I’ll wait until they come in. But yes, good news. The Kansas City community has spoken loudly in favor of forgiving Cally. Look here: long lists of opinions printed in the KC *Star* on her behalf. The decision will be up to the judge, but perhaps she and Felicity can go home sooner than we thought! That’s good, since I have only one more week off before my New York concert series begins in Albany May 3 and New York City May 6, 7, and 8.”

“Then Oakwood School May 10. Thank you for this, Charlie,” said Sarah.

“I’m glad I can do it,” said Charlie. “Then Baltimore May 13 and 14. Here, read this.”

“‘What kind of people would we be, to punish a young girl—a mother at that—for doing something under great duress she didn’t even realize was wrong?’” Sarah read aloud.

“Here’s another,” said Charlie. “‘If Mr. Graham is suffering financial need, perhaps the community could take up a collection for him. But if he is simply greedy, shame on him! How could he want such ill to befall this beautiful girl and her child? Has our society fallen so low?’”

“‘Clearly this young lady was not a typical horse thief, nor ought she be treated as one. I salute Dr. Tann for his courage and his charity,’” read Sarah.

"Oh, there you are, Cally," said Charlie. "I think you'll be happy with these newspaper clippings, just arrived from Thomas."

"Felicity went to show her new book to Nathanael." Cally blushed as she read. "These people don't know me. They only know a few things about me."

"Well, if they did know you, they would feel even more strongly that you should be protected, Cally," said Charlie. "Thomas and Cora both sent letters as well. Oh my."

"What is it, Charlie?"

"I'm not sure yet. Let me sit down and read this more carefully."

"A cup of tea in your hand, Charlie and Cally?" asked Sarah.

"Oh, thank you, Sarah. Come help me decipher this, Cally. Do you remember hearing about our eccentric Uncle William? I think I told you about Margaret's wedding, when he tried to steal from my father."

"You, Thomas, and Cora foiled his plan!"

Charlie laughed. "We did, yes. That's when Thomas first heard Cora's name."

"I didn't know that," said Cally.

"So, let me read what Thomas says: 'Uncle William died way back in '92. For almost two years before that, no one knew where he was. Apparently, without telling anyone, after Margaret's wedding, he sailed to the United States and wandered west to the territory of Idaho.'"

"Where is Idaho?" asked Cally.

"It's way out west; a new state as of 1890. Thomas says, 'Uncle William left a will in Idaho as well as his official one in Waterford, to be claimed by the first Malcomson to show up in Boise City, Idaho. No one in Ireland has wanted to travel so far.'"

"If your uncle died in 1892, why are you just learning about this now?"

"Hmm, let me see. Here it is: He instructed his bank in Boise City not to open his safe until a member of the Malcomson family showed up. An invitation circulated through the extended family in order of proximity to Uncle William, which took a long time. Finally, it reached our branch of the family. After Daniel rejected the invitation, he mailed it to Mummy at Margaret's, and she sent it to Thomas."

"Must Thomas go to Idaho to open the will?"

"It's more complicated than that," said Charlie. "Thomas says, 'Uncle William must have had spare time on his hands, because he devised a treasure hunt for one of us Malcomsons to follow if we wish to discover what he left in his will. The first clue is at the bank in Boise City."

"A treasure hunt?"

"I'm as puzzled as you, Cally. I suppose the first clue leads to a second, and so forth, until someone finds the treasure, whatever it is. 'What a lark!' Thomas says."

"I've never imagined such a thing!"

"Thomas wonders whether we should laugh at this—one more story to tell about funny old Uncle William. Or whether one of us should travel to Idaho and try to follow the clues."

"What an odd family!"

Charlie chuckled and stood. "I think Uncle William wins odd fellow of the century. Here's a letter for you from Cora, one for Felicity from Shauna, and one for you from Germany."

"The Anthonys! Thank you!"

"I have a supper appointment with a scheduler from the New York Philharmonic. You can entertain Nathanael and Sarah with Uncle William's enigmatic proposal."

"Have a nice evening, Charlie. Oh—is this your meeting with Laoise?"

"No. That's not until next month, June third. Cally, think about how we should respond to Thomas. You're part of this family! 'Bye."

Cally shook her head as the front door closed. *I am and am not part of this family. There's so much the Malcomsons share that I don't know. Thomas and Cora's little family though—there I do feel at home. All because of Cora's kindness.* She settled back on the sofa and read Cora's beautiful script.

Cally, I miss you so much! I can't wait for this kerfuffle to end so you can come back home. We all miss you. The children don't know how to deal with being only three. Josie sets places at the table for you and Felicity. After you left, she came to me saying "I can't find Felicity anywhere." She doesn't understand how far away you are.

I'm delighted with the outpouring of support for you in the papers. Thomas says it may influence the judge's decision. I wish we knew how long we'll have to wait for him to clear your name. Mr. Graham's and Mr. Finelli's attitudes seem barbaric to me. Perhaps your case will help change our laws toward penalties more civilized than long imprisonment. Or what the vigilantes do: shooting horse thieves on sight!

Thomas and I met with Richard and Athena Williams, hoping to think of some way to help you, but it seems we can only wait. Dr. Tann returned the award money to Mr. Finelli. Some people say he should use it to aid you and Felicity. We'll see...

Meanwhile, what do you think of traveling to Idaho? Thomas is halfway inclined to use his vacation time to pursue this eccentricity of Uncle William's.

All for now, my dear. I'll write again soon.

Sending you my love,

Your sister Cora

CHAPTER 4

TOO-CLOSE ENCOUNTER

New York City, Wednesday, April 27

"THAT'S PRETTY, CALLY. Is it for Felicity?" asked Charlie.

"No, this dress is for Shauna. Almost finished."

"How did you learn to sew?"

"Aisling taught me to make doll clothes. The rest I taught myself. Do you want to sit down, Charlie?" Cally moved over on the sofa.

"Sure. I've been puzzling over Uncle William's treasure hunt."

"Before we talk about that, I have something for you. A belated birthday gift." Cally pointed to a large, beautifully wrapped package on a side table.

"A new case for my music! Cally, this is perfect! I guess you noticed my old one has become disreputable. Thank you very much."

"Look inside."

"An elegant new cravat! You are truly gifted with a needle, Cally! I love the grey and cream combination. Thank you!"

"You're welcome. I'm sorry it's late."

"Never too late for such special gifts." Charlie sat again on the sofa and hugged her.

"You and Thomas can decide about the treasure hunt. Thomas sent me a letter from Aunt Mary saying she and Miss Anthony will be back in

Rochester next Tuesday. I want to visit them next week while you're playing your concerts."

"Good idea, Cally. I have a concert Tuesday in Albany. We could ride to Albany together, and then you can switch to the train for Rochester. Or you could stay overnight with me at Cousin Johnny's so you can attend my concert at their church. I always stay with them when I'm in Albany. Cally—is something wrong?"

"A wash of memories. I went to that church every Sunday when Teddy and I were with the gang. Sometimes I saw your cousin."

"Did he recognize you?" asked Charlie.

"Oh no. I was a boy then, remember? Teddy and I were part of a crowd of ragged lads, not dressed up fancy like we were when he met us with your family. One reason I decided to be Calvin is so our cousins Roisin and Malachy wouldn't recognize me. But I never saw them again, after your father talked to them at your concert."

Charlie touched her arm. "Why did you run away from us, Cally? Can we talk about that sometime? It's a piece of the puzzle I've never understood."

Cally dropped her head. "I don't know. Maybe ... Someday ..." *I feel panicky when anyone asks about us running away from the Malcomsons in Albany. Will I ever get over this?*

Charlie pulled her into another hug. "I won't force or pressure you, Cally. But I care. I hope one day you can trust me with this."

"It's not that I don't trust you, Charlie. It's just—hard. And once I say it, I can't unsay it."

"All right. But what do you think? Shall we travel to Albany together on Tuesday?"

"Yes! I'll check the train schedule to decide about staying for your concert."

"Thanks again for my beautiful birthday gift!"

Albany, Wednesday, May 4

As Johnny's carriage rumbled back toward the Albany train station the morning after the concert, Charlie said, "Cally, I'm riding with you and Felicity to Rochester. You're worried about something, otherwise you wouldn't be wearing Cora's mourning dress and veil. We're a long way from Kansas City."

"But do you have time, Charlie? I know we'll be fine. I just feel safer in disguise."

"Safer? What are you afraid of?"

"Of—maybe of my own memories." *I don't want to talk about Jeb.* "You didn't answer my question."

"I don't have another concert until Friday. So yes. I have time." Charlie warmed to his own idea. "And I want to go with you. I would love to meet the Anthony sisters who were so good to you. Susan B. Anthony has become a household name in America!"

"She's old now—84. That's one reason I want to go. I may not have another opportunity to see her. Aunt Mary is younger."

"If your friends have room for me, I'll stay overnight and return to New York City tomorrow. Is that acceptable?"

"I think so, Charlie. They always have other people living with them. We'll find out when we get there whether they have space."

"Here we are at the station. I'll buy three tickets to Rochester."

"Goodbye, Cousin Johnny. Thank you for your hospitality!"

⁂

"Rochester will take four hours, since the train makes so many stops," said Charlie.

"So long?" groaned Felicity.

"It's a lot faster than on the barge, Felicity!" Cally laughed. "The mules walked about four miles an hour, so it took us several days to make this trip."

"I miss Lizzy!" said Felicity.

Cally kept her focus on Charlie and Felicity, bothered by a young man across the aisle who kept staring at her. *He seems familiar somehow . . .*

Felicity scooted to the opposite bench beside Charlie so he could read to her. Cally took out her embroidery. *This will give me something to do with my hands and my eyes.*

After the conductor collected their tickets, the young man stood. "May I?" he asked, sitting beside Cally before Charlie had the chance to protest. "It's the lassie who tipped me off. She's the spittin' image of a lass I once knew, named Cally. Or Calvin."

"Paddy? Is it really you?"

"In the flesh, ma'am. I'm sorry for yer loss."

"Oh. Thank you."

"This lassie must be yer child."

Felicity stared, her eyes flicking to her mother, then back to the stranger.

"Yes! Felicity, this is Paddy—or are you Patrick now? And this is my brother Charlie."

"Yer brother? I didn't know ye had any brothers besides Teddy."

"Charlie is my adopted brother."

Charlie extended his hand. "I'm pleased to meet you, Patrick. Shall Felicity and I give you two a few minutes? I would like some coffee."

"It will be quick. I'm getting off at Amsterdam. I live there now, Cally. I've been in Albany for business."

As they walked away, Cally heard Felicity say, "Uncle Charlie, what does adopted mean?" *She's never known life apart from the Malcomsons.*

Cally turned to Paddy. "What kind of work do you do now?"

"I sell insurance for New York Life."

Cally laughed. "I think you could sell anything to anyone, Paddy."

"It's going well. Enough to keep my wife and family happy."

"You're married and have children?"

"Yes! My wife is Fiona. We have a lad and a lassie, Brody and Cate. Come visit us!"

"I would love to, Paddy. What fun to run into you like this!"

"But tell me about ye. Is it yer husband ye have lost? Do ye still live in Rochester?"

"Oh no. I left Rochester many years ago, before Felicity was born. I live in Kansas City."

"Where is that?"

"A long way from here, in the middle of the country. People call it the heart of America."

"I never saw ye again in Albany after Cap died."

"Yes, that was sad."

"Does Teddy live in Kansas City with ye?"

"No, he lives in Oklahoma Territory with the Oneida. He's happy with them. I visit when I can." The train slowed.

"Please come visit so we can catch up properly, Cally. Here's my card. Weekends are best. Yer Felicity can play with my Brody. And Cate is just learning to walk. Goodbye, Cally. It's good to see ye again."

"Goodbye, Paddy."

Cally only began to tremble after Paddy left her. *I wonder if he knows anything about Jeb...* She heard Felicity's voice before she saw Charlie's head above the confusion of Amsterdam passengers in the aisle. "Do you think that man might be my daddy?" Felicity asked.

Oh no. She's never asked me before about her father. This trip is bringing up questions that didn't occur to her at home. What shall I tell her?

"Mummy, we got you a lemonade! Is that man gone? Can you read to me now? Uncle Charlie has to work."

"Certainly, sweetheart. Let me just finish embroidering this flower—three more stitches."

"Will you teach me to sew, Mummy?"

When the conductor announced Rochester, Cally breathed deeply. *Felicity never asked me more about Paddy. Whatever Charlie said to her must have been enough. For now.*

I could walk this path in my sleep. Cally switched her small valise to her other hand and smiled at Felicity who skipped ahead then back to her, excited to be off the train. *How kind the Anthonys were to me! I didn't fully realize as a child how generous they were.*

They turned the corner onto the Anthonys' street. Cally gasped and took off running.

"What's wrong, Cally? Oh … Felicity, stay by me."

A large house swarmed with police. Neighbors gathered in groups on the sidewalk. Cally darted between them, ignored a policeman's shout, and ran into the house. Miss Anthony and Aunt Mary sat side by side on a couch as Dr. Hempfield bandaged Aunt Mary's right arm. Her face was scratched, her dress spattered in red.

Cally jerked off her veil and sank to her knees beside Miss Anthony. "What happened? Are you all right?"

"Cally, dear, how good of you to come today, of all days," said Miss Anthony. "We've been vandalized. Mary caught the thief in the act and has a fractured arm to show for it. But she did knock him out, and he is in custody. My guess is that he broke into the house and stayed here while we were in Germany, taking things and selling them a few at a time."

Miss Anthony stopped, breathless. Aunt Mary took up the tale. "He must not have known we were back, because he walked in as if he owned the place. We were upstairs working. I heard the door—you know how it creaks—and crept down the back stairs. Caught him defacing the kitchen wall—painting ugly words all over it. This isn't blood on my dress—it's paint."

"Mary, that's all I can do for you now," said Dr. Hempfield. "The swelling must go down before I can cast your arm properly. Use this sling and come to my surgery three days from now. If the pain is bad, you may use laudanum."

"Thank you, Doctor. No, I don't want laudanum. I prefer pain to a fuzzy brain."

As the doctor left, Cally saw Charlie and Felicity standing in the doorway. She shook her head.

"Felicity, let's go for a walk by the river. It's such a beautiful day," said Charlie. Cally smiled her thanks.

Miss Anthony said, "This seems to be a personal crime, Cally. The thief apparently doesn't appreciate our efforts toward women's suffrage. But there's more to it than that. Don't go into the kitchen. I'll ask Abner to paint over the words."

"I'm not a child anymore, Miss Anthony," said Cally. She walked straight back to the kitchen, a policeman following her, Aunt Mary in his wake. Huge red letters shouted across the wall: WHERE'S THE WHORE? SHE'S MINE, MINE!

"Jeb," Cally whispered, and fell to the floor in a dead faint.

"We can't stay here," Cally heard Aunt Mary say, as she regained consciousness on the couch the Anthonys had occupied minutes before. "The police have told us so. We'll go to the guesthouse on Mount Hope Avenue, near Highland Park. Abner has already gone for the carriage. Oh, you're waking up, Cally."

"My dear, I did tell you not to go to the kitchen," said Miss Anthony, her blue-veined hands fluttering. "You were more obedient when you lived with us. We called Dr. Hempfield to come back, and these two strangers came in too."

"I'm sorry, Miss Anthony." Cally sat up, relaxing when she caught sight of Charlie across the room, tear-stained Felicity in his lap. "Have you met my brother Charlie and my daughter Felicity?"

"Your brother?" said Aunt Mary. "Never mind; you can tell us later. Welcome, young man, young lady. I'm sorry you've found us in such a state."

"Allow me to check you over, please, Callandra. You've suffered a shock." The doctor bent over her.

"I'm fine, truly, Doctor."

"You must rest." He turned toward Aunt Mary, an envelope of powder in his hand. "Oh, your arm . . . "

"I can do it," Miss Anthony said. "Tell me exactly what to do."

"Mix half of this into a glass of water. Callandra should drink it all over the next ten minutes or so. And likewise, the other half, an hour from now." Dr. Hempfield glanced around. "Does anyone else here need my services? Then I'll be going. Again. Mary, you absolutely must not use that arm for anything, is that clear in your mind? Let this young man here know what you need. He looks amenable to helping out."

"Indeed, sir. Whatever I can do," said Charlie.

"You know where to find me if you need me, Mary. Susan. Good afternoon."

"We will stay at the guesthouse until the police allow us to come home, Dr. Hempfield," said Miss Anthony.

"So I heard, Susan. That's good. All of you need rest. Good afternoon." The doctor bowed and escaped.

"There's Abner now. Young man—Charlie, is it?—will you please go upstairs to fetch our bags? You'll find one in each of the two front bedrooms. We've been so out of kilter since returning from Germany we haven't unpacked." said Aunt Mary.

"Right away, ma'am," said Charlie.

"Abner, you remember Cally? Of course, you do, though she used to be Calvin," said Aunt Mary.

Abner's eyes widened as he stared at Cally, mumbling, "A pleasure to see you again."

"Abner, assist Cally and her daughter to the carriage, along with their things. Then come back for Susan and me. We'll be crowded, but it will be better than making two trips. The young man—Charles, is it?—will sit on the bench with you. The city has grown since you were here, Cally. The traffic is insufferable." Aunt Mary fanned herself with her good hand.

"Who could have guessed all this would happen the very day our Cally comes to visit us after all these years?" marveled Miss Anthony. "Oh, thank you, young man."

When the women were settled in the carriage, Charlie asked Miss Anthony, "Ma'am, would you like me to stay here at the house tonight, to keep an eye on things?"

"Thank you for offering, but there's no need, Charles. The doors are not damaged, and the police will keep watch overnight. I'm not worried, because the thief is behind bars." Miss Anthony shifted, seeking a more comfortable position in the crowded space.

"Yes, ma'am." Charlie climbed up beside Abner and the carriage moved away.

"That reminds me, Cally. The police wish to speak to you tomorrow. They are wondering what made you faint when you read the words on the kitchen wall. I was unable to tell them, apart from the shock of their vulgarity. I arranged for you to meet them in the Poet's Garden, off Reservoir Avenue in Highland Park at ten o'clock tomorrow morning. Near the guest house."

Tears sprang to Cally's eyes. "Yes, Aunt Mary," she said.

"Now, you must introduce us properly to this beautiful child, and tell us about Charles. You never told us you had another brother. Do you know, she looks just like you, though you were a little older when we first met you, Cally."

"This is my daughter, Felicity Rose. I am so happy you can meet her." Cally settled Felicity more comfortably on her lap. She had not said a word since her mother recovered from her faint. "Felicity, these ladies are my precious friends, Miss Anthony and Miss Mary. I used to live with them. Can you say hello?"

Felicity looked at each of the women in turn but said nothing. She buried her face in her mother's shoulder.

"All in good time, Cally. Fret not," said Miss Anthony.

"Don't press her," said Aunt Mary. "I expect she'll relax once we're in a more normal environment. The guesthouse is quite nice. You and your mother will have your own room, Felicity." Felicity did not respond.

"Things have been in such a tumble I haven't yet understood why you called Charles your brother. Oh, Mary, I'm sorry I bumped your arm," said Miss Anthony as Mary squeaked.

"Fret not. Those were your words, weren't they?" said Aunt Mary. "You were saying, Cally...?"

"Charlie's brother Thomas Malcomson and sister-in-law Cora adopted me and Felicity, so by extension, Charlie is also my brother. Felicity and I have lived with Thomas and Cora and their children in Kansas City all her life." Cally stroked Felicity's back. "But I first met Charlie on the ship coming over from Ireland when I was seven. His father was the ship's captain, and Charlie befriended Teddy and me."

"You never mentioned them when you lived with us, Cally."

"I—true. It's a long story, Miss Anthony."

"We'll have plenty of time for stories, Cally," interjected Aunt Mary, as Felicity frowned. "We're almost there. We chose this guesthouse because it's near Highland Park, a lovely place for Felicity to play. Perhaps we can picnic there tomorrow. Would you like that, dear?"

"We love picnics, Aunt Mary. Thank you," said Cally.

"At home we have picnics at West Terrace Park," Felicity blurted, then pulled back again behind Cally's arm.

"We do, yes. Felicity loves to feed the ducks in the pond there," said Cally.

"And ride the ponies," Felicity added.

"We don't have pony rides here," Aunt Mary said. "But our gardens are famous for their flowers. I think you will like them." She smiled at Felicity and received a timid smile in return. She lifted the window flap and said, "Here we are!"

The carriage slowed and turned into a curved driveway. The scent of lilacs greeted them as Abner opened the door of the carriage.

"Look at all the flowers, Felicity!" Cally exclaimed. Felicity ran to smell the lavender blooms. "I think she's relaxing already, Aunt Mary. Thank you both for your kindness to us."

"You're our girl, Cally. We've missed you."

Cally descended the stairs to the guesthouse lobby. "Felicity is asleep," she told Charlie, who rose from a sofa.

"The Anthonys' room is next to yours," Charlie said. "They will hear Felicity if she wakes, don't you think? Perhaps we could take a short walk."

"Maybe a short one, Charlie. I don't want to leave her for long. And I'm tired too, ready for an early bedtime."

As they walked outside into the warm, fragrant air, Charlie observed, "Felicity seemed almost back to her normal self by the end of supper."

"This is a lovely place," Cally said, and burst into tears. "I ran away from trouble in Kansas City, and now I'm in the middle of trouble here," she sobbed. "Why do I always cause trouble wherever I go? I don't mean to, truly I don't."

Charlie hugged her. "Of course, you don't. None of this is your fault, Cally, here or in Kansas City."

"It's happening because of m—me," Cally hiccupped.

"You're upset, Cally, understandably so. I think everything will look different in the morning. How about some warm milk before you go to bed? I'm sure we can ask for that in the guesthouse. They have been so accommodating."

"That sounds nice, Charlie."

"I'm noticing the people in this town will do most anything for Susan B. and Mary Anthony. My Mummy always gave me warm milk when I was upset, or hot cocoa. It helped," said Charlie. "I'll have some too. We can both sleep and start everything over in the morning."

Cally smiled. "If your mother were here, she would say, 'God's mercies are new every morning.' Wouldn't she, Charlie?"

"That's exactly what she would say."

"I'm glad you came with us to Rochester, Charlie. Thank you."

"With all that's going on here, I've decided to stay an extra day. I'll return to New York City on Friday."

"But your concert is that evening!"

"It will be fine. I'll take the first train Friday and get to New York in plenty of time."

The elderly policeman who met Cally at the Poet's Garden the next morning was gentle and patient. By the time the interview ended, Cally told him everything.

"I've never talked about this with anyone before, not even my closest friends and family," Cally said, concern creasing her forehead.

"Don't worry, ma'am. They won't hear it from me. Your story is invaluable to us. We will use your testimony only as we must, to convict the thief of his many crimes. This is not the first time he's been apprehended, ma'am. He has made a nuisance of himself in these parts for the last six years but has always managed to get away."

"How awful."

"Yes. As terrible as this has been for the Misses Anthony, it will be a relief to the community that they caught him red-handed. He must answer for a long list of offenses, apart from what he did to you, Miss. I am sorry for your suffering, and grateful for your assistance. I hope it will be a relief to know Jeb is no longer free." The officer tucked his notebook and pencil into his satchel.

"I hope so too. Thank you, Officer." Cally took a step away, then turned back. "May—may I ask you a question, sir?"

"Of course, ma'am."

"Why would Jeb do this now? It's been so many years since he—"

"Since he attacked you?"

"Yes."

"I can only speculate, ma'am. Perhaps he had been watching the Anthonys' house and saw them leave with enough luggage to be gone for a long trip. Perhaps despoiling their home felt to him like some kind of vengeance related to you."

"But—I mean—why would Jeb still remember me? Why would I still matter to him, even in such a horrible way?"

"I can't say, ma'am. Sometimes troubled men fixate on a particular woman, believing she belongs to them in some fashion. Sometimes this happens when they haven't even met the woman they claim as theirs."

"I don't understand."

"Neither do I, I'm afraid, ma'am. It's not your fault, though. Don't ever believe it is."

"Thank you for saying so, sir."

"Is that your friend come to meet you? I've noticed him watching us."

Cally turned. Charlie and Felicity sat on a bench across the garden. "My brother and my daughter," she said. "Can I do anything more for you, Officer?"

"No, you are free to go. I wish you well, ma'am. Thank you for speaking with me."

"Thank you, sir."

As Cally moved toward them, Felicity jumped up and ran to throw herself in Cally's arms. Charlie followed and hugged them both.

Cally turned. The policeman, watching them, smiled.

"You must tell us, Cally," said Miss Anthony after Charlie left for the park with Felicity after breakfast the next morning. "It's our wall bearing that horrible message—though I do hope the police have allowed Abner to paint over it by now."

"Must I? It's not a happy story, Miss Anthony."

"It's your story, Cally. That means it's part of us, too, because we love you. And we're proud of you, Cally. That won't change, no matter what the details may be. We want to grieve with you, dear, knowing the facts, rather than only imagining them," said Miss Anthony.

"We suspect, Cally, that this Jeb may be Felicity's father. Is that the case, dear?" asked Aunt Mary.

Cally burst into tears and sobbed for so long, the sisters looked at each other in alarm.

"Tell us what happened, Cally. Put it into words. Perhaps that will help release it from your soul," said Aunt Mary.

The interview with the policeman was like a dress rehearsal. This is so much harder. I don't want to hurt them. But it seems I must tell them.

For the second time, hesitant at first, and with more tears, Cally told her story: Seeing Jeb, formerly a member of Paddy's gang in Albany, at the Rochester New Year's Eve fireworks. Jeb stalking her on her daily visits to the mules at Abner's. The terror of his physical strength, when he attacked her, tied her up and gagged her and threw her into an alley. The overwhelming memories of Roisin and Malachy's kidnapping as she lay there for hours, helpless. Jeb coming back and raping her. Her single-minded obsession with finding Teddy once someone untied her. Who? She couldn't remember. The long journey on the mule Harry. The farmers who helped her. The guilt she felt for ruining Harry's health, riding him too hard.

And the rest of the story, through Cora's invitation to live with her family, and the happy reunion with Charlie and his mother, Cathleen. The joy of her child's birth. Finding herself weeping when she first saw Felicity Rose, remembering another wee newborn, almost ten years before, her baby sister, too small to live.

In the middle of this long recital, Charlie and Felicity returned from the park. Cally heard Charlie say, "Let's eat lunch, Pipsqueak. I'm hungry, aren't you?" She found them, later, both sound asleep on a blanket behind the guesthouse grape arbor. Cally stood for a moment gazing at them, her heart lighter than it had been since before Felicity was born.

"I'll play in Poughkeepsie next Tuesday, so I'll come back for you and Felicity Wednesday, Cally. Would that be satisfactory?" Charlie looked so intent, so concerned for her, that Cally laughed, then hugged him.

"We'll be fine, Charlie. By then, the Anthonys should be back in their house, don't you think? Look for us there first. And don't worry. The worst is over. I intend to enjoy these days. Aren't Aunt Mary and Miss Anthony lovely?"

"Yes. I've noticed Miss Anthony is not to be trifled with. No wonder she's been able to advance the cause of women's suffrage. I doubt anyone less determined could accomplish that."

"Imagine what she was like in her prime, Charlie. But progress comes at great personal cost. It makes me sad to think she may not live to see the cause she so sacrificially gave her life to finally succeed."

"That is sad, Cally. There's the carriage."

"Give Nathanael and Sarah my love, Charlie."

"Goodbye, sis."

CHAPTER 5

PADDY

Rochester, Saturday, May 7

"HOW IS THE WORK AT THE HOUSE GOING, Aunt Mary?" Cally asked as they sat on a sofa in the parlor, after Felicity and Miss Anthony went to their naps.

"It's coming along, slower than I hoped, but isn't that always the case? The kitchen is back to rights. That was our first objective." Mary sipped her second cup of tea.

Cally froze. *Those awful words. Jeb. I must tell Paddy.*

"I have an idea, Aunt Mary."

"Oh?"

"On the train coming here I ran into Paddy, the leader of the gang in Albany, the one who insisted I become Calvin instead of Cally. Jeb was his right-hand man. I think I should let Paddy know Jeb is in jail. Paddy invited Felicity and me to visit him and his family in Amsterdam."

"Hmm. After all that has happened, I don't think it's wise for you to go alone, Cally. Can't you visit him with Charlie on your way back?" Mary set her empty cup on a side table.

Cally frowned. "Paddy isn't like Jeb, Aunt Mary. He's kind. He was always good to me and Teddy, until he told us we couldn't stay with the gang and made us go with Cap."

"That was years ago, Cally. You can't know very much from a few minutes' conversation on a train. Please, for Susan's sake and mine, wait for Charlie and make this visit with him. Our old nerves can't handle another crisis."

Cally gave Aunt Mary a warm hug. "I understand, Aunt Mary. I need to ask you a question. Will you forgive me for running away without telling you what had happened or where I was going? Now that I have a daughter, I realize I must have caused you great anxiety."

"You have no idea, Cally. We were frantic. We advised the police you were missing, of course, and we soon learned from Abner the mule Harry was missing. We were sure something dreadful had happened to you. We even hired a detective to search for you. We didn't know which direction you had gone, though, and the detective failed to find you."

"Oh, Aunt Mary, I am so very sorry. I never wished to cause you pain."

"Now that you told us what happened, Cally, we understand why you ran away. I am so relieved we caught Jeb in the act of robbing our home. We should discuss whether you will press charges for what he did to you."

"I've been thinking about that, Aunt Mary. But it was so long ago, how could I prove anything? He could say I'm lying, and it would be my word against his."

"You have tears in your eyes, Cally. Please tell me what you are thinking."

"I couldn't bear to see him again, Aunt Mary. I couldn't!" Cally found herself sobbing and buried her head in Aunt Mary's embrace.

"There, there, dear." Aunt Mary patted Cally's shoulder until the flood of tears eased.

"I'm sorry. I didn't know I had more crying left inside me."

"Tears are a gift, Cally. Don't ever be ashamed of them. You buried your grief deep inside far too long. Crossing paths with Jeb again after all these years is bound to bring tears up from where you buried them."

"Mummy? Are you all right?"

Oh! I didn't hear Felicity come in!

Cally held out her arms. "I'm just fine, sweetheart. How was your nap?"

"Fine. What are we going to do this afternoon, Mummy?"

Aunt Mary responded. "It's such a beautiful day, I thought we could drive to the Genesee River and enjoy a picnic supper. Susan has a meeting, but the rest of us can go. Would you like that, Felicity?"

"Yes!" Felicity clapped her hands.

"Abner will be here with the carriage in twenty minutes. Will you help me pack the picnic basket, Felicity?" Aunt Mary glanced at Cally over Felicity's head.

Aunt Mary is so thoughtful. I can spend these twenty minutes resting. All that crying made me tired.

"So, Cally, there's something I've been wondering." Aunt Mary turned her head from watching Felicity attempt to skip rocks into the river.

"Yes, Aunt Mary?"

"Let's walk by the river." Mary took Cally's arm. "When you stayed with us as a child, you were full of ideas about what you would do when you grew up. You wanted to be a doctor and write books. You read almost every book we own. But it seems the Cally who had dreams and ambitions has disappeared. Where has she gone? Is she still alive?"

"Oh, Aunt Mary, you're going to make me cry again. How can I think about dreams for myself when I have a daughter to raise alone? I'm dependent on Thomas and Cora for every bite we eat. All my time goes toward helping Cora and mothering Felicity."

"Have you spoken with Cora and Thomas about your dreams?"

"No. How can I? It seems selfish and wrong, after all they've done for me."

"Then what are you thinking about your future? Do you plan to live with Thomas and Cora indefinitely?"

"I don't know, Aunt Mary. For me, a single mother, the idea of working in a profession seems impossible. I'm quite sure no one would want to marry me, much less support me in going to college or developing a career. I've actually had no formal schooling—only what you and Miss Anthony gave me."

Felicity ran to show them an oddly shaped stick. "It's an F, like my name!"

"You are so ready to learn to read, Felicity!" said Aunt Mary. "Can you find any more letters?"

Felicity ran back to examine the sticks on the ground under a grove of trees.

Mary turned to Cally. "I can't believe, Cally, that a girl as resilient and resourceful as you would not be able to overcome any obstacle, if you really want to. The question is, what do you want? Once that's clear, you can figure out how to achieve it."

"There's something blocking me, Aunt Mary. It's like I lost confidence in myself because of—of what Jeb did. I feel—how can I explain it? Like what he did was my fault, and it proves I don't deserve anything in life. I should have been able to prevent it somehow. I feel the same about Teddy running away from me, that I should have been able to love him well enough to not lose him. My father's last words to me instructed me to take care of Teddy. But I couldn't, or at least didn't, do it well enough. Do you understand? I love my daughter. I can't imagine my life without her. Yet—"

"Yet the circumstances of her birth complicate your life. I think I understand, Cally. For my part, and I know I can speak for Susan as well, you have been a gift to us. Your life has enriched ours in many ways. There's nothing you could do or not do that would make us love you less or make us less grateful for sharing parts of your journey." Mary turned around. "We shouldn't walk too far from Felicity."

"You are so kind, Aunt Mary."

"From what you've said about Thomas and Cora, I imagine they feel about you as we do. You should talk with them about your future, Cally. Isn't it true Cora herself has overcome obstacles as a professional female? Don't you think she would be sympathetic?"

"Perhaps. But she took me in as a servant. Despite their adopting me as their sister, and the loving way they treat me, I'm in a different category from them." Cally stopped. *I've never tried to say this out loud before.*

"How so, Cally?"

"I grew up on a small farm, and became an orphan, and lived in the streets. The Malcomsons have wealth and education and respected positions in society. Right now, I am on trial for my life, Aunt Mary! A judge could decide I deserve to be in prison. As safe as I feel here with you, and with Nathanael and Sarah, a trial awaits me in Kansas City. Oh, there comes Felicity. How did you get all wet, young lady?"

"I threw the biggest stone I could find into the river, and it splashed me. Mummy, can we eat? I'm hungry."

"Of course, child," said Aunt Mary. "Cally, we will continue this discussion later. Which would you like, Felicity, fried chicken or a sandwich?"

"Both!"

Aunt Mary laughed. "Your mother can have both as well, I believe. In life as well as food."

ঙ্গ

"So, Charlie will return Wednesday afternoon?" Miss Anthony asked at breakfast the next morning. Cally nodded, her mouth full of muffin.

"Then we'll have a lovely dinner together at our house before you leave Thursday morning. I'm pleased you'll be able to see our home restored and in order. Mary, don't let me forget to speak with Charlie about scheduling a concert here in Rochester," said Miss Anthony.

"Oh, thank you, Miss Anthony! I'm so glad you were able to return from Germany in time for me to see you again. I want to hear more about your time there," said Cally.

"Where is Germany?" asked Felicity.

"It's far away across the ocean," said Miss Anthony.

"You would have been proud of Susan, Cally," Aunt Mary said. "Honored by women from so many countries. And what a speech she gave! The audience rose as one, cheering and waving handkerchiefs. Unforgettable, and so well deserved."

"It matters not a whit if we don't achieve suffrage, Cally. I fear I may not live to see it."

The Anthony home, Wednesday evening, May 11

Cally jumped when the telephone rang, spilling her water on Aunt Mary's lovely tablecloth. "I didn't know you have a telephone here in your house!"

"Yes, we got it a year ago. It makes Susan's life so much easier," Mary said over her shoulder as she went to answer it.

"Lift the vase of roses so we can soak up some of the water," said Miss Anthony.

"It's for you, Cally," called Aunt Mary. "Your friend Paddy. He wants to confirm your plans for tomorrow. No, hold the telephone like this. Go ahead and speak. Say hello."

"Hello?"

Paddy's voice blared. "Cally, I got your telegram. Are you still coming tomorrow, you and Felicity and Charlie? And you'll be staying overnight?"

"Ye—yes. I've never talked on a telephone before. I can tell it's you!" said Cally.

"I know. It surprised me my first time too. I'll meet you at the train station. Goodbye."

"What can you tell Felicity and me about your friend Paddy?"

Charlie asked Cally after they hugged the Anthonys goodbye and found their seats on the train.

"Well, I met Paddy when I was seven, just a couple of years older than you, Felicity. He was kind to me and Uncle Teddy after our da died and let us stay in his house." *Someday I'll tell her his house was a boxcar.* "We had adventures with him and his friends. Now Paddy is married and has two young children—younger than you, Felicity. I think you'll like him."

"Did you live with him a long time, Mummy?"

"About two months. Then Paddy introduced us to his friend Captain Flannery, and we went to live with him on his barge to take care of his mules, Carson and Harry. We did that for almost seven years. I was sad when the mules got old and died."

"What's a barge?"

"It's a flat boat that floats on the canal," said Cally.

"What happened after that?" asked Felicity.

"After that I went to live with Uncle Thomas and Aunt Cora. And then you were born!"

Cally's eyes met Charlie. *I know you want the details. Maybe. Someday.*

"There you are!" exclaimed Paddy as Cally, Charlie, and Felicity stepped down from the train. "Thank you for coming to visit me. I borrowed a carriage for the day so I can show you around my town.

"We're delighted," said Cally.

"This is our street. Brody and Cate will be watching for us. Their nanny will have the afternoon off today. You'll meet Fiona at supper. Brody is almost four, and Cate is one. You're five, is that right, Felicity? Here we are! Please come back in half an hour, Hank. Thank you."

Multicolored tulips bloomed around Paddy's small, neat house. "Amsterdam. Tulips. Do you understand? Fiona had to explain it to me," said Paddy. "Come meet Brody and Cate, the joys of my life."

"Here we go then," said Paddy, as everyone squeezed into the carriage. "We'll go first to the lock, for old time's sake, eh, Cally? The canal is used mostly for pleasure boats now."

"There wasn't much business going on even when Teddy and I lived on the canal. Cap used to say he lived the end of a wonderful chapter of American life."

"Yes. I heard him say that, Cally. Without the canal, though, Amsterdam probably wouldn't have grown into such a large city. We'll drive past some of the fancy houses of the rich people who own Amsterdam's factories. Did you know more carpets and rugs are made in Amsterdam than any other city in the country? Buttons, too. That's where Fiona works, making buttons. Then we can see the Armory, and you'll like this, Cally: we have a library! It opened just last year." Paddy stopped. "I'm babbling."

Cally put her hand on his arm. "Relax, Paddy! We're friends, aren't we?"

"Yes of course. Although the last time I saw you, Cally, not counting on the train ..."

"I know. You weren't very nice to me. I forgive you. Oh, Paddy. Cap stopped here many times, but I never knew Amsterdam was such a big city!"

"Yes, we have about 25,000 people living here, from many different countries. Fiona works with people who speak half a dozen different languages, everyone trying to learn the English. Remember those days, Cally?"

Cally laughed. "I still say funny things in English. Charlie teases me."

"This morning she called a rotund man at the train station 'tall around,'" said Charlie, grinning. "And called herself 'thick as champ' when I tried to teach her a new card game."

Paddy turned to Felicity. "When I met your mother, she only knew Irish. I made her and Teddy learn English as fast as they could."

"Now Uncle Teddy speaks Oneida. I don't understand Oneida or Irish," said Felicity.

ଔ

"There! We should have an hour or so to talk before the children wake from their naps. Would you like a cup of tea in your hands?"

"That would be lovely, Paddy. Let me help."

When they were settled, Charlie asked, "How did you and Fiona meet, Patrick?"

Paddy chuckled and told his story. "But now I want to hear where you've been all these years, Cally."

"If we hadn't run into each other on the train, we might never have reconnected, Paddy. What happened to the gang?" asked Cally.

Paddy took a sip of his tea. "Short story or long?"

"As much as you want to tell us."

"Well, one Sunday Father Callahan asked me to stay back after his reading class. You remember those classes, Cally?"

"Of course! I loved them."

"Father Callahan asked me whether I would like a job. He told me a parishioner of the church wanted to interview me. Father Callahan told him I was a good organizer, compassionate, and a great salesman.'" Paddy blushed. "First though, I had to care for my lads. Father Callahan persuaded the younger ones to take the orphan trains. Do you know about them, Cally?"

"Yes. The magic word was 'family.' Do you know how things worked out for them, Paddy?"

"No, sadly, I never heard anything more about them."

"What about the older ones?" asked Cally.

"By then, Jeb had left us. He and I weren't getting along. He did things behind my back, causing problems for the whole gang. One day he disappeared. I was sad but not sorry, if you know what I mean."

Cally glanced at Charlie. "We should talk more about Jeb. But finish your story first."

"Father Callahan found jobs for the other boys like he did for me, some in factories, some on farms. Once they all had a place, I went to work for Mr. Mueller. After a year or so, he sent me to Amsterdam, and I've been here ever since. I sometimes see one or another of the lads who stayed in Albany when I report to Mr. Mueller once a month. Now it's your turn. Tell me more about you, Cally."

"First, did you know Jeb is in jail?"

"Yes. I read it in the paper. I wish I could have cared better for him. He was already pushing against me by the time you left the gang, Cally. I had to treat you rudely because of the things he was saying about you. I worried he might harm you if you came near the gang. I'm sorry I couldn't explain it to you, Cally. I saw on your face that I hurt you."

Cally looked at Charlie, then got up and poured more tea. *I don't know what to do. Should I tell him or not? What will it mean either way, to Paddy and Charlie and to me? I've never talked about this except to Aunt Mary and Miss Anthony.*

"Jeb found me in Rochester, Paddy. I haven't told Charlie about this. I'm sorry if I shock you, Charlie. Jeb is Felicity's father, not by my choice. I was so terrified I ran away and ended up, through the kindness of many people, with Charlie's brother's family in Kansas City."

"Oh Cally. I'm so sorry. How awful for you," said Paddy, tears running down his cheeks. "I feel even more my failure as Jeb's leader. And you paid the price. I am so very sorry."

"It wasn't your fault, Paddy. And Aunt Mary told me it wasn't my fault either, though I find that harder to believe," said Cally.

Charlie too brushed away tears. "I feel like this whole story is my fault somehow. For some reason you ran away from us, Cally, when all we wanted was to protect you. I tried so hard to identify what I had done to make you reject us."

Cally set down her teacup and hugged Charlie. "Oh, Charlie. I never imagined you would feel that way. It's my turn to be sorry. It wasn't you at all, Charlie. You always treated me with such kindness. It was Captain

Malcomson, insisting he would take us back to Killeagh. I couldn't do that, much as Teddy wanted me to. It wasn't your fault."

"That's what Mummy said." Charlie pulled out his handkerchief and blew his nose. "But it didn't make sense to me. You talked about Dugan and Aisling with such affection."

"Cally, despite the awfulness of what Jeb did to you, I have to say Felicity is wonderful," said Paddy. "She looks just like you when I first met you, even her mannerisms. Does Jeb know about her?"

"No, and I don't want him *ever* to know," said Cally. "Please, promise me, Paddy, you won't tell him you've seen me. I have nightmares about Jeb finding Felicity and doing to her what he did—what he did—" Cally couldn't continue. She buried her face in her hands and wept.

Charlie stood and walked to the window, his body stiff.

Paddy put his hand on Cally's shoulder. "I understand, Cally. I do. If I ever see Jeb again, I won't tell him. I promise. I'm a father now and my heart will break in pieces if my Cate ever suffers as you have."

Paddy rose and walked the length of the room, stood there for a moment, then smacked his fist into his other hand. He turned with an expression that shocked Cally. She looked at Charlie for help and saw the same intense anger in his face.

"What I want is to find Jeb and kill him. If he weren't in jail already, I would be after finding him as soon as you board the train tomorrow."

Cally jumped to her feet and gripped Paddy's arm, looking back and forth from him to Charlie. "Promise me, both of you, not to do any such thing, even if Jeb gets out of jail. It could destroy your lives. It could destroy your family, Paddy, and your career, Charlie. We must let Jeb's badness stop with him. I've had years to think about this. If we take revenge, the wrongness and hurt and pain will get bigger and bigger. We must live the opposite way, so evil doesn't grow inside of us too. Do you understand what I'm saying, Paddy? Charlie? The only way to win is to be good and kind ourselves. That's how I feel."

"Even though you still suffer so much, Cally? I've heard you scream in your nightmares," said Charlie.

"That's even more reason, Charlie. I want to heal and live a good life. I don't want my mind and heart twisted around revenge and anger and pain. And I don't want yours to be either. That's why I haven't wanted to talk about this."

"Well, it's a good thing Jeb is in jail," said Paddy. "And looking at Felicity, I wonder what kind of person Jeb would be if he had been loved and cared for since he was born. It's like she received whatever good is in him."

"I hope so, Paddy. I love her dearly. But I wish I could have had her under different circumstances. She's started asking me who her father is, and I don't know what to tell her."

"That's hard. I hope God will give you wisdom," said Paddy. "It's nice to see you as a woman, Cally. I can hardly believe now I insisted you pretend to be a lad. But I had no idea what to do with a lassie."

"Being a lad kept me safe for many years, Paddy. It is nice, though, to be who I really am, without constant worry about someone discovering the truth. That was the hardest part, all the pretending."

"Tell me about Teddy," said Paddy.

"Teddy was angry I didn't take him back to Ireland. As he grew up, he became more and more resentful. Finally, he ran away. I thought he had returned to Ireland. Later I discovered he had gone to live with the Oneida. They call him Blue Eyes. He's one of them now."

"Oneida? Who are they?"

"The Oneida are the people who originally lived in New York state. But white people took their lands and forced them to move away. When they went to Oklahoma Territory, Teddy went with them. He just married a lovely Oneida lass. I'm happy for him. We became friends again after he realized I wouldn't try to take him away, or as he says, be his boss anymore. I visit him and Starlight whenever I can, at least twice a year. The train makes it easy. He's never come to visit me in Kansas

City, though. I hope one day he will want to."

"How did you come to live with Charlie's family?"

Cally laughed. "Long story or short?"

Paddy grinned. "As much as you want to tell me."

I can't believe I'm telling this story again! "When I ran away from Jeb, the only thing in my head was to find Teddy. ..." Cally spoke quickly, telling Paddy only the facts. *I don't want to upset him again!*

"What a story!" exclaimed Paddy when Cally paused.

"Yes. Well, after the doctor discovered I was a lassie, and pregnant as well as sick with typhoid fever, the Williams family nursed me back to health. Cora had been corresponding with Mrs. Williams and invited me to live with her and Thomas to help care for her three children—twins and a younger girl. It just so happened—"

"It just so happened that both I and my mother were visiting Thomas and Cora at the time Cora brought Cally home," said Charlie. "Imagine the joy of that reunion!"

"After Felicity was born, Thomas and Cora decided to adopt us," said Cally. "So, Charlie became my brother, and Felicity has grown up as a Malcomson. Oh, I hear the baby."

"Happily ever after, then. I'm glad, Cally. I'll get Cate and peek in at the other two. Brody doesn't usually sleep this long. I guess we wore them out."

Cally smiled as Felicity rushed into her arms. "Did you have a good sleep, sweetheart?"

"Yes, and Brody told me a story when we woke up."

Charlie chuckled as Paddy walked in cuddling Cate with one arm and holding Brody's hand with the other. Cally had a sudden, vivid memory of Da holding Teddy while she toddled, clinging to Da's pointer finger. To hide her emotion, she buried her face in Felicity's hair, fragrant from Aunt Mary's soap.

"Brody has his father's charm. That's evident already," Charlie said.

"Fiona will be home soon," said Paddy. "If you two don't mind entertaining the wee ones, I'll start organizing our supper."

"Well, that was delightful. I've learned so much about you on this trip, Cally," said Charlie on the train the next morning.

"More than anyone else in the Malcomson family knows. Thank you for caring, Charlie. Sometimes I feel like I don't fit into your family, because I lived such a different life for fourteen years. And there's so much I don't know about your life growing up."

"We could help remedy that with a trip to Ireland. I want to take you back, Cally."

Cally opened her mouth, closed it, frowned, and turned to look out the window. *I can't handle talking any more about my story. It's been too many people, too much. I feel naked and vulnerable. I want to crawl in a hole and stay there for a long time.*

"I know you're not ready, sis. But when you are, let me know. All right?"

"All right, Charlie. Felicity, shall I read you a story? We have another hour on the train before we get to New York City."

"After that, I have something else to discuss with you, Cally. News from Kansas City."

Cally finished reading *Squirrel Nutkin,* then set Felicity to drawing squirrels, bunnies, and Old Brown the owl on the empty seat across from them. "You have news from Kansas City, Charlie? Good news or bad?"

"Well, mixed, I would say. Your trial has been put off until August because Judge Jones had a heart attack. He insists this case is his and won't pass it off to another judge. Since reporting this, the newspapers are no longer writing about your case. I guess the trial is too distant now to hold people's interest. But Thomas says the Wanted posters are still up around town, so he doesn't think you should go home."

"I don't see any good news in all that," said Cally.

"Thomas has decided to take on old Uncle William's curious

treasure hunt. He says if there is treasure at the end of it, he wants you to have it to invest in your future. I think that's good news, don't you?"

"Maybe ... But you say Uncle William was both eccentric and unpredictable. Who knows what the treasure will be or whether there even is one? Is Thomas going to Idaho, then?"

"Yes, but he's not free to go right away. He asked me whether I can arrange my schedule to take a couple of weeks to pick up whatever Uncle William left at the bank in Boise and pursue the first steps of the treasure hunt, assuming that's how it's organized. He suggests you and I and Felicity go together, and he'll join us as soon as he can. Cora and my mother are intrigued and might go as well once Mummy arrives, depending on what we find out."

"But what about your concerts?" asked Cally.

"After this weekend, I'm free the next three weeks. I had reserved that time to prepare for my concert tour in Europe. I've inquired about performing at St. Michael's Episcopal Church in Boise while we're there, to help pay the expenses of the trip."

"What is Idaho like?" asked Cally.

"I've never been that far west, but I will have a series of concerts in California in August."

"When would we leave?"

"I'll play in Baltimore tonight and tomorrow night, return to New York Sunday, and we can leave for Idaho Monday morning. The concerts in Baltimore are fundraisers for people who lost their homes in the great fire. Did you know there was a huge fire in Toronto too, just before my birthday? The hall where I played just six months ago was destroyed, along with most of downtown."

"I'm sorry, Charlie." *I don't know where Toronto is. Or Baltimore, for that matter.*

"Mummy, look at my pictures," said Felicity.

"Nice job, sweetheart. I could tell the whole story from what you've drawn," said Cally.

"When I grow up, I'm going to draw pictures for books," said Felicity.

"What a good idea, Pipsqueak!" said Charlie.

"Mummy, can I walk to the water closet by myself?"

"May I ... yes, you may, but come right back here."

"So, what do you think, Cally? Do you want to adventure in Idaho with me?" asked Charlie. "Until I have to leave for my Europe tour. By then, Thomas will be with you."

"I have no idea what we'd be getting into. But since I can't go home yet ... I guess so."

"Knowing Uncle William, I admit it's possible the whole thing is a ruse. But we'll never know if we don't take the first step. And if the 'treasure' does turn out to be money, I agree with Thomas: it could finance whatever preparation you need for your future. Give it some thought, Cally. Felicity will start school soon. You'll have freedom to invest in yourself, for a change."

"You and Thomas think I can do something with my life, Charlie?"

"Of course, Cally. You're intelligent, resilient, resourceful, well-read. . . There are all kinds of things you can do!"

"Miss Anthony and Aunt Mary asked about my plans and were not pleased that I don't have any. I guess it's time to think about more than Felicity's wellbeing. I still want to support Cora and her career though," said Cally.

"One step at a time. But think about it."

"I will." *Am I capable of doing anything other than housekeeping, sewing, and nannying? I was so sure as a child I could do anything I wanted. But life isn't that easy.*

"Shall I buy train tickets for Monday from New York City to Boise, then? It will be a five-day trip. Four nights on the train. We'll have to be creative about entertaining Felicity for that long. I'll think about what I can contribute."

"I heard that, Uncle Charlie," said Felicity, sliding back onto her seat. *"Five days* on another train? Can I stay in New York and play with Lizzy?"

Charlie laughed and tickled Felicity. "We'll make it fun for you, I promise. We'll arrive in Boise early Friday and stay at the Idanha Hotel."

"What's an Idanha?" asked Felicity.

"I don't know," said Charlie. "Friday after we arrive we can go to the bank for whatever Uncle William left for us, but I must find a place to practice Friday afternoon and several hours on Saturday as well for the concert at St. Michael's that evening."

"You've put a lot of thought into this already, Charlie," said Cally.

Charlie laughed. "You and your mummy can explore Boise City, Pipsqueak. I, however, must spend a good part of each of our travel days working."

"I have an idea of something I think you'll like, Felicity. I'll make it this weekend while you're playing with Lizzy," said Cally.

Felicity looked at them as if considering whether to make a fuss. Instead, she drew a picture of a girl with red curls and a pouty face.

CHAPTER 6

BOISE CITY

On the train from New York City to Boise City, Monday, May 16

"FELICITY, I MADE A BOOK FOR YOU," said Charlie.

"You did, Uncle Charlie? Can I see it?"

"May I see it," said Cally.

"Certainly," said Charlie.

"But it's empty. It doesn't have any writing or pictures," said Felicity.

"That's because this is a special book for you to write and illustrate yourself. Your mummy and I can help you with the writing part, but we'll only write what you tell us. And you can draw pictures to go along with what you decide to write. When you finish, you can choose a title to write on the front. This can be the first illustrated story by Felicity Rose Malcomson."

"You're funny, Uncle Charlie. What will I write about?"

"Well, you could write about this long trip we're taking. I figured out we'll be traveling through eleven states and eleven cities to reach Boise City. So, I have another book for you."

"This one has writing and pictures!"

"Yes! It tells about the states and the cities. As we travel, we can read to you about the places we're going and you can include in the book you're writing whatever you find interesting. What do you think? Would you like to become an author?"

"What's an author?"

"An author is a person who writes books," Cally said. "Now let me show you what I made to help you with your book." She handed Felicity a purple cloth satchel with several pockets and "Felicity Rose" embroidered across the top in bright colors. "You can keep your book in here when you're not working on it. That way it will stay nice."

"Can I—I mean, may I look in the pockets?"

"Yes, you may."

"Uncle Charlie, look! Paints and paintbrushes! And this pocket has scissors, and paper. And colored pencils. What's this, Mummy?"

"Those are called crayons. They're an invention Cousin Matilda showed me. She bought some for Lizzy for her birthday. I think you'll like them. They're simpler to use than paints."

"Oh. And here's some colored paper, and—these look like cookie cutters. There's a round one, a crinkly round one, a star, and a heart. Will we make cookies on the train, Mummy?"

Cally laughed. "No. I thought you might like to draw around them to make shapes to cut out and glue into your book. For example, if we travel through a city that's a state capital, maybe you'll want to cut out a star for that page."

"But I don't have—oh, I do have glue. You thought of everything, Mummy!"

"Did you look in all the pockets?" asked Charlie.

"Almost. This one has pencils and erasers. And this one has—what is this, Mummy?"

"That's called a ruler. You can use it to draw straight lines, or to measure. For example, if you want to divide a page in half, you can use your ruler to do it. We can help you."

"So many things."

"There's another pocket, I think, Felicity," said Charlie.

"There is? I think I looked in them all, Uncle Charlie."

"Did you see the one on the back of the satchel?"

"Oh. What is this?"

"It's a map of the United States. It will help us keep track of where we're going. Here is New York City, and here is Boise. See how far we're going? I marked the cities we'll visit on the way. Capital cities have stars. These dotted lines show the outlines of the states."

"I'll be very busy using all these things. I can't wait to show my book to Lizzy!"

"Yes, well, you'll have to write it first. But Uncle Charlie and I will help you. I think you missed a pocket, though, Felicity. Look inside the satchel." Cally watched Felicity's face.

"Oh! It's a dolly!" Felicity hugged the small rag doll, then held her out for a better look. "You're so pretty. You even have red hair, like me and Mummy. I'll call you Lizzy because I miss my friend Lizzy from New York. Look out the window—see, the big buildings are gone. Look at that pretty meadow. Wave to that little boy and his dog."

Cally beamed, and Charlie gave her a thumbs up. "Shall we put all these things away for now and go have breakfast in the dining car?"

"Yes, we're hungry! Lizzy and I want a doughnut!"

Charlie laughed. "We'll see if they have any, Pipsqueak! Maybe not the healthiest breakfast, eh, Cally? But this is a special day, the beginning of our grand adventure!"

Wednesday morning, Cally emerged from her sleeping car wearing Cora's mourning dress and veil.

"Good choice, Cally. We'll arrive in Kansas City in two hours. Max will meet me at the station with things from Thomas and Cora, but you should stay on the train," said Charlie.

"I finished Shauna's dress. Please give it to Max to take to her. And my letter to Cora."

"I want to see Shauna and Shane and Josie!" said Felicity.

"I know you do, Felicity, but they're at school. I miss them too. In a few weeks they'll come see us in Idaho! Do you want me to send them a letter? What shall I write for you?"

"A few weeks is a long time. Why do we have to go to Idaho?"

"We're going to search for treasure, Felicity!"

"I don't want treasure. I want to go home," said Felicity.

ଔ

"Here's a package for you from Cora, Cally," said Charlie.

"It's like Christmas!" said Cally. "Look, Felicity, some books for you: *The Princess and the Goblin* and *The Princess and Curdie.* And one for me by the same author, George MacDonald. It's called *Sir Gibbie.*"

"She sent me one too, called *Robert Falconer*," said Charlie. "Cora must be enjoying this author. I've never heard of him. Have you?"

"Yes! We read *At the Back of the North Wind* to the children last year."

"Diamond was friends with the wind," said Felicity.

"I can read these Princess books to you while we travel," said Charlie.

"I'll finish sewing Josie's birthday dress while you read," said Cally.

ଔ

The conductor announced, "Boise City, next stop!"

"Hurrah! We're almost there!" said Cally.

Felicity sighed and threw her arms up. "I don't EVER want to ride in a train again!"

"Such drama, Pipsqueak! But it has been a long trip," said Charlie.

"Felicity, will Lizzy like this little dress, matching Josie's? You could sew on the buttons before we reach Boise City."

"I'm too tired, Mummy. Lizzy can wear a different dress. You woke me up *so* early." Felicity pressed her nose against the window. "All I see is brown and a funny color of green. What are those bushy things called again?"

"They're called sage, or sagebrush, Felicity. We're in a high desert. Aunt Cora will need a special color palette to paint in Idaho. But I think Boise City will surprise us," said Charlie.

"What's a palette?"

"A palette is a selection of colors. Haven't you seen the round board Aunt Cora holds when she paints, with the colors she needs for the painting she's working on?"

"It has a hole for her thumb."

"Yes. So, to paint scenes in Idaho, she'll need brown and green. Will she need to make different shades of brown and green?"

Felicity considered. "Some are lighter, and some are darker. Yellow, too, for those flowers. And blue for the sky. Does Idaho sky ever have clouds?"

"Not often, I guess. Some people call this blue sky country."

"Charlie, what do you know about Boise City?" asked Cally.

"Let's see what your book says, Felicity. Its population in 1900 was 6,000. Fifty years ago, people traveled through Boise City on the Oregon Trail and some of them stayed. I'll tell you how the town got its name after we first see it. I don't want to spoil the surprise."

"How will we find the hotel, Uncle Charlie?"

"We'll ask for directions at the train station. The Idanha is three years old. Let's see what else your book says, Felicity. Oh, there are hot springs nearby. Hot water bubbles up out of the ground! I'm sure we'll learn a lot more today and tomorrow."

"Is that why this is an adventure, because we don't know very much?"

Charlie and Cally both laughed. "That's exactly right, Pipsqueak. Oh! Quick—look out the window!"

"Trees! With flowers on them! There haven't been trees for hours and hours."

"That's how Boise City got its name. French explorers drove their wagons up a cliff and in the valley below saw a river lined with trees. The French word for trees sounds like Boise."

"I might like being here," said Felicity.

"I think we'll all like it," said Charlie. "I'm not sure I've ever seen such blue, blue sky."

ଔ

"How nice to have a sitting area between our rooms." Cally yawned. "I don't know why I'm so tired. All we've done for the last four days is sit. I think Felicity is asleep already. She flopped onto her bed, shoes and all."

"How about a leisurely bath and a rest before we go to the bank? Unless you want me to go by myself so you can rest longer."

"No, we'll go. Thank you, Charlie."

ଔ

"Even through the scaffolding, I can tell this is a beautiful building," said Cally. She stood with Charlie and Felicity gazing at the activity and mess surrounding the Boise City National Bank. A uniformed official gestured for them to enter through a side door, since the main entrance was blocked.

"Pardon the confusion, sir, ma'am. We are adding a fourth floor to our building. It will be lovely in the end, but meanwhile we must put up with noise and inconvenience. May I ask the nature of your business here today?" the bank official asked.

"I have a letter from my great-uncle," said Charlie as he withdrew it from his case. "I'm to speak with a Mr. Eastman."

"Ah, the bank's director. Please have a seat while I inquire whether he is free."

"Thank you, sir."

Cally, Felicity, and Lizzy gazed at marble floors and counters, sparkling chandeliers and upholstered furnishings. From inside, they could hear construction noise only faintly. The various tellers spoke in subdued tones.

"What that man said applies to us, Cally," said Charlie.

"What do you mean?"

"The inconveniences are necessary for a lovely outcome. That's true for us too, sis, don't you think? We're under construction too, you and I. We're already wise, and patient, and strong—our first three floors. We're adding a fourth story, joyful in troubles ..." Charlie grinned.

Cally poked Charlie and giggled. "Speak for yourself, oh wise one. I'd gladly stick with just three stories, thank you very much."

Charlie poked her back. "Not ready for joy yet, eh?"

"Uncle Charlie, the man is back," said Felicity.

"Mr. Eastman will meet you in the consultation room, sir. Through here. Sit wherever you like. May I serve you tea or coffee while you wait?"

"Just water for me, thank you, sir. Cally and Felicity?"

"Water, please. Thank you."

The man returned with three glasses of water and one lollipop on a velvet-covered tray. "Can I, Mummy?" asked Felicity.

"May I. Yes, you may."

A few minutes later, a portly gentleman entered the room. "I am Hosea Eastman. I understand you are related to William Malcomson?"

"Yes, he was my great-uncle. I am Charles Malcomson. This is my sister Callandra and my niece Felicity."

"Ah. Your father is Peter Malcomson?"

"Was, yes. You are well informed. My father died suddenly four years ago."

"I've waited years for someone from your family to appear."

"Yes, sir. It took a while for the information to reach us. I believe it circulated through the extended Malcomson family before my mother sent it to my older brother Thomas. He lives in this country, in Kansas City. He was not free to come, so he sent us."

"Do you also live in the United States, Mr. Malcomson?"

"No, sir. I come periodically on musical tours. I am a pianist."

"Oh yes. My wife mentioned a concert at St. Michael's tomorrow evening. If she has her way, we will be there."

"I hope you will enjoy it, sir. Is there a musical tradition in Boise I can consider as I plan the concert?"

"We like dance music, Mr. Malcomson. This is the 'wild west,' you know. Most of us didn't grow up with classical music. Your concert will be unusual for us, young man."

"How delightful! I'm fond of dance myself, especially ragtime. I believe you may be pleased, Mr. Eastman," said Charlie.

"So, the materials you have come for are in a lockbox in our vault, a floor below us. A bank guard will accompany us. Perhaps you and your daughter will be comfortable here, ma'am?" asked Mr. Eastman.

"Did you personally know Uncle William, sir?" asked Charlie as they left the room.

"Why couldn't we go, Mummy?" asked Felicity.

"Maybe it would be too crowded. Shall I read you a story? This one is called *The Tale of Benjamin Bunny.* It just came out. I saw it in the hotel gift shop."

☙❧

"This small packet—that's it!" said Charlie, returning without Mr. Eastman. "The bank could have mailed it to Thomas, I would think, but oh well, we're here now. Please take it back to the hotel, Cally, so it won't distract me. I've seldom in my life gone so many days without touching a piano. I'll see you at supper, all right?"

"Enjoy practicing, Charlie."

☙❧

"You two slept so long, perhaps we should have supper first, and a walk after. Shall we eat in the hotel restaurant to keep things simple this first day?" asked Charlie.

"Good idea, Charlie. I feel much better after taking a nap in the morning and this afternoon. Don't you, Felicity?"

"Yes. Lizzy's hungry. Can she come?"

"Of course. Shall we ride the elevator again? This is the first building in Boise to have an elevator," said Charlie. "Lobby, please, sir."

Felicity pointed. "Look, Uncle Charlie! The elevator has a paper with your picture on it!"

"Oh! It's advertising the concert tomorrow night!" Charlie said.

"Uncle Charlie is famous, Felicity." Cally grinned at her and the elevator man.

"Not here," said Charlie.

"No doubt that will soon change," said the elevator man.

A waiter wearing colorful clothing seated them. "Look at this, Cally. The menu features Basque dishes. There's a growing Basque community in Boise City and nearby. They have their own language and customs. Many of them are sheepherders."

"Where are Basque people from?" asked Cally.

"They're from France and Spain. They first came during the Silver Springs gold rush about thirty years ago. Shall we try some of their food?"

"Is this part of our adventure?" asked Felicity.

"It is! Hmm, the menu offers something called lamb empanadas, lamb curry, lamb stew ... Shall we each get a different dish and try each other's? And something called flan for dessert," said Charlie.

"I've never eaten lamb in my life," said Cally.

"They have ordinary food too, but where's the adventure in that?"

"Mummy, look at those people. They have clothes like our waiter. Are they Basque?"

"I think they're going to dance for us, Felicity! This is delightful!"

Felicity jumped from her chair and tried to imitate the smiling dancers on the stage. One noticed and beckoned her to join them. Felicity sat back down and scooted close to Cally, hugging Lizzy, but her eyes never left the choreography unfolding in front of them. "Lizzy and I will do it when we get back to our room," Felicity whispered.

"I will too," Cally whispered back. "Here, try some of this stew. This food is delicious!"

"Yum. I like flan!" said Charlie, taking another bite. "The Boise River is nearby. We're to walk toward a row of cottonwoods. Do you know what cottonwoods are, Cally?"

"Maybe a kind of tree? Let's go find out!"

"Another adventure!" said Felicity to her doll. "Lizzy wants to come too."

"Ah, I see," said Charlie after they walked about three blocks.

"Look at the white fluffy stuff on those trees. It looks like cotton," said Cally.

"That must be the river!" Felicity took off running, and Cally ran after her. They threw themselves down on the grass at the edge of the water.

"Beautiful!" said Charlie.

"Such a big river in the middle of the desert! No wonder people want to live here! I see little red blossoms, in between the cotton," said Cally.

"Look, there are people in boats. Can I ride in a boat, Mummy?"

"You two can take a boat ride while I practice at St. Michael's tomorrow," said Charlie.

"Look at Felicity, Charlie. She's falling asleep."

"I'll carry her back. We're all ready for an early bedtime, I think."

Charlie eased Felicity into her bed, then joined Cally in the sitting room.

"Charlie, thank you for all you do for us. You make this adventure fun and easy."

"It's a grand change of pace for me, Cally. And I would not be able to rest if you were alone in this ridiculous exile from Kansas City. I know it's hard, sis. We 'll get through it together, you, me, Thomas, and Cora. We love you."

Cally wiped her eyes. "All I do these days is cry."

"Come here, sis."

Cally scooted over to Charlie and burst into tears as he hugged her.

"I know, I know," he murmured. "I've been through times when on the outside I tried to be normal but, on the inside, I felt such pressure I thought I would burst. Let the pressure out, Cally. It's too much for you to carry. You're not alone. You're not alone."

"What will we do all day, Mummy?" asked Felicity at breakfast.

"Tell me what you and Lizzy would prefer. We can walk back to the river and then up it a little way until we get to a famous orchard. Or we can hire a carriage to take us to the hot springs, and bathe in warm water coming out of the ground."

"What's an orchard?"

"It's a farm that grows fruit. The Davis Orchards mostly grow apples and plums. The trees are blossoming right now, so the orchard is pretty."

"Can I eat some fruit?"

"*May* I ... I don't know, Felicity. The trees don't have fruit on them yet. But maybe they saved some apples from last year's harvest."

"Let's go see! I want Uncle Charlie to go with us to the hot springs."

"All right. Are you ready to go?"

"I'm enjoying the Basque spices, aren't you? I've never imagined anything like the *solomo*," said Cally as the elevator lifted them to the fourth floor of the hotel after an early supper.

"Lizzy likes rice pudding," said Felicity.

"I prefer the flan," said Charlie with a yawn. "Whew, I'm tired. Wake me in half an hour? I know we haven't opened Uncle William's packet yet, but we can do it tomorrow, right?"

Cally stayed in her seat as the concert ended, hoping Charlie would carry sleeping Felicity back to the hotel. *She did well during the first half.*

Cally watched the long line of people greeting Charlie slowly dwindle. *They liked Charlie's playing despite Mr. Eastman's misgivings. Oh, there he is—the last man in line! The woman with him must be his wife.*

Charlie bowed to the banker and his wife then joined Cally. "The Eastmans invited us for tea tomorrow afternoon." He handed Cally his satchel and lifted Felicity.

"Lovely," said Cally. "I've never heard music like you played in the first half."

"I added ragtime rhythms to classical tunes," said Charlie. "A musician named Scott Joplin taught me to do that years ago. It's great fun. I thought the people here would like it."

"They loved it. They even stayed through the second half. What was that you played as an encore? Everyone was on their feet for that one."

Charlie laughed. "The musicians at the hotel taught me a Basque piece. Did you like it?"

"I loved it. I'd have been dancing along with the crowd if Felicity hadn't fallen asleep on me. I doubt Boise citizens will ever forget this."

"It's a bridge, perhaps, to music Boise City hasn't yet learned to appreciate. I've found if I start with music people recognize and already like, I can introduce them to a wider repertoire. Several asked for another concert. We'll see." Charlie yawned.

"You're so gifted, Charlie. Let me get the door for you."

Cally dreamed she was lost. Every direction she walked circled back to a dark, damp cave filled with frightening, unidentifiable noises. She woke to Felicity crying, "Mummy, Mummy, wake up!" Charlie appeared at their door, framed by the sitting room light he had flipped on as he came through.

"Wha—what happened?" Cally asked, sitting up and trying to get her bearings.

"You tell us, Cally. You were screaming," Charlie said.

"Oh, I'm so sorry. It was just a bad dream. I'm fine, Felicity, truly." Cally pulled the sobbing little girl into her lap, rocking her like a baby. "I was asleep, sweetheart. I didn't know I was screaming. I wish I didn't do that. Go back to sleep, Charlie. We'll be fine."

"If you're sure."

"I'm sure. Please leave the light on and the door open a little bit. Thanks."

"Call me if you need anything. Promise?"

"I will."

Charlie stumbled back to bed, closing the door to his room. Cally talked and sang to Felicity until she fell asleep, then carried her to her bed.

Thoroughly awake, Cally grabbed her robe and walked to the sitting room, tears in her eyes. *Why do these nightmares keep happening? They're terrible for me, but even worse for Felicity. Please, God, make them stop. Why did I dream about a cave? The only cave I remember is the one Teddy and I slept in after we escaped from Roisin and Malachy. But it was pleasant, a refuge. Not horrible like the one in my dream.*

Cally paced around the sitting room. *The cave in my dream felt like . . . I know, like waking up inside Roisin and Malachy's horrible sack! Can dreams do that—take the emotions of real life and represent them with a different confusing image? I'm so disoriented!*

Cally slumped on the sofa and picked up her George MacDonald book. *Perhaps this will distract me from the images of my dream.*

The sun shone through the sitting room windows, yet the electric light was still on when Charlie opened the door from his room. Cally lay with her face buried in the back cushions of a couch, a book on the floor beside her. He extended a hand and breathed a prayer over her, crossed himself, then slipped out the door for a pre-breakfast walk. *Later this morning we can look at Uncle William's packet.*

ঃঃ

In the sitting room two hours later, Charlie handed Cally a paper. "See if you can make sense of this."

Cally read in shaky longhand:

Early winter chased the Saints in 1863.
They huddled for protection in a place called Clover Creek.
They thought they were in Utah and their leader Brigham Young
Envisioned greatness and decreed a name of Frenchee tongue.
A village still when I was there; most people looked askance
At such ambition for a town not worth a second glance.
Yet one by one folks said, "I'm done with wagon trains and travel.
Two thousand miles of dirt and grime have worn me to a frazzle.
I crossed South Pass and took an oath the first place that I saw
I'd claim my stake and build my home no matter any flaw."
The village has a banker now; you'd best inquire there.
You're certain to pursue this clue if treasure you would share.

Cally blinked and read it again. "I have no idea, Charlie. Maybe the Eastmans can help us. Did Uncle William say anything else?"

"There is a map of sorts, but it's as oblique to me as the poem." Charlie extended a "map" with a single irregular line. "If it is a map, I don't know whether it runs north-south, east-west, or neither. Clearly, Uncle William intended this treasure hunt to be challenging. And we've no idea whether the so-called treasure will be worth anything!"

"Are you having second thoughts about pursuing this?"

"I don't know. The only other thing in the packet is equally confusing, at least to me." Charlie handed Cally a thick, sealed envelope labeled "For Billy." Across the bottom, large letters vowed vengeance on anyone but Billy who dared open the envelope.

"Billy is a nickname for William, isn't it? I wonder if that's any kind of clue. The Billy we need to find and give this to must have known your Uncle William."

"Let's take it all to tea and ask the Eastmans for help."

"This is delicious! I've never had lemon ice cream," Cally told Mrs. Eastman.

"No? It's called sherbet, a creamier version of sorbet. We're close enough to California to benefit from their citrus," said Mrs. Eastman. "Please, call me Mary Ann."

"Charles, when can we schedule another concert? A dozen people at least have asked me about this," said Mr. Eastman.

"Let me think. In two weeks, I'll travel back to Europe for a two-week tour. Then I'll be home in Ireland for several weeks before returning here. Perhaps we could schedule the end of July? It will be tight, but I have July 30 free before a tour already planned for California."

"July 30. I should have realized you are much in demand," said Mr. Eastman.

"Our experience last night was extraordinary, wasn't it, dear?" said Mary Ann.

Charlie inclined his head. "Thank you for saying so. We have some questions, Mr. Eastman, about the materials you gave us from Uncle William."

"Oh? I'll help if I can. Your uncle did not share with me the contents of the packet he left in the bank's keeping," said Mr. Eastman.

"Before we begin this conversation, Hosea, let me offer Felicity something more interesting than adult chatter. Would you like to see my granddaughter's dollhouse, Felicity?"

"Can I, Mummy? I mean, may I."

"Yes, you may."

"Now then," said Mary Ann.

"Uncle William has devised a treasure hunt of sorts for us," said Charlie. "He left a map—at least, I surmise it is a map, though it makes no sense to me. And a rhyme, our first clue, I believe. And a package for someone named Billy."

"How delightful!" exclaimed Mary Ann. "I love mysteries."

"Perhaps you would like to read the rhyme yourselves." Charlie handed the paper to Mary Ann, who read it aloud.

"The Saints must be the Mormons. A group of them settled here in Boise City. Yes, Brigham Young was their leader until he died—when, Hosea? 1870-something."

"Clover Creek," said Mr. Eastman. "Isn't that what Montpelier used to be called? It was the first stop on the Oregon Trail after crossing into Utah from Wyoming. I helped Ezra Martin establish the bank there in 1890. I can write him an introduction if you like, Charles."

"That would be helpful. Thank you," said Charlie.

"You're fortunate: the railroad reached Montpelier in 1892, turning the village into a town. I'll go write that letter."

"This has been so helpful," Cally told Mary Ann. "We were stumped."

"Glad to help. Hosea is from New Hampshire, but I've lived here all my life," said Mary Ann. "I would love to hear how you progress with this treasure hunt! Will you write me?"

Cally laughed. "I'll be glad to, Mary Ann. We have no idea what we're getting into. I'm happy with the thought you and Mr. Eastman will know where we are!"

"Is there is a train to Montpelier tomorrow?" asked Charlie.

"One daily train travels each direction through the southern towns of our state, Charles, from Boise to Montpelier and points in between. It departs Boise City at 8:00 a.m. Oh, there you are, Hosea."

Mr. Eastman handed an envelope to Charlie. "I should tell you: Ezra has some quirks."

"Quirks, Mr. Eastman?" asked Charlie.

"Perhaps I shouldn't have said anything. He's a fine banker."

"We would appreciate any information that might help us."

"Let's just say he's friendly with Indians and other odd folks. Not a popular stance in our state. That's why the bank sent him to no man's land, as it was considered at the time, before the railroad chose that route."

"I see."

"You mentioned a map, Charles?"

"Well, it might be a map ..."

"Yes, of course. Hold it this way. Boise City is here, Montpelier at the opposite end here. The uneven line connecting them is roughly the route of the old Oregon Trail. Your Uncle William was fascinated by the Oregon Trail story, thousands of people uprooting in the East to start life new on the Western frontier. Perhaps your treasure hunt will start in the east and end back here in Boise City. I have a map I can loan you showing the points in between. It may help you decipher future clues. I'll get it."

"You can telephone us if you get stuck or in trouble," said Mary Ann. "We have telephones here as well as the bank. Ask the operator for the Boise City Eastmans at home. I'm intrigued by this treasure hunt. What do you suppose might be the treasure?"

"We have no idea," said Cally.

CHAPTER 7

MONTPELIER

[Note: for a map, see "Montpelier" under Historical Links on HorseThief1898.blog.]

Almost midnight, Montpelier, ID, Monday, May 23

CALLY JERKED AWAKE. Someone pounded on the door of her room in the boardinghouse above the tavern on Montpelier's Fourth Street. A woman shrieked, "Let me in! Let me in! My mother is in there! She needs me!"

Felicity whimpered, and Cally cuddled her. *Are we in the wrong room? The woman sounds desperate. Should I let her in? Will someone else hear and take care of her?*

The doorknob rattled as the shouting and pounding continued. *What if she's so angry she becomes violent? I must protect Felicity! The woman sounds drunk. Or something. What should I do? She sounds so distressed.*

"Mummy, you should help her," whispered Felicity.

"She does sound very upset. But I'm not sure we're the best people to help her. We're new to this town."

"But she's pounding on our door," said Felicity.

"You're right. I wonder where Charlie is." Cally reached for her robe and started toward the door. But the pounding stopped. As she stood listening, Cally realized pounding now sounded from the floor above her. *That's Charlie's room. I think.*

Cally opened her door and looked out. A woman down the hall did the same. "Is there someone we should call?" she asked, stepping toward Cally.

"I don't know. I'm new here. We arrived this afternoon."

"Me too. I'm the new schoolteacher. I was going to ask whether this is a common occurrence in Montpelier, but you wouldn't know."

"My name is Cally. Oh, Felicity, this lady is a schoolteacher."

"Nice to meet you. I'm Sherilyn. I arrived two days ago from Denver. The teacher here had a baby, so I'll fill in for the rest of the term. I start tomorrow—or today, I guess it is. Will you be in school today, Felicity?"

"Oh, no," Cally responded. "We only expect to be in town a couple of days."

"Uncle Charlie's talking to the woman, Mummy," said Felicity. "I hope he can help her. Oh, they're coming down the stairs."

As Charlie appeared, guiding a woman down the stairs, Sherilyn called, "I think the boardinghouse owner lives behind the tavern. Maybe he'll know what to do."

"Thank you, ma'am. You can all go back to bed."

A slender man with thick glasses extended his hand to Charlie at the bank the next morning. "Welcome to Montpelier. I'm Ezra Martin. I received a telegram from Hosea Eastman advising me to expect you. How can I help?"

Charlie shook the banker's hand and looked around the small lobby. "Is there a place we can talk, Mr. Martin?"

"Of course. Come into my office. Please, sit."

"Mr. Martin, my name is Charles Malcomson. This will sound strange, but—"

"You are a Malcomson? I haven't heard that name in years! I had ceased to expect—just a moment."

The banker rose and spoke to someone outside the office. Cally yawned.

"You couldn't get back to sleep last night, Cally?" asked Charlie.

"No. Did you?"

"Eventually, yes." Mr. Martin returned as Charlie spoke.

"Is there a problem, Mr. Malcomson?"

"No, sir. It seems you knew my Uncle William?"

"I did, yes. It's a long story. Shall I join you for supper at the tavern so we can talk more? My assistant is fetching a packet William left for any Malcomson who might show up asking for it. I confess I was tempted to open the packet myself after so many years passed. What could it contain that would attract someone to our little town from across the ocean? I am baffled. Here it is. Thank you, Damaris."

The packet Damaris gave Mr. Martin looked much like the one Uncle William had left at the bank in Boise City. Charlie rose. "Perhaps we'll be able to satisfy your curiosity at supper, Mr. Martin. But I suspect this packet will raise more questions than it answers. Until then."

"Until then, Mr. Malcomson. Ma'am. Young lady." Mr. Martin bowed.

Outside, Charlie turned to Cally and Felicity. "Shall we wander down Fourth Street to evaluate our options for lunch? I can tell you what I know about what happened last night, and we can investigate this packet." He shivered and buttoned his coat.

"It's cold here for spring, don't you think?" Cally said as they walked.

"We're at a high elevation—almost six thousand feet, a man at the boardinghouse told me. Lovely farming country. We're in the Bear River Valley."

"The mountains are beautiful. And Sherilyn told us at breakfast there's a lake close by. We should find out how to get there."

"Perhaps Mr. Martin can tell us the town's story at supper. What makes it important enough to be a railroad stop? The train whistled right through several other small communities."

"Sherilyn told us Montpelier is the largest town in the county. Fifteen hundred people and growing."

Felicity smiled at a girl her size walking by with her mother.

"Can I go to school, Mummy?" she said. "Miss Sherilyn is nice."

"I don't think you can go to school for just two days, Felicity."

Felicity sighed. "I miss Shauna and Josie. And Lizzy. I want someone to play with."

"I brought your travel journal. You can work on it while Uncle Charlie and I talk. Imagine the fun of sharing it with Shauna and Josie when they join us in a couple of weeks."

After they ordered at a diner, Cally asked, "What happened with that poor woman you helped last night, Charlie?"

"Mr. Dawson knew her. He apologized but didn't seem surprised at her behavior. He said he would walk her home," said Charlie.

"Strange. Shall I open Uncle William's packet?"

Cally pulled out a hand-drawn map, a WM-monogrammed handkerchief, a fat sealed envelope addressed to Minnie, and a rhyme labeled #2.

Charlie took the map and looked at it from every direction. "Does this map make any sense to you?" he asked the waitress when she brought their plates.

"Sure. This here is Bear Lake, and that's the road to Montpelier from Dingle through Preston. The star might be Dingle—yes, I think that's about right. The M for sure is Montpelier."

"So, if we drive through Preston and Dingle, we'll reach Bear Lake?"

"Yes. It's about eight miles to Dingle, I think. Maybe four more to the lake."

"Where can we rent a carriage? And can you pack a picnic lunch for us tomorrow? What time do you open in the morning?"

"We serve breakfast starting at 7:00. You can rent a carriage on Second Street, three blocks down. Simon's the name."

Cally caught her breath, then looked at the lettering on the handkerchief to cover her emotion. *Simon. What a good friend you were to me. I wish we could have brought you with us to America. But what would Dugan and Aisling have done without a good horse?*

"We wanted to see the lake, didn't we?" said Charlie. "Though Uncle William is only sending us as far as Dingle, apparently."

"We'll inquire in Dingle for a person named Minnie, I suppose?" asked Cally.

"I suppose. This seems straightfor—"

Gunshots exploded nearby. Cally jerked to her feet, upsetting her chair. Charlie and other diners rushed to the front window. Cally yelled, "Stay close to me, Felicity."

They pushed through to the window just as several men pounded by on horses, shooting into the sky and yelling "Yee-haw! Butch Cassidy's Wild Bunch rides again! Yee-haw!" The last horseman waved as he leaped to his feet on the racing horse's back, then flipped to face backwards. He somersaulted over the back of the horse and pulled himself back up by grabbing its tail. Another rider yodeled, and the rest responded.

The diner crowd rushed into the street, staring after the horsemen. Three riders, one with a star on his chest, galloped by in pursuit. "You'll never catch 'em," shouted a man in front of a barber shop across the street, his face half-covered with shaving cream. "That copycat Wild Bunch'll hide out in the mountains. Them're the best horsemen in all

Idaho."

"What'd they do this time?" yelled another man. He ran in the direction the gang had come from. Most of the spectators took off after him, turning the corner on Main Street.

"I bet it's the bank," said Charlie. "Poor Mr. Martin. We may not see him for supper after all. We can't help, though. Have you had enough lunch, Cally and Felicity? Let's head back to the boardinghouse."

When Charlie pushed open the door of the tavern that evening, Mr. Martin was there, sipping a glass of ale. A woman sat beside him.

"Isn't that—" murmured Cally.

"Yes. She looks different in daylight," Charlie whispered back.

"Good evening, Mr. Martin. We are sorry for your losses at the bank," said Charlie.

Mr. Martin and the woman both rose. "Good evening, Mr. Malcomson. Ma'am. This is my daughter, Constance O'Brien. Connie, the Malcomsons are visitors in our town. I did some work for their great-uncle many years ago."

"I'm pleased to meet you," said Mrs. O'Brien, inclining her head. "Please, sit. I hope you will enjoy your stay in Montpelier. Do you plan to be here long?"

"Not long," said Cally. "Uncle William left us a couple of tasks to accomplish, and then we'll move on. This is my daughter, Felicity."

"Tasks? How intriguing," said Mrs. O'Brien. "Can we be of any help? It's nice to meet you, Felicity."

"I imagine you have enough on your plate, with the bank robbery today, Mr. Martin," said Charlie.

"My hands are tied until Hosea arrives from Boise with a new vault, and he can't come until Thursday. Everyone in town knows the gang made a clean sweep of our assets. This may be the last straw for those Cassidy copycats. I wanted to ride out with the posse, but they may be days in the effort, and I must set the bank to rights as quickly as possible."

"I recommend the potato soup. It's quite good," said Mrs. O'Brien.

When their soup arrived, Cally began, "This reminds me of—" "Champ!" Charlie said at the same moment.

"You're familiar with champ?" asked Mrs. O'Brien.

"Of course! We're from Ireland!" replied Charlie.

"I learned about champ from my husband. He's presently in Denver on business."

"Oh? What is his business, if I may ask, Mrs. O'Brien?" asked Charlie.

"Please call me Connie. He and a friend have an idea of building a dam on Bear Lake to create electricity and irrigation. The idea is sound—it would transform our valley—but it's a huge undertaking and dreadfully expensive. Michael is visiting businessmen hoping to raise funds. I keep telling him to go east. That's where the big money is. But he's never been east and hasn't yet worked up his courage."

"Connie is a seamstress," said Mr. Martin. "She owns the dress shop on Fourth Street. Michael has a good heart and a great imagination but hasn't yet settled into a solid career."

"He will, though," smiled Connie.

"Mummy sews dresses," said Felicity. "She makes all my clothes, and Shauna's and Josie's and Aunt Cora's. She makes shirts and pants for Shane, too."

"The dress you are wearing is lovely. Did she make that one?" asked Connie.

"Yes, but I chose the cloth," said Felicity.

"You do excellent work, Mrs.—"

"Please call me Cally. Thank you."

"If you lived here, I would hire you," said Connie.

Cally smiled. "Working with you would be a pleasure, Connie.

Charlie and I want to learn more about your town, and why Uncle William came here. Can you tell us, Mr. Martin?"

"Mormon pioneers founded the village of Clover Creek in 1863. Later settlers changed the name to Belmont, but our leader Brigham Young renamed it Montpelier, after his hometown in Vermont."

"You said, 'our leader,'" observed Charlie. "Are you Mormon, then?"

"Lapsed Mormon," chuckled Mr. Martin.

"It's not funny, Daddy," said Connie.

"No, I suppose not. I've never said that phrase before, so I found it amusing." He turned to Charlie. "I became disenchanted with the Saints because of the Bear River massacre. Are you familiar with that piece of our history?"

"I'm afraid not," said Charlie.

"The background is a complex mosaic of aggression, broken treaties and betrayal, but here's the short version: In January 1863, Utah Mormons cooperated with the United States Army under Colonel Patrick Connor to attack Chief Bear Hunter's starving Shoshone at their winter camp. They killed hundreds of men, women, and children. Colonel Connor was hailed as a hero and promoted to Brigadier General. He went on to kill hundreds of Sioux and Cheyenne as well, with acclamation from the Mormon Church. I could not associate myself with that point of view. The Saints excommunicated me for being vocal about my dissent."

"What a sad story," said Charlie.

"Yes, well, in Montpelier everything changed when the railroad arrived in 1892, bringing what the Saints call 'Gentiles' to live among us. The town settled out into two sections. The Saints have plans to build a huge tabernacle here, hoping to attract more Mormon settlement. There's already a large tabernacle in nearby Paris."

"Are the Saints and the Mormons the same thing?" asked Cally.

"Yes. The official name is The Church of Jesus Christ of Latter-Day Saints. Their sacred Scripture is called the Book of Mormon. The faithful are known by both names."

"I see," said Cally.

"How did you meet Uncle William, Mr. Martin?" asked Charlie.

"One day in 1890, a man walked into the bank asking for assistance. He had with him a woman from Pocatello."

"Named Minnie?" asked Cally.

"Why yes. How did you know?" asked Mr. Martin.

"The packet you gave us included an envelope we are to deliver to her, with a map indicating a place called Dingle," said Charlie. "Does that make sense? I've hired a carriage to take us there tomorrow and ordered a picnic lunch at the diner."

"So that's where she ended up. I never knew. I hope she's still alive," said Mr. Martin. "You see, Minnie had—has, I hope—dark skin. Montpelier did not welcome her. Your uncle appealed to me for help because—"

"Because my father helps anyone in trouble, no matter the color of their skin or the language they speak," said Connie. "Neither Mormons nor Gentiles know what to make of Ezra Martin. But they all need his services. My father's an excellent banker."

"Thank you, my dear," said Mr. Martin. He turned to Charlie. "I had to advise your uncle not to expect an attitude of kindness toward Minnie here. They left, but a few months later your uncle walked into the bank and asked me to keep a packet for him until some Malcomson showed up to claim it. He paid for a locked box for fifteen years. Come to think of it, I owe you the remaining cost of —"

"Don't even think about that," said Charlie. "Consider it a small expression of thanks for your graciousness to us."

"I wonder—would you permit me to accompany you to Dingle tomorrow? I have time, since the bank is closed, and I would dearly love to help you find Minnie, if she's still alive. I've often wondered what happened to her. It's a disgrace to our state how unfriendly we are to people who look different from us."

"Yes! Join us!" said Charlie. "Mr. Martin, the packet from Uncle William we picked up in Boise included an envelope addressed to 'Billy.' Do you know who that might be?"

"Billy. Hmm. It's a common name, but it must be someone who knew your uncle. Can you think of anyone, Connie?" asked Mr. Martin.

"No, no one comes to mind," said Connie. "Perhaps Minnie may know."

"You've both been very kind. Now I must take Felicity to bed. No, no protests, young lady. I've seen you yawning. I'm tired too," said Cally.

"I have one more question, Mr. Martin," said Charlie. "I see the piano. Might I be able to use it in the morning before we leave for Dingle at 8:00? I would love to practice from 6:30 to 7:30, unless that would disturb someone."

"I don't imagine that would be a problem," said Mr. Martin, glancing around the room. "There's Steve Dawson, the owner, at the table in the corner. Why don't you ask him while I settle our bill?"

"Thank you, but I wish to pay. You've been so helpful."

"No, I insist. Good night. I'll meet you here at 8:00 tomorrow morning for our ride to Dingle and will be happy to share your picnic lunch."

"Good night," responded the others.

Charlie and Mr. Martin sat inside the carriage with the picnic basket, while Cally, at her request, guided the horses. Felicity perched on the bench beside her. They trundled south on a rough road from Preston to Dingle through lovely green, flower-covered hillsides, a surprise after the endless miles of sage they had come to expect in the high desert.

"Mr. Martin, I don't quite know how to ask ..." said Charlie.

"Just ask, Charles."

"Your daughter—"

"I expected this question," said Mr. Martin. "It's all right. I'll tell you the story, though it's not a pleasant one."

"I don't mean to intrude," said Charlie.

"No, no. You deserve an explanation after seeing her as she was Monday night at the boardinghouse. Connie has spells, you see. That's what we call them. She enters some different state of consciousness and has no memory later of what she did or said. We never know when this will happen. That's why she stays with me when her husband is out of town."

"Do—do you know what causes these spells? It was difficult seeing her so distressed the other night. And then seeing her completely at ease last evening with you ..."

"I understand your confusion. My only clue is that when she is altered as you saw her Monday night, she sometimes references a terrible experience she had as a child. It's like she's reliving it again in the present. It must be horrible for her. I wish I knew some way to relieve her of these awful episodes."

Charlie gripped the map in his hands, wrinkling it. *Like what happens to me in storms and sometimes on ships.* "May I ask what happened to her as a child?"

"I don't often talk about this. Do you remember what I told you about the Bear River massacre?"

"Yes."

"A group of Shoshone attacked citizens of Montpelier to avenge the massacre. My wife was one of the victims. Connie was only two years old. She was knocked down and injured in the raid. We surmise she saw her mother murdered. In all the confusion, it took us hours to find little Connie, wandering in a daze some distance from town."

"You speak of this horrible tragedy without bitterness."

"Oh, I grieved. I still miss my wife so much it takes my breath away at times. I have never cared to remarry. But I know—I *know*, we white people deserved retribution, after our horrible treatment of them. One day I realized my wife suffered on behalf of our people, a sort of atonement, I suppose. I determined not to let her sacrifice go to waste. I seek to live out restitution however I can, by extending kindness to all people, whatever their color, creed, or social position."

"I'm impressed."

"I do this for my Hannah, in her name. In this way I have found meaning in her death. The only hope I see for our country is resolution of the terrible animosities that divide us into color and class, privilege and misery. I know Hannah would approve of my stance. She was the most loving person I have ever known."

"I imagine—that is, I suppose—many people do not understand you."

Mr. Martin smiled wryly. "You have a gift for courteous understatement. I have chosen not to let the sting of misunderstanding take root in my heart. I came close enough to bitterness after Hannah's death to know I don't want to live that way. Instead, when someone demeans me, I pray for their soul."

"That is lovely."

"This prayer practice has slowly generated compassion in me, where once I nurtured anger and resentment. When people speak contemptuously, I learn more about the condition of their hearts and minds than about the object of their scorn. I grieve for them."

"You are a remarkable man, Mr. Martin. Thank you for sharing this with me. Can nothing be done for Connie?"

"I don't know, though I pray daily for her release and for healing of the childish emotions I believe trapped inside her. Connie claims not to remember her mother's death, and I have no doubt that is true at a conscious level. But I think her body remembers. Does that make any sense to you? The impact of such an event on a young child's soul must be the more terrible because she did not have words, perspective, or experience to help her objectify or express or make sense of what she witnessed."

"Her husband must be aware ..."

"Oh yes. Michael grew up with her. He loves her dearly and is as distressed as I when these spells come upon her. His loving attitude has taught the town to be tolerant and gracious toward her as well. I am so grateful."

"The mysteries of the soul are far deeper than we as a society have begun to plumb."

Mr. Martin studied Charlie's face. "I believe you speak from experiences of your own."

"You are perceptive. I suppose every person becomes overwhelmed at one time or another, don't you think? Music is what helps me with what I call my demons." Charlie noticed the carriage slowing. "Oh, we seem to be arriving. I see several cottages."

"Yes. Dingle is a tiny community. Let's inquire about Uncle William's friend Minnie."

"Thank you for helping us today, Ebony," said Cally.

"Miz Minnie!" Ebony knocked gently on the door of a cabin so old it looked ready to crumble. Pink, red, and lavender bee balm bordered the cabin. Beyond it a neat vegetable garden flourished. "Miz Minnie, I'm coming in. Folks here want to see you."

Charlie, Cally, Felicity, and Mr. Martin stood back while Ebony entered. They heard conversation but couldn't distinguish words. After a time, Ebony emerged supporting a woman with a limp, blinking in the bright sunshine. Cally stepped forward to take her other arm.

"Miz Minnie doesn't hear so good, but her mind is sharp. I'll help you talk to her. We can sit on these stumps," said Ebony.

Cally chose one nearby and drew Felicity onto her lap. "May I call you Miss Minnie, ma'am? My name is Cally. This is my daughter Felicity and my brother Charlie. I believe you met Mr. Martin some years ago at his bank."

Minnie looked slowly from one face to another, settling her gaze on Mr. Martin. "I remember you. I was with William."

Mr. Martin knelt on a level with Minnie's face. "That's right, Miss Minnie. I've wondered ever since what happened to you."

"You wanted to help us but didn't know how."

"That's true. Isn't this—wasn't this old Peg Leg's place? I came here once when I was a boy, ten or eleven years old, before my parents settled in what we then called Clover Creek." Mr. Martin gazed around him. "I remember because my father allowed me to purchase penny candy at Peg Leg's trading post, a rare treat for me. The trek across Wyoming was hard, and this valley felt like a paradise. Until the winter snows, that is."

"Old Peg Leg is long gone. Soon I will be too. There's no penny candy here for you now, young man. I never heard from William again after he left me here in 1890."

What word describes her voice? Apple cider, maybe. Rich and sweet. Cally released Felicity to chase a butterfly and shifted on her stump. *Perhaps these trees were cut to build the cabin.*

"I saw William once more, Minnie," said Mr. Martin. "He came on the train and left a packet with me at the bank. He told me he was going home to Ireland, and I should hold the packet until someone from his family came to fetch it. Charles here is the one who did."

"I am Charles Malcomson, Miss Minnie," said Charlie. "William was my great-uncle."

"You must be the boy who called the police and interrupted his attempt to rob your father," said Minnie. "William told me all about that. His wife left him after she found out what he tried to do. He was so embarrassed and ashamed he left Ireland and came here."

"Oh. We never knew why Uncle William disappeared or where he went," said Charlie. "My father thought he had made amends for the family's unkind treatment of Uncle William, but when no one could find him, his wife went abroad. After he returned to Ireland, he joined her in London, and they were together for a few months there until he died."

"The packet Uncle William left with Mr. Martin contained an envelope for you, Miss Minnie," said Cally. Charlie handed the envelope to Minnie.

"Oh. Oh my. He shouldn't have. Read the letter to me, Ebony. My vision isn't what it once was."

Ebony read:

My very dear friend Minnie,

I am sorry I had to return to my own country without saying goodbye. If you are reading this, I have gone ahead of you to Heaven. Thank you for showing me how to be free of bitterness and shame. You changed my life and moved my heart toward reconciliation with my wife. I don't yet know whether she will listen to me, but if she does, I owe it to you. Thank you for taking me to the cross and for your intercession for me. I will pray for your family, especially for your missing son Cecil. I hope this money will ease your way in your latter years.

God bless you,

William.

"Cecil was conscripted into the Union army, a young boy in the wrong place at the wrong time," said Minnie. "We didn't know what had happened until the war was over."

"Then he came home and now he's my daddy," said Ebony,

grinning at the group in general. "He's the one taught me to read."

"How did you meet my great-uncle William, Miss Minnie?" asked Charlie.

"That was in Pocatello," said Minnie. "Times were hard, and our family was starving. I fought for her not to do it, but my daughter Melody was pulled into the night life, and before I knew it, she was locked into the Walled City, those terrible houses of ill repute—a prison, really. William met her there at a low time in his life. He bought her out, though the owner of that awful place threatened him. She told him, 'Please take care of my mother, Minnie,' and he did. My husband had died years before, building the railroad out west, long before it came to Montpelier."

"Aunt Melody still lives in Pocatello," said Ebony. "I only met her once. She's a beautiful lady."

"That she is, that she is," said Minnie. "But she forgot beauty is as beauty does. Don't you ever forget that, Ebony, hear?"

"Yes, ma'am, Miz Minnie."

"I don't let her call me grandma," said Minnie. "Makes me feel old." She laughed, so everyone else did too.

"I've heard age is more a matter of the heart than the body," said Cally. *Though I've never seen anyone with so many wrinkles.*

"But you are old. Aren't you?" asked Felicity.

"Bless you, child, of course I am. But I don't need Ebony to rub it in now, do I?"

Cally smiled at Felicity, who pulled back in confusion.

"Miss Minnie, we brought a picnic along with us," said Charlie, after a glance at Cally. "We would love to share it with you and Ebony, if that's all right with you."

"I'll get the basket!" said Cally.

Felicity ran after her to the carriage. "Why doesn't Miss Minnie want to be called old, Mummy? She *is* old."

"Perhaps inside she's not quite ready to be old, Felicity. We'll talk more later."

Felicity pouted a moment, then looked up with a bright smile. "I'll help you pass around the food!"

ଓଃ

"Lizzy and I like seeing trees and grass again," said Felicity, gazing across Bear Lake an hour after they said goodbye to Ebony and Minnie. She skipped to the shore and found a pebble to throw in the water.

"Yes, this valley has potential," said Mr. Martin. "Michael's idea of a dam and irrigation canals might be a good one, if only it weren't so costly."

Thou shalt be like a watered garden.

Cally's eyes widened. *Where did that thought come from? It must be something Aisling used to say.*

ଓଃ

"There's a part of Uncle William's packet we haven't talked about," said Charlie as they trundled back toward Montpelier. Felicity lay with her head in his lap, sound asleep. Cally insisted on driving the carriage.

"Oh? Is it something I can help with?" asked Mr. Martin.

"I hope so. It makes no sense to me," said Charlie, pulling Uncle William's rhyme out of his pocket. "It's only four words."

Mr. Martin read aloud, "Fizzy. Dizzy. Busy Lizzy."

"Cryptic. As Uncle William often was," said Charlie, stroking Felicity's head to soothe her after the carriage hit a bump.

"Fizzy. Dizzy." Mr. Martin repeated slowly. "Fizzy makes me think of Soda Springs."

"Soda Springs?"

"Yes. Fizzy water straight out of the ground. Travelers on the Oregon Trail used to mix it with sugar or jam and drink it. Nowadays folks add lemon and sugar. It's not bad, if you can get it chilled. Mineral water from Soda Springs is shipped all over the world."

"You grow lemons around here?"

"Oh no. But the railroad makes it easy to import them from California."

"Where is Soda Springs in relation to Montpelier? Does the railroad go there?"

"It's thirty miles northwest. The Oregon Short Line reached Soda Springs in 1882. You'll enjoy the ride through beautiful Bear River Valley. Now, what could the word dizzy have to do with Soda Springs? It does have a reputation as a wild west town, a jumping-off place for miners to the Carriboo Mountains. Perhaps William found life there dizzying."

"Any thoughts about 'Busy Lizzy'? Or about where we can stay in Soda Springs?"

"I'd only be guessing. A photographer named Elizabeth Johnson lived in Soda Springs in Uncle William's day. She moved to Pocatello in 1896 to work with Benedicte Wrensted. Have you seen her work? Miss Wrensted is well known in southeast Idaho, especially for her photographs of native Americans. If Elizabeth Johnson is William's Busy Lizzy, you'll have to look for her in Pocatello. But of course, you can inquire in Soda Springs about other Lizzys. That's all I have to offer. I suggest you stay at the famous Idanha Hotel."

"Idanha? That's the name of the hotel where we stayed in Boise!" said Charlie.

"Ah, yes. But the Soda Springs Idanha came first, built in 1887 with electric lights and natural gas heating—the fanciest, most modern building in the wild west. Hundreds of tourists stay there each year. Many of them travel to Soda Springs for the water cure. Soaking in the medicinal waters is said to heal whatever ails you. The Boise Idanha is a copycat. Ah, here we are. Strange how a return trip always seems shorter than going."

Charlie laughed. "From what you say, Soda Springs will be an adventure. We'll catch the train tomorrow morning. Thank you, Mr. Martin. You have been most gracious. I hope you'll soon have a secure bank vault for the citizens of Montpelier."

"It is I who thank you. I've wondered for years what became of Minnie and whether she was still alive. I'm delighted to know William provided for her old age. I hope you will visit Montpelier again, and perhaps play the piano for us."

"That would be a pleasure, Mr. Martin. I think I'll ask Mr. Dawson whether he and his guests would mind if I play for a while this evening. I'm not used to going so many days without several hours of practice."

"Then Connie and I will go hear you. Goodbye until then."

CHAPTER 8

SODA SPRINGS

[Note: For a map, see "Soda Springs" under Historical Links on HorseThief1898.blog.]

Soda Springs, Thursday, May 26

"IT IS FIZZY!" EXCLAIMED FELICITY. "I never had fizzy lemonade."

"I haven't either," said Cally. "I've never imagined water coming out of the ground already carbonated. After lunch and a rest, shall we explore this new place?"

"Why can't Uncle Charlie go with us?"

"He needs to practice. Uncle Charlie is a pianist, Felicity. You know that, right? The hotel has asked him to play this weekend. He said yes, to help us with the costs of staying at this fancy place. But he must prepare. Have you had enough to eat?"

"Yes."

"Then let's go upstairs for our rest time. Felicity, look at the people gathering around the piano to listen to Uncle Charlie practice! I liked to do that when I was a little girl. It's probably the best way he can advertise his concerts. Oh my."

"What, Mummy?"

"I just noticed the name of the bar. It's called 'Dizzy Lizzy!'"

"Dizzy Lizzy?" Felicity clutched her doll. "Lizzy isn't dizzy!"

"I'll explain later, sweetheart. Let's ask whether anyone here knew Uncle William."

"That man has funny skin," said Felicity.

"Shh, Felicity." Cally frowned at her daughter, then turned toward the elderly barman. "Sir, do you have time to speak with me?"

"Certainly, ma'am. How can I help you?"

"I have rather a strange question. I'm looking for someone who might have known my great-uncle years ago. His name was William Malcomson."

"Why, it's about time you showed up, young lady! We'd begun to think no Malcomsons would take old William up on his crazy treasure hunt! But the person you need to speak to isn't here. She retired long since. This bar is named after her. She's a legend in this town."

"Not related to a photographer named Elizabeth Johnson, then," said Cally.

"No, no. No relation at all. Lizzy lives up near China Peak on Caribou Mountain, what the locals call China Hat. Here, let me show you."

The barman ushered Cally and Felicity across the lobby to a huge window. "See there, in the distance? Doesn't that look like a Chinaman's hat? Near ten thousand feet high, that China Hat is. Lizzy lives halfway up that mountain, past Gray's Lake, near one of the old mines. You can take a carriage the first five hours or so, but you'll have to walk the last couple of miles."

"Is this an adventure, Mummy?" asked Felicity.

"It certainly is. Can you tell us more, sir?"

"Lizzy's cousin was a miner. When he left, he deeded her his cabin, which she furnished from her old boardinghouse. She hasn't been down to Soda Springs in years. Perhaps she's no longer mobile. I think she and your Uncle William were well-nigh the same age. She seemed ancient to me fifteen years ago."

"You've been so helpful! We could go up the mountain tomorrow, I think. Thank you, sir. May I ask your name?"

"Name's Calico, on account of my skin. Not my real name, of course, but that's what everyone calls me. Don't bother me none."

"What does calico mean, Mummy?" asked Felicity.

"Calico is a kind of fabric, Felicity," said Cally.

"But the fur of a calico cat has patches of different colors," said the barman. "Like my skin, see? I was born like this."

"Thank you, sir. Shall we tell Lizzy Calico sent us to her?" asked Cally.

"Yes, with my regards. We miss her. You'll see what I mean," said Calico.

"Sir, can you think of anything Lizzy would appreciate us taking to her?

"She always was partial to Idanha mineral water. Here. Take her these bottles, courtesy of the hotel. She'll like that."

"Thank you. I'll ask my brother Charlie to stop by for directions. Is that all right?"

"Yes, yes. Order a carriage at the front desk and ask the kitchen to pack food for you. Truly, I began to think this day would never come, when a Malcomson would show up here." Calico sighed. "I would love to see Lizzy again."

"Why don't you go with us? I'm sure that would be fine with Charlie, sir."

"Well then, I'll find someone to watch the bar tomorrow. Tell your brother we'll need an early start if we hope to make the trip and return the same day. It'll be cold, so dress warmly."

"Thank you, sir."

As they walked toward the stairs, Felicity asked, "Why is his skin like that, Mummy?" Cally heard the man chuckle.

"I've never seen so many sheep!" exclaimed Cally, several hours into their ride to the Caribou Mountain.

"Yes, thousands of them graze in the Grays Lake area," said Calico.

"And the lake is so blue!" said Charlie. "Oh, look, Cally! There's an old wagon. An old, covered wagon, like pioneers must have used on the Oregon Trail."

"I wonder what happened to the family it belonged to. Can we stop for a few minutes, Calico? I want to fix this scene in my mind. The mountains, the lake, the wagon ..."

"Sure, Cally," said Calico, signaling the driver. "We have at least another hour to ride, so it will be good to stretch a bit."

"Can I run down by the water, Mummy?" asked Felicity.

"I'll go with you, Pipsqueak. If that's all right, Cally," said Charlie.

"Just for a few minutes," said Calico.

"I want to look more closely at the wagon," said Cally. "Imagine a wagon this size being home to a family for weeks on end, never knowing what kind of danger they might encounter. All with the hope of a better life at the end of the trail."

"This family must have decided to leave the Oregon Trail for some reason, to come this far north," said Calico. "Perhaps they settled nearby, rather than trekking all the way to Oregon. Perhaps they were tempted by the Cariboo gold rush."

"I can see why they would want to stay here," said Cally. "This is beautiful."

"Especially this time of year. We're nearing the end of the spring blooms. A few weeks ago, the hillsides were covered with flowers. Don't let them fool you, though. Winter is long, spring and summer short around here. We can have frosts at night in the middle of summer."

Thou shalt be like a watered garden.

Cally startled. *Why do I keep thinking of that? What does it mean?*

"The wildflowers are resilient. They come back in the spring though winter be bitter cold," continued Calico. "We don't know what happened to this family, but I hope they were as resilient as the flowers. Life here isn't easy."

"Thank you for warning us it would be chilly," said Cally. "I hope it will be warmer by the time we walk. I never thought of packing winter clothes for this trip."

"Lizzy or her daughter will serve us hot tea to warm us up," said Calico. "Shall we resume our journey?"

"All right," said Cally, taking one more look at the old wagon while Calico called Charlie and Felicity. *I wish I knew what happened to this family thirty or forty years ago.*

"Lizzy's daughter lives with her? Can you tell us more about them?" Cally asked Calico as they bumped along the trail once more.

"Why sure. Lizzy crossed over from China along with hundreds of miners when the word 'gold' made its way across the ocean. They knew exactly what they were doing, those Chinamen. Found more gold than any white men. Lizzy ran a boardinghouse and tavern in Soda Springs, a booming business during the goldrush."

"She must be an interesting person," said Cally.

"That she is. Folks called her Busy Lizzy because she was always running to catch up with the demand at her boardinghouse. Course her real name's something Chinese no one remembers. When the Union Pacific built the Idanha in 1887, they invited her to run the bar—to attract the locals, you see. Lizzy knew everyone in town. More Chinamen here than white men in the old mining days, until the gold ran out. Most of them returned to China. But Lizzy stayed on. Because of her daughter, some said."

"Oh?"

"May Lee is only half Chinese. Lizzy never said who her father was. Neither Chinamen nor whites wanted to marry the girl, even with the shortage of women at the time. May Lee worked with Lizzy and moved to the mountain with her. Quiet woman, standoffish, though some of us tried to befriend her. Very different from Lizzy, but they were devoted to each other."

"How long until we walk, Calico?" asked Charlie.

"Not long now—maybe forty minutes. Time for a nap, if you like."

"Calico! What a surprise! And you have people with you," said the woman who responded to Calico's knock.

"May Lee, how nice to see you. May we come in? I'll introduce my friends to you and Lizzy at the same time," said Calico.

"Come in, of course, but Mother isn't dressed yet. She's doing poorly, Calico. Not long for this world, she tells me. But she'll be happy you came to visit. Your friends are shivering. I'll put the tea kettle on and help Mother dress," said May Lee. "Here is the teapot and tea and sugar and cups. Please make your own when the teakettle whistles."

"Mmm, so good," said Cally as they sipped their tea a few minutes later.

"Lizzy likes it too, Mummy," said Felicity, holding her cup against her doll's mouth.

The bedroom door opened. "Will you help us, Calico?" asked May Lee. "I'm sorry, but Mother will need the space on the couch. And we only have the two chairs."

Cally, Charlie, and Felicity all jumped to their feet. "Sit here, Cally," said Charlie.

"And my Lizzy will sit with me on Mummy's lap," said Felicity.

Calico emerged from the bedroom carrying a tiny woman, whom he lay gently on the couch. May Lee tucked a pillow under her head and spread a blanket over her. The woman's bright eyes took in her visitors.

"Who are these people, Calico?" she asked. "Why did they climb all this way to see me?"

"They are Charles Malcomson, his sister Cally, and her daughter Felicity," said Calico.

"And my friend Lizzy—the same name as you!" said Felicity, holding up her doll.

"She is charming, child. Malcomson ... You must be related to William Malcomson."

"He was my great-uncle," said Charlie.

"May Lee, look in my bottom drawer, under everything, at the back, for a small packet."

"Yes, Mother."

"I've been thinking you would show up soon. I couldn't die before completing this task for my friend William."

"How did you know my Uncle William, Miss Lizzy?" asked Charlie.

"Your Uncle William came here at a time of duress, with his friend Melody. He wanted a room at the Idanha, but the hotel wouldn't accept her. So, I invited them to stay with me and May Lee. They were with us long enough for Melody's child to be born."

"Her child?" said Cally.

"Yes. I never asked the whole story, and they never told me. But William brought Melody here from Pocatello when they found out she was pregnant, to spare her judgment from her people there, I gathered. She couldn't escape judgment, could she, but May Lee and I cared for them. They named the baby William, so I assume the baby was his. We called him Billy."

"Billy!" exclaimed Charlie and Cally at the same time.

"The name means something to you? May Lee, serve our guests more tea."

"Uncle William left us something to give Billy, but we didn't know who he was," said Charlie. "Do you know where we can find him?"

"No idea, none at all," said Lizzy. "William and Melody left Soda Springs when the baby was a few weeks old. As far as I know, they returned to Pocatello. That's where I would look first. Billy would be—what year is this, May Lee?"

"Today is May 27, 1904, Mother."

"Then Billy will be fourteen the fourth of July," said Lizzy. "His birthday is easy to remember. He was born in 1890."

"Uncle William wanted us to know Billy, all these years later. Thank you, Lizzy," said Charlie. "And thank you for your kindness to Uncle William. This is hard to take in. My father had a young cousin he never knew. And never can know. We had no idea."

"Your father no longer lives?"

"No, ma'am. He died suddenly four years ago," said Charlie. "We miss him."

"We brought you water!" said Felicity. "I don't think it's a very good present, but Mr. Calico said you would like it."

"He was right, child. There's no taste so pure as Idanha water. Thank you, Calico."

"Ma'am, if it's not too rude to ask: May we know how old you are?" asked Charlie.

May Lee smiled, and Lizzy laughed. "You won't believe me if I tell you. I'm one hundred and six."

"What's your secret?" asked Cally.

"Vegetables. Clean water. Tea. A free and happy heart. No regrets, no grudges. My wonderful May Lee's excellent care and company," said Lizzy. "And now I must rest. Thank you for coming, and for relieving my mind about William's package. I can die now in peace."

"But Mother—" said May Lee.

"Now dear, we've been talking about this. No one lives forever, and my time is coming soon. I need a nap, and then we'll talk more. Calico, will you kindly carry me back to my bed?"

"Mother, what do you want me to do with this packet?" asked May Lee.

"See how forgetful I am? Give it to this young man. Charles, you called him, Calico?"

"Yes. He's a famous pianist," said Calico.

"How nice," said Lizzy. "Now, Calico—"

Calico lifted the tiny woman in his arms. "It's a joy to see you again, Lizzy."

"Thank you for bringing these people all the way from Soda Springs. You must leave soon to get back before dark," said Lizzy.

"Yes, ma'am," said Charlie. "Thank you. God bless you and May Lee. Goodbye."

"Goodbye. When you find Billy, tell him the woman who midwifed him into this world wishes him to live with no regrets and no grudges. And to eat his vegetables," said Lizzy.

Charlie smiled. "Yes, ma'am. Goodbye, May Lee."

"Thank you for the tea," said Cally.

"My Lizzy hopes she'll someday be as old as you," said Felicity. "She likes old people."

Lizzy chuckled. "On your way, now. Goodbye."

"Uncle William is full of surprises," said Cally as they began their trek down the mountain.

"Billy is the greatest surprise of them all," said Charlie. "We'll open the new packet after we get back to the carriage. Perhaps Pocatello will be our next stop."

"A telegram for you, sir," the Idanha receptionist informed Charlie when they walked, weary, into the hotel lobby.

"Thank you, sir. Cally, it's from Thomas. He and Shane will begin their journey to Idaho tomorrow. He's asking what their destination should be. We don't know yet because Uncle William's new clue is as cryptic as always."

"We should have asked Calico while we were with him. We got too distracted talking about Lizzy and Billy and wondering how Uncle William's sons will react when they find out they have a half-brother," said Cally. "Then Felicity fell asleep, and I dozed too."

"Too much has happened too fast," said Charlie. "I can't quite absorb what Uncle William is telling us."

"We should write it all down, so we don't lose track of the pieces," said Cally.

"Good idea. Since we're tired, and have the concert tomorrow night, what if we stay here over Sunday and enjoy the warm springs? I'll leave early Monday to return to New York City for my ship to Lisbon. I'll tell Thomas to come here. You'll be all right for a few hours until they arrive, won't you?"

"Of course. You'll meet with the New York Philharmonic before you ship out, right?" Cally grinned at Charlie, and he blushed. She patted his arm. "A couple more days here will be nice. We need time to figure out the next clue." She yawned. "I don't want to think about the treasure hunt any more tonight. We'll miss you while you're in Europe, Charlie."

"I expect to be back by the end of July. Go on to bed, Cally. I'll send Thomas a telegram. Good night, Felicity. Did you enjoy meeting Miss Lizzy?"

Felicity yawned too. "Yes, but she's really, really old, like Miz Minnie. Uncle William's friends are the oldest I ever met. Good night, Uncle Charlie."

"What's this?" asked Cally as they sat down to a late breakfast.

"Open it," said Charlie.

"A notebook?"

"Yes, for Uncle William's story. I want you to keep track of all the details, since I'll miss the next few weeks of discoveries. It will be good to have everything written in orderly fashion, to pass on to Cousins William, Llewellyn, and Hubert."

"Thank you, Charlie. I can't wait to get started. Felicity, you can finish your travel book while I work on this story."

"Anxious as we are to find Billy, the next clue doesn't sound like Pocatello," said Charlie, opening Lizzy's packet. "I'll read it again." He read out loud,

Joe Rainey knows the place
Where old Fort Hall resourced the Trail
We buried the next chapter
Of this treasure seeker's tale.

"Hmm. We can consult Calico, for starters," said Cally.

"Would you and Felicity mind talking to him after your soak at the spa? I need to decide what I'm playing for the concert tonight."

"We'll be glad to. Is there more in the packet? Yesterday we only looked at the clue."

"There's an envelope labeled 'For the treasure seekers.' Would you like to open it, Felicity? You're one of the treasure seekers."

"It's money, Uncle Charlie, and a letter," said Felicity.

"A brief note," said Cally. "It says, 'In case by now you need reinforcement. The Idanha isn't cheap.' Signed William."

"Considerate of him," said Charlie. "How did he guess we would stay at the Idanha? This will tide us over until Thomas arrives with more money. Here, Cally, take half. Why don't you two spend the day as you like, and I'll join you for supper at 6:00. See you then."

"Felicity, I think Lizzy should stay in our room while we're at the spa. I don't want her to get wet. Let's go pack a change of clothes. I don't know what people wear to soak in the warm water. But this will be fun!"

Felicity spoke into Lizzy's ear, and then held the doll's face to her own ear. "She says she'll stay if she can have fizzy lemonade for lunch."

Cally laughed. "I think that will be fine."

ꕥ

Charlie walked not to the piano but to the hotel gardens. *I need a minute to sort out my feelings. It's all well and good for Uncle William to offer us support in this endeavor. But if he hadn't bankrupted Malcomson Brothers, we wouldn't have any worries about money. The more I see him giving away, the more resentful I feel. But I need to bury these feelings for Cally's sake. I don't want to complicate things for Thomas, either. Soon he'll be here instead of me.*

Charlie circled back to the front door. *I'll do what Mr. Paderewski taught me years ago: let my angst flow out into my music.*

ꕥ

"Does Calico know Joe Rainey?" asked Charlie, after they ordered supper.

"He said the name sounds familiar, but he wasn't sure," said Cally. "He's going to ask the hotel manager whether he can check back through the register to find out whether he was ever a guest here. Especially in the early 90s when Uncle William was in town."

"I wish now we had taken time to open the packet while we were with Miss Lizzy," said Charlie. "From what Calico has told us, not much in this town got past her."

"You're right. That is what we should have done," said Cally. "I can't quite picture us making the trip back up the mountain. Perhaps Calico will discover something."

"Well, Thomas and Shane might enjoy the hike. Aren't you glad we met Miss Lizzy and May Lee, Felicity?" said Charlie.

"I think my dolly Lizzy will look like Miss Lizzy when she gets old," said Felicity.

Cally smiled. "I'm glad we met her when we did. One riddle to solve after another—that's the nature of treasure hunts, I suppose. I'm fascinated by how Uncle William is telling us the story of his lost years, when no one in your family knew where he was."

"How was the spa? Did you soak away all your worries and cares?" asked Charlie.

"Jenny and I splashed some ladies. They said, 'Calm down.' They didn't want their hair wet," said Felicity.

"Felicity met Jenny at the spa. Her family lives in Boise City," said Cally. "Imagine water coming out of the ground a perfect temperature for bathing! It relaxed us so much we took a long nap this afternoon. What special music do you have planned for tonight, Charlie?"

"I'll blend classics with ragtime again. Idahoans seem to like that."

"It's an unusual blend!" said Cally.

"Tonight, I'll listen," said Felicity. "I was too tired those other times."

"Please tell me whether you like it, Squidget," said Charlie. "By the way, I heard there are interesting caves to explore here in Soda Springs. I bet Shane would enjoy that even more than the spa. Since you're staying an extra day, you could check it out."

"Lizzy and I are afraid of caves. We can't make light shine like the Light Princess."

"I think they have lanterns," said Cally.

"We have half an hour before the concert," said Charlie. Would you two ladies join me on a walk in the Idanha gardens?"

"Sure, Uncle Charlie!"

CHAPTER 9

CARIBOU MOUNTAIN

[For a map, see "Caribou Mountain" under Historical Links on HorseThief1898.blog.]

Soda Springs, Sunday, May 29

"MUMMY, MAY LIZZY AND I PLAY WITH JENNY?" asked Felicity after breakfast.

"What does her mother say? Oh, good morning, Mrs. Hanover."

"Good morning. Please call me Tamara," said a stylishly dressed woman with a small girl in tow. "Jenny is asking whether Felicity can play with her this morning. Would that be all right with you? Since it's raining, I expect we'll stay in the hotel."

"Of course, she may. And my name is Cally."

"Shall we see you at luncheon then, Cally?"

"Yes. My room is 305, should you need me," said Cally

"And mine is 208. We'll probably spend time in the playroom. Please tell your brother we enjoyed the concert last night."

"Thank you. I will. Have fun, girls!" said Cally.

It was a lovely concert. I'm not surprised the hotel invited him to play again tonight. Charlie is so personable and charming. People kept asking for one more, just one more ...

"Ma'am, I have a message for you," said the desk clerk.

"Thank you, sir."

Cally read, "Charlie and Cally, I found that Joe Rainey was a guest at the Idanha in 1889. He gave his address as Malad, Idaho. That's a long way from here, about sixty-five miles. I suggest you send a telegram to Malad to find out whether he's still there. If so, perhaps you can arrange to meet him wherever this old Fort Hall is located (if he knows).

"Perhaps Lizzy could tell you more. I can't go back up the mountain this week after taking off a whole day Friday. But the driver who took us will remember the way to the place where you have to walk. Follow the trail straight uphill like we did before. If it were me, I would do it. We'll lose a trove of history and random information when that dear woman dies! Best wishes, Calico"

Good idea. I hope Thomas and Shane will be up for climbing to Lizzy's cabin. The soonest we can do it is Tuesday. I'll send Joe Rainey a telegram in Malad. What a strange name—I wonder where it came from!

"Sir, I need to send a telegram."

And now, since Charlie is with that fiddler he met last night, the rest of the morning is all mine! Imagine that! I could read, or write more of Uncle William's story, or complete the tucking on Josie's dress, or write letters to the Anthonys and Nathanael and Sarah, or journal about my dreams for the future, as Charlie asked. And I could write a letter to Mary Ann Eastman, catching her up with what happened in Montpelier and in Soda Springs.

Cally wandered to the lobby window and looked out at the rain, vaguely aware of Charlie and the violinist practicing in the background. *If I could do anything at all with my life, with no concerns about a child or about money, what would I do? Charlie told me to list the things I love, that give me energy. I'll do that now. I can write letters tomorrow.*

ʢʫ

"Ma'am, you've received a telegram," said the desk clerk as Cally walked toward the dining room to meet Tamara, Jenny and Felicity for luncheon.

"Already? Thank you!"

"`Yes, I live in Malad`," the telegram said. "`Call me this afternoon at 4:00 at the LDS social hall. Joe Rainey`."

"Sir," said Cally, showing the telegram to the clerk. "Do you know what LDS means?"

"Latter Day Saints. It's another name for Mormon," responded the clerk. "I'll reserve telephone time for you at 4:00." He indicated a small room behind the desk.

"Thank you, sir."

Either Joe Rainey is Mormon or there aren't many telephones in Malad. My, that's beautiful music. I've never heard Charlie play with a violinist. What fun for him to offer a different experience to the hotel guests this evening! Charlie didn't just happen to bring the scores for piano-violin duets along with him. This must be a piece he might play with Laoise for the New York Philharmonic! I wish I could be a fly on the wall when he reconnects with her.

Cally settled into the chair beside Felicity at the Hanovers' table and waved to Charlie as he entered the dining room with his new friend. *I wonder if we'll have time before he leaves tomorrow to talk about the work I did this morning, identifying the things I love. I'll miss him. But it will be good to see Thomas and Shane again, and soon the rest of the family!*

"The violinist is from Weiser," Mr. Hanover was saying. "They have a tradition of great fiddling. Remember, Tamara, when we heard a string group from Weiser play in Boise City? We're in for a treat tonight!"

"Yes. Weiser is famous for its fiddling contests." Tamara turned to her daughter. "Jenny, you must take a nap after lunch if you want to stay up for the concert."

"You too, Felicity," Cally said.

Cally grabbed her notebook and opened the door to a gentle knock, putting her finger to her lips as she slipped out to the hallway. "Felicity is napping. Do you have time to talk for a few minutes, Charlie?"

"Let's go to the sitting area on the landing," said Charlie. "How was your morning?"

"I did what you asked—I listed the things I love," said Cally.

"I'm glad you took time for this," said Charlie, reading through her notes. "Do you feel it gives you direction? What steps do you think you should take once you return to Kansas City?"

"Before we talk about that, can you join me for a telephone call with Joe Rainey this afternoon at 4:00?"

"No, I'm sorry. I'll be in the middle of another practice session with Mr. Gregory," said Charlie. "I'm sure you'll handle it well, Cally. Write down any arrangements you make."

"Calico thinks we should go back up the mountain to ask Lizzy about Joe Rainey."

"You're thinking about making the trip again then, Cally? It's such a long way!"

"Yes, but Calico is convinced it will be worth our while. I've already arranged for the carriage with the same driver. I think Thomas and Shane will enjoy it. By the way, you didn't just happen to have piano-violin music with you ..."

Charlie blushed and twiddled his cravat.

"It's fun to tease you," said Cally. "I wish I could meet Laoise."

"I'm worried, actually," said Charlie. "We didn't leave on good terms. I hurt her badly." Tears sprung to his eyes, and he brushed them away.

"I didn't know that. I'm sorry, Charlie. What happened?" asked Cally.

"Short story or long?"

"That's up to you, Charlie."

"We liked each other, but something happened, and I rejected her friendship." Tears flooded his cheeks. A hotel guest opened his door and walked toward them. Charlie pulled a handkerchief from his pocket. "I can't tell you the whole story now, Cally. But seeing Laoise again is all I can think about."

Cally smiled at the man as he passed them. "I understand. Perhaps we can talk more this evening after the concert, once Felicity is asleep?"

"Sure."

"Can you rest a bit before you practice again with Mr. Gregory?"

"I'll do that. I would go for a walk, but it's still raining."

"What time is your train tomorrow morning?"

"It's early—7:00. The hotel will pack a breakfast for me."

"I'll see you at the concert."

"Thank you, sis."

"You'll meet us in the lobby of the Pocatello train station Thursday morning," said Cally, jotting notes as she listened to Mr. Rainey on the telephone. "Thank you, sir. And we'll take a wagon from there to old Fort Hall. Wouldn't a carriage be more comfortable? ... Oh, you think we'll need a wagon. And you want us to arrange for it, since we'll arrive before you. I understand. There will be four of us, myself, my brother Thomas and two children. With you, that's five. The children and I can ride in the wagon while you and Thomas sit on the bench ... This trip won't be appropriate for the children? But I have nowhere to leave them, Mr. Rainey. You'll bring a shovel? Why will we need a shovel? ... All right, we'll talk about it when we meet you in Pocatello. Thank you, sir. Until Thursday."

Frowning, Cally hung up. *What could make this trip inappropriate for the children? I suppose Thomas will go with Mr. Rainey alone, while I stay somewhere with Shane and Felicity. I'm even more motivated to talk with Lizzy about this Joe Rainey. And why this side trip, since Melody and Billy are probably in Pocatello? What is this about, Uncle William?*

Early morning, Monday, May 30

"Charlie, we'll miss you so much! Thank you for taking all these days to help us with this crazy treasure hunt."

"Thank you for my train book, Uncle Charlie," said Felicity, throwing herself into Charlie's arms. "Lizzy is sad you're going away."

"I'll miss you, Pipsqueak," said Charlie. "I'll see you in about a month, all right?"

"Write to me, Charlie! I want to know everything!"

Charlie colored. "I will. Goodbye, Cally. Goodbye, Felicity. Goodbye, Lizzy."

"Thomas! Shane! It's so good to see you both!" Cally hugged each of them in turn, while Felicity jumped up and down and clapped her hands. "How was your trip?"

"It went by fast," said Thomas. "I've never seen desert landscapes before."

"Not so fast for me," said Shane. "I got bored."

"Well, you won't be bored now," said Cally. "There's so much going on here, it's hard to keep track of everything."

"You can tell us all about it at supper," said Thomas. "Right now, I would love to find our room and clean up a bit. Shall we meet you in the dining room in half an hour?"

ଓଃ

"Try the fizzy lemonade," Felicity told Uncle Thomas and Shane.

"Fizzy? What makes it fizzy?" asked Shane.

"Try it first, then I'll tell you," said Felicity. "And there's warm water to play in that comes out of the ground. And there are caves! And tomorrow we're going to visit Miss Lizzy again. And—"

"I'm hungry. Let's order, then you can tell me everything," said Shane.

"Who is Miss Lizzy?" asked Thomas after their food arrived.

"Perhaps we should start at the beginning," said Cally. "What have you already heard from Charlie?"

"You were leaving Montpelier for Soda Springs," said Thomas. "Catch us up."

"I brought the clues we've received from Uncle William so far," said Cally.

"Uncle William is telling us his story," said Felicity. "Mummy said so."

ଓଃ

"So," Cally concluded an hour later. "Tomorrow we'll get up early to travel up Caribou Mountain to talk with Lizzy about Joe Rainey, then we'll have Wednesday to rest and play, and Thursday early we'll take the train to Pocatello to meet Mr. Rainey."

"Fascinating," said Thomas. "I wonder why we're not going to look for Billy first, if he lives in Pocatello, instead of sidetracking to old Fort Hall."

"My question, too," said Cally. "Is Uncle William playing games with us?"

"Maybe Uncle William buried something he wants us to dig up and give to Billy," suggested Shane.

"But why would it be inappropriate for children?" wondered Cally.

"I'm still trying to get my head around meeting a relative we never knew existed. My father's young cousin. Well, in three days we'll know more than we do now," said Thomas. "I see that yawn, Shane. An early night sounds good to me, since we'll be up at dawn tomorrow. I'll telephone Cora to let her know we've arrived safely, and then we'll be off to bed."

"Tomorrow wear everything you have that's warm. It's cold on Caribou Mountain," said Cally.

"What a lark!" said Thomas, turning around on the mountain path to look back toward Soda Springs. "Thank you, Uncle William, for thinking up this crazy treasure hunt."

"We're almost there," said Felicity. "The cabin is behind those big rocks."

"The trek seems easier this time, maybe because I knew what to expect," said Cally.

Felicity ran ahead and knocked. The others caught up before May Lee opened the door.

"May Lee, we—oh. Is something wrong?"

May Lee stood like a statue. For a long moment she said nothing, just gazed at the sky. Then she wailed, a loud, piercing cry. "My mother. My mother died. Last night. She is gone."

"May Lee, I'm so sorry," said Cally. She put her arms around May Lee, but the woman stood stiff and unresponsive. "May Lee, this is my brother, Thomas, and his son Shane."

Slowly, May Lee turned toward Thomas and nodded, then returned to gazing at the sky.

"I think she's in shock, Cally. Perhaps we can help her to the sofa," said Thomas.

"I'll make some tea," said Cally. "It's so cold in here. Felicity, can you look in May Lee's room for a blanket to wrap around her? Thomas, perhaps you and Shane could make a fire in the fireplace?"

It seemed a long time before May Lee shook herself and seemed to notice for the first time the four people gathered around her. "Who are you?" she said.

"I'm Cally, and this is my daughter Felicity. We came to see you and your mother last week. Do you remember us? And this is my brother Thomas, and his son Shane."

"Not the same. The other was—lighter hair, I think," said May Lee.

"Yes. Our brother Charlie came last week, along with your friend Calico."

"Calico, yes. My mother gave you something."

"She did, and that's why we came back, to ask her for more information," said Cally.

"She is gone. Gone." Once again, May Lee wailed, then stopped and froze, her eyes apparently unseeing.

All four of the others had caught their breath, and slowly let it out.

"I think she needs someone she knows better," said Cally.

"But we are the ones who are here," said Thomas. "I don't think we should leave her alone, do you?"

"Your mother would say God brought us here today," said Cally.

Thomas smiled. "She would, wouldn't she. It is rather remarkable." He stood for a moment, silent.

"Are you thinking of your father?" asked Cally.

"Yes. It's still hard to believe he is gone."

"I've been thinking of my da too."

"I think Shane and I should go back to the hotel to find someone who knows May Lee," said Thomas.

"Calico will know what to do. Ask for him," said Cally. "Felicity, do you want to stay here with me, or return to the hotel to play with Jenny?"

"I want to play with Jenny," said Felicity.

"Then I'll stay with May Lee," said Cally. "Thomas, ask at the hotel for Tamara Hanover in room 208. I believe she'll be happy to care for Felicity."

"I'll leave you the food we brought for our lunch. We can eat at the hotel. We'll be back as soon as we can with someone to help," said Thomas.

I don't know anything about Chinese customs. But when Da died, I didn't want to talk. Maybe May Lee feels that way too. What a terrible loss for her.

Cally put a piece of wood on the fire and filled the teakettle. The spotless cabin required no attention. She pulled a chair close to the fire. May Lee sat unmoving; her tea grown cold. *I remember a woman sang to me after Da died. I wonder whether May Lee would like that, even though I don't know any Chinese songs.*

Cally sang an Irish lullaby, tears falling as she remembered Da. May Lee did not move. Cally sang another, and then another. Still May Lee sat, as if disconnected from all around her.

"I was like that too, when my father died, May Lee," said Cally. "It's so much to take in, that the person we love the most in the world is no longer with us. It's hard, terribly hard."

May Lee did not move.

"My da was like your mother, kind and wise," said Cally. "I miss him terribly. It hurt so much to think I would never see him again."

May Lee blinked.

"You've never known life without your mother. I had never known life without my father. It's been almost fourteen years since my da died.

But it still seems like yesterday." *I don't know whether she hears me or I'm talking to myself. Maybe both.*

May Lee crumpled against the sofa and began to weep. Cally put her arms around the grieving woman, crooning as if to a small child until her sobs eased.

I think she may be asleep. Cally brought a small pillow from May Lee's room and eased it under her head, tucking the blanket around her.

I wonder where May Lee will want to bury Lizzy. I'll look around outside.

A large, tidy vegetable garden sprouted. *Thou shalt be like a watered garden.*

Cally stood still, staring at the vegetable patch. *There it is again, that phrase that keeps coming to my mind. What can it mean?*

She peeked inside a small, low stone structure at the back of the garden. It was half-filled with potatoes, carrots, yams, turnips, and other root vegetables she didn't recognize. *Such an interesting assortment of shapes and colors. A garden nourishes both body and soul. This must be how they live through the winter. But how do they not freeze?*

Flowers surrounded the cabin, some already blooming. Cally walked slowly around the small home. *I recognize a few of these, because Cora grows them too: buttercups, primrose, lilies, phlox, goldenrod, coneflowers, iris, asters. The others I don't know.*

Circling back to the vegetable garden, Cally stood and gazed around her. *What beauty these two women have created! But they are so isolated. As far as I can see, there is not a single other dwelling. I wonder whether May Lee will stay here alone or return to Soda Springs.*

Cally bent to pull a weed, then stopped. *Perhaps that isn't a weed. Lizzy and May Lee must have unique gardening abilities, to make all this grow in such a cold, dry climate. I better check on her.*

May Lee lay in the same position, apparently still asleep. Cally gazed at her a moment, then walked quietly toward Lizzy's bedroom and peeked in. A small hump in the bed was all she could see. *May Lee pulled the covers over her mother's head. I wish I knew something about Chinese customs related to death.*

In one corner of the room an easel bore a half-finished painting. *It's the view from the front door of the cabin! Such soft, lovely colors. Is Lizzy the artist, or May Lee? Oh, I hadn't even noticed—the walls are covered with paintings.* Without thinking, Cally took a step forward to examine the one closest to the door, a detailed rendition of a gray wolf, with the signature May Lee. *He looks so intelligent, like he's speaking to me. What are you saying, mister wolf?*

May Lee stirred, and Cally jumped. *I shouldn't be in here.* She closed the door and walked back to her chair by the fire, adding wood before she sat down. *May Lee has an amazing gift. She could support herself by selling her paintings if she would be willing to part with them. I would love to own one and I'm sure others would also.*

She looked around. *How interesting that there are no paintings in the living room or kitchen. It's like May Lee is keeping her gift a secret, even from the few visitors they must occasionally receive.*

May Lee turned over and sat up. Cally sat back and waited. May Lee rubbed her eyes and looked around, confusion on her face. When she saw Cally, she startled. Then her face crumpled. "My mother ..."

"Yes," said Cally. "I am sorry for your great loss. My brother has taken the children back to the hotel to find someone who can come help you."

"The Chens," said May Lee.

"I hope he has found them," said Cally. "Thomas should be back soon. I have food. Will you eat with me?"

"No, I will not eat," said May Lee. "I will send food with my mother into the afterlife."

"Do you know where you want to bury her?"

"Yes. My mother chose the place."

"Good. I'm sure Thomas will help you dig the grave, May Lee."

"I must think what else she will need. Excuse me, please." May Lee walked into her mother's bedroom and closed the door.

I guess I'll eat while she's occupied. How interesting that the Chinese dead take food and other things with them.

It was late afternoon before Thomas returned, with a Chinese couple who looked to be about May Lee's age. Thomas carried a shovel and a bag. The Chinese couple also carried bags. With a cry, May Lee rushed out to meet them and wept for some time on the woman's shoulder. Thomas left them and walked into the cabin.

"Shane?" asked Cally.

"The Hanovers planned to go caving this afternoon and that appealed to Shane," said Thomas. "They seem very nice people."

"They are. Who did you bring with you?"

"The Chens. Calico told me they are good friends of May Lee and Lizzy. He gave me directions to their home," said Thomas.

"I'm glad. May Lee told me after you left that's who she wanted. You did well, Thomas."

"Thanks. They say they will stay for the seven days of the funeral, and possibly the 49 days of mourning if May Lee wishes them to. Apparently, there will be a final ceremony at one hundred days, when other friends may join them here."

"The Chinese certainly honor their dead. Thomas, I discovered May Lee is an incredible artist. Dozens of her paintings hang in her mother's room. I would love to buy one, but should I mention it? I discovered them while May Lee was asleep. I don't want to offend her."

"I'll ask Mr. Chen while we dig Lizzy's grave," said Thomas. "I think he'll tell us what is appropriate. Here they come."

"I have made tea," said Cally after introductions.

"Thomas and I must dig the grave," said Mr. Chen. "May Lee has shown me where Lizzy wants it. I will use her garden shovel."

"How can I help?" asked Cally.

"Your presence and caring are already a help," said Mrs. Chen. "Thank you for being here with May Lee, so she would not be alone. Now she and I must prepare Lizzy's body." They walked into Lizzy's bedroom carrying a basin of water and shut the door.

Well, I guess I'll watch the grave digging. I don't know what else to do. Thomas and I must leave soon to make it back to the hotel before dark.

"I asked Mr. Chen about the paintings," said Thomas as they walked down the trail an hour later. "He said this is not the right time to ask May Lee. I'm sorry, Cally."

"I will carry their beauty in my memory," said Cally. "Well, we learned nothing about Joe Rainey, but I'm glad we made this trip. Tomorrow, I want a long soak in warm spring water."

"Felicity, you must say goodbye to Jenny now, because we'll leave early tomorrow morning," Cally told her daughter at bedtime Wednesday evening.

"I don't want to say goodbye."

"I know it's hard, but we plan to see the Hanovers again. Remember? They invited us to visit them in Boise City when we return there."

"All right. Goodbye, Jenny."

"Goodbye, Felicity. Goodbye, Shane," said Jenny.

CHAPTER 10

OLD FORT HALL

[For a map, see "Old Fort Hall" under Historical Links on HorseThief1898.blog.]

Pocatello, Thursday, June 2

"CALLY, WHY DON'T YOU STAY WITH SHANE and Felicity and our luggage while I rent a wagon," said Thomas, looking around the Pocatello train station. "Then we can put everything in the wagon and explore a bit, since we have a couple of hours to wait for Mr. Rainey."

"All right, but I think we should find a hotel first. We don't know how long it will take you to do whatever needs to be done at old Fort Hall. And I'm pretty sure our next directive will be to look for Melody and Billy here in Pocatello. We don't know how long we'll be here."

"That's a good idea," said Thomas. "The Pacific Hotel is right next to the station. It was built by the Union Pacific Railroad. But it might be noisy. Let me ask the ticket seller for other hotel recommendations."

He soon returned "The man says we won't want to stay in the Triangle, whatever that is. There aren't any other hotels. But there is a boardinghouse that doubles as an inn, on Cleveland Avenue not far from the center of town. He gave me directions. We can check there first."

"All right," said Cally. "I'd like to find someone to ask about Melody, Billy's mother. I wish we had known when we were with Minnie that we would need to find her daughter. We didn't realize until talking with Lizzy that Melody was so important to Uncle William."

"One step at a time. I'm wondering about buying or borrowing another shovel, so I can help Mr. Rainey dig for whatever Uncle William buried at old Fort Hall."

"Perhaps the boardinghouse has a shovel you could borrow," said Cally.

"What a lark!" said Thomas.

Shane and Felicity were already in bed when Thomas walked into the Cleveland Avenue Boardinghouse late that evening. Cally sat in the front room sewing and waiting for him.

"Whew! I need a bath," said Thomas. "Is there a way I can do that, Cally? Then we can catch up with each other's day."

"There's a tub in a room next to the kitchen," said Cally. "We can heat water on the stove. Mrs. Brady showed me."

"That will be great," said Thomas. "Could you start the water heating while I visit the outhouse? Thanks, Cally."

"Of course. Come to the kitchen when you get back."

"Any luck with finding Melody?" asked Thomas, walking into the front room still towel-drying his hair. "Oh, hello, sir."

"Hello." The man went back to reading his book.

"Let's talk on the porch," said Cally. "It's not too cold out there, is it?"

"No. Good idea," said Thomas. "So—"

"No luck yet," said Cally. "I was told emphatically not to go by myself to the part of Pocatello where she probably lives. Tell me about Joe Rainey and old Fort Hall."

"It's quite a story," said Thomas. "I can hardly believe it, and I was there. Joe was right to insist this wasn't a trip for the children."

"What happened?"

"First of all, two other men were at the station to meet Joe Rainey. I didn't realize it until a man walked up and greeted a man dressed as an Indian as he got off the train. I heard him say, 'Joe Rainey, it's good to see you, though the circumstances be sad ones.' The other man was a policeman."

"Sad ones?"

"Yes. Turns out he was the father of a boy Uncle William murdered."

"Wait. What? Did you just say Uncle William killed a boy?"

"Yes. He did. I told you I can hardly believe it. Look at this, written by Uncle William. Joe Rainey gave it to me. He held it for us all these years."

Cally read in the light of the lantern on the porch:

Like Moses, my anger rose hot.
A white youth was beating my boy.
I killed him in rage—I forgot
He too was somebody's child, the one whom I shot.

Like Moses, my deed was observed.
I fled west with the corpse. Joe saw
Yet offered me grace undeserved,
Helped me face and confess what occurred.

Not life, but his body I now can restore
To his family. I grieve my grave sin.

And my guilt I can't longer ignore.

Joe Rainey, please help me once more.

Cally looked at Thomas. "How horrible! I never imagined anything like this."

"I know. The boy was only twelve. His name was Andy. His father, Mack, told me their family was frantic when he disappeared. They searched everywhere. But they had no clues at all. If someone saw the murder, per Uncle William's poem—if we can dignify it as poetry—he never said anything. I showed Mack the poem. He thought for a while and then said perhaps the person who observed it was black, like Billy. If so, he might have felt a white boy deserved what he got, for beating up a two-year-old."

"That's how old Billy was?"

"Yes. Mack was shocked, but not surprised, if you know what I mean. In his anguish at finding out what happened, Mack said this was partly his fault, for teaching his children to despise black people as he had been taught by his own father. He said it wasn't the first time his son had mistreated black children, and he had never disciplined him for it. At the time, Mack didn't think black people even belonged in Idaho. It confounds me that Mack responded with grief and contrition instead of anger at Uncle William. Seems impossible. But he seemed glad just to know what had happened."

"How do you account for that?"

"I believe Joe Rainey has influenced Mack over the years. Joe is half Indian, as Billy is half black. Joe is respected, I've learned, by everyone, white, black, Chinese, and Indian, because he lives such a kind, honest life, helping everyone no matter the color of their skin."

"Amazing," said Cally. "Makes me think of Mr. Martin in Montpelier. Charlie told you about him, right?"

"Yes. It's been a remarkable experience, spending the day with Joe, despite the sadness of our task," said Thomas. "I've never before had to dig up a corpse buried almost twelve years ago. It wasn't pleasant. Joe brought a coffin with him on the train. Tomorrow Mack and his family will bury Andy in the Pocatello cemetery, laying to rest the tragic mystery which has haunted their family all these years."

"Uncle William wanted us to know what he did," said Cally. "Do you suppose it was a way for him to ease his own conscience, all those years ago? But why do you think he waited so long? How terrible for Mack and his family."

"Uncle William feared for his own life, if he confessed," said Thomas. "He talked it over with Joe and decided to return to Ireland."

"How did Joe come into the picture?" asked Cally.

"Joe lived with his Indian relatives out at old Fort Hall," said Thomas. "It had already been abandoned. Everything of value was taken by a young man named J. N. Ireland to build a Holladay Stage Line station a few miles away on Spring Creek. But the Indian settlement continued there for many years. Joe saw an old man digging and went to offer help. It wasn't uncommon for people to dig around the old Fort Hall site. They often found useful things, like pots or dishes."

"But this old man—Uncle William—was digging a grave," said Cally.

"Yes. Joe helped him. Later, Uncle William confessed to the chief what he had done. He stayed for some time with the Indian community, trying to figure out what he should do. He was afraid to go back to Pocatello, because the person who saw him kill the boy might turn him in. By the way, you'll be surprised at the name of the area around the old Fort Hall site—Oneida."

"Oneida! Like Teddy's tribe!" said Cally. "But so far from where the Oneida lived."

"Yes. But some of the first white settlers were from Oneida, New York."

"An interesting coincidence. So, Thomas, does Mack consider the death of his boy settled? Does he feel justice has been done, or will he want further retribution?"

"According to the policeman—oh, I don't think I told you. A Pocatello officer went with us, at Joe's request. He—his name is Peter—told me Pocatello has a reputation for being one of the wildest wild west towns."

"We were told that about Soda Springs," said Cally.

"Well, at the time Uncle William killed Andy, Idaho had just recently become a state, and official systems of law enforcement were just developing. Most men owned guns, and shootings were not uncommon. It was up to family or friends to seek justice."

"That sounds terrifying," said Cally.

"Peter said we must look at this situation according to the customs of the time, rather than the way justice would be viewed now. The death went unchallenged for all these years. Who would the family pursue, since Uncle William is dead?"

"Maybe—us? Since we're his family?"

"That's the logical answer. But I don't think Mack has the heart to avenge Andy's death. He seemed relieved today to learn the truth of what happened. I have no idea how his feelings may evolve, though. He invited us to Andy's funeral tomorrow. I think that's a good sign. And he thanked me for helping him recover his boy's remains." Thomas stopped for a moment, staring at the wall. "I keep imagining how I would feel if it was Shane."

"Shane would never beat up a child, no matter what color his or her skin," said Cally.

"No, of course not. But he has not been taught, as Andy was, to despise members of another race, or that violence is acceptable behavior."

"Clearly there was wrongdoing on both sides, but a beating is not equivalent to a murder," said Cally.

"True. But we don't know how badly Andy might have hurt Billy had he not been stopped. I wonder what a two-year-old could have done to make Andy angry enough to resort to violence." Thomas sighed. "We'll never know, Cally. It's a terrible tragedy, no matter how we look at it. Do you want to go to Andy's funeral?"

"Can I think about it overnight? What would we tell the children? They will want to know what you did all day without them. Especially Shane," said Cally.

"I need to think about *that* overnight," said Thomas. "Who knew this treasure hunt would involve so much drama? I assumed it would just be a lark, an amusing adventure."

"Yes, coming at a convenient time, when I had to be away from Kansas City," agreed Cally. "So, what's next in the treasure hunt? Is it time to try to find Melody and Billy?"

"Joe Rainey has a packet for us. He'll give it to me at the funeral." Thomas chuckled. "I think it's Joe's way of ensuring I attend. I'm glad he didn't give it to me today. I feel overwhelmed already with digging up a corpse that Uncle William buried—my father's uncle. Think about it, Cally. I can't seem to absorb it."

"I don't understand why Joe Rainey sat on this for all these years, knowing Andy's family didn't know what had become of their son," said Cally.

"I think if Joe had come forward with this knowledge, blaming a murder on someone who couldn't be found nor his account about Uncle William verified, he ran a high risk of being blamed for the death himself. Especially because white people in general didn't trust Indian people in general. Perhaps the funeral tomorrow will shed more light on all this."

"That fits with what Mr. Martin told us about how Indians have been treated. How sad."

"Mack asked Joe to speak, so I don't think he bears him ill will. On the contrary, Mack holds Joe in high regard. Joe kept the horses and wagon and offered to come by for me in the morning, since I don't know how to find the cemetery. He'll take us all, if you decide to go."

"I wonder if Joe thinks he can help fashion some kind of agreement between Andy's family and ours," said Cally.

"Maybe so. He does have an envelope from Uncle William to give to the family, as well as the packet for us," said Thomas. "I'm bushed, Cally. Can you show me the way to my room?"

"We're fortunate the boardinghouse had space for us," said Cally. "Keep that in mind when you see the accommodations. But the owner—Mrs. Brady—has been wonderful. She loves children and will be flexible with us in terms of meals, if we'll clean up after ourselves. We're to eat in the kitchen, not in the dining room with the regular boarders. They have specific mealtimes and their own rhythms."

"Right now, all I care about is a quiet place to sleep," said Thomas. "Two deaths in two days—it's two too many for me."

"We're all going," said Cally when Thomas found them on the front porch the next morning. "We've had breakfast. Yours is in the kitchen. I'll show you."

"What did you tell Shane and Felicity?" asked Thomas when the door closed behind them.

"I told them some new friends had lost their twelve-year-old son, and invited us to the funeral," said Cally. "They didn't know what a funeral was. When I explained it, they felt sad for the family and wanted to go. I didn't tell them it has anything to do with Uncle William."

"All right. Joe should be here soon." Thomas stretched. "My arms and back are sore. I'm not used to digging graves."

"Let me introduce you," said Joe. "Thomas and Mack, you already know each other. Cally, this is Eileen, Mack's wife."

"I'm sorry for your loss, ma'am," said Cally.

"And these are their children, Betsy, Christopher, Donald, Evelyn, and Floyd."

"Their names are in order of the alphabet," Shane whispered to Felicity. "Andy must have been the oldest."

Cally frowned and put her finger to her lips. "This is Thomas's son Shane, and my daughter Felicity."

"Are you both widowers, then?" asked Eileen.

"No, ma'am. Cally is my sister," said Thomas. "Shane and Felicity are cousins."

"The preacher is getting ready to start," said Mack.

Cally looked around. A large group had gathered around the fresh grave. *Around fifty, I think. Mostly white, but not all.*

The pastor reflected on the sadness of the occasion, then invited Joe Rainey to speak.

"While we are sad," said Joe, "it's a comfort to the family to understand at last what happened to Andy, and why. Mack and Eileen have asked me to say they are at peace and have entrusted their son to the mercy of God. Surely, if we feel sympathy toward those involved in this situation, God is even more able to have compassion for our weaknesses. Let us together, as a community bound by his love, affirm our support for one another. Not one of us knows what we are capable of in extreme circumstances, and how much we may need one another before our own lives end. Thank you."

"Let us reaffirm our dependence on God and our trust in him through saying together the prayer the Lord Jesus taught us," said the pastor. "Our Father, who art in heaven ... "

"Thank you for coming, Thomas and Cally," said Eileen. "Because of you we found out what happened to our boy, and we are grateful."

"Your Uncle William gave us a most generous apology in the form of a large financial gift," said Mack. "Let me read you what he wrote: 'This in no way replaces the life I took from you, the precious life of your son. But I pray it may ease in some way the burdens you carry. Sincerely, William Malcomson.'"

"That was right good of him," said Eileen, "given how our boy mistreated his son. We intend to use it in some way to better the lives of black families in Pocatello, as our own way to make up for what Andy did."

"I must leave now to catch my train," said Joe. He bowed and walked toward the wagon, where Shane and Felicity played with Mack and Eileen's youngest children. Thomas and Cally said goodbye and followed Joe. Thomas took up the reins.

"Here is the packet from your Uncle William," Joe said as they arrived at the train station. "I took the liberty of writing on the envelope the last information I have about Melody and Billy. And now I must go. Goodbye."

"Thank you, Joe," said Thomas and Cally at the same time. Joe smiled, raised his hand, and hurried into the station.

CHAPTER 11

LAOISE

[Reminder: Laoise is pronounced *lee-sha.*]

New York City, Friday, June 3

CHARLIE DRUMMED HIS FINGERS ON HIS LEG. *I haven't felt this nervous ever. Even playing in London and Paris and Prague. I'm glad the Philharmonic representative will be with us and doesn't know our history. God, please don't let me hurt Laoise again. Please. Here we are.*

Charlie paid for his taxi, straightened his suit, and walked toward a back entrance to Carnegie Hall. He gave a few coins to a child beggar, pressed the doorbell, and greeted the attendant, who escorted him to the director's office.

Laoise rose as he entered. Charlie drank in the beauty of her blue eyes and stammered a greeting.

"Hello, Charlie. Herr Strauss has been delayed. He wishes personally to meet with us," said Laoise. "He hopes to appeal to the large Irish population of the whole state of New York through our concerts, so he wishes to participate in our selection of the program. Though I'm sure you've given it much thought and have arrived with a proposal."

"As, no doubt, have you," said Charlie. "You've done well, Laoise. Very well. I've followed your career."

"You have?" said Laoise, blushing. "Thank you. I guess I—well, I didn't expect that."

"You are so gifted. I'm delighted every time I imagine people listening to you play."

"Oh, Charlie!" she stammered. "But how about you? It's been such a long time."

"It has. Almost eight years since we graduated from Dublin Academy." Charlie took a deep breath. "Laoise, after this meeting, do you have plans? Would you like to eat dinner with me? It would delight me to catch up a bit before I leave tomorrow for Europe."

Charlie saw Laoise hesitate. *I can't blame her. Not at all. Meeting professionally is one thing but going out together is entirely different. Perhaps I was too bold, too hasty. Perhaps—*

"I'll go to dinner with you on one condition, Charlie. Will you tell me what happened to you at Christmas time, 1894?" Laoise looked at him steadily, her expression indecipherable.

It was Charlie's turn to hesitate. "Laoise, I—I don't know whether I can."

Laoise let out her breath and turned away.

Think, man. Do you want to lose her again, before you've even had a chance? But what if she's too shocked, too offended by what happened? What if that becomes all she can see when she looks at me? Would I even be able to go through with these shared concerts?

"Laoise, I—I want to. Truly I do. I just—I don't know whether it will be too hard."

"For me, or for you?" asked Laoise.

"For both of us. It's not a pretty story."

"Knowing would be better for me than imagining, as I've done for all these years, Charlie. Won't you give me a chance? I'm not fifteen anymore."

Charlie hesitated again. "All right, Laoise. But I can't do it in a restaurant, with other people around. I don't know how I will behave."

"I'm staying with a friend at the Washington Square Hotel in Greenwich Village. It has a rooftop garden. If it's free, we could eat our dinner and talk there. I'll write the address for you. Give me a fifteen-minute lead time after we finish our meeting before you come, so I can find out whether we can be there undisturbed. If not, I'll meet you in the hotel lobby and we can come up with a different plan."

"All right, Laoise," Charlie said again. "I hope you won't be sorry you asked."

The door opened. Master Richard Strauss strode in, followed by a Carnegie Hall attendant laden with music scores. The next hour was all business, comparing the advantages of the variety of pieces Charlie and Laoise suggested, and finally agreeing on a program.

We've ended up with almost exactly what Laoise proposed to begin with—which matched my ideas in all but two instances!

"Can you two run through this program with the orchestra tomorrow, while you're both in New York City?" the maestro asked.

"If it's early," said Charlie. "My ship for Lisbon departs at 2:00 tomorrow afternoon."

"And mine for Brest at 1:00," said Laoise.

"We will begin practice with this program," said Master Strauss to his assistant.

"Sir, most of the musicians will not have seen this music before."

"We will give them an hour to familiarize themselves. Charles and Laoise, meet our photographer here at exactly 9:00 for our advertising of the concerts. Rehearsal at 10:00. Plan to go to your ships directly from here."

"Yes, sir," they said at the same time.

"Until tomorrow, then," said Master Strauss. Charlie and Laoise bowed and left the room.

"Don't forget my fifteen-minute lead time," said Laoise. "If I'm not in the lobby, take the elevator to the top floor of the hotel. You'll see signs directing you to the stairs up to the roof garden." She smiled at him over her shoulder and walked away.

I'm trembling. Fear or happiness? Both: pure terror and pure joy.

❧

"This is lovely, Laoise," said Charlie, walking to the edge of the roof and gazing out at the city. "It's such a beautiful evening. Not yet as muggy as the city gets in the summer."

"It's impossible to see the stars, with all the city lights. Otherwise, yes, it is nice. Do you come often to New York City?"

"Fairly often, yes. I stay with cousins here."

"I've only come three times," said Laoise. "I'm not fond of the voyage. Let's sit down."

Me either. Crossing the ocean is the bane of my life.

"This looks delicious, Laoise! How did you come up with this meal on short notice?"

"True confession?"

"Please," said Charlie.

"I planned this ahead of time, in case you would say yes. I've been longing to see you, Charlie. I've missed you all these years, ever since—"

"Ever since I was so cruel to you. I'm sorry, Laoise. I've been sorry every single day since I said those terrible words that hurt you so deeply."

"Then why did you?" Laoise's hand trembled as she stretched it toward him.

Charlie sighed and for a moment covered her hand with his own. "Is it time for me to tell you what happened?"

"Past time, Charlie."

Charlie told the whole sad story, leaving nothing out. By the time he finished they both wept. Charlie found his handkerchief for Laoise, but she already used her napkin.

"I don't know how to explain how this affected me," said Charlie. "I don't understand it myself. Logically, I see that it wasn't my fault. Not even his death by his own hand a few weeks later. Emotionally, though, I felt it was my fault. I felt confused about myself—about who I was. I had nightmares about the same thing happening again, and again, and again. I lost confidence in my relationships. I didn't believe anyone could truly love me. Including you. I felt ruined, somehow. Soiled. Afraid of hurting others as I believed I had hurt Mr. Barrow. Especially, I was afraid of hurting you. And I cared about you too much to take that chance."

Charlie ran out of words. He pushed away his plate and buried his face in his arms on the table, his shoulders heaving. *Am I hurting her by telling this story? What must she think of me? I feel like I've jumped off a cliff and can't see the bottom. Oh. ... Oh my. ... That feels so good.*

Charlie lifted his head, turned, and caught her hands in his, hands that had been kneading the tension from his back and neck. "Laoise, do you understand? I've never stopped loving you. I've been so afraid of hurting you. I—"

Laoise bent and stopped the flow of his words with her lips. Stunned, Charlie sat very still for a moment, then pulled her onto his lap, her head against his heart, and wept again. This time, tears of relief and joy.

"Good, I have enough individual pictures of each of you. Now, may I take a few of you together? Laoise, look up at Charles. Yes, lovely. Now stand by him at the piano, with your violin. Perfect. One more, sitting on the piano bench together. Good. I think I have what I need. You two better run, or Maestro Richard will have my head. Soon these photos will adorn advertisements of these concerts across the city. Oh, Laoise, give me one more, holding your violin and leaning against the piano, without Charles this time."

This would have felt unbearably awkward if we hadn't had our true confessions time last night. One thing I learned, Laoise is a stickler for discipline. She didn't let me stay one minute past midnight. Her personal boundary, she said, because she depends on her sleep.

"All right, off you two go to dazzle the orchestra. Don't expect to dazzle the maestro. Nothing seems to impress him. Goodbye."

I've no doubt Mr. Strauss will be impressed today, whether he says so or not. I can't wait to hear Laoise play again.

☙

"I'm grateful you snagged this taxi, Charlie. There are so few automobiles, and I don't think we'd make it in time by carriage."

"I'm glad you sail before I do, so I can see you off. Can we compare notes about our schedules the next few weeks? Perhaps they'll overlap. Here's mine; I wrote it out for you."

"Hmm. Lisbon, Madrid, Barcelona, Marseille ... You've scheduled yourself tightly, Charlie. I wouldn't be able to handle so many concerts in a row."

"It is too many, I agree. I do it because I spend so much time in America I must make up for the travel days," said Charlie. "I'll travel between cities by night. I learned this from my teacher, Mr. Paderewski."

"You'll be tired ... Here's one overlap, Charlie! I'll be in Munich while you're in Zurich, and I have the next two days off before traveling to London. I can attend your concert in Frankfurt, and we could have the day together there on Monday the 20th. Yes?"

"Wonderful!" smiled Charlie.

"And could you stay over in Dublin a few days after your concerts there? I'll arrive home Sunday morning the 26th. Come to my home for dinner that evening."

"I would love to, if your parents are amenable," said Charlie.

"Of course! They will remember you from our Dublin student days. I play in Dublin the next weekend, July 1st and 2nd. Here's an idea, Charlie. Could you stay over the week, and play encores with me at my concerts? It will be good preparation for New York in September!"

"I'll need practice time during the week ..." said Charlie.

"So will I. It will be simplest if you stay in my home. Then we can easily rehearse together, and—"

"Are you sure your parents will approve this plan?"

"I'll ask them, but I'm confident they will be delighted," said Laoise.

"Then when I arrive in Lisbon, I'll send a telegram to my sister in Waterford telling her not to expect me until July 4th. I'll still have two weeks to rest and prepare for the fall before I return to the United States," said Charlie.

"Oh, I'm glad. I have so many questions to ask you. I want to hear everything about what you've been doing, thinking, feeling, dreaming the last eight years. May I keep this schedule? Here, I'll copy mine for you."

"My tour will go fast, with so much to look forward to." Charlie caught the taxi driver smiling at them in his mirror. He smiled back.

This is the most relaxed I've ever felt about boarding a ship. Only fifteen days and eight concerts until I can see Laoise again!

CHAPTER 12

POCATELLO

[Note: For a map, see "Pocatello" under Historical Links on HorseThief1898.blog.]

Pocatello, Friday, June 3

"WHAT A WONDERFUL NAP," Cally said, rolling her neck as she walked into the front room of the boardinghouse. "Did you rest, Thomas?"

"I tried. Let's go out to the porch," said Thomas, nodding toward a man polishing his shoes. "My, it's hot, but a drier hot than Kansas City in the summer. Anyway, yes, I tried to rest. But the facts we've learned about Uncle William kept whirling in my head. He murdered a child! He betrayed his marriage vows! He fathered a son with a prostitute! And we're the only ones in the family who know about this. It seems a heavy burden to bear."

"It's beyond shocking. Worse for you because you knew Uncle William," said Cally.

"Yes. On one of my last encounters with him he tried to rob my father, his idea of justice for what he viewed as unfair treatment by his Malcomson relatives. My father extended compassion and friendship to him, but now I'm wondering whether that was ill-considered."

"What is the story behind Uncle William's belief he was mistreated by the family?"

Thomas stood up from the front step and paced in front of the house. "After Grandfather Joseph died, Uncle William took the helm of Malcomson Brothers, and through a series of disastrous independent decisions, bankrupted the family enterprises. That's not all, but it's the bottom line. Then he resented the family for getting upset with him."

Cally leaned against the porch railing. "Oh my. I didn't know," said Cally. "There's so much I don't know about your—I mean, our—family."

"How could you know? I'm discovering there are things about this family I don't *want* to know. I'm tempted to abandon this so-called 'treasure' hunt, afraid of what else Uncle William may tell us. Think about it: the only 'treasure' we've discovered so far is a child's corpse."

"I know, Thomas. But there is another side to all this. Uncle William did try to make amends to the people he hurt. We helped Andy's family solve the mystery of his disappearance. We delivered money to Minnie and to Lizzy. We were there when May Lee needed us."

Cally buried her nose in a red rose blooming beside the porch. "Mmm, nice. We've met wonderful people along the way, Thomas. Mr. Martin in Montpelier, the Hanovers and Calico in Soda Springs, Joe Rainey here. The Eastmans. We're seeing a part of America we'd never have imagined. If we give up—I'm just thinking out loud—we won't ever know the whole story, only the worst parts of it. Assuming we've already seen the worst."

"That's just it. We don't know what's coming. I've only been doing this with you for four days and already I feel emotionally exhausted."

"I understand. It has been hard. Worse for you and Charlie than for me," said Cally. She put her hand on his arm. "But Thomas, what about Billy? None of this is his fault. We've been carrying Uncle William's packet for him since Boise. What would we do with it?"

"I know, but—" Thomas sat again on the porch step and rested his head in his hands. After a moment, he sighed and looked up at Cally. "How about this: let's take the rest of the day off and do something fun with Shane and Felicity. Tomorrow morning we'll open the new packet Joe gave us and decide whether to keep going."

He stood. "While the children are still napping, Cally, I want to call Cora. She's so good at stabilizing me—both my overexuberance when I'm excited about something and my discouragement when things don't go well."

"You always think things should go well, don't you, Thomas."

"Don't you? I'll have to find a telephone. Do you mind staying with Shane and Felicity? Think about what they might enjoy. I won't be long. Thanks, sis."

Thomas stuck his head into the front room of the boardinghouse and smiled at Shane and Felicity, cutting out paper dolls on the floor. Cally set aside her book.

"I need a drink of water, but I have some ideas for the rest of the day. I'll be right back," said Thomas.

"Daddy has the best ideas," said Shane. "Better than paper dolls."

"So," said Thomas when he returned. "Cora sends love and greetings to each of you."

"I wanted to talk to Mummy," said Shane.

"I'll be sure you can next time," said Thomas. "Did you three come up with a fun plan for the afternoon?"

"No," said Felicity. "We're waiting for you."

"Well then. As I walked, I remembered Peter, a policeman who went with Joe and Mack and me to old Fort Hall. He mentioned his sister's photography studio. I decided to check it out. It's on this street, 132 S. Cleveland Avenue. The owner, Benedicte Wrensted, let me use her telephone."

Thomas sat on the couch beside Cally. "Miss Wrensted's photography shop is fascinating. The walls are covered with her pictures, almost like a museum. Most of them are photos of Indians. They're fun to look at, especially when Benedicte explains them. I suggest we go there until time for a baseball game between Pocatello and a nearby town called Blackfoot. If there aren't food venders, I'll look for something to eat. What do you think?"

"I heard about Benedicte Wrensted in Soda Springs. She used to live there," said Cally. "I think she moved here about ten years ago. I would love to see her work."

"I want to watch the baseball game," said Shane.

"I want to eat!" said Felicity. Everyone laughed.

"Something for everyone, Thomas. Well done," smiled Cally.

"Off we go then. Anyone need the outhouse before we leave?"

"We already did," said Felicity. "I screamed because of a spider. Shane laughed at me."

"But you know I love you, cuz, since I cut out dolls for you," said Shane, tickling her.

"Let's go!" said Cally.

"What a fun outing!" said Cally as they walked back to the boardinghouse. "Benedicte's photos are powerful. Thank you for buying one for me, Thomas. It will be a wonderful memento of this trip. I can imagine Cora turning the photo into a gorgeous desert mountain painting."

"She may well do that, helping all of us appreciate the beauty of this strange-to-us landscape," said Thomas.

Shane and Felicity yawned.

"Since the children are sleeping late, shall we gather our courage and open the next packet from dear Uncle William?" asked Thomas the next morning over coffee.

"I'm ready," said Cally.

"It's a long letter," said Thomas. "Shaky, but legible. Here we go:

In a village whose name rhymes with yellow—no, you don't need another of my amateur rhymes at this point.

"It's hardly a village anymore," said Cally. "I heard someone say four thousand people live in Pocatello."

"And it's growing fast," agreed Thomas. "I'll continue:

My guess is that you're in Pocatello, and have completed the terrible task I assigned you, of returning to his family the boy I killed. I'm sure, since you are reading this, that Joe Rainey helped you, as so many times he helped me. Even so, it must be a terrible shock to discover your uncle is the worst kind of criminal. I cannot excuse what I did. In a few weeks I hope to be back in Ireland with my wife, and I intend to confess all of it to her and beg for her forgiveness. I believe this is what I should do, for the sake of my marriage vows and the fact that, for better or worse, I am my adult sons' father, and must do my part to mend the breach between us.

Yet it pains me greatly to leave my Billy, for however wrongly I acted in his conception, he is precious to me. I will try to keep in touch with his mother and with Billy from Ireland. I hope you can find him and tell him with this letter and with the envelope you carry for him how much I love him. I hope as well that his mother, Melody, has kept the promises she made to me regarding his care.

Thomas stood. "I told you this is a long letter. I've barely started. I'll read a bit more and then you can take a turn." He paced around the kitchen as he read, nodding occasionally to boarders who came for their coffee and bread.

I want to explain to you what happened. I left Ireland severely depressed, feeling rejected by those who meant most to me. My wife and my sons made it clear they wanted nothing more to do with me. I caught a ship to America not knowing whether I would reach its destination or in my distress throw myself overboard. A man befriended me aboard ship and urged me to give God a chance with my life. While dismissing the "God" part—for I believed He too had rejected me—I decided to explore this new country and take whatever adventure befell me. I boarded a train to the frontier west, thinking of it as a blank canvas where anything might be possible. You have now seen some of what I encountered in this strange Idaho Territory.

I was tired of the train by the time I reached Pocatello, discouraged and lonely. I was an easy target for this village's chief trades: prostitution, alcohol, opium, and gambling. 'My wife and family care nothing for me,' I told myself to justify my indulgences. The Chinese here run a lucrative opium business. All these vices offered a kind of relief to me, a space to grieve without feeling all the pain. Inside the Walled City, I met a beautiful woman—a young girl, to be truthful. I was appalled at the conditions those women endured, a kind of slavery, for they could never earn enough from their trade to pay off their clothing and housing and food. Many of them, perhaps most, were deliberately addicted by their masters to the opium, an additional enslavement.

"Your turn, Cally. Start on the next page."

This young woman, you are already guessing, was Melody, who in time bore my son Billy. When I learned she was pregnant, I bought her out, freeing her from the tyranny of the Walled City. For a time, she was grateful, and we lived together happily, but in truth, she did not know how to live outside of the 'home' she had known since a young girl.

I took Melody to Soda Springs for the birth of our child. You have already met the wonderful woman who took us in, when others drew back at the shade of Melody's skin. My mother—blessed be her memory—would say Lizzy was a godsend, that is, sent by God to befriend us when we had no friends. I bless Lizzy for her kindness.

When we returned to Pocatello, Melody informed me she had no vocation for being a mother. I aided her in every way I could, for the baby enchanted me. I could not nurse Billy, but otherwise his care fell almost entirely to me. Melody was restless. Finally, she told me she wanted to return to the Walled City! I was appalled. Talking with people as I walked the streets with Billy, I learned there were women who offer sexual favors to men outside of that horrible place, through a "genteel" establishment in the Triangle. This would be better than the Walled City, I thought. By then, I had concluded I could not be Melody's savior, for she did not want to be saved.

Melody welcomed the prospect of continuing the life she knew, though living in better circumstances and serving a higher-class clientele. The house willingly accepted Billy to gain Melody, for truly she is beautiful and charming (when she is not angry and spiteful). This will be good for Billy, I thought. A whole houseful of women to love and care for him. Surely most other women are more motherly by nature than Melody.

This is the last I know about Melody and about Billy. Look for them at the Serenity House in the Triangle. I hope you will find them, and learn for my sake how my son fares, and what he needs. Once you have done so and deliver the envelope you picked up for him in Boise, you can open the envelope enclosed with this letter, which will tell you what to do next.

Gratefully,

William

P.S. Billy's full legal name is William Joseph Malcomson, named not for my brother but for my friend Joe Rainey. I always just called him Billy. His birthdate is July 4, 1890.

P.S.S. To understand Pocatello, you must think geometrically. This town is framed by hard straight lines, shutting people in or out. The train tracks create a natural barrier between the haves and the have nots, creating two incompatible halves to this city. The Triangle, of course, is literally on "the wrong side of the tracks," dominated by the square Walled City. The police with their five-sided badges, headquartered but a block from the Walled City, profit from an arrangement with the pimps, charging each prostitute six dollars twice per month to continue their illicit trade. Beware. There is little law and less order to be found in Pocatello, as my crime attests.

P.S.S.S. Melody does not know I killed a child, and Billy was too young to remember. I see no benefit to anyone for that to change.

"Goodness!" said Thomas.

Cally spread the pages of the letter on the kitchen table. "I wish we had known all this when we met Minnie, Melody's mother, in Montpelier. In Dingle, I should say, because Minnie wasn't welcome in Montpelier. Minnie could have told us how to find Melody. What did Joe write on the envelope?"

"Only that Melody might still be at the Serenity House in the Triangle," said Thomas.

"Billy is almost fourteen," Cally mused. "Do you think he would still live with his mother in a brothel, high class as it may be? I wouldn't be surprised if he's run away, especially if his mother cares for him as little as Uncle William thought. Minnie never mentioned Billy. Perhaps she doesn't know her daughter has a child. Don't you want to try to find them, Thomas?"

"I'll give it a couple of days. But I don't want to take our children into the Triangle, much less to this so-called Serenity House, or into the Walled City. And I'm not keen on you going to those places either. So, I think you'll need to care for the children while I search."

Cally smiled. "I'm used to that, Thomas. I just thought of something. Do you think the policeman you met, Benedicte's brother, would help you?"

"Peter, yes. That's an interesting thought. I could ask for him at the police station."

"I'm glad you're willing to pursue the leads we have, Thomas, for Billy's sake."

"I wonder how Billy has survived growing up in a context of drinking, opium, and prostitution. The whole situation beggars belief."

"Yet many people are born, grow up, live, and die in that kind of environment, don't they? I've been thinking: if people with money, or greedy for money, did not support their services, places like the Walled City would not exist. In this town, even the police are complicit."

"I'm sure you're right, Cally. Well, this task will not become more agreeable by putting it off. I'll find the nearest place to cross the tracks. Don't expect me back until evening, sis. I hope you and the children find ways to enjoy your day."

"It feels hot already. I think we'll go to the Portneuf River with a picnic. Benedicte told me there's a nice park a few blocks from here. Don't worry about us. But do be careful, Thomas, all right?" *I'll also find time to write letters to Mary Ann and Charlie while Thomas is gone.*

"I will. 'Bye."

ﾉ

"I couldn't find them, Cally," said Thomas as he ate a late supper Saturday evening. "Serenity House no longer exists. I asked a lot of people, including at the Walled City, but Melody seems to have vanished. No one told us her last name, did they? Did Minnie tell you?"

"No. But I don't imagine there are many gorgeous black women named Melody."

"And you told me Minnie believes Melody still lives in Pocatello."

"That was true the last time Minnie had contact with her, but anything could have happened since then. Hmm, I wonder whether Melody's brother Cecil would know anything ... Perhaps we could send a telegram to Dingle. Were you able to talk to Peter the policeman?"

"Today was Peter's day off. I should be able to find him on Monday."

"What is the Triangle like?" asked Cally.

Thomas smiled. "In some ways it's very appealing. Children of many nationalities play together in the streets, while their mothers chat on their front steps. I saw and heard Chinese, German, Spanish, Italian, Greek, French, even Irish. Maybe Japanese and others I didn't recognize. All imaginable colors of skin and manners of dress. You would never in your life know from this side of the river that the whole world inhabits the other side!"

"So, it didn't feel scary."

"No, it didn't. The first settlers, I learned, came to herd or farm. Then came the miners, hoping to strike gold. But today, most Triangle residents work for the railroad. I'm happy my profession is providing jobs for people clearly in need of them. On the surface at least the Triangle seems a bustling, happy place. I think you and the children can safely go with me and will find it fascinating."

"Yet beneath the surface ..."

"Well, yes. There is a darker side. For example, in the first block I counted nine saloons, all of them overflowing with men by the end of the day. I suspect, Cally, the women—most of them—must work very hard to care for their families and raise them to a higher standard. I didn't investigate, but I saw signs indicating opium dens. And of course, there's the Walled City."

"Did you find any other 'genteel' establishments like Serenity House?"

"I found several, but none of them claimed to know a woman named Melody. We can continue the search together on Monday. I know Shane will be fascinated by the street games the boys were playing."

"All right. What shall we do tomorrow?"

"Let's rent a carriage and drive into the countryside. Did you know there are lava fields?"

"What's a lava field?"

"It's the remains of an old volcano. The lava hardens almost like glass, sharp and hard. Wouldn't you like to see something like that?"

"Not fun to walk on, I imagine. I'll ask Mrs. Brady to pack our lunch to go with us. May I drive the horses?"

Thomas laughed. "Of course." He stretched and yawned. "I'm tired. I want to go to bed early. Good night, Cally."

"Good night, Thomas. I'm reading a book I found in our room—left by a previous tenant, I suspect. It's a good story. I'll go to bed soon."

"Oh. What is it?"

"*Great Expectations,* by Charles Dickens."

The truth is, I want to fill my mind with a happy ending before I go to sleep. Perhaps that will stave off my bad dreams.

"That was a memorable day to me, for it made great changes in me," Cally read. "But it is the same with any life. Imagine one selected day struck out of it and think how different its course would have been.

Pause you who read this and think for a moment of the long chain of iron or gold, of thorns or flowers, that would never have bound you, but for the formation of the first link on one memorable day."

Like my decision not to return to Uncle Dugan and Aisling ...

"Shane and Felicity, your grandmother Cathleen will sail from Waterford today," said Thomas at breakfast on Monday. "She'll spend next weekend with Nathanael and Sarah in New York City, then catch the train to Kansas City, and then to you!"

"And Mummy and the girls too, right, Daddy? For Josie's birthday!"

"That's right, Shane," said Thomas. "I'm sure you'll find a fun way to celebrate, wherever you are on June 21st."

"Play in the hot springs!" said Felicity.

"Explore another cave!" said Shane. "It's called spelunking. Mr. Hanover told me."

"Those are great ideas," said Thomas. "But we don't know where the treasure hunt will take us by then. Today we'll explore more of Pocatello."

"That doesn't sound fun," said Felicity. "It's just buildings."

"Daddy told me the children play interesting games in the streets," said Shane.

"Can I take Lizzy?" asked Felicity.

"May I," said Cally. "I think it would be best to leave Lizzy at home, Felicity. Then you won't have to keep track of her or worry about dropping her in the street and getting her dusty."

"We'll be trying to find Melody, Felicity," said Thomas.

"Who is Melody?" asked Felicity.

"Remember Minnie and her granddaughter Ebony?" said Cally. "We met them in Dingle."

"I remember," said Felicity. "Miz Minnie was as old as Miss Lizzy. Even more wrinkly. Shane didn't meet her."

"Melody is Miz Minnie's daughter," said Cally. "We want to find her."

"Ebony said she's a beautiful lady. I would like to see a beautiful lady," said Felicity.

"All right then. Everyone ready?" said Thomas. "First, we'll stop at the police station to ask Peter Wrensted whether he knows Melody or how we can find her. It will be a hot day. I'm glad we all have hats."

"I heard you during the night," Thomas said quietly to Cally as the children skipped ahead. "A bad one?"

"Yes. I wish I knew how to stop having nightmares," said Cally. "I'm sorry you heard me. I hope I didn't disturb anyone else."

"Shane slept right through it," said Thomas. "And you've taught me not to worry, so I prayed for you and went back to sleep. Yes, turn right, Shane. Hold your mummy's hand crossing the tracks, please, Felicity."

A puppy bounded up to them as they walked down a street into the Triangle. Felicity squealed. "Oh, he's so cute. Can we keep him, Mummy? Please?" She dropped to her knees and the puppy licked her face. "You like me, don't you, sweet thing. I'm going to call you Billy until we find the real Billy."

"How do you know about Billy, Felicity?" asked Cally.

"Me and Shane heard you and Uncle Thomas talking. Billy is our cousin. He's the real reason we want to find Melody." Felicity jumped up and ran in circles around the others, the puppy chasing after her.

"Well. Were you two going to tell us?" asked Thomas.

"No. You were trying to have a secret from us, so we decided to have a secret from you. But Felicity isn't good at keeping secrets," said Shane. "Anyway, we can help look for Billy. How will we know who he is? How will he know who we are?"

"That's a good question. We hope he's with his mother, Melody. If so, she can introduce him to us, right?" said Thomas.

"And if he's not?" asked Shane.

"Then we'll think about what to do next."

A man came out of a shop and whistled. The puppy bounded away and walked down the street with the man. Felicity burst into tears.

"I'm sorry, sweetheart. The puppy was too well cared for to be a street dog," said Cally.

"Goodbye, Billy," said Felicity, her voice catching. "Mummy, when we go home to Kansas City, can I have a puppy?"

"May I—we'll see, Felicity. We need to talk with Thomas and Cora about that."

"Felicity, come look!" yelled Shane. "These children are dancing!"

A woman standing by looked up and smiled. "They're practicing for Juneteenth," she said. "The children dance better every year."

"What is Juneteenth?" Shane asked.

"It's the day in 1865 when Black slaves in Texas found out they were free," said the woman. "The Emancipation Proclamation took place on January 1, 1863, but it took more than two years for the slaves in Texas to hear the news. Emancipation means freedom."

"What is a slave?" asked Felicity.

"A slave is a person owned by someone he or she has to work for," said the woman.

"That doesn't sound nice," said Felicity, frowning.

"No, it's not nice. That's why on Juneteenth we celebrate the end of slavery. That will be two weeks from now."

"If we're still here, can we come?" asked Felicity.

"Bless you, child. Of course, you may. Juneteenth is for everyone," said the woman, smiling.

"Can I dance too? I like to dance," said Felicity.

"Well, why don't you join the children then," said the woman.

"Come on, Shane!" yelled Felicity, running toward the dancers.

"I'll watch you," said Shane.

"Thomas, is the police station nearby? Perhaps you could talk with Peter while Shane and I stay here with Felicity," said Cally.

"No, I want to go with you, Daddy," said Shane.

"All right, son. Stay on this block, Cally, even if the dancing ends before we get back," said Thomas. "Look at her—she joined right in."

"And she's learning the steps very quickly," said Cally, clapping to the rhythm of a drummer. "That's my girl."

"Did you find Peter the policeman?" Cally asked.

"Yes. He told us where to look for Melody," said Shane.

"We'll go now, if you ladies are ready," said Thomas. "It's just a few blocks from here."

"That was fun!" said Felicity. "They invited me to come back to practice again next Monday. Can I?"

"May I. If we're still in Pocatello, yes," said Cally. "If we find Melody and Billy quickly, we'll probably have another clue to follow before June Nineteenth."

"Then I'm not going to look for them anymore," said Felicity, sitting down. "I want to dance at the Juneteenth party."

"Aren't you glad we came, Felicity? You had two fun things already, the puppy and the dancing," said Shane.

"Yes." Felicity jumped up. "Mummy, look, that man is selling candy. Can I have some?"

"May I have some."

"May I, Mummy? Please?"

"Two lemon twists, please," said Thomas to the vendor. "Do you want one, Cally?"

"No thanks."

"Here you are, children," said Thomas. "Sit on those steps while you eat them. Try not to get too sticky. The house where we're to look for Melody is a block away. Shall I inquire, Cally, while the children eat their candy?"

"Good idea," said Cally, sitting down by Felicity.

Thomas approached a door with no markings, set back a few feet from the street. A string hung from a hole in the door. *I guess they pull the string inside when they're not open for business.* He pulled the string, and a gong sounded inside. A few minutes later, the door opened a few inches, and someone peered through.

"Yes?" said a gruff voice.

"I'm looking for a woman named Melody," said Thomas.

"Her hours begin at 4:00. Come back then." The door slammed.

Thomas pulled the string again.

"What is it?" the person said, without opening the door.

"I'm a friend of her mother's," said Thomas. *Well, not exactly true, since I've never met Minnie, but—*

"Then tell me her mother's name," said the voice.

"Her mother's name is Minnie. Her brother's name is Cecil. Her niece's name is Ebony," said Thomas. *I won't say "Her son's name is Billy." I don't know what the people at this house know about Melody.*

"What is your name?"

"My name is Thomas Malcomson. My great-uncle William Malcomson is a friend of hers."

"I'll ask her if she wants to see you."

The person was gone for a long time. *I would have been more polite, but I couldn't tell whether the voice was male or female. I wonder whether she or he is waking Melody. Perhaps she's used to sleeping late.*

"She'll see you at 3:00," the voice said on the other side of the door. "Come back then."

"I will," said Thomas. "Thank you." There was no response. He sighed and walked back toward Cally and the children. *Well, it seems we've found Melody. I hope there's not more than one woman with that name in this part of town.*

"We have several hours," said Thomas after he explained his appointment to Cally. "I suggest we return to the boardinghouse for lunch and a rest. Then we can decide how many of us will come back to talk with Melody."

"I wonder whether she'll feel more comfortable if I'm with you," said Cally. "Perhaps Mrs. Brady would allow the children to stay with her for an hour or so."

"Good idea. We can ask her."

"Didn't Shane look funny in that apron?" laughed Cally, as she and Thomas walked toward the tracks after lunch and a nap. "Mrs. Brady was brilliant, asking him and Felicity to help her make bread and cookies."

"I doubt they'll want any supper," said Thomas.

"Mrs. Brady told me the Pocatello Triangle is the most diverse population in the state of Idaho," said Cally. "She lived there until she married Mr. Brady. We haven't met him."

"No. Mrs. Brady told me yesterday he died in an accident, working on the railroad. Too many people have," said Thomas. "I told Mrs. Brady I was sorry. She looked me up and down and said, 'Sorry is as sorry does, young man. Has the railroad improved its care of its workers?' I must investigate that when I get back to Kansas City headquarters."

"Did you learn anything else from her?"

"Yes. She told me black people are banned from renting or purchasing property outside the Triangle. She said, 'No one knows I'm black. My skin is light, so I can pass for white. It's my secret way to take revenge on white people after my child died from dysentery with no help from the railroad. Don't you tell anyone my secret, now.' I told her

I wouldn't. But why do you suppose she told me that? She risks losing her boardinghouse, right?"

"People naturally trust you, Thomas. But how sad."

"Kansas City isn't different, though, Cally. Do you think people with dark skin would be welcome in our neighborhood?"

"I've never thought about it."

"I can tell you: they wouldn't. When we bought our house, the realtor relayed it as a point of pride. It bothered me. But I grew comfortable and accepted the status quo. Irish people are just as unwelcome in some places, if they don't have money."

"Do you think we can influence our neighbors to think differently?" asked Cally.

"I don't know. The question has never come up. I'll ask Cora," said Thomas. "Here we are. Do you want to pull the string? It rings a bell inside."

Cally pulled the string and heard a bell clang. "They might open the door just a crack," said Thomas, as the door swung wide.

"You're William's kin?" said a woman. "Is he still alive? I haven't heard from him for a long time."

"Ma'am, I presume you are Melody? I am Thomas Malcomson, and this is my sister, Cally. May we come in?"

"No," said the woman. "I'll come out." She swept through the door and walked down the street, her head down. Thomas and Cally hurried after her. When she looked up to avoid running into a child with a hoop, Cally saw tears on her cheeks.

"I'm sorry we brought you bad news," said Cally. "Uncle William died twelve years ago, in 1892."

"No one told me," said the woman in a small voice.

"I'm sorry, ma'am. We didn't know about you," said Thomas.

"How did you find me, then?" she asked.

"Ma'am, is there a place we could sit and talk? A tea shop, perhaps? A café?"

"Not likely," said Melody. "They wouldn't serve me, being what I am, even in the Triangle. I'm taking you to the China gardens. There's a place I know—" She ducked her head as they walked past a man and a woman.

She said nothing more until they had walked past the buildings, into the countryside. Abruptly she turned right down a small lane between fruit trees.

"How beautiful!" said Cally.

"This is where I come when I need peace," said Melody. "No one bothers me here." She continued walking until they came to a pond with grass and trees around it. She sat and stared at the water.

"I see a fish!" said Thomas. "Several of them!" He walked to the edge of the pond to see them more clearly.

Cally sat next to Melody. Thomas remained standing, a few feet away.

"Uncle William left a letter, asking us to find you," said Cally. "He left it with a man named Joe Rainey. Joe gave it to us last week. We've been looking for you since then."

"Good old Joe," said Melody. "I haven't seen him for a long while either. Why did William want you to find me?"

"We have a letter from Uncle William for your son, Billy," said Cally.

"Billy ran away on his thirteenth birthday," said Melody. "I haven't heard one word from or about him for almost a year. My free time is up. I must be getting back."

"May we talk with you again, Melody?"

"Same time tomorrow—3:00. No, I'll go back by myself. Enjoy the gardens."

CHAPTER 13

MELODY

Pocatello, Tuesday, June 7

"WHAT SHALL WE DO with Shane and Felicity today, while we talk with Melody?" asked Cally, drinking coffee with Thomas on the front porch before the children woke up.

"Maybe I should stay with them, and you go alone, Cally. She might feel more comfortable talking just to you. I could take the children on an outing. There's a place called Lava Hot Springs about 35 miles away, close enough by train. Do you remember that stop on the way here from Soda Springs? We could make a day outing of it. You would have time to yourself until time to meet Melody. What do you think?"

"I think the children will love it, and I'll be a wee bit sad to miss the outing. But it's a good plan, Thomas. I don't want Shane and Felicity to start resenting this treasure hunt."

"I agree, though it seems with Billy's disappearance we've hit a dead end. Maybe he has our next clue—or even confirmation of the end of the hunt."

"No, it doesn't make sense for him to have a packet for us, Thomas. He was just a toddler when Uncle William left him to return to Ireland! Melody may have something for us, though."

"Do you feel all right about going to see her alone?"

"Yes. This morning I want to shop for a gift for Mrs. Brady. She's been so kind. Maybe one of Benedicte's photographs. I'll ask Mrs. Brady to pack a lunch for your outing."

ଔଓ

"You came alone," said Melody when she opened the door.

"Yes. One of us needed to care for the children—Thomas's son and my daughter. So, we decided to send him on an outing with the children while I came back to talk with you."

"I didn't know you had children with you. Shall we go again to the gardens?"

"That would be lovely. How are you today, Melody?" asked Cally as they walked.

"I've reached my limit with this life I am leading. I can't do it anymore."

"I would like to know more about your life, Melody, if you're willing to tell me."

"You mean my life now, or the story of my life?" asked Melody.

"Both. Whatever you wish to talk about. Your mother Minnie told us you live in Pocatello, but not much more."

"I've lived in the Pocatello Triangle all my life. Never traveled, except when William took me to Soda Springs for a few weeks."

"We met Lizzy. She told us about Billy's birth," said Cally.

"She was one nice lady," said Melody. "I haven't known anyone else like her."

"She died last week," said Cally. "She was 106. I asked her secret and she said vegetables, clean water, tea, a free and happy heart, no regrets, no grudges, and her wonderful daughter May Lee."

"Humph! A free and happy heart. No regrets, no grudges. Those words mean nothing to me. A foreign language. That Lizzy lived a more charmed life than I realized. I'm not free and I'm full of regrets and grudges. Here we are." Melody sighed as she eased herself to the ground. "My body aches today. I'm sick. Dying, though I don't know how long it will take."

"Oh. I'm sorry. I didn't know."

Melody gave a short laugh. "Girl like you, born with a silver spoon in your mouth, how could you know the afflictions of the life I live?"

"What does that mean, the silver spoon thing?" asked Cally. "I'm sorry. I spoke Irish as a child and my English isn't as good as it should be."

"It means you were born into a rich family that cared for all your needs without you lifting a finger," said Melody.

"Oh no. It wasn't like that at all," Cally said. "I was born into a poor farm family in southern Ireland. My mother died birthing my baby sister when I was five and my brother was three. I had to care for him and our cottage and cook and clean from then on."

"You're fooling with me. Look at you now! Fancy clothes. A real lady."

"Thomas and his wife Cora adopted me as their sister when I was fifteen, after my daughter was born," Cally said. "After my father died, I pretended I was a boy so I could be a member of a street gang in Albany, New York. Then I worked on the Erie Canal as a hoggee."

"What's a hoggee?" asked Melody.

"A hoggee takes care of mules," said Cally. *She might never have seen a canal.*

"If you pretended to be a boy, how did you get pregnant?"

"A member of the gang discovered I was a girl. When I was fourteen, he found me and attacked me," said Cally. "I don't like to think about it. But I love my daughter."

"I was attacked too," said Melody. "But I was only eight. I never told my mother. She would have blamed me, and I couldn't bear that. Soon I realized that's all I was good for. The only thing boys and men ever cared about was my face and my body. Until William. That old man William. I think he truly cared about me. But I didn't know how to live the kind of life he wanted. It scared me. And I didn't know how to be a mother. William was father and mother to Billy until he went away, back to his wife and his life in Ireland."

"I'm sorry," said Cally. "It must have been lonely for you."

"I don't want to talk about it anymore," said Melody.

"All right. Can you tell me about Billy?"

"Billy missed his father terribly after William left. I lived with several women who always wished to be mothers. They cared for him. Good thing, since I didn't know how and didn't want to learn. Billy liked all the attention. But he grew restless. He kept saying he would run away to find his father. And finally, he did."

"My brother ran away from me, too, when he was eleven. Do you think Billy went to Ireland to find his father? Did he know Ireland is far away, across this huge country and then across the ocean?"

"I don't know what he knew or where he went or whether he's still alive. I didn't know I loved him until he was gone. No regrets, no grudges, ha!"

"Lizzy didn't have an easy life either, Melody. I agree, it's a wonder she lived like that in her old age. Free and happy. I wonder whether that's possible for me, or for you."

"Not for me. I won't live that long. Old age isn't an option for women in my profession. Well, Cally, you're an interesting woman, but I must go. Tell Thomas I have something for him. He can come again tomorrow, three o'clock. No, don't walk back with me. Enjoy the gardens."

Cally sat by the pond a long time after Melody left, thinking about her regrets.

Thou shalt be like a watered garden.

Cally startled. *What does that MEAN? Why do I keep thinking it? A watered garden would be a garden made beautiful by rain. But these gardens are beautiful, and it doesn't rain much here. I wonder ..."*

Cally got up and walked around the pond. *Aha. I was right. This ditch takes water from the pond to the gardens on this side. There must be another ditch on the other side. Hmm. A garden with frequent rains, like ours in Kansas City, is like the silver spoon child Melody thought I was. I'm like these gardens that would die without these water ditches. I depend on others for what I need to survive. Maybe that's why I'm restless sometimes. I want to be able to provide for myself and for Felicity. Yet much has been given me. Melody is right about that. Aisling and Cathleen would say it was God, not just Thomas and Cora and other kind people along the way, like the Anthonys.*

Cally walked the rest of the way around the pond, then headed back to Mrs. Brady's, passing Melody's door on the way. *Is she really dying? She says she wants a change. Might she consider going home to her mother Minnie? Maybe Thomas can ask her that tomorrow."*

Cally stepped to the side of the street as a farm wagon trundled past. *Like Melody, I wonder about Lizzy. How did she come to have a free and happy heart, no regrets and no grudges? Her life was not easy, especially in regard to May Lee. I wish I knew ...*

ꕥ

After Shane and Felicity, sunburned and happy, settled to sleep, Cally told Thomas in detail about her conversation with Melody. "I was right. She does have something to give us. She said she would give it to you at 3:00 tomorrow."

"All right."

"Thomas, do you think Melody could go live with Minnie?"

"In the tiny, dark hovel you've described? I don't think Melody would like that, Cally."

"I wonder if we could communicate with Minnie somehow. Perhaps Mr. Martin could tell me how to get a message to her," mused Cally. "Minnie may not be strong enough to travel, but perhaps Cecil could come and take Melody to see their mother, at least for a visit."

"You can call Mr. Martin, Cally, but don't get your hopes up. Melody is used to living her own life, making her own decisions. She hasn't lived with her mother since she was very young. It might be too much for both of them."

"You're probably right. Still, I'd like to try."

"I imagine Benedicte would let you use her telephone. You could call Mr. Martin tomorrow morning before I see Melody again. In case there's something we can tell her about her mother and brother."

"I'll do that."

***

"Mr. Martin? This is Cally Malcomson. Do you remember me? I was in Montpelier for a couple of days with my brother Charlie. You went with us to Dingle to visit Minnie."

"Of course, I remember. How are you? Is there something I can do for you?" Mr. Martin's voice sounded surprisingly clear over the telephone.

"I'm with my other brother, Thomas, now, because Charlie left for a concert tour of Europe," said Cally. "Thomas and I are in Pocatello. We've been getting to know Minnie's daughter, Melody, and I've been thinking—"

"This is serendipitous!" said Mr. Martin. *Seren—what?* "I've spent a fair amount of time with Minnie the last few weeks."

"You have? Is she all right?"

"More than all right. Remember that shack she lived in when you were here? Well, Minnie sent her son Cecil to ask me whether the money your Uncle William gave her would be enough for her to buy a proper house. I was about to put a cottage on the market. The bank held the title, and the former renter moved back east."

"Amazing timing!" said Cally.

"Yes," said Mr. Martin. 'I have a house,' I told Cecil, 'But it would be too big for just your mother.' To shorten the story, William's money was enough to pay half the cost of the house, and I gave Cecil a loan for the other half, with terms he believes he can meet. Connie and I helped him, his wife, his daughter Ebony, and Minnie move in last weekend. Minnie was like a child, she was so excited. Can you imagine the change for her, from that dark hut to a lovely cottage on Bear Lake? Your uncle's generosity made this possible for her, Cally."

"What work does Cecil do?"

"He's a fisherman, so this is perfect for him. The house is in a village called Fish Haven where the main business is—"

"Fishing," said Cally.

"Fish Haven supplies the small towns in the area, including Montpelier," said Mr. Martin. "I'm delighted with the whole situation. It's the part of banking I love the most—helping people fulfill their dreams."

"I wonder ..."

"Yes?"

"Well, it seems unlikely, but would there be space in Minnie's new house for Melody, if she were to visit?"

"Oh, yes. The house is spacious."

"This is truly wonderful, Mr. Martin. I'll ask Melody to consider a visit. If she decides to go, could I get a message to Minnie through you?"

"You could, yes. Thank you for calling so I could tell you about the cottage. Please let me know whether Melody will visit, so I'm not left wondering!"

"Of course. Goodbye, Mr. Martin. I'll be in touch."

Back at the boardinghouse, Cally told Thomas, "I want to go with you today. We can all go. I have something to tell Melody."

꧁

Melody opened the door promptly when Shane pulled the string. She walked out holding a packet. "Oh, you are all here today."

"Melody, this is my son Shane," said Thomas.

"And my daughter Felicity," said Cally.

"Can we meet our cousin Billy?" asked Felicity.

"I'm sorry, child. He's not here right now." said Melody. "Are we walking to the gardens today, or—"

"Yes, please," said Shane. "Aunt Cally told me about the irrigation. I'd like to see it."

"All right then," said Melody. "Here's the packet, Thomas."

"Is it another clue for the treasure hunt?" asked Felicity.

Melody startled. "What treasure hunt, child?"

"Uncle William's treasure hunt. We think Cousin Billy is the treasure but we're not sure until we find him," said Felicity.

Thomas and Cally looked at each other. Each shrugged.

"We didn't know we have a cousin named Billy," Felicity continued. "Shane and I are cousins, and Shauna and Josie are my cousins. I didn't know I could have even more cousins."

"I have many cousins too," said Melody. "We all grew up together right here in Pocatello. Some of them moved away when they got old enough."

"Are you going to move away?" asked Shane.

"I would like to, yes I would," said Melody. "If I can figure out a way to do it."

"I want to talk to you about that," said Cally. "Yesterday I learned something wonderful. Your mother has a new home, with lots of space. Thomas and I would like to pay your train fare so you can go visit her. If you would like that."

Melody stopped walking. "I don't believe she wants to see me," she said in a small voice. "She spoke harsh words the last time I saw her."

"She might feel differently now," said Cally. "I believe she would be happy to see you."

"She's old," said Felicity. "I thought she was the oldest person in the world until I met Miss Lizzy. But Miss Lizzy died. So, your mother might die too."

"Oh my," said Cally, blushing. "I'm sorry, Melody. Felicity doesn't know yet how to be discreet."

"What does discreet mean, Mummy?" asked Felicity.

"It means knowing what to say when," said Cally. "Melody might not want to talk about her mother dying."

"Oh. Because that would be sad. Like for May Lee it was sad when Miss Lizzy died."

"Yes."

"Mummy! Look how pretty the flowers are!" Felicity and Shane ran toward the gardens.

"Well, think about it, Melody. Visiting your mother would be a way to take a break from your work here," said Cally.

"Unfortunately, we don't expect to be in Pocatello much longer," said Thomas. "This packet likely tells us to go somewhere else."

"This is interesting," said Melody. "Can you open the packet now? I'm curious. A treasure hunt, you said? Nothing interesting happens in my life. Not since William. And Billy."

Thomas glanced at Cally, who nodded. "All right. Let's sit down. It looks like Shane and Felicity are running around the pond. We can keep an eye on them from here."

He opened the packet and withdrew an envelope labeled "Melody." "Well, here you go. It's a good thing we opened this while we're still with you."

Melody took the envelope and stared at her name. "He didn't forget me. I thought he had." She held the envelope with both hands against her chest. An expression of sadness crossed her face. "What's there for you two?"

"It's probably the next clue." Thomas opened an envelope and withdrew a single sheet. "Do you know anyone named Flora, Melody?"

"Flora? No. Should I be jealous?" said Melody.

"I don't know, but there's an envelope labeled Flora and this poem:

In nature, Flora and Fauna share Life
Twin realms of gestation and growth.
But Life too depends on water and air
Twin foundations of all that exists.
Twas water first linked us, that fateful day
Twin cascades of rainbow-hued might
Carvers of Snake River's cliffs
Twin mockers of hubris and gall.

"William and his poems!" exclaimed Melody. "He was always writing them. Most times I had no idea what they meant. Like this one. He might as well be speaking a foreign language."

"He never said anything to you about someone named Flora?" asked Thomas.

"Flora, Flora. Hmm. There's something niggling my mind ... Oh, now I remember! When I was birthing Billy, William kept saying he wished Flora was there; she would know what to do. Maybe Flora is a midwife? I don't know. That's all I can tell you."

"Flora, possibly a midwife, in a place with waterfalls and deep cliffs. Maybe twin waterfalls. I wonder who would know if there's a place like that," said Thomas.

"We could ask Mrs. Brady when we get back to the boardinghouse," said Cally. "And she could ask her boarders at supper.

Many of them have traveled. I heard her say so, that her house attracts the drifters."

"It's a place to start," said Thomas. "Speaking of supper, aren't you staying late today, Melody? It's past four o'clock. Will you get in trouble?"

"I don't care if I do. I'm leaving this place. William is freeing me again. I'll go visit my mother, and if she doesn't want me, I'll look for a place nearby where I can at least see my brother and his family. I'm worn out, like a desert inside, all dry and dusty. I want to find some peace before I die."

"I'm glad to hear this, Melody! You won't be sorry. I'm sure of it," said Cally.

"Since William gave me this gift, I can pay for the train myself. I don't need your help. Tell me again where my mother's new house is?"

"A place called Fish Haven, on Bear Lake. Take the train to Montpelier. Fish Haven is one stop before Garden City," said Thomas.

"Watch me and get off one stop before I do, is it," said Melody drily. "Well then. It's time to say goodbye."

"First can we talk a little more about Billy?" asked Thomas. "What sorts of things does he like? Did he go to school? Who were his friends? What did he talk about? Anything you can tell us will be a help. Uncle William assumed, I think, he would be here with you, but since he isn't, we need clues for how to find him."

"Of course, Billy went to school, at Bonneville Elementary—you'll pass it on your way back to the tracks. No rules against black children or Italian or Chinese or Irish or German or Greek, just all the little ones mixed up together, same as they play in the streets. A smart one, my Billy, always at the top of his class. He read anything he could get his hands on, which wasn't much, sad to say. He started lecturing me about the dangers of my lifestyle long before I knew I was sick. I don't know how he came by that knowledge—must have been from the other women in the house. He's vain, too, because he was fussed over by so many mothers in the house where we lived. He had a bee in his bonnet about his father, wanting to know about him, wanting to find him. Finally, he left. I think he might have tried to go to Ireland."

After this outpouring, Melody covered her mouth with her hand. "I haven't said so much at once to anyone as long as I can remember."

"I can tell Billy matters a great deal to you, Melody," said Cally.

"We'll do all we can to find him," said Thomas. "What you've said is helpful. It gives us an idea of the person we're looking for. Do you have any photographs of him?"

"Not since William left, no."

"All right. Well, my mother—her name is Cathleen—is a big believer in prayer. We'll ask her to pray for us to find Billy," said Thomas.

"My mother is a big pray-er too," said Melody.

"I have a good feeling about your plan to visit your family," said Cally.

"Melody, we need a way to keep in touch with each other, in case either of us learns something about Billy," said Thomas. "You could send me a telegram in Kansas City, and I'll always know where Cally is. Here is my card."

"If my visit to Fish Haven goes well, I'll stay with my mother there," said Melody. "If it doesn't, I don't know yet where I'll go. But I'll let you know, Thomas."

"Thank you for spending so much time with us, Melody. Goodbye," said Cally.

"Goodbye," said Melody. "I'm going to sit for a while here by the pond. Best wishes finding Flora and Fauna."

"Thanks," said Thomas. "Shane! Felicity! It's time to go!"

"I don't know," said Mrs. Brady. "But why don't you join my boarders at supper tonight and ask them?"

"Thank you. I would love to hear anything they have to say," said Thomas.

"Will Cally join us as well?"

"No, she wants to bathe the children and put them to bed early. But thank you!"

ঔ

"That's easy," said a man sitting across from Thomas. "Miz Flora doctors all the folks around her. Has her clinic at the Strickers' by the old Rock Creek stage station until the family gets back from Germany. Treats all alike, Indians, whites, whoever. Pet wolf called Fauna seldom leaves her side, not since Miz Flora healed her broken leg when she was a pup. Ask anyone how to find her."

"An odd one, Miz Flora," said another man. "Believes all people are equal in God's sight, women same as men. Twin Falls didn't welcome her, so she moved to the town of Rock Creek. Folks didn't think a woman could be a doctor, and they still call her Miz Flora. But even the stubborn ones run to her when they need help."

"So, there's a town of Rock Creek and a station called Rock Creek?" asked Thomas.

"Yes. Rock Creek town is about two miles upstream of the Stricker homesite, where the old Rock Creek station used to serve travelers on the Oregon Trail. Not many folks go by there anymore. The station still stands, near the Strickers' new house where Miz Flora is while the family is gone. Rock Creek itself flows nearby."

"Thank you," said Thomas. "You've been very helpful."

ঔ

"Mrs. Brady, you have been kind and generous to us," said Thomas. "I want to settle our bill, so we won't disturb you at breakfast. We'll take the early train to Twin Falls."

"It has been a pleasure to have you. Your children are delightful."

"Thank you, Mrs. Brady. They still talk about making bread and cookies," said Thomas. "Cally asked me to give you this gift in appreciation of your kindness to us."

"Why, thank you. Take some cookies along on your trip. Twin Falls is a long way. I'll make sandwiches for you before I cook breakfast in the morning. Get a good sleep now."

"Thank you, ma'am. Good night."

CHAPTER 14

ROCK CREEK STATION

[Note: For a map, see "Rock Creek Station/Stricker Homesite" on HorseThief1898.blog.]

On the train to Twin Falls, Wednesday June 8

"I SUSPECT DR. FLORA TREATED HIM MEDICALLY," said Cally, rereading Uncle William's poem.

"Yes, maybe a fall in the Snake River Canyon," said Thomas. "I hope she's at home. Have you ever heard of someone having a pet wolf?"

"Never," said Cally. "I'm glad you're with us! I wonder how far the Rock Creek station is from Twin Falls."

"We'll ask," said Thomas. "I hope not too far. My train for Kansas City departs Twin Falls mid-morning Friday. I'm looking forward to a day at home with Cora and the girls before they leave early Monday to join you. You're sure you'll be all right by yourself with both children until Cora arrives, Cally?"

"Who knows where we'll be a week from now," said Cally, smiling at Felicity's worried expression. "It's an adventure, sweetheart. We've been fine so far, right?"

"I'm not scared of wolves," said Shane.

A passenger across the aisle cleared his throat. "Excuse me. I heard you talking about Miz Flora and Rock Creek. This train makes several unofficial stops on the way to Twin Falls, to serve folks working on the irrigation canal from Milner Dam west. Take the next stop after I get off. It's a small settlement, but you may be able to hire a wagon to take you the seven miles to the old Rock Creek stage station. Twin Falls would be more like twelve miles. Worth a try."

"Thank you, sir," said Thomas.

"There's quite a project going on. The Twin Falls Land and Water Company means to transform this desert into fertile farmland, can you believe that? If it works, it'll be a miracle. The dam is almost finished, and the canal is making good progress. Over five hundred men working on it, so I've heard. Come back next year to see whether the Snake River Plain has succumbed to the magic of water."

"In Montpelier we heard the same idea using the Bear River," said Cally.

"I heard about that," said the man. "Fella couldn't get enough funding. It's been a struggle for the TFLWC too."

"TFLWC—oh, the Twin Falls Land and Water Company," said Thomas. "If it works here, I imagine other places will follow."

"Could be," said the man. "Well, I'm going to snooze. Nice talking to you."

"We appreciate your advice," said Thomas.

ઉ઱

"There's not much here," said Thomas, looking around at a collection of tents. "Perhaps we should have gone on to Twin Falls. Oh, sir," he called to a man walking slowly by. "We need to find Miz Flora. Do you know where we can rent a wagon?"

"No," said the man. "Wagons at diggings. You hurt or sick?"

"No. Just visiting," said Thomas.

"Seven miles to Rock Creek station. You walk."

"We could, I suppose," said Thomas, glancing at Cally. "But we have all this luggage, and it's terribly hot. And we don't know where we're going."

"Why get off train here? Just canal workers. Not for women and children."

"A man on the train told us it's closer to Rock Creek station than Twin Falls," said Thomas. "Have we made a mistake?"

"Yes. Wagons at Twin Falls." The man removed his cap and wiped sweat with his sleeve.

"When does the train next stop here?"

"Saturday."

Thomas glanced at Cally's worried face. "Do you have any suggestions for us, sir?"

The man scratched his head, scrunching up his face. "Miz Flora has wagon. Leave woman, children. Walk to Rock Creek station. Bring wagon for things."

"My, it's hot. And no trees for shade," Cally said. She sat on her trunk, pulled Felicity onto her lap, and waved her hand in front of her daughter's flushed face. *The man chops his words as if it takes too much energy to form complete sentences. Can't say I blame him.*

"Can you give me directions, sir?" asked Thomas.

"Walk an hour south across canal. Then half hour to Rock Creek. Wagon trail east to station. Stricker's house behind it."

"We appreciate your help, sir. My name is Thomas."

"Donny. Miz Flora's pet wolf called Fauna. Get it? Flora and Fauna."

"Got it. Donny, where can my sister and children be more comfortable until I get back?"

"Not here," said Donny, looking around at the tents as if he hoped something new would appear. "Rancher near river, mile northeast. Trail to house. Name Jenner. Good folks."

"Thank you," said Thomas. "Is there a place we could leave this luggage?"

"My tent," said the man. "No bother. Mate working. I hurt back. Dig tomorrow. No work, no pay."

Thomas looked at Cally. Her eyes were wide, but she said, "Thank you, sir."

"Can't help move things," said the man.

"Your back," said Thomas. "I understand, Donny. If you'll just show us the way."

"It will take more than one trip," said Cally. "Felicity and Lizzy, please stay here with our extra things until we come back for them. Thank you."

"Not far," said Donny, waving his arm. "Mommy right back, little girl."

Thomas, Cally, and Shane, carrying all they could manage, followed Donny to a tent in the middle of the empty settlement.

"You won't have much room to rest, Donny, with our things in here," said Thomas.

"Use friend's tent. Working hours yet," said Donny. "You back before night."

"Thank you so much," said Cally, after they crammed the second load of luggage into Donny's tent. "You have helped us."

"Mother said spread kindness," said Donny. "Water barrel yonder. Take."

"Thank you, Donny. That's a grand gift," said Cally.

"Go now," said Donny.

"Is this an adventure?" asked Felicity as Thomas started walking south, and she, Shane, and Cally followed a trail northeast through sage and scrub.

"A big one," said Shane. "I hope we find a real wolf! Not a tame one like Miz Flora has."

"Water could make this land like Miss Melody's garden!" said

Felicity.

"You understood what the man said about the irrigation canal, didn't you!" said Cally. "Let's try to imagine the land full of trees and flowers and crops."

"And a pond," said Shane.

"With ducks!" said Felicity.

"And fish," said Shane.

"And shade," said Cally.

ଔଡ଼

Half an hour later, Cally and the children dragged themselves up the steps onto the porch of a two-story house. Cally knocked on the frame of the open front door.

"My goodness, y'all startled me!" said the woman who came to the door. "We don't get many visitors. Y'all look tuckered out. Not used to the heat, eh? Come in! Abigail! Bring lemonade for our guests! My name is Priscilla. Y'all are—?"

"My name is Cally. This is my daughter Felicity and my nephew Shane. I'm sorry we're barging in on you."

"Well, y'all are a surprise," said Priscilla.

"Apparently we got off the train at the wrong stop," said Cally. "A man suggested we ask you for shelter while my brother walks to Rock Creek station to borrow a wagon from Miz Flora to collect our things from a man's tent. It's a bit confusing."

"You poor things. Sit down. Or do y'all need the outhouse first? Y'all can stay for as long as you need. We're delighted to see people, aren't we, Abigail? We're alone most of the time, with only the sheep for company. Are y'all hungry? We'll have a meal in about an hour, but do y'all need something sooner? Abigail, what can we offer these poor pilgrims?"

ଔଡ଼

Gazing at the canal workers digging furiously while their overseers shouted at them, Thomas pulled off his hat and wiped the sweat from his face with his handkerchief. *I had no idea the canal would be so big. They will need a lot of water to irrigate all this dry land. Well, I better keep going. I hope Cally and the children found refuge.*

Carefully following Donny's directions, Thomas found himself an hour later in front of the abandoned Rock Creek stage station. Several outbuildings and old wagons flanked the station. A log cabin sat a short distance to the right. A large house ahead and to the left was shaded by trees. *I hear whimpering. In that big house, I think. Such a fancy house here in the middle of nowhere! Two front doors. Miz Flora must be home. The door on the right is open.*

As Thomas approached, the whimpering became a howl, and a large grey wolf bounded through the door. *That must be Fauna. Can a wolf be tamed?* Thomas hesitated, surprised when Miz Flora did not follow Fauna. The wolf ran toward him, and Thomas scrambled into a wagon.

Fauna leaped into the wagon and pushed him out. Thomas hit the ground in a heap. Fauna nudged him until he stood, then butted him toward the house.

Something must be wrong with Miz Flora. Thomas ran, the wolf loping beside him. Whimpering, Fauna ran to a woman collapsed on the floor of a large sitting room.

Oh my. Thomas squatted and touched Flora's cheek. *Burning hot. At least she's not dead.*

He looked around. *I see a kitchen through that door. This one is ... yes, a bedroom. It looks lived in, so perhaps it's hers. I'll carry her in. She's so hot! She looks dressed for cold, not the heat of this day.*

"Ma'am, can you hear me? My name is Thomas. Don't worry, I won't hurt you. I'm taking off your jacket. You must have had chills before this fever."

Flora stirred and mumbled something.

"Fauna, where can I find water?" Thomas walked outside. *That looks like a pump. Now, something to hold water. Hmm, the other front door is labeled 'Clinic, Tuesdays and Thursdays, 1:00-4:00.' I wonder if it's open. Nope.* He walked into the kitchen. *This basin will do.* Outside at the pump, Thomas filled it with water.

"Now, Fauna, I need a rag or towel, something like that." *Yes, here we go.* He took one from a neat stack of clean cloths in the kitchen.

Flora had not moved. As Thomas bathed her face and arms, she stirred, and her eyes blinked open.

"Who are you?" she whispered.

"My name is Thomas. You're a doctor, ma'am. Can you tell me what's wrong with you and how I can help?"

"Don't know. Fever. Headache. Nausea. Could be anything. Dehydrated. Need drink." Flora tried to sit up but fell back on her pillow. "Glasses and pitcher, cabinet in kitchen."

Second time today someone's chopping off their sentences. "Yes, ma'am. I'll be right back." Thomas almost tripped over Fauna as he hurried to follow Flora's directions. The doctor seemed unconscious again but moved when he spoke and touched her shoulder.

"Cabinet by stove. Large pinch sugar small pinch salt in glass. Stir."

When Thomas returned, Flora turned her face to the side. "Drink slowly ... Thanks." Fauna's gaze did not leave her face. "Yes, hold glass like that."

"You're shaking, ma'am," said Thomas.

"Chills. Fever going up. May pass out. Drink more. Who are you?"

"My name is Thomas. We can talk about why I'm here once you're better. How can we treat your fever?"

"Pinch willow bark powder in water. Middle shelf right of door in clinic. Thomas—"

"Yes?"

"Take off more clothes. Bathe cold water. No modesty."

"Ma'am, the clinic door is locked," said Thomas, returning to see her whole body shaking.

"Open pocket door front room," said Flora.

"All right. I'll be back with the willow bark." *What a gorgeous carved door.* Fauna followed Thomas into the clinic and back to Flora's bedside.

Oh no. She's unconscious again. I wish you were here, Cally! You would know how to do this. Might she wake up enough to drink this willow bark if I sit her up? Fauna watches me as if waiting for instructions.

Thomas lifted Flora with one arm, holding the glass in the other. Fauna leaped on the bed and pushed against Flora's back. Thomas lifted Flora's chin and dribbled water into her mouth. She coughed, opened her eyes, and took several swallows before her eyes closed and her body sagged. Fauna jumped to the floor and Thomas eased her back on the bed.

This is awkward, undressing a woman I just met. But here we go. She's hot as blazes. I wish I had a way to communicate with you, Cally. I won't be back for you today, that's for sure.

Thomas chatted with Fauna while he pulled off Flora's skirt and blouse. "If we had not gotten off the train where we did, I wouldn't be here now trying to help Dr. Flora. My mother would say God is involved with this somehow. What do you think about that idea, Fauna?"

଼

The afternoon waned and with it the intense heat. Cally grew concerned. She walked outside to where Priscilla unpinned laundry from a line. "Priscilla, how long should it take for my brother to walk to Rock Creek station and drive a wagon back to us?"

"Hmm, let me think. Perhaps two hours to reach Miz Flora and two hours back. He should be here by now, no question. But y'all are welcome to stay overnight if he's delayed."

"I think something is wrong," said Cally. "Here, let me help you."

"Well, perhaps Flora was out on a call. She travels all over this area, y'know."

"Ah, perhaps that's it. I'm rested now. How can I help with your chores?"

"Do y'all mind folding this laundry? And I'll start supper. Jerry should be in soon."

Cally picked up the heavy basket and walked toward the house with Priscilla. "Jerry is your husband?"

"Yes. Jeremiah, but we call him Jerry."

"All of your names are from the Old Testament."

"Yes. We are Mormon. We were headed to Salt Lake City, but Jerry saw this valley and fell in love with it. That was twenty years ago and we're still here."

"I have a question about the river," Cally said. She set the basket on the kitchen table and pulled out a shirt. "I thought the Snake River flowed through a deep canyon."

Priscilla smiled. "That's true, further west. Over time, I guess, the waterfalls carved out those deep cliffs. But here—well, y'all have seen it. The river valley here is lovely for sheep."

"We've seen how quickly the desert takes over, away from the river."

"Yes. That's the reason for the new dam and the canals, to change the desert into farmland. I reckon many people will move here then. I'm looking forward to it. I get lonely, and Abigail is our only child."

"She's a lovely girl."

"She is. We're sending her to Salt Lake City in the fall. She needs friends."

"I know you'll miss her terribly." Cally glanced out the window for the hundredth time, hoping to see Thomas pull up in a wagon. "Shall I carry this basket upstairs?"

"No, Jerry'll do that. Just set it on the floor by the stairway. Thanks, Cally."

"I'll check on Shane and Felicity. It was kind of Abigail to take them to the river."

Thomas rubbed his eyes. *I didn't realize I fell asleep. It's getting light already.* He lifted the lantern and touched Flora's cheek. *Cooler. And Fauna slept. She must sense Flora is better.*

Flora turned over and sighed. *I think she's sleeping. I'm going to stretch my legs and think about what I should do. I wonder what the horses need.*

Thomas walked to the barn behind the house, stretching his arms over his head. *It's cool this morning! What a long night. Flora frightened me when I couldn't get her fever down and she talked nonsense. I'm no nurse! I hope Cally and the children are all right and not too worried.*

One mare stamped and whinnied as Thomas opened the barn door. "There now, my beauty, everything is fine, even though you didn't have supper last night. Come on outside. I'll give you hay and water and you can run around your enclosure. Later perhaps I'll take you for a ride. I can tell Flora takes excellent care of you. ... Now I must check on Flora and find something to eat. I'll be back later."

Thomas peeked into Flora's bedroom. Flora and Fauna slept on. He found bread and honey and made himself a cup of tea. *What should I do? Flora isn't well enough yet for me to leave her. It would take me four hours at least to pick up Cally and the children and our things and return. Maybe Flora will be all right that long. I don't know. And I have no idea what to feed a wolf.*

Thomas took his bread and tea outside to the front porch. *This is a nice house. I wonder where the owners are. The Stricker family, I think Donny said.* After breakfast, he put his head under the pump, caught his breath, and scrubbed his face and hands. *Whew, that's cold. I'm certainly awake now!*

Fauna ran out of the house and pushed him toward the door. "Flora is awake now and needs me? I didn't know wolves were so intelligent." Thomas shook the water from his hair, wiped his face on his sleeve, and entered Flora's bedroom.

"Thomas, I'm sorry, I need your help again. I know it was awkward last night helping me with my necessaries, but I must ask you to do it again. I tried to get up but I'm not strong enough. My legs hurt. And look at this rash on my arms. I think I have what we call spotted fever. See there—the rash is on my legs too. I wouldn't still be alive if you hadn't come along."

"Can I get you something to eat?" asked Thomas.

"No, I'm not hungry. But a cup of tea with honey sounds nice. I'm glad to have a break from the fever. It must have been a long night for you. Did you sleep at all?"

"A little, yes, toward morning. I'll make the tea. Anything else?"

"Can you help me get under my blankets? I'm a bit chilled."

"I should have thought of that when it got cool during the night. But you felt so hot from the fever ... Flora, how do I care for Fauna? What does she eat?"

"She fends for herself. Keep her water bowl filled and don't restrain her. Don't worry if she disappears. She hunts, for rabbits mostly, I think. So far, she always comes back. Leave a door partially open so she can come and go as she likes."

Thomas raised his eyebrows, but said only, "I'll get your tea."

When he returned, Flora was asleep. *I truly don't know what to do. Cally and the children must be very worried.*

Late morning, Fauna ran outside. Thomas followed and soon heard the clip-clop of horses' feet and the creak of wooden wheels. *If it's someone seeking Dr. Flora, I won't know how to help. ... Oh, thank God.*

It's Cally and the children!"

Shane shared the wagon seat with a man. "Cally, children, I am so glad to see you!"

Thomas rushed to help them from the wagon, gave them all hugs, and turned to the man, who had started lifting Cally's trunk. "Thank you, sir. Let me help." Together, they set the trunk on the front porch. Thomas extended his hand. "My name is Thomas."

Cally reached the porch with a load from the wagon. "Thomas, this is Jeremiah Jenner. His family cared for us last night. When you didn't come, Jerry offered to bring us to you."

"I am grateful, sir. Dr. Flora is very ill. Had I not stayed, she might not have survived the night. I had no way to communicate with you, Cally."

"I'm sorry to hear that. I'll tell Priscilla," said Jerry. "Will y'all be all right?"

"I—I don't know," said Thomas. "I'm not sure about food, and—"

"Priscilla packed food for you, enough for several days. I see lettuce and radishes in Flora's garden. Beans and peas soon. Fruit in the orchard. Eggs from the chickens. Hansen's store in Rock Creek town, two miles upstream."

"That's good, but Jerry, if—if Dr. Flora gets worse—what should we do?" asked Thomas. *I don't want him to go. I've seldom felt so insecure.*

"Y'all have neighbors closer than us," said Jerry. "See the tree line behind the house? That's Rock Creek. Walk east along the creek half a mile to the Ingram farm. They'll help you." He had climbed back onto the wagon seat while he talked. His "Goodbye" floated back on the dust stirred by the horses' hooves.

"Uncle Thomas, we didn't know what happened to you." Felicity burst into tears.

"I told her there was a reason you didn't come, Daddy," said Shane, eying Fauna. "Is that Miz Flora's wolf?"

"Yes. She's friendly, as long as you do what she tells you," smiled Thomas as he hugged his niece. "Felicity. I'm sorry. I had no way to tell you what happened."

"How is Dr. Flora now?" asked Cally.

"She was sleeping before you came. Children, stay here on the porch for a minute while Cally and I check on Flora. I expect Fauna will go with us."

"All right, Daddy," said Shane. Felicity put her hand in Shane's and nodded.

"I never imagined playing nurse," said Thomas. "She's very sick, Cally. She thinks it's spotted fever."

"Rocky Mountain spotted fever? I've read about that," said Cally. "It spreads through tick bites. We should make sure there are no ticks on Flora's body or on Fauna."

Flora's eyes were open, but the bed shook. "Chills, Thomas. Fever going up again. Please give me more willow bark. Don't let me sleep until I drink a full glass of water with sugar and salt. Oh, hello."

"Flora, this is my sister, Cally. She'll be a much better nurse than I have been."

"Welcome," said Flora. "Sorry not to be more hospitable. My head aches terribly."

"I'm so sorry," said Cally. "We'll care for you as well as we can. Thomas, show me how to fix her drink."

"What shall we do?" Thomas asked Cally once Flora slept, her fever abated for the moment. "I must return to Kansas City. But I don't want to leave you alone with Flora and Fauna and the horse and chickens and the children."

"You could find the neighbors Jerry mentioned. The children might enjoy a walk."

"Good idea. It would be a relief to find some help! We'll go now."

A half hour later, Thomas and the children returned in a wagon guided by a middle-aged woman. She bustled into the house, introduced herself briefly to Cally as Margaret, then hurried to Flora's bedroom. Flora stirred and turned her head.

"So, even the doctor can get sick. Spotted fever, eh?" Quickly Margaret assessed Flora head to toe.

What a relief to have someone who knows what she's doing!

"I'll take turns with Cally here to care for you and the animals, since Thomas must return to Kansas City tomorrow. Looks like he's done a good job. What do you need right now?"

Cally watched Margaret efficiently bathe Flora and dress her in a nightgown. "More comfortable? But we wore you out. Drink this and then you can rest. While you sleep, Cally and I and Thomas will devise a plan."

In the front room, Thomas asked, "Could you come early tomorrow, Margaret, so Cally can take me to the train station in Twin Falls? I'm sorry I must leave. I feel so much better though, knowing Cally won't be alone. Thank you."

"What are neighbors for? Flora has cared for our family more than once," said Margaret. "Will you two be all right the rest of the day? Clearly you need sleep, Thomas. I'll come back at sundown to spend the night and stay until you get back from Twin Falls, Cally. I'll sleep on the front room sofa so I can hear Flora. You can leave the children with me. I can bring my grandson Tucker to play with them. We'll take it one day at a time."

"My wife Cora and my two daughters plan to arrive Tuesday," said Thomas. "We need to figure out where everyone can sleep. Perhaps we could use the clinic waiting room?"

"That will work for tonight. Herman and Lucy left the five bedrooms upstairs locked and we don't have the key," said Margaret. "Their foreman and his wife live in the log cabin. They're out tracking cattle with the cowboys. A thousand acres is a lot to cover. Tomorrow we can clean out the station. Stage passengers used to sleep there. We'll figure it out. There's always a way."

"Thank you," said Thomas. "You are a godsend."

"From what I can tell, it's you whom God sent," said Margaret. "You stumbled into this situation. Perhaps later you'll tell me who you are and why you're here."

"We have questions, too," said Thomas. "Including whether the Strickers—is that the family's name who own the house?—will mind us staying here for a while."

"No way to know, since they're in Germany. Under the circumstances, what else can you do?" replied Margaret.

Monday, June 13

Shane and Felicity raced around the property with Fauna and four-year-old Tucker. Cally and Margaret supported Flora through the door and eased her into a chair on the front porch. Fauna rushed to Flora's side. Cally pulled Felicity down to her lap on the grass and patted the space beside her for the boys. Margaret brought another chair and sat beside Flora.

"Beautiful morning isn't it," said Margaret. "You're making progress, Flora!"

Flora took a deep breath and smiled. "Thanks to you and Cally. I keep wondering, Cally, why you're here. And why your brother showed up when he did, other than to save my life."

"We're on a treasure hunt!" said Felicity. "It's an adventure!"

"A treasure hunt?" queried Margaret.

"Billy might be the treasure. But we can't find him," said Felicity.

"Let me show you something," said Cally. She pushed Felicity off her lap and walked to the station. Returning, she put Uncle William's poem into Flora's hands.

"This was written by our great-uncle William," said Cally. "It led us to you."

"It's clue number six," said Shane. "We think you might have a clue for us too. And Aunt Cally has an envelope for you."

"William Malcomson ... amazing. After all these years, you arrived at the precise moment I needed help," said Flora. "It's almost enough to make a person believe in Providence."

"We're curious what happened between you and Uncle William," said Cally. "The poem made us suspect you treated him medically."

"I did," said Flora. "I still lived in Twin Falls. William tried to climb down the cliff by one of the falls, fell, and broke his leg. People saw it happen and brought him to me. It was quite an experience, knowing your Uncle William."

"I never met him," said Cally. "He died when I was small. But he left this for you." She extended the envelope labeled Dr. Flora.

Flora scanned the note tucked into the envelope. "It's money to help supply my clinic. While he was here, William encouraged me. Many people resisted the idea of a female doctor."

"I might be a doctor when I grow up," said Felicity. "Or an artist. Or a mommy."

"Perhaps you can be all three," said Flora. She rubbed her forehead and stretched. "My energy has run out. But this has been lovely. Thank you."

"I look forward to hearing more about Uncle William after you've rested," said Cally.

"William did leave a packet for 'anyone from the Malcomson family who shows up,'" said Flora, making quotation marks in the air. "I'll look for it. So many years have passed ..."

"There's no hurry," said Cally, helping her into bed. "Tomorrow Cora and the girls will arrive. It will be fun for them to be present when we learn the next clue for our treasure hunt."

"A treasure hunt across southern Idaho. Unbelievable," said Margaret.

"Grandma, what's a treasure hunt?" asked Tucker.

"Perhaps we'll find out. Right now, we must figure out beds for the new folks arriving tomorrow."

CHAPTER 15

FLORA

Stricker homesite, Tuesday, June 14

"FLORA'S STILL SLEEPING," Cally told Margaret. "She had a restless night. Thanks for keeping Shane while Felicity and I go to Twin Falls for Cora and the girls. He'd rather play with Tucker than ride for hours in the wagon."

"Glad to," said Margaret. "While Flora sleeps, Tucker, Shane, and I can clear some weeds from her garden."

"You'll have to teach Shane," said Cally.

"No problem," said Margaret. "Tucker's a good little weeder, once I tell him what to pull and what to leave." Margaret tousled his hair. "You might want to have lunch in Twin Falls before you start back. I'll make soup for your supper. Three more places at the table, right?"

"Yes. My sister-in-law Cora is lovely. Shauna is ten; she's Shane's twin. And Josie will be seven a week from today. We would love for you and Tucker to come to her birthday party!"

"Can I, Grandma?" asked Tucker.

"We'll check with your parents, Tucker. Off you go, Cally. I'm glad you have experience with horses. Why Flora named her mare Chamomile, I don't understand. She's feisty."

"Oh—I thought her name was Cammie."

"Her nickname. Simpler than Chamomile, don't you think?"

Cally held on to Felicity with one arm and Cammie's reins with the other, letting the mare have her head. They whooped and the wagon rattled. Cally reveled in the speed and the wind blowing her auburn curls from their pins.

After racing across the desert for several miles, Cammie finally slowed, blowing and panting. "That was fun, Mummy!" exclaimed Felicity.

"Cammie won't run so fast on the way back. Whew, it's already getting hot," said Cally.

"I can't wait to see Shauna and Josie," said Felicity, bouncing on the seat. "How long since I saw them, Mummy?"

"A long time. Two months," said Cally. "Have you enjoyed our adventures so far?"

"Mostly," said Felicity, wrinkling her forehead. "I didn't like Miss Lizzy dying. And Andy dying. And Billy being lost. And Flora being sick. And that lady—what was her name? Pounding on our door in nighttime. And your bad dreams. And Uncle Charlie leaving."

"The lady's name was Connie. What did you like so far?"

"Playing with Uncle Charlie. Miz Minnie's sparkly eyes even though she is sooo old. My cousin Lizzy in New York. My doll and travel book. Miss Anthony and Aunt Mary, but they're old too. You have lots of old friends, Mummy."

"That's true. They've been good to me. Anything else?"

"Fizzy lemonade. Warm baths and caving with Jenny and her mommy. Uncle Thomas and Shane. Tucker and Fauna. Lots of things!"

"Now we'll share our adventures with Cora, Shauna and Josie."

"And Grandma Cathleen!"

"In a few more days, yes."

"Mummy, does Tucker have a daddy?"

"Yes. His mummy and daddy are farmers and work very hard. So, his grandmother Margaret often takes care of Tucker."

"Why don't I have a daddy?" asked Felicity.

Cally looked down at Felicity's flushed face. "This question bothers you, doesn't it."

"Yes. Why won't you ever tell me?"

Cally sighed. "Your father is not a good man, Felicity. He's in jail because he hurt many people. But you know quite a few good men, sweetheart. Who are some of the good men you know?"

"Uncle Thomas. Uncle Charlie."

"Yes. They both love you very much. Anyone else?"

Felicity considered. "Cousin Nathanael. Cousin Lizzy's daddy. That banker man loved Miz Connie, I could tell. And Miz Minnie too."

"Mr. Martin. I agree. Anyone else?" asked Cally.

"That Indian man. And Andy's daddy. He was sad Andy died. But he wasn't mad."

"You've been watching the daddies, haven't you. Yes, I agree. The Indian man's name is Joe Rainey. He was kind to everyone."

"I want a nice daddy for me," said Felicity. "Not anyone else's daddy. My own."

"Then here's what you can do, Felicity," said Cally. "At night when you say your prayers, you can ask God to give you a nice daddy."

"Can God hear me?"

"Yes. He hears every word you say to him. And he loves you very much."

"All right. Look, Mummy, I see the train tracks!"

"Yes, we're almost to the station. Listen. Can you hear the train?"

"I think so! But it's far away."

"We got here just in time. I'll ask this boy to watch Cammie and the wagon so we can go to the platform."

ঔ

The girls jabbered all through lunch at the Twin Falls Diner. Halfway home in the wagon, Shauna exclaimed, "Uncle Charlie's in love!"

Cally's eyebrows shot up. "Charlie's in love?" she asked Cora, beside her on the bench.

Cora laughed. "I'll let you read his letter. He wrote you, too. The letter's in my suitcase, along with one from Mary Anthony. Charlie reconnected with a lass he knew at the music academy in Dublin. Her name is Laoise. She's a performer too, on the violin."

"Has he mentioned her before?" asked Cally. *So, things went well! I'm so glad! I hope he wrote me all the details!*

"Not to me," said Cora. "My, it's hot."

"Yes, but it cools down at night, and the early mornings are lovely."

"Have you gotten used to this strange country, Cally? I've never been anywhere so dry. What are these bushy things I see everywhere?"

"They're called sage."

"I can't wait to paint this. Look at the blue, blue sky. Almost cerulean. How much longer until we get to Flora's house?"

"About an hour. Cammie is picking up her pace. She's as eager to arrive as we are."

"Cally, have you thought about Josie's birthday? How shall we celebrate out here?"

"I have one idea. This road is part of the old Oregon Trail. Flora told me about it. Thousands of people from the east and south of the United States traveled west hoping to find land and a better life. Kansas City was one of their departure places. Look, right there are ruts from their wagons. Traveling across Idaho we've seen many of those ruts."

"I've heard of the Oregon Trail, but never imagined the west to be like this."

"It's not all like this. There are mountains and springs and rivers and lakes. All kinds of landscapes. Anyway, for Josie's party, what do you think of pretending we're pioneers on the Oregon Trail, and the log cabin is a trading post as it used to be? The house where Flora is staying belongs to the Stricker family, who ran the store until 1897. Rock Creek station was the first and largest stage stop on the Oregon Trail between Fort Hall and Fort Boise. Travelers could camp there, water their animals from the creek, pick up mail, and trade for things they needed from the Strickers and from the Indians before continuing their journey west."

"How intriguing!" said Cora.

"Each of us could choose the character we want to play. Cathleen could be the station manager with letters for the settlers. Perhaps Margaret—you'll meet her soon—could pretend to be Mrs. Stricker, and the goods she has to trade could be Josie's gifts and treats for the children."

"You've put a lot of thought into this!"

"What do you think? Our children are imaginative. Getting ready will be half the fun!"

"It's a charming idea. Certainly, different from any birthday Josie would have back in Kansas City!" said Cora. "Perhaps we could spend today settling in and talk to Josie about it tomorrow. I'm sure Cathleen will go along with it."

"All right. Whoa, Cammie. Would you like a wild ride, Cora? She's chomping at the bit."

"Is it safe?"

"As long as everyone holds on!"

"I'm sorry to tell you Flora has taken a turn for the worse," said Margaret, after the introductions. "She's in pain and hasn't gotten out of bed at all today."

"Oh no!" said Cally. "I'll quicky show Cora and the children the station so they can get settled, then I can see Flora."

"Already covered," said Margaret, pointing to Tucker and Shane trooping across the grass with the girls and Cora. "I'll welcome ideas for helping Flora. I don't know what to do."

Flora groaned as the two women entered her room. "I'm not doing well," she managed.

"I'm so sorry," said Cally. "What can we do?"

"I can't think of anything we haven't tried already. I want to consult Falling Water," said Flora. "Can you help me turn over?"

"Falling Water is a Shoshone healer," said Margaret as they eased Flora into a more comfortable position. "Flora, are the Shoshone still camped by Cottonwood Creek?"

"Yes, but they'll soon be forced to move. The irrigation project will divert the creek." Flora moaned again.

"I'll go for her," said Margaret. "Will you watch Tucker, Cally?"

"Of course. He can play with the other children."

"I made stew for your supper. I'll be back with Falling Water as soon as I can, Flora."

"Water," said Flora.

"I'll pump some fresh," said Cally. She almost fell over Fauna as she hurried outside.

"Falling Water brought a satchel full of leaves and powders, prepared to stay until Flora is better," said Margaret. "She wasn't surprised by this turn for the worse. She'll watch Flora tonight. We can take turns caring for her tomorrow so Falling Water can sleep during the day."

"I'm relieved," said Cally. "I hate seeing Flora in so much pain. How does Falling Water know so much English?"

"Her grandson has been teaching her what he learns on the irrigation project."

"I hope her medicine will help," said Cally.

"The Shoshone have been dealing with spotted fever for

centuries," said Margaret. "I'll take Tucker on home now. His parents will be getting worried."

"Thank you, Margaret. For everything. I don't know what I would have done without you. Flora might not still be alive."

"Well, she's still very sick. Pray for her, Cally. I will too."

Cally was surprised the next morning to see Flora stripped to her underclothes, sitting in a chair, Fauna at her feet, while Falling Water pulled the bedclothes from her bed. "You wash her sheets," she said, pressing the bundle into Cally's arms. "I will help Flora bathe. She's better."

"I see that," said Cally. "I'm so happy."

"Better, but still sick," said Flora. "Cally, please take Falling Water to the clinic. Show her where the clean sheets are. Falling Water, I want you to see whether I have anything useful for you. And you can sleep on the clinic bed."

"I brought my mat," said Falling Water. "I'm used to sleeping on the floor."

"Margaret should be here soon, Falling Water," said Cally. "After we hang the laundry, Cora and I will take the children to the river to play and picnic, so it will be quiet around here." *I hope to find time to write Charlie, the Anthonys, and Mary Ann.*

"Flora will sleep today too. That will help her most now," said Falling Water.

Friday, June 17

"Cally, when you go to Twin Falls tomorrow to meet Cathleen, can you send this telegram for me?" requested Flora. "Falling Water says I need a long rest and the best place is Soda Springs. I'm asking my sister in Oregon City to take me there for a few weeks."

"You have a sister in Oregon City?"

"Yes. The rest of my family lives there. It's a long story. They object to me being a doctor. But I think Florence will come."

"I'll be glad to send the telegram. How soon might you travel to Soda Springs?"

"Whenever Florence is free to join me. Margaret will check on Fauna and the homesite."

"If you meet Calico at the Dizzy Lizzy Bar of the Idanha Hotel, please greet him for us," said Cally. "And a Chinese woman named May Lee."

"Do you think your Uncle William would mind if I use some of his money to pay for the hotel?" asked Flora. "I'll replace it as soon as I can."

"I'm sure Uncle William only wanted what's best for you."

"When she comes, I'll ask Florence to help me search for the packet William left for you. I'm sorry I haven't been well enough to do it myself."

"We've been too busy to think about that," said Cally.

"I know you have," said Flora. "I'm grateful your brother showed up when he did. And for the care you and Cora and Margaret and Falling Water have poured out on me."

"It's amazing to think we're here because of a man who died twelve years ago."

CHAPTER 16

CATHLEEN

[Note: Aisling is pronounced *ash-ling.*]

Stricker Homesite, early Saturday, June 18

"YOUR MUMMY LEFT EARLY to pick up Grandma Cathleen in Twin Falls," Cora told Felicity. "Remember? We're going to make plans for Josie's birthday party and play in the creek."

"Mummy and I asked Miz Falling Water if she and her family could come to be real Indians," said Shane.

"What did Miz Falling Water say, Shane?" asked Shauna.

"She said yes! Some of her family will camp here, like they did in the old times," said Shane. "They will bring crafts to trade with us. And they will let us see how they live inside their special tent. It's called a wickiup. It's made of woven grass."

"I'll go make space in the station for Grandma's bed," said Shauna.

"Thank you, Shauna. But Grandma will sleep at Margaret's house. We think she'll rest better there after her very long trip across the ocean from Ireland and across this big country," said Cora.

"Oh," said Shauna. "I thought she would sleep with us."

"We could invite her for a sleepover!" said Josie.

"We'll see, sweetheart," said Cora. "Let's say a prayer for Cally and Grandma's trip and for Flora and be very quiet in the house so she can rest."

"I'm praying God will give me a daddy," said Felicity.

Cally stood to the side, watching passengers step off the train. *I feel shy. I haven't been alone with Cathleen for a long time. There she is. Here we go.* She stepped forward with a smile and returned Cathleen's warm hug.

"Cally, you are more beautiful every time I see you," said Cathleen. "My, it's hot. Let me take off this jacket." She looked around. "Are you here alone?"

"Yes. The trip is three hours each way. Cora and I agreed she would stay with the children, since I've made this journey enough times to know what I'm doing. Mr. Foster, the station manager, will help with your luggage."

"I'm afraid my trunk is quite heavy, Mr. Foster."

Mr. Foster tipped his hat and hefted Cathleen's trunk.

"This way," said Cally. "We'll eat lunch here in Twin Falls and then begin our drive. You must be exhausted, Cathleen."

"I am tired, yes. But delighted to be part of this adventure! Thank you for coming so far for me, Cally. If the *Lion III* had not been delayed. I'd have traveled from Kansas City with Cora. How is Dr. Flora?"

"She is better, thanks to the care of an Indian healer named Falling Water. She's lovely and skillful. You'll meet them both in a few hours."

"We have so much to catch up on, Cally," said Cathleen as they climbed to the wagon seat after lunch at the diner. "I think this ride will not be long enough. First, tell me where I'll be sleeping, so I can prepare myself. I understand your accommodations are rather rustic."

Cally laughed. "You could say that! You'll stay at the home of a wonderful neighbor named Margaret Ingram. You can be with us as much each day as you choose."

"That is thoughtful, Cally. At sixty-two I'm not as flexible as I once was. But I understood the Stricker house is large."

"It is, yes. The family cleared one bedroom for Flora downstairs and locked their valuables into the five bedrooms upstairs. Flora uses what was Herman and Lucy's sitting room and bedroom as her clinic. I hope the Strickers won't be upset when they find out we've been here! I don't think we've done any damage, at least so far."

"I see what I've been hearing about the desert. Sagebrush, it's called?"

"Yes," said Cally. "You'll enjoy Cora's paintings."

"Tell me more about the family where I'll be staying."

"Margaret has been a lifesaver, helping us care for Flora, weed the garden, cook, do laundry. She lives with her son George and his wife Betsy and their delightful four-year-old Tucker. Margaret lost her husband in an accident a few years ago. I think you'll find you have many things in common," said Cally.

"I like her already, just from her name," said Cathleen.

"How is your Margaret? And Percy and the children?"

Cathleen sighed. "Sometimes I think we raised our daughter too indulgently. She would not consider an adventure like this one. She's never experienced want or privation. Yet she has a kind, generous heart. She's been a great comfort since Peter's death. Her children entertain me endlessly. I've missed Peter more on this journey than I have for years."

"The children can't wait to see you, but we'll let you have a long rest at Margaret's tonight and tomorrow. You can bathe and settle in. When you're ready, Margaret will walk with you the half mile to us from her house for supper. Does that sound all right?"

"You've thought of everything. Thank you, my dear. Tell me, how has this so-called treasure hunt been for you so far? I mean for you personally, having to leave Kansas City so suddenly and under such extraordinary circumstances. It can't have been easy."

Cally burst into tears. *Where did that come from? I had no intention—*

"My dear, take my handkerchief. Weeping helps us women so much, don't you think?"

"I—I'm sorry. No one has asked me that question," said Cally.

"I would be beside myself, Cally. Please tell me all about it. We have plenty of time, I believe, so you've no need to leave out the details."

"If you're sure ..."

"Absolutely."

So, Cally told Cathleen how it felt to disguise herself and run away again. About Jeb and the events in Rochester. About her visit to Paddy. About her nightmares. About Felicity asking about her father. About her uncertain future as a single mother, believing she should establish herself on her own, yet not knowing how to accomplish that and care well for Felicity.

She poured it all out, to this woman whose kindness she had shunned by running away as a child, but who, astonishingly, bore her only good will. This woman whom she could not bring herself to call mother, despite her adoption into the Malcomson family.

"Dear Cally," Cathleen said, when the torrent of words finally stopped. "All I know to do is to leave all of this at the foot of the cross. It's too much, too heavy for you to carry. You are even more precious to our Lord than you are to me. Will you let me help you give it all to him?"

"I—I'm not sure what you mean," said Cally.

"May I take the reins? Cammie seems to know exactly where she's going."

"All right," said Cally.

"Now, close your eyes. I want you to imagine Jesus right here with you."

"All I see is the crucifix in our church in Killeagh," said Cally.

"I will ask him to come down from the cross," said Cathleen. "Please do this for Cally, Lord Jesus."

Cally gasped. "He did it! He's walking toward me!"

"He is so good, child. Look into his eyes. Can you see how much he loves you?"

Tears streamed down Cally's cheeks. "I—I didn't know," she whispered.

"Now, hold your hands out to Jesus and let him take from you all the burdens you have just shared with me. Is he taking them?"

"Yes," said Cally, a while later. "I feel so light! But now he's taken my hands and wants me to dance with him. Oh my," said Cally, and didn't say anything else for a long time. Cathleen, glancing from time to time at Cally's radiant face, felt her own weariness slip away.

Thank you, Lord Jesus. You are so good, so good to us.

"Cally, you're different somehow," said Margaret, after settling Cathleen in her room.

"I'll tell you about it later," said Cally, smiling. "I need to let everyone at the homesite know Cathleen has arrived safely. Thank you for welcoming her, Margaret."

"If we're not there by suppertime, go ahead to serve the children. She must be exhausted after such a long trip."

"Yes, but she wants to greet everyone today. Cora will walk back with her after supper."

"And Falling Water will take the night shift. That woman is a marvel."

"As are you, Margaret." Cally surprised them both by giving the older woman a hug.

Felicity, nestled into Grandma's embrace, clapped her hands when shouts of "Grandma, Grandma, Grandma" reached them. Shane, Shauna, and Josie raced to where Cathleen sat at the makeshift table Margaret and Cora had erected in front of the Stricker house. Cathleen gathered them in, all three chattering at once. Cora smiled her welcome. "We were playing in the creek, Grandma. We'll take you there!"

"I have something special to show you," said Cathleen, taking a folded sheet of newsprint from her pocket. "Do you know who this is?"

"It's Uncle Charlie and a beautiful lady," said Shauna.

"She has a violin," said Shane, reading. "'Irish Classics. September 2-4. New York Phil—Phil—"

"Philharmonic. It's an orchestra. The lady is Uncle Charlie's friend, Laoise."

"Our first sighting of Laoise!" said Cora. "She is beautiful. What newspaper is this from, Cathleen?"

"The *New York Times.* Nathanael gave it to me. There was a poster in the lounge of the *Lion III* too. Makes sense, since most of the passengers traveling to New York are Irish."

Cora's eyes widened. "Look!" she said, pointing toward the door of the house. Falling Water and Cally emerged, supporting Flora between them. In her excitement, Fauna almost tripped them up.

Easing Flora to her chair on the porch, Cally gestured to Cathleen. The children burst into cheers, quickly joined by the adults. Flora clapped with them, grinning, then turned to Cathleen.

"Welcome, Mrs. Malcomson. Please pardon the scratchiness of my voice."

"Flora, I am delighted to meet you. And you must be Falling Water," Cathleen said, turning toward her. "Your name is like the grace that pours from your life. Cally, Cora, and Margaret have all told me how grateful they are." Falling Water inclined her head.

"Not nearly as grateful as I am," said Flora. "Fauna, settle down. All is well." The wolf lay down at her feet, Flora's hand on her head.

"I won't stay through supper, but I may try to eat a little," said Flora. "Your stew smells marvelous, Cora."

"I hope you don't mind I raided your garden for early vegetables," said Cora.

"What are they for if not to eat?" said Flora.

"I made cornbread to go with the stew," said Cally, walking from the kitchen with a pan in her hand. Does that sound good to you, Flora?"

"Perhaps a small piece. Please, serve your family. I will sit here and rest for a moment."

"Cathleen, will you say grace?" asked Cally.

"With pleasure. Father, this is a day of rejoicing. Please continue to heal dear Flora and bless us all through the bounty of this table. Amen."

After supper, Cora took the children to tuck them in. Cathleen pulled several envelopes from her pocket and handed two to Cally. "Aisling gave me this letter for you about a month ago, Cally. I believe she enclosed a note for Teddy as well. Can you mail it to him?"

"Next time I go to Rock Creek, yes. So, you're still in touch with Aisling and Dugan?"

"Yes, as often as possible. I'm the children's honorary grandmother, ever since Aisling's father died. You knew him, didn't you? She misses him terribly," said Cathleen.

Cora returned from the station. "Eating outside worked well, don't you think?"

"Yes! We should have thought of this sooner," said Cally.

"Cathleen, are you ready to walk over to Margaret's, or would you prefer riding? You must be exhausted," said Cora.

"Walking is a delight, after so many days on the train. Thomas sent a letter for you, Cora, and one for Josie for her birthday."

"Lovely! Thank you," said Cora, slipping the envelopes into her pocket.

"Before we go, Cora, I have a question for you both," said Cathleen. "What would you think of inviting Margaret's family to supper tomorrow? And follow it with evening prayer? I would be happy to lead. I imagine Margaret would contribute to the supper."

"That would be a lovely way to express our appreciation to the family for all Margaret has done for us," said Cally. Cora nodded.

"Thank you. I'll ask them," said Cathleen. "I'll show up tomorrow after a good rest, perhaps sometime in the afternoon. Is that acceptable?"

"Certainly. Take all the time you need," said Cally.

"Good night then, my dear."

Cally gave Cathleen a hug. "Sleep well."

As Cora and Cathleen walked away, Cally gazed after them. *Who can explain the love and kindness those two women so consistently offer me? Such a wonder.*

She shook herself, cleared up supper, checked on the children, told Flora she had sent her telegram to Florence, said good night to her and Falling Water, and folded the day's laundry. When Cora returned from Margaret's house, the two women discussed what they could serve for supper the next day and how to enlarge the outdoor table, then Cora went to tell Flora good night. Cally yawned. Darkness settled over the quiet homesite. *I'll read Aisling's and Charlie's letters tomorrow. I'm too tired to light a lantern tonight.*

CHAPTER 17

SUNDAY SUPPER

[Note: Caoimhe is pronounced *kee-va.*]

Stricker Homesite, Sunday evening, June 19

"MUMMY, A WAGON IS COMING! Two wagons!" yelled Felicity.

Cally turned her chicken and potatoes down to keep warm and ran out the back door. *Perhaps it's someone seeking Dr. Flora.* She wiped her face on her sleeve and tucked strands of hair back into her hairpins. *The man driving the first wagon looks familiar ... Oh, I know! It's Mr. Jenner! But I don't recognize the man beside him. Looks like he's holding a baby.*

Felicity ran toward the wagons. Cally hurried to catch up. From the second wagon, a woman called, "Hello, Cally! Remember us?"

"Of course, Priscilla. Hello, Abigail. How nice to see you both again," said Cally.

"We didn't know y'all were still here, until Margaret invited us for y'all's dinner," said Priscilla, as she and Abigail climbed down from the wagon.

Oh no! We won't have enough food! Flora only let us kill one chicken.

Priscilla continued, "We invited our neighbors, the Robisons, also. Silas and Eden couldn't come, since she will give birth any time now. Come meet a new friend, children. This little girl is named Felicity."

Two boys and a girl scrambled down from the wagon bed. "Felicity, this big boy is Todd. And this is Gabby. She's your age, I think. And this boy is Freddy. He and Tucker are friends."

Felicity and Gabby stared at each other until Gabby said, "I like your pretty doll, Felicity. May I hold her?"

"Her name is Lizzy," said Felicity. "I wish I could have a real baby, like you."

"Our other children have been playing in the creek," Cally told Todd and Freddy.

"Is Margaret here yet?" asked Priscilla.

"She should arrive soon. You are all very welcome." *Though I have no idea what we will feed everyone.*

"I want to hear your news, Cally," said Priscilla. "I persuaded Abigail to bring along the dress she's making. She's hit a snag and I know you can help her. Oh, we invited another neighbor as well, Ryan Byrne. We told him about your family being Irish and all. Sadly, his wife died in childbirth three months ago."

Cally froze, her mind flooded with images. *Mammy screaming. Blood everywhere. Da holding the wee blue babe—*

Priscilla turned toward the men's wagon. "Come, Ryan. Show off your little Brian."

Felicity grabbed Cally's hand and pulled her toward the wagon, where Jerry had begun to unload several bundles. "Brian rhymes with Ryan. Look, the baby is smiling!"

More than can be said about his father. But who can blame him? How sad he lost his wife, and the baby lost his mother.

"Can I hold him? Please?" begged Felicity. "I mean, may I, Mummy?"

Cally smiled. "We'll have to ask his father, Felicity. Perhaps if my daughter sits down, she could hold the baby on her lap, Mr.—"

"Byrne. Call me Ryan," said the man. "Yes, sitting down is a good idea. Felicity, is it?"

"Yes, and my Mummy's name is Cally."

"The rest of the family will be along soon," said Cally. "We could sit by the table."

"I helped make supper," said Felicity. "We never had company before. Except my grandma, but she's not really company."

"Sit here, Felicity. May I, Ryan?" Cally took the baby and supported him on her daughter's lap while Felicity cooed and smiled. *How will we feed all these people? How strange that Margaret invited them without telling us. It must be an Idaho custom. Or maybe a farmer custom since everyone lives so far apart.*

"Where shall we put the food?" asked Jerry, coming from the wagon with a huge pot.

"Oh! You—you brought food?" stammered Cally.

"Of course," laughed Priscilla. "It's an Idaho custom. I don't think this table is large enough, though. Can y'all do something about that, Jerry and Ryan? Abigail can help me unload the wagon. I hear Tucker's voice! And there come the other children."

I hope this won't be too much for Flora.

Baby Brian fussed, then cried. "What's wrong?" wailed Felicity as Cally picked him up to comfort him. "Doesn't he like me?"

"Of course, he likes you," said Cally. "Maybe he's hungry or tired."

"I wish we had a baby," said Felicity. "I want Josie to see him." She ran toward her cousin as Margaret and her family and Cathleen emerged from the trees by the creek and Falling Water opened the door of the house to help Flora to her chair, Fauna getting in their way.

"One, two, three, ..." counted Shauna out loud. "Mummy, there are twenty people and a baby and a wolf!"

"A baby is a person too," said Shane.

"Is not," said Shauna. "A baby just lies there. I remember Felicity—"

"A baby is a small person," said Cora. "But he doesn't need a chair, and everyone else does. Can you bring some of those stumps over to the table for people to sit on, Shane? If they're too heavy, Shauna can help you roll them over. Maybe these other children can help too."

"I want my daddy," said Josie, and burst into tears. "Why must I have my birthday with all these people instead of him?"

"Come here, sweetheart," said Cora, hugging Josie. "Daddy will come as soon as he can. Remember we talked about that? But Grandma is here. Why don't you tell her about our plans for your party while I help Cally with supper?"

"Grandma is talking to Miz Flora and Miz Priscilla and Miz Falling Water. Miz Margaret is talking to Abigail," said Shauna.

"How do you feel Ryan is doing, Priscilla?" Flora asked.

"Better, I think. This is the first time he's left his farm since Bethany's death. He refuses to let anyone else take care of the baby, even me. He's neglecting his animals. Jerry is helping as much as he can. We think he came today so you can tell him how Brian is doing."

"The baby looks healthy from here," said Flora. Falling Water, Cathleen, and Priscilla all turned to watch Cally humming to baby Brian.

"Come see him, Josie. He's so cute!" coaxed Felicity, grabbing Josie's hand.

"Yes, go," said Cora. "Tell his daddy I need Cally to serve supper."

"What lovely people," said Cathleen, sipping tea with the other ladies after the Jenners and their guests left, Tucker's parents took him home to bed, and the Malcomson children were tucked in. "Your potato casserole was delicious, Margaret! It tasted like our Irish—"

"Champ!" Cally and Cora chimed in.

"I'm glad you liked it," said Margaret with a small bow. "I've never been to Ireland!"

"Jerry has a way of roasting lamb I've never managed to duplicate," said Flora.

"When those two wagons showed up, I couldn't imagine how we would feed so many people!" said Cally.

"That's because you're not from Idaho," said Margaret. "We always take food along when we visit someone at mealtime."

"A grand custom," said Cora. "Especially if your hosts don't expect you."

"It's not easy to communicate with each other here," said Margaret. "So, if we have an excuse to see someone, we just go. Evening Prayer was lovely, Cathleen. Thank you. You saw everyone's enthusiasm for doing it again. You have such a gentle manner I think they all felt included, despite being from different traditions."

"I'm delighted to hear that," said Cathleen. "Is anyone other than Ryan Catholic?"

"Not even him," said Margaret. "Ryan is Quaker. Or at least his parents were."

"Oh! I assumed, since he's Irish ... Can you tell us his story, Margaret?"

"Flora knew his family. I didn't," said Margaret.

"Ryan's parents caught cholera on their way to join a settlement in Oregon," said Flora. "They stopped in Twin Falls to get well, thinking they could join the next Quaker wagon train. Sadly, the cholera spread to their children. I did my best to care for them, but Ryan is the only one from the family who survived."

"How terrible!" said Cathleen.

"Yes. Ryan was the youngest, four years old I think, though I never knew his birth date. Ryan only spoke Irish. I cared for him until Priscilla Jenner showed up one day needing help with a toothache. She and Jerry had wanted a child for years, and she eagerly took Ryan home to be their own. Abigail was born several years later."

"Ah, that explains the Jenners' relationship with Ryan," said Cathleen. "They treat him like their own son."

"Yes, and they considered his sweet wife Bethany a second daughter. Don't let Jerry's gruffness fool you. They have huge hearts," said Flora.

"We experienced their hospitality," said Cally. "I didn't know they had so recently suffered such a huge loss."

"Folks in Idaho don't share intimate emotions with people they've just met," said Flora. "Ladies, the evening has been delightful, but I must rest."

"This is the longest I've seen you up," said Cally.

"I will help her to bed," said Falling Water. "Tomorrow, I return to my family. But we will see you on Tuesday for the birthday party."

"Thank you, Falling Water. I learn so much from you," said Cally.

"Good night, Falling Water," said Cathleen. When Flora and Falling Water disappeared into the house, she mused, "So, Ryan's family was Quaker. I wonder whether he remembers anything about their beliefs or practices."

"We don't have many Catholics hereabout," said Margaret. "The Jenners and Robisons are Mormon. Our family was once Methodist. I think Flora's family in Oregon is Anglican. I don't know what to call Falling Water's beliefs, though I believe she has a soul."

"You thought Falling Water didn't have a soul?" exclaimed Cora.

"So my family taught me," said Margaret. "When we came on the Oregon Trail, we believed the Indian people were savages, somewhere between animals and people. I think that belief justified killing them and taking over their lands."

"Oh my," said Cathleen. "The English said that about the Irish when I was a child."

"Knowing Falling Water and her family has changed my mind," said Margaret. "Now I mourn the terrible way her people have been treated."

"How did Ryan meet his wife?" asked Cora, changing the subject.

"Bethany was the daughter of a farm family near Twin Falls," said Margaret. "Ryan met her at the harvest festival two years ago. Lovely girl. Lutheran, I think. You'd have thought them the happiest couple in the county. I don't know how he will go on, with both a baby and his sheep to tend, even with Jerry's help."

"He didn't say a word all through dinner, except briefly when I asked him a direct question," said Cora. "I feel so sad for him."

"So do I," said Cally. *But twice when I happened to look his direction, it seemed like he was staring at me. It made me self-conscious. He seemed embarrassed too.*

"I should take you home to bed, Cathleen," said Margaret. "You're discreet, but I've caught you yawning three times."

"Good night, then, girls. You hosted this meal wonderfully. Thank you for indulging my desire to worship God together," said Cathleen.

"It was lovely," said Cora. "I'm glad everyone wants to come again next Sunday."

"If people keep bringing food, we can do it!" said Cally. "Good night, Cathleen. Come whenever you like tomorrow. We'll be getting ready for Josie's party."

"Priscilla and Abigail will bring three Robison children," said Cora. "Added to our four plus Tucker. And Falling Water's grandchildren. This will be a celebration to remember!"

ଓଃ

Cally opened her eyes Monday morning, seeing Cora still asleep beside her on the floor of the station's back room. *Can I slip out without waking her? I need some time to myself.*

Cally picked up the clothes, journal, and pencil piled to the side of the folded Indian blanket serving as her mattress. She eased open the door into the front room of the station and blinked in the bright sunlight streaming in through the door, half-open for air. She stopped for a moment to gaze at the four children lined up asleep on the floor. Felicity clutched her doll. Next to her, Shauna's hand rested on a dogeared notebook.

Shauna is so much like me at her age, wanting to record her thoughts and feelings and experiences. I'm sad I lost my old journals when I ran away from Rochester.

Josie slept with the birthday letter from her father held next to her heart. Shane had placed his blanket-mattress as far from the girls—about six feet—as the room allowed. He slept on his stomach, one arm over his face. *As if he's finding privacy the only way he can. He's been a good sport through all this.*

Cally breathed a prayer of blessing over them and tiptoed to the door, stopping with her hand on the doorknob. *Where did that prayer come from? I haven't prayed for or with the children for a long time, other than their bedtime prayers.*

Cally stepped outside and walked to "her" spot by the river, a large flat stone shaded by trees. She pulled a small mirror from her pocket. *Am I different? I feel different. Maybe if I write down the new thoughts and feelings I've noticed since Cathleen came, I can make some sense of them. But first I'll read Charlie's letter, and Aisling's. I didn't manage it yesterday.*

Cally slipped her mirror back in her pocket and drew out the two envelopes.

Cally, this will be short. I'll post it to Thomas, since I don't know where you'll be. I'm about to catch the train to Lisbon for my first concert. I had plenty of practice time on the voyage, sorely needed after the days on the train from Soda Springs to New York. Seeing Laoise again was amazing. We spent the evening together after our appointment with the Philharmonic and have become friends again. I'll see her in Frankfurt on June 19th—can't wait! I know you will love her, Cally. She's gentle, kind, sensitive, beautiful, and incredibly gifted on the violin. I can't wait for you to meet her. She has forgiven me for the way I treated her in Dublin so many years ago. I'll tell you more when I can. I hope Thomas and Shane are enjoying the treasure hunt with you, and Cora, the girls, and Mummy after he returns home.

Love,

Charlie.

I wonder when I'll be able to meet Laoise! She sounds perfect for Charlie! Now Aisling.

Precious Cally,

Ye can't know how often I think of ye and pray for ye and Teddy, and how my heart yearns to see ye again. It's been so long since ye left us—almost thirteen years, Cally! Ye are a young woman now, a mother, as I am. We have so much we could share. I ask God every day for the chance to know ye as ye are now, and to meet yer Felicity, and for ye to meet our Caoimhe, Cathal, and Christopher, growing up fast. Will that day come, Cally?

Cathleen has been a blessing to us since my father died. Our children are always delighted to see "Grandma Cathleen." I hope yer time with her will be rich. She speaks to me often about ye, Cally, always with love and admiration. It eases the pain in my heart, and the unanswered questions, Why did ye not come back to us? Did ye not know how much we loved ye? Perhaps one day I can know the answer to these plaguing questions.

I haven't time to write more now, dear Cally. I must post this letter and one for Teddy today. There's always room for ye in our home and at our table and in our hearts.

Aisling

Tears dripped down Cally's cheeks, and she let them flow. *I don't have an answer that will make sense to Aisling and Dugan. Can you make a way for me back to them, God?*

Cally raised her head, startled once again. *That prayer rose inside me, as if it has a life of its own. What's happening? Perhaps Cathleen can tell me. I feel like my life has started over. I feel—quiet. At peace. A feeling I haven't known since Da died.*

Cally sat for a long time, not writing, just gazing at the flow of water, the sunlight through the leaves dappling the ground around her, an emerald dragonfly darting over the water. Finally, she stretched, picked up her journal, and returned to the people and tasks awaiting her.

CHAPTER 18

FRANKFURT

[Reminder: Laoise is pronounced *lee-sha.*]

Alte Oper Concert Hall, Frankfurt, June 19

"CHARLIE, YOUR ENCORE WAS WONDERFUL!" Laoise threw her arms around Charlie as he exited backstage, the roar of the audience still reverberating behind him. "Listen!"

"I would rather listen to you, in a quiet place somewhere," said Charlie, holding her close. "Thank you for traveling to Frankfurt. The thought of meeting you here has kept me going since we were together in New York."

"But you must give your adoring fans some attention," said Laoise. "We'll have the whole day together tomorrow."

"Laoise, the orchestra put me up at the Steigenberger. Do you know it? I took the liberty of reserving a room there for you as well. This is one of the rare nights on this tour I won't spend on a train! You could settle in at the hotel, and I'll join you as soon as I can."

"I would rather wait for you, Charlie. It's a short walk and a beautiful evening."

"All right. I hope I won't be long."

"Don't worry. I understand." Laoise kissed his cheek and stepped back.

"I know you understand. As few others would. Thank you, Laoise." Charlie squared his shoulders and went to greet the concertgoers awaiting him.

"What a beautiful hotel this is! Thank you, Charlie. My room is luxurious," said Laoise, as he rose to seat her for breakfast in the hotel dining room. She looked at him. "It was so special to walk with you in the moonlight after your concert."

"It was wonderful for me too," Charlie said, stifling a yawn as he took her hand. "I'm sorry. I could sleep the day away, but then I would miss this rare time with you."

"I don't know anyone who schedules themselves as tightly as you do. Has your tour gone well so far?"

"It has. Let's order, then I'll tell you about a surprise at my concert in Zurich."

After their waiter bowed and walked away, Charlie said, "In Zurich, my mentor, Ignacy Paderewski, attended my concert! I didn't find out he was there until the intermission, when he poked his head around my door backstage. What a delight! I haven't seen him for a very long time. He agreed to play an encore for me. The crowd went wild."

"If last night was any indication, your audience was already excited," said Laoise. "I've never met Maestro Paderewski. But of course, his fame is known everywhere."

"He's been a friend to me, even more than a teacher," said Charlie. "I hope I can introduce you someday."

"I hope so, too, but I don't often travel to Switzerland."

"Perhaps someday you can play there with me." Charlie smiled as the waiter brought them rolls, salami, cheese, jam, and coffee. "Any thoughts about the day?"

"One idea. I would love to see the Impressionist art collection at the Städel Fine Arts Museum. I'm curious whether they have any of Mary Cassatt's works."

"Mary Cassatt? The American painter who was awarded the Order of Chevalier last month?" asked Charlie.

"You're well informed. Yes. She's lived in France most of her life. I got to meet her when I played in Paris two years ago! She greeted me after the concert, and I impulsively asked if I could visit her studio. She was painting *Mère et Enfant.* I fell in love with it. I would love, love, love someday to have a copy to hang in Mummy's room. The painting captures such a tender, loving moment between a mother and her daughter. It expresses the way I feel about my mother. I wonder what became of that painting."

"Likely it's been sold, don't you think? But yes, the Impressionist painters intrigue me too. Especially Degas. Let's go see what the Städel offers us!"

"Degas is a close friend of Mary Cassatt. The day I met her she planned to have dinner with him."

"Let's ask at the desk what time the museum opens. And as Americans say, go from there."

"Let the rest of the day develop after that without a specific plan?" smiled Laoise.

An hour later, Charlie and Laoise stood before Edgard Degas' *Musicians in the Orchestra.* "How interesting," said Charlie. "The other ballerina paintings we've seen take the perspective of the dancers. But this one is a view from the audience."

"All male musicians," said Laoise. "Will that change, with time? Will women one day perform in more diverse roles? Degas loves his ballerinas! Look at the detail in her costume."

"You're always welcome to play on my stage, Laoise," said Charlie. "Shall we find food for a picnic at Metzler Park?"

"Right on the river? Lovely!" said Laoise. "This will be my treat."

Charlie frowned. "Can't I take care of my best girl?"

"You'd best get used to the fact that I've taken care of myself all these years," said Laoise. "Let me do this, and you can host me for dinner."

"My father would be shaking his head," said Charlie.

"Tell me about your father," requested Laoise, as they left the museum later.

"He was captain of an ocean liner, the *Lion III*. He loved his work and tried to interest each of his three sons in sailing. You know how successful that was with me. When he died suddenly of a heart attack four years ago, we learned from his will he had chosen his sailor Paudeen to succeed him as captain. Paudeen is still a good friend to all of us."

"Does Paudeen now own the ship?"

"No, it still belongs to the Malcomson family. I take the *Lion III* whenever I sail from Waterford, as Mummy did two weeks ago. I'll take it back to America in July. Would this wee shop have what you want for our picnic, Laoise?"

"So," said Laoise, after making her purchases. "If your father sailed all the time, you couldn't often have seen him as a child."

"True," said Charlie. "It made me want to excel, so he would receive a good report about me whenever he came home. I was in awe of him. He was a stern man, but he mellowed with time and we became friends. Your father seems more approachable than mine was."

"Yes. My da is an easy man to love," said Laoise. "You needn't have any fears about meeting him. Or Mummy. My brother, though—he's the one you'll need to impress. He's always been protective of me in the male suitor department."

"I imagine there have been many of those!" said Charlie.

"A few would-be's, yes, musicians and others. But no one who captured my heart. Only one pianist has ever done that."

Their picnic lay unattended for quite some time.

CSꝸ

"It's gone too fast! said Laoise as they waited that evening to board different trains. "But it's been a marvelous day. Thank you, Charlie. I'll see you Sunday in Dublin! Goodbye!"

"Goodbye, sweetheart. God be with you."

CHAPTER 19

JOSIE'S PARTY

Stricker Homesite, Tuesday, June 21

"I HEAR HORSES!" said Cally as the family finished breakfast at the long table outside.

The children ran to the curve in the trail, Fauna beside them. "It's Miz Falling Water's family!" Josie yelled.

They watched the Shoshone family raise a large woven grass wickiup across from the station. Several young children gazed back at them through bright, dark eyes. Falling Water walked into the house, where Cora frosted Josie's birthday cake and Cally washed fruit from the orchard.

"We have enough wagons for all the children, though they'll have to imagine the 'covered' part," said Cora. "Good morning, Falling Water. Thank you for coming! Could two of your horses pull a wagon? That way we'll have three: Flora's, Priscilla's, and one of the abandoned wagons here. We examined them all and chose the one that seems in the best condition."

"My son Walter can drive," said Falling Water.

"Thank you," said Cora. "We'll go just to Margaret's farm and back. We'll give each child coins to trade at the wickiup and with Margaret on the trading post porch. And they can check for letters at the post office window at the house. Cathleen will be the postmistress. She's written letters to each of the children, pretending to be a relative back east. If anyone pretends to have medical needs, they can see Dr. Flora. Do you have any other ideas, Falling Water? You are the only one of us who experienced seeing a caravan of covered wagons arrive at this station."

"My children never rode in a covered wagon," said Falling Water. "There was so much distance between us and the white pioneers. Shall we cook salmon for the children at a fire outside? My sons caught salmon yesterday. We will be happy to share them with you."

Cally clapped her hands. "That's a wonderful idea, Falling Water! Thank you! My father's cousin used to fish for salmon in Ireland. I haven't eaten it since coming to this country."

"Salmon live across the ocean?" asked Falling Water.

"Yes. Until now, I didn't know there are salmon here," said Cally.

"They are one of our main foods," said Falling Water. "I should tell you our young children don't speak English. They will learn it when they go to school. My sons' names, Walter and Raymond, were given to them in school. Will the mothers ride in the wagons?"

"Yes, if they wish," said Cora. "Cally and I will ride with our children. What have I forgotten, Cally? Supper is already prepared, so that will be quick when we decide it's time."

"The white pioneer children played in the creek, like yours," said Falling Water.

"Yes, but we don't want everyone getting wet and dirty during the party," said Cally. "I know what we're missing: music! I've read about fiddlers and other musicians playing at settler gathering places. Too bad my brother Teddy isn't here with his harmonica."

"Well," said Flora, walking into the kitchen. "I play the violin. I know some music the children could dance to."

"You do?" exclaimed Cora and Cally together.

"But do you have enough energy to play?" asked Cally.

"I can try, and if I get tired, I'll stop," said Flora. "I don't actually expect to have many 'patients' to attend. The children will be having too much fun with everything else. I wish Lucy's children were here. They would have loved this."

"If you're up for it, Flora, we could have a dancing time before supper," said Cora.

"'For the good are always the merry ..." began Cally. Cora joined her. "'Save by an evil chance, And the merry love the fiddle, and the merry love to dance.'" They both laughed.

"What is that?" asked Flora.

"It's from a poem called 'The Fiddler of Dooney' by William Butler Yeats," said Cally.

"It ends, 'And dance like a wave of the sea,'" said Cora. "I imagine most people who grew up in Ireland can recite that poem."

"What musical instruments does your family play?" Cally asked Falling Water.

"We brought a drum to show the children" said Falling Water. "My son Raymond is a good drummer. The children can ride our horses before the others come. Would they like that?"

"Oh yes! Thank you, Falling Water. This will be a party to remember," said Cora. "I'm grateful to you all. We suggested three o'clock to Margaret and Priscilla."

"I need to rest until the party begins," said Flora.

"May I meet your family, Falling Water?" asked Cally. "I want to show Walter which wagon we think is in the best condition and see whether he agrees."

"It's almost time for the party!" said Cally, tying a green bow in Felicity's hair. "I think—Oh, let me see, Josie. Do you like it?"

Josie pirouetted in her new lavender birthday dress. "I love it!" She ran to hug Cally.

A shriek shattered the moment. A boy shouted "Help! Help!" and Fauna howled.

"It's Shauna and Shane!" exclaimed Felicity. Cally had already dropped the hairbrush and rushed to open the station door. Walter and Raymond reached the children before she did.

"A—a snake!" panted Shane. "Shauna tripped on a rock, and a snake bit her!"

Raymond scanned the ground and started off toward the trees by the river. Walter lifted Shauna and carried her to the house. Flora directed him to the bed in the clinic. "Where's my mummy?" whimpered Shauna. "I want my mummy!"

Cally hurried in. "Shh, shhh. She'll be right back, Shauna. She's gathering flowers by the creek to decorate the table. Show Doctor Flora where the snake bit you."

"On my leg," said Shauna, pulling up her dress. "It hurts, Aunt Cally."

Flora tightened a tourniquet above the bite on Shauna's calf. "I need to know what kind of snake it was, Walter."

Shane, hovering in the doorway, shouted "I saw it! It was brown and white and big!"

"Did you hear a rattle?" asked Walter.

"What do you mean?" said Shane.

"Two snakes have similar markings and are about the same size," explained Walter. "But the rattlesnake is poisonous, and the gopher snake is not, even though its bite can hurt."

"I'll find it!" yelled Shane, running out the door.

"My brother will soon find it, if the boy is not too loud," said Walter.

Raymond entered, with Shane close behind him. A large, dead snake hung from his arms. "It's just a gopher snake, Miz Flora," he said.

"That's good news. Thank you, Raymond," said Flora. "It's not poisonous, Shauna. I can remove this tourniquet. Your leg will hurt for a while, but you'll be fine."

"Shauna, look at the snake that bit you! May I touch it?" asked Shane.

Shauna turned her head away. "I want my mummy," she whispered.

"Shall I sing you a song while we wait for your mummy?" asked Cally.

"This poultice will soothe your pain, Shauna," said Flora. "You've had a pioneer experience! Snakebite was common on the Oregon Trail."

"I don't like it," said Shauna, closing her eyes. "Please sing to me, Aunt Cally."

"I'll make willow bark tea," said Flora. "Then I must rest, Cally. I have something to tell you and Cora, but it can wait until after the party."

"Dr. Flora!" shouted Shane. He ran into the house and knocked on her bedroom door, Fauna beside him. "Come quick! There's been an accident!"

"What happened, Shane?" asked Flora, adjusting her skirt as she opened her door. "Catch your breath and tell me."

"A wheel came off that wagon—the old one we used from here," panted Shane. "The wagon tipped over and hurt Freddy's leg. Walter sent me for you."

"How far away, Shane?"

"Not far. I asked Walter to drive fast, to beat the other wagons. We were almost here. Walter doesn't want to move Freddy until you see his leg."

"I can't walk fast, Shane. Take this blanket and cover Freddy with it. If he broke his leg, he may go into shock. I'll be there as quickly as I can."

"I'll tell them, Dr. Flora!" Shane raced down the track and around the curve.

"I may not have the energy to fiddle," Flora told Fauna. "What do you imagine will happen next?"

☙

"Do you want me to take you home, Freddy?" asked Priscilla, once Flora had set, splinted, and wrapped his broken leg at the site of the accident.

"No! I want to stay," said Freddy. "It doesn't hurt anymore. Well, not much. I want to do all the things. Please, Auntie Priscilla."

"Walter can carry you around," said Falling Water, glaring at her son. "A small penance for driving too fast."

"I'll help, Walter," said Shane. "It was my fault, Miz Falling Water. I begged Walter."

"You can't just carry him, Walter." Flora turned to Freddy. "You must keep your leg straight and still. We'll have to tie you to a board. Do you understand?"

"Walter and I can use part of the broken wagon to make a cart for you," said Shane.

"Can you, Walter?" asked Flora.

"If you have tools," said Walter.

"In the barn," said Flora. "Priscilla, please stay with Freddy and keep him still until Walter and Shane have the cart ready. You'll have time to do all the things, Freddy, don't worry. I'll make willow bark tea for the pain. I know it hurts, more than you're saying, young man."

"Let me prepare the willow bark, Flora," said Falling Water. "You must rest."

"A broken wagon wheel—another experience common to Oregon Trail caravans," muttered Flora, walking slowly back to the house. "I hope that's the end of it."

☙

"Flora, I'm terribly sorry to bother you," whispered Cally, walking into the doctor's darkened bedroom.

"What happened?" asked Flora, struggling to sit up.

"I'll show you." Cally opened the curtain and extended her right hand.

"Oh my. That's a severe burn, Cally. You must soak your hand in cold water to stop the burning. Ask someone to look in the wet cellar. The ice may be mostly melted but it will be colder than river water. You must sit at the table and leave your hand in cold water for at least a couple of hours."

"I'm sorry to disturb your rest, Flora."

"I was waking up anyway. Ask someone for help with the cold water, Cally. You'll be amazed by how it eases the pain. I'll check on you in an hour."

"A snakebite. A broken wagon and broken leg. A burn. If you hoped for an Oregon Trail experience at this party, you're getting it! What happened?" said Flora, examining Cally's hand an hour later.

"Falling Water served me a delicious-looking piece of salmon and it slid off my plate into the fire," said Cally. "I wanted it so much I reached for it. All I got for my greed was this burn." She stopped. "Listen a moment, Flora."

"I hear happy children, all over this homesite," said Flora. "It's such a delight to me. I confess it's lonely here at times, with just Fauna for company. I know you won't be here much longer, but I'm so glad you came. And not just because Thomas saved my life."

"Why do you think we won't be here much longer?" asked Cally.

"When I took my violin out of my closet, I found this," said Flora, pulling a packet from her pocket.

"The next clue from Uncle William!" said Cally. "But we won't leave you until you're well, Flora."

"I know. But I'm stronger every day. It won't be long. I expect my sister to come soon."

"Flora, will Freddy's leg be all right?"

"I expect so, if he can manage to stay off it for a while. It's a simple fracture, nothing unusual. You look so worried, Cally. What's wrong?"

"I . . . I . . ." Cally stopped and then tried again, her voice so soft Flora had to strain to hear it. "I think it was my fault."

"Your fault? No. If anyone is to blame, it was Walter. He should have known better than to drive so fast. And Shane shares the blame, for egging him on. How can it be your fault?"

"I examined the wagons and chose that one," said Cally.

"There's more to this than you've told me so far," said Flora. "Do you have some experience with broken legs, Cally?"

"My brother," said Cally, her eyes brimming. "He broke his leg when he was the same age as Freddy. I was distracted, talking to my father instead of watching him. Teddy had a surgery, but it didn't heal right, and he's had a painful limp ever since. When I saw Freddy lying there, it all came rushing back. I knew it was my fault."

"Cally, the two situations are not related to each other. I suspect only you thought you were responsible for your brother's accident. And no one here blames you for this one. Blaming yourself doesn't help Freddy. Can you let this go?"

"I'll try," said Cally, wiping her eyes with the hand not soaking in water.

"Don't sit there ruminating," said Flora. "Listen to the happy voices all around you."

CHAPTER 20

FLORENCE

Stricker Homesite, Wednesday, June 22

"MUMMY, YOU HAVE PAINT ON YOUR NOSE," said Josie as the family gathered at the outside table for lunch.

"I do? What color is it?"

"Greenish," said Josie.

Shauna squinched her face, considering. "Brown and green and gray," she said finally. "I know! It's the color of the plants that grow in the desert!"

"Yes, sage," said Cora, swiping at her nose. "Do you think I got it right?"

"Perfect!" said Shauna. "I want to see what you painted."

"All right. After lunch I'll show you," said Cora.

"I hear a wagon!" said Shane as they finished their sandwiches.

"I hope it's not a medical emergency," said Cora. "Flora's so worn out from yesterday she hasn't gotten out of bed today."

"It's not a wagon. It's a carriage," observed Cally, as two fine bays trotted around the curve. "I wonder who that could be?"

"Oh no!" said Cora, scrubbing her nose.

"Let me help," said Cally.

"I'll go see who it is!" said Shane. He was off before his mother could stop him. "It's a fancy lady!" he yelled back to the group at the table. He trotted beside the carriage as it pulled up opposite the station.

A woman in a lovely pale blue dress emerged from the carriage. "Please wait until I ascertain whether I've reached the correct destination," she said to the driver, her voice carrying in the still, hot air.

Cally walked over to greet her. "My name is Cally. May I help you in any way?"

The woman looked her up and down. Cally blushed, realizing she had not changed since doing laundry and weeding the garden that morning. *I must look a sight.* She raised her unbandaged hand to her face.

The woman brushed her own skirt at about the same place Cally had a smudge. "My name is Florence Gardner. I'm looking for my sister, Dr. Flora Spencer. But I must have arrived at the wrong place."

"No, Flora is here. I'm happy to meet you, Mrs. Gardner. Flora will be delighted you have come. Shall we unload your luggage?"

"I will talk to Flora before I make any decisions," said Florence, staring at the log cabin. "Surely, she can't live in a place like this. There must be some mistake. Take me to her at once."

"Certainly," said Cally, with a small curtsey, raising her eyebrows to Cora who had walked over beside her. "Flora lives in the house over there."

"That's a relief. I was afraid she was living in that—that hovel." Florence shuddered.

As Cally escorted Florence to the house, she heard Cora say to the driver, "We have stew left from lunch. May I serve you a bowl, sir?"

"As you know, Flora has been very ill," Cally told Florence. "She may be asleep. She had a strenuous day yesterday and has been resting today."

Florence marched into the house and started up the stairs.

"Um . . . Mrs. Gardner, Flora's bedroom is down here," said Cally. She knocked and then opened the door to Flora's darkened room. Fauna, already on her feet, emitted a low growl. Florence startled and tripped over a leg of the bed, falling on top of Flora. Cally opened the curtains and used her good hand to calm the wolf, who continued to growl. "It's all right, Fauna. This is Flora's sister!"

"Flora! What is that monster? What is this horrible place? Who are these people?"

"It's lovely to see you, too, Florence," said Flora, managing to sit up.

Cora appeared in the doorway. "I brought a chair for you, Mrs. Gardner. May I serve you lemonade? Have you had lunch?"

"Go away, all of you, and let me talk to my sister! And take that monster with you!" yelled Florence. "Flora, what is the meaning of this?"

Flora nodded to Cally and Cora, and said "Go on, girl" to Fauna, who settled herself in the doorway, refusing to budge so Cally could close the door.

"Fauna and these people are my dear friends," Cally heard Flora say before she walked outside to wipe the table as Cora cleared it.

"Perhaps it's good Falling Water isn't here today," Cora said. "She might have been one shock too many for poor Florence. I'll invite the carriage driver in out of the sun."

"Good idea," said Cally. "I'll pour him some more lemonade."

"Wait—where are the children?" asked Cora.

"Oh-oh. I suspect—yes, there they are," Cally said, rounding the house and pointing. All four huddled under Flora's open window. "Will it cause more of a ruckus to call them away, or let them be? I can't imagine the conversation will entertain them for very long."

"Florence livened up our day!" said Cora, grinning. "A dollar says she won't stay."

"You're on, Cora. I think she will. She's Flora's sister, after all," said Cally. "But I hope Florence won't see Shane's face in the window."

"I'm planning my lecture for the children about eavesdropping," said Cora.

"It seems Flora hasn't told her family much about her circumstances. But Hotel Idanha at Soda Springs is fancy enough for anyone. It will be a lovely place for Flora to regain strength."

"We need to make plans, Cally. With Florence's arrival, Flora won't need us anymore."

"It's time we find out where the treasure hunt will take us next. Flora asked me to go with her tomorrow to check on Eden and examine Freddy's leg. I don't imagine Flora will leave for Soda Springs until the baby is safely born. Eden had a difficult delivery the last time."

Shane and the girls ran toward them, laughing. "What's so funny, Shane?" asked Cora.

Shane gasped, and tried to discipline his face, but burst out laughing again.

"The lady tried to pull Miz Flora out of her bed, and Fauna pushed her into a corner," said Josie. "She's still there. Fauna won't listen to Miz Flora."

"You should see the lady's face!" said Shauna.

The children went into gales of laughter. Cally and Cora rushed into the house. They found Flora laughing too, while Fauna sat on her haunches staring at Florence pressed into the corner of the room, her face ashen.

"Oh, it's too funny," Flora wheezed, waving her hand toward Fauna and her sister. "Florence will never forgive me, but I can't stop laughing. Maybe you two can persuade Fauna that Florence is not a threat to me."

"But are you all right, Flora?" asked Cora.

"I'm fine. Cally, please do what you can for poor Florence." Flora wiped her eyes and lay down, her body shaking with mirth.

Cally walked to Fauna and sat down beside her. "It's all right, Fauna," she said softly. "You can let her go. Flora is fine. We'll protect her." Cally stretched out a hand. "See—Florence isn't hurting me. Everyone is safe, Fauna."

Fauna looked at Florence, then turned toward Flora, who said, "Come here, girl."

With a last look at Florence, Fauna trotted to Flora's bedside. Cally rose and extended her good hand to Florence. "Come with me," she said. "I think you'll feel better outside. Fauna will stay with Flora."

Leaning on Cally, Florence stumbled past the carriage driver resting on the couch, and out to the porch.

"Sit here," said Cally. "This is Flora's chair. Cora will bring you a drink."

Cally brought a chair from the outside table and sat beside Florence. "Take slow, deep breaths, Mrs. Gardner. I know Fauna frightened you, but everyone is safe, I promise."

Cally took a deep breath and slowly released it. Florence, her eyes fixed on Cally, followed suit. Her trembling gradually eased.

"I hear Tucker's voice," said Cally. "That means Cathleen and Margaret are coming." *This is good. Florence will have some neutral parties to share her woes with. Older women who surely are more sensible than Cora and me and Flora.*

Cally watched the children converge on their grandmother as she emerged from the trees beside the river, all talking excitedly. Cathleen looked her direction. Cally smiled and waved, then watched Florence track the approach of the two older women.

Cathleen and Margaret brought chairs and greeted Florence. She said nothing.

"You've had a long journey today, Mrs. Gardner, and the children tell me you've had a fright," said Cathleen. "I'm sorry this happened to you. Please let Margaret and me help you. Fauna is bonded to your sister very strongly, as you experienced."

"I offer you the hospitality of my home," said Margaret. "It's nearby. Your carriage driver can take you. We can make room for you with Cathleen."

Florence finally spoke. "That horrible beast—" She shuddered and began to scream. The other women looked at each other. The screaming stopped as suddenly as it had begun. Florence gulped, took a drink of lemonade, and stood.

"I'm here to take my sister to Soda Springs. If you wish to help me, talk sense into her. She says she won't leave until some woman has a baby. Clearly, she's in no condition to deliver anyone's child."

"The baby is due any day now," said Cally. "Flora will soon be ready to leave for Soda Springs."

"One of you, pack her things for an extended stay away," said Florence, as if Cally hadn't spoken. She sat again in Flora's chair. "We'll spend tonight in Twin Falls and take the train to Soda Springs tomorrow morning. One of you, advise the driver to be ready within half an hour. Whatever the horses need should be attended to now."

"Shane has cared for the horses," said Cally.

"My husband offered to come. I should have accepted. He would not allow Flora to talk nonsense about delivering a baby," said Florence.

"I can assist Flora with her packing," offered Margaret. She walked into the house.

"You are from Oregon City, are you not?" Cathleen asked Florence. "I've not yet been that far west, but I've heard it is lovely."

"Yes, it is beautiful. I've lived there most of my life," responded Florence, some energy coming back into her voice. "Flora could come back and have a wonderful life there, but no, she had this foolish notion of becoming a doctor, a profession totally unsuitable for a lady, as I'm sure you agree. I hope this illness will persuade her to give up her romantic notions and return home. Our parents are aging and long to have their youngest child with them once again."

"I understand," said Cathleen. "We parents find ourselves in a dilemma, wanting our children to live their best lives and at the same time wishing them to be near us."

"Clearly you are a high-born woman," said Florence. "Surely you do not have children living in this—this wilderness."

"Not as yet," said Cathleen. "Three of my children live in Ireland, and two in lovely Kansas City. I cherish every bit of time I can have with any of them."

Cally's cheeks warmed. *Cathleen claimed me as one of her children. But what did she mean by "as yet"? Could Thomas and Cora be thinking—surely not ..."*

Margaret appeared in the doorway of the house, Flora leaning heavily on her arm, Fauna behind them. "Sit here, Flora," offered Cally.

"Florence, my friend and neighbor, Margaret Ingram, offers you hospitality," said Flora. "Cathleen is staying with her already, so you would be in good company."

"Have you not packed Flora's things, as I asked?" demanded Florence, glaring at Margaret. "I've no wish to spend another minute here, Flora."

Flora sighed and accepted a glass of lemonade from Cora. "I will not leave until Eden's baby is safely born, Florence. She had a breech delivery last time. She could die without adequate assistance, leaving her other four children without a mother. I can't take that risk. I'm only asking for a few more days."

Florence leaned forward. "Nonsense, Flora. You're not indispensable. What if the baby had been born while you were so ill? You couldn't have helped then."

"True, but it would have grieved me the rest of my life," said Flora. "This matters to me, Florence. I genuinely care about my patients."

"I'm here to take you to Soda Springs to regain your strength. And persuade you to give up this ridiculous life and return home." Florence stood and pulled Flora's arm. Fauna growled. Florence released Flora's arm and stepped back.

Flora handed her empty glass to Cora and sat up straight. "Florence, you have three choices. You can stay with Margaret until after Eden's baby is born. Or you can wait for me at the Idanha Hotel. Cally will put me safely on the train to you. Or you can return to Oregon City. Any of the three will be fine."

"But—" said Florence.

"I appreciate your desire to help me recuperate, Florence, and would like to join you in Soda Springs. But not until after Eden's baby is born. That's my final word on the matter." Flora sat back and crossed her arms.

Florence's voice rose. "Why must you be so stubborn? You've been this way since you were a child, rejecting what is best for you, Flora Elizabeth. Well then, have it your way. I will endeavor to explain to our parents why you refused to allow me to take you to Soda Springs."

Florence leaned close to Flora. "The disappointment and worry may take them to their graves when I describe the conditions under which you live. That will be your fault, not mine."

Florence straightened and looked from Margaret to Cally to Cathleen. "One of you, call my driver. I will stay the night in Twin Falls and take the train home tomorrow. I have done my best for you, Flora. You bear the consequences on your own head."

"I packed sandwiches for you and your driver," said Cora, walking out of the house with a brown paper packet. The driver followed, carrying a similar packet. "I wish you Godspeed."

“Humph. I don’t understand you people,” said Florence. She walked to the carriage without taking the sandwiches, climbed in without saying goodbye to Flora, closed the carriage door hard, and ordered the driver to proceed. Cora handed her sandwiches to the driver. The women watched in silence as the carriage disappeared in a cloud of dust.

“Well,” said Flora. “That was invigorating. I believe I will pack my bag for my visit to Eden and Freddy tomorrow. You will accompany me, Cally?”

“Yes,” said Cally. “What time do you want to leave?”

“As early as possible,” said Flora. “Cora and Cathleen, you mustn’t worry if Cally and I are gone overnight. I don’t know what I’ll find when we get to the Robison’s. We won’t leave Eden until we know she and the baby are stable and well.”

“Then I’ll spend some time with Felicity before we go,” said Cally.

“And I have a lecture about eavesdropping to deliver to my children,” said Cora.

“Cathleen, you were telling me about your son Charlie,” said Margaret.

“Yes. Then I want to hear how you met your husband. So, Foxwell was good for Charlie in many ways …” Cathleen’s voice faded as Cally walked toward the station looking for her daughter.

CHAPTER 21

EDEN

The Robison home, Thursday, June 23

"MAMA, MIZ FLORA IS HERE!"

A child's high voice announced their arrival as Cally climbed down from the wagon and helped Flora gather her supplies.

"Thank God you came. How did you know I was in trouble?" Eden asked, pulling a bandanna from her eyes as Flora embraced her on the couch.

"Intuition, I suppose," said Flora, turning to survey the room. "Hello, children. Todd's out working with Silas, I suppose? Freddy, how are you, love? I'll check your leg in a minute."

Flora turned back to Eden, sprawled on the sofa, her face flushed. "Eden, this is my friend Cally. She's come to help any way she can."

"Nice to meet you," said Eden. "Silas is my husband. He wants to finish the haying before this baby is born."

"I see your feet are swollen, and your face and hands too. Tell me what you're feeling, Eden," said Flora.

"I feel dizzy, and my vision is blurry. Can't hardly stand the light. Seems like I swelled up all at once. And I have a vicious headache. Don't remember any of this with my other babies," said Eden. "I had just decided to ask Silas to fetch you, once he comes in for his dinner. And here you are! I'm that grateful." She wiped a tear from her eye. "I feel fragile-like. Want to cry at the least thing. Can't seem to catch my breath."

"I think you have a condition called pre-eclampsia," said Flora. "I'll confirm it by checking your blood pressure." Flora pulled a sphygmomanometer from her bag. "Children, could you be quiet just for a minute so I can hear? Thank you."

Cally smiled at the children, her finger to her lips, as Flora pumped up the device and listened, a frown on her face.

"Yes, as I suspected, your blood pressure is elevated, Eden. We must deliver this child. Have you felt any contractions?"

"Nothing worth mentioning, no. Just those warming-up pinches," said Eden.

"Let me check the baby. Gabby, could you bring me your mommy's pillow?"

Gabby pushed two-year-old Dinah off her lap and ran from the room. Cally moved to pick up the toddler before she started to cry. Dinah leaned into Cally and stuck her thumb in her mouth. Cally sat on the floor near Freddy as she cuddled Dinah. *It wasn't my fault. It wasn't my fault. Freddy's broken leg was not my fault. Eden's trouble is not my fault.*

"Thank you, Gabby. Let's make your mommy more comfortable," said Flora. "Better, Eden? Please get her a drink of water, Gabby."

Gabby hurried to the kitchen, while Flora carefully felt for the position of the baby, then listened through her stethoscope.

"Good news, Eden. The baby's positioned correctly and has a steady heartbeat."

Eden started to cry. "I've been so worried it might be breech like Dinah."

"No. This delivery will be easier. Eden, I must rupture your membranes to induce labor. At the same time, I'll check to see how prepared your cervix is for delivery. Cally, perhaps you could take the children to the river? Freddy, we'll find something for you to do here."

Whew, thank you, Flora. I can't sit here another minute. What if Eden starts bleeding? What if the baby—

"But I can walk now," said Freddy. "Pa made a crutch for me."

"Let me see you walk. ... All right, just be sure to keep your weight off that leg, Freddy. It still needs time to heal. You don't want to break it again, right?" asked Flora.

"No, ma'am."

"Gabby, before you go, please get me towels, as many clean ones as you have."

"I haven't managed to do the wash," said Eden.

"Then any kind of clean cloth you can find, Gabby," said Flora. "Don't worry—we'll wash everything before we go. I should have thought to bring towels. But we'll be fine."

Gabby returned with an assortment of dresses, shirts, and underwear, dumped them on the end of the sofa, then ran out the door to join Cally, Freddy, and Dinah. "Let's show Miz Cally the marmot hole we saw yesterday. If we're quiet maybe it will come out."

૪

An hour later, Flora met Cally and the children at the porch steps, finger to her lips.

"Cally, Eden has fallen asleep," Flora said softly. "She'll need her rest for the labor to come. Could you take the children to Priscilla to care for until the baby is born?"

"I'm sorry, I don't think I know the way. But that's brilliant, Flora. They love Priscilla." *The children won't have to witness whatever happens next with Eden. I wish I hadn't—*

"I can take them," said Silas, who had turned the corner from the barn. "Todd is watering the horses. How is Eden?"

"She should go into labor soon. Cally, please find out whether Eden managed to cook anything this morning. If not, figure out something to feed us. I'll explain the situation to Silas."

Cally walked quietly into the house, past the semi-closed door of Eden's bedroom and into the kitchen. The remains of breakfast sat on the table, a sticky pot from oatmeal on the stove. Cally glanced at the pantry shelves and through the cupboards, then out the window to the kitchen garden. She ran outside and caught Silas helping his children into the wagon.

"Silas, my name is Cally. I'm a friend of Flora's."

"Heard about you from the children," said Silas. "You burned your hand at the party."

"It's healing well," Cally smiled, touching the bandage on her hand. "Silas, we don't have any clean towels or sheets. And not much food in the kitchen. Perhaps Priscilla could send something for your dinner? Eden won't be able to cook for a couple of days at least."

Silas's face changed. He grunted and drove away without responding.

"I heard that," said Flora, walking toward her from the porch. "Silas likes to fend for himself. I suggest you check the hen house. There may be eggs that haven't been collected yet today. We could start with those."

"How is Eden?" asked Cally.

"Still sleeping. A blessing," said Flora. "We must watch her closely. Her blood pressure is so high I'm concerned she may seize. While we wait for her labor to start, I must rest a bit."

"I'll check for eggs and figure out Eden's system for washing clothes. How would you have managed all this if you had come by yourself?"

"Usually, I'm not recovering from illness myself," said Flora. "And Falling Water might have come with me. There's always a way. But I'm grateful you're here, Cally. Thank you."

"Rest as long as you can until Silas and Todd return," said Cally.

I saw a few potatoes and goat cheese in the kitchen, so they must have a goat. If I can coax her to give me a little milk, I can make champ!

From the kitchen, Cally heard Eden moan. She quickly washed bits of herbs from her hands and eased into Eden's bedroom, not wanting to wake Flora on the couch.

Eden's eyes were open, but she seemed not to see Cally. Suddenly her body stiffened, her back and neck arched, and her body jerked. "Flora!" Cally screamed.

"She's having a seizure," said Flora. "There's nothing we can do except—" She doubled an old dress under Eden just as a flood of urine poured out.

"No blood," Flora observed. "So far, the placenta is still intact."

As suddenly as the seizure began, it slowed and stopped. Eden lay unresponsive. Flora wiped a trickle of blood from her chin.

"She must have bitten her tongue. If you believe in prayer, Cally, pray Eden will quickly go into labor and deliver this baby. The sooner Eden's body is free from the pregnancy, the sooner it can start its journey back to normal. And more chance the baby will survive."

Please, God. Help.

Eden groaned and her eyes flickered. Flora took her hand and said, "I'm here with you, Eden. Rest, now."

Eden's eyes closed, but a moment later she tried to sit up. "Where? What?"

"You've had a seizure, Eden. But it's over, and now you can rest."

"Ooooh," moaned Eden.

Flora placed a hand on her abdomen and let her breath out in a whoosh. "You're in labor, Eden. You and the babe may yet pull out of this."

May yet? This is scary.

The front door opened and closed, and footsteps crossed the living room. Silas stood at the bedroom door. "I'm back, Eden. Abigail will care for the children. I let Todd stay there. I'll unload the wagon. Priscilla sent food."

"I'll help," said Cally.

Flora followed them out. "Eden is in grave danger, Silas, both she and the baby. She's just had a seizure. Thankfully, her labor has begun. Pray to your God the labor will go quickly and the baby born safely before she has another seizure."

"What could another seizure do?" asked Silas.

"It could cause the placenta to separate from the uterus. If this happens during labor, the baby won't have a source of oxygen. And Eden will hemorrhage."

"I'll say a prayer for her," said Silas, returning to the bedroom. Flora and Cally waited, to give them some privacy. He emerged wiping his eyes and walked straight out the door.

ଓଃ

Flora did not leave Eden's side. She asked Cally to make a soup of spinach, potatoes with their skins, broccoli, and carrots, all available in the family garden. "I don't know why scientifically, but these vegetables have something in them known to help with eclampsia. Falling Water taught me this. Yogurt, too, and pumpkin seeds. Can you make yogurt?"

"We have seeds from last year's pumpkins," said Silas, walking in while Flora was talking. "Eden bakes them with salt. We had so many we got tired of eating them."

"Wonderful! Eden, could you eat a few pumpkin seeds?" Flora asked.

"I'll try," said Eden. "I'm not hungry. My entire body hurts, even between contractions."

"That's because of the seizure, Eden. I want you to eat things that might help you not have another one. I wish I had a magic pill to give you, but I don't."

"One or two more contractions, and you'll meet your child, Eden."

"That's good. I'm done in," said Eden. "Ohhhh!"

"Take a deep breath, hold it, and push as hard as you can," said Flora.

The baby slithered into Flora's waiting hands. And with it a flood of blood.

Cally ran screaming out of the house.

Huddled by a tree on the riverbank, Cally looked up to see Silas approaching. He carried a small bundle. Cally burst into tears.

"Cally, why do you weep? The baby is fine. Small, but fine. Will you look?"

Cally scrubbed her eyes with her hands, breathed deeply, and stood. Silas pulled back the blanket to show her a sleeping infant, his skin pink, breaths lifting his small chest. Cally reached out a finger and touched his cheek, tears streaming down her face.

"And—and Eden?" she whispered.

"Still alive," said Silas. "Miz Flora worked hard to stop the bleeding and must rest now. Will you take the baby? We're naming him Isaac. It means laughter. I'll feed Eden more soup."

Laughter? After all Eden has been through? When she still might die?

Cally accepted the tiny bundle and sat again under the tree. A song came to her mind and, unbidden, from her mouth as she gazed at

Isaac's face. "In peace I will lie down and sleep, for you alone, O Lord, will keep me safe."

Aisling's prayer. I didn't know I still remember the way the Williams' maid Florence sang it when I was sick with typhoid fever.

ঔ

Cally tiptoed into the quiet house with Isaac fussing and squirming. Flora slept on the couch, one arm flung over her head. Cally peeked around Eden's half-open door and saw Silas beside his wife's bed, his lips moving soundlessly. Eden's face was almost as white as her pillowcase. Her eyes fluttered open when Cally walked in.

"Hungry, is he?" said Silas. "Can you feed him, Eden?"

Eden nodded and raised a hand toward her son. The effort was too much, and her arm flopped back against the covers. Silas took Isaac and positioned him beside Eden's breast. He latched on eagerly.

"Wants to live, that one," said Silas. "Soon he'll grow big and strong as his brothers. Will you sit with Eden for a while, Cally, so I can do the chores? Miz Flora is tuckered out. Eden should eat more soup when she's done nursing."

Cally nodded and sat in the seat Silas vacated. Eden glanced at her and smiled before her eyes closed again.

Everything is clean and tidy as if—as if what happened never happened. How did Flora do it? How did she stop the blood?

Tears welled and Cally pressed her palms against her eyes, willing them to stop. *What happened to me? It's like I was back there in that room with Mammy and Da and the dead baby and all the blood and Da saying "Ye're too late!" I couldn't bear it.*

Cally looked carefully around the simple, clean, comfortable room; the sun's last pink glory visible through the window. *This is different. It's not happening all over again. Flora was here. She knew what to do. The baby is alive. Eden can get well now. It's not the same. It's life, not death. It's beauty and order, not chaos and confusion. It's hope, not despair. Isaac. Laughter.*

The baby stopped sucking, his mouth releasing the nipple. Eden opened her eyes. "Soup?" she said. "I finally feel hungry."

"I'll get it," said Cally. "Shall I move Isaac, or—"

"Let him stay," said Eden. "When he wakes again, he'll need a clean nappy."

"I'll be right back," said Cally.

"I'll be here," said Eden.

"The baby?" asked Cally the next morning, after greeting Eden, who sat propped up by pillows, eating the soup Flora fed her.

Flora pointed to her other side. "He's doing well. Greedy little fellow."

Cally peered around Flora to see Isaac sleeping in a dresser drawer on the floor by the wall, one hand curled against his cheek. A well of love surged in her chest.

"Cally, will you be Isaac's godmother?" asked Eden. "I would ask Flora, but she's already Freddy's godmother."

Cally's eyes widened and her hand flew to her mouth. "Oh my. I would love that. But it's not fair to Isaac. I don't know how long I'll be here. Maybe just a couple more weeks."

"Well, you have time to think about it," said Eden. "That's all I can eat right now, Flora."

"Cally, I've been thinking," said Flora Monday morning. "Eden doesn't need both of us anymore, at least while her other children are with Priscilla. Baby Isaac is doing well."

"I've noticed Eden's swelling has decreased. Is there anything I should watch out for that might still happen to her medically?"

"Well, eclampsia can be tricky. It can seem resolved and then suddenly cause seizures again. But if that happens, there isn't much you can do. Her bleeding has normalized, and her blood pressure is much better, though still a bit high. I think if she were going to have more seizures, she'd have done so already. I'm tired, Cally. Silas will bring his other children home today. Do you feel up to having the whole crew here if Abigail comes to help?"

"If Abigail comes, yes. Perhaps Silas can ask Priscilla for the ingredients for Eden's soup? I've stripped the garden here."

"Good thinking. I want Eden to have a couple of bowls of that soup every day, for as long as we have the vegetables to make it. And she must drink plenty of water to help her body replace the blood she lost. Cally—

"Yes?"

"What happened to you during the delivery?"

Cally sucked in a breath. "Umm—I don't know exactly."

"Some people can't stand the sight of blood. But I suspect there was more to it than that. No pressure, though, Cally. Whenever you're ready, I hope you will tell me."

"Thank you, Flora."

"You've been amazing, Cally, doing everything everywhere at once. You have good instincts about what's needed in each situation. Thank you for coming, and for staying these extra days. I hope you will accept being Isaac's godmother, because you'll come back to visit him, and I'll be able to see you again!"

"It seems an unusual offer, since they hardly know me."

"You were here at a time of great need in their lives," said Flora. "And I've noticed the affection you have for Isaac."

"It's true. Maybe because it seemed like he might not survive. In some deep way, he represents life to me. And hope."

"I'm glad. Well, I'll gather my things and be on my way. Expect Silas with Abigail and the four children to show up by lunch time."

Cally was changing Isaac when she heard a wagon and then footsteps on the porch. She frowned. *That sounds like a man's step, but I don't hear the children.*

She fastened Isaac's nappy carefully around the stump of the umbilical cord and tucked him into the drawer for a nap, then walked softly past Eden, sound asleep, into the front room, pulling the door almost closed behind her. Through the open door she saw a horse and wagon. *Who could this be?*

Cally peered around the side of the house, then walked toward the garden. A man bent over the vegetables, pulling weeds. He raised his head and smiled at her.

"Forgive me for not announcing myself, Miz Cally. I suspected you were attending the baby or Miz Eden."

"Ryan? What are you doing here? Where is Brian?" asked Cally.

Ryan nodded toward a blanket spread in the shade of the house, where the baby lay sleeping, his thumb in his mouth.

"He looks enormous, compared to baby Isaac," said Cally.

"Priscilla told us at the Sunday dinner what happened with Miz Eden. I came by to lend a hand. I can't stay long, but I can clean up this patch and maybe help you hang some laundry? I noticed the tub by the clothesline. Those wet sheets are heavy."

"Thank you. Everyone helps each other with such kindness," said Cally.

"It's not like that in the city?" asked Ryan. "Perhaps because there are few of us, we value each of our neighbors more. Don't feel you have to stay with me. I know you have plenty to do in the house. Miz Flora is gone?"

"Yes. She needs rest. Abigail will come with the children to help for a few days. When I heard your wagon, I thought it was them."

"Knowing Priscilla, she'll send food for a week!" laughed Ryan.

"I expect them soon. Will you stay for lunch, Ryan?"

"No, thanks. I'll finish the weeding, hang the laundry, and be on my way."

"You're a fast weeder," said Cally.

"Been doing this since I was not much bigger than Brian," said Ryan. "Perhaps I'll see you at the next Sunday supper?"

"They've become a regular event, have they?" smiled Cally. "I worried when you and Jerry and then Priscilla drove up the first time. I had no idea how I would feed you all."

"Hang around and you'll learn how things work around here," said Ryan. "There's Abigail now."

Cally turned to see children jumping from every side of the wagon. To her great surprise, Felicity was one of them.

"Mummy, Mummy, I haven't seen you for such a long time!" shouted Felicity, running toward her. Cally swept her up and whirled her around, giving her a big kiss before setting her back on the ground.

"I've missed you, too! I didn't know you were at the Jenners' house, Felicity!"

"They took me to their house after Sunday supper, because I wanted to see you so much,"

"I'm glad, sweetheart. Do you remember Mr. Ryan and baby Brian?" asked Cally.

"Of course. I held Brian at the supper. He likes me." Felicity walked over and looked down at the sleeping child.

"Don't wake him, Felicity," cautioned Cally. "Mr. Ryan wants to work while he's asleep. I'm going inside now."

Abigail greeted Cally in the front room. "Eden is asking for you, Cally. I'll leave her care and the baby's to you. I can do chores with the help of these two." She poked Todd and Gabby and they giggled. "Freddy's resting his leg—he says it hurts a little. Eden's letting him hold baby Isaac while she gives some attention to Dinah. My mother sent food for lunch."

Cally heard Eden laugh. *That makes me happy all the way to my toes.*

CHAPTER 22

DUBLIN

The Murphy home, Dublin, June 26

"MUM, DA, YOU REMEMBER CHARLIE, don't you?" said Laoise as she escorted Charlie into the sitting room of her parents' home in Dublin.

Mrs. Murphy inclined her head. "Of course, Charles. You were Laoise's friend at the music academy. Welcome back to our home. It's been a long time."

"Thank you, Mrs. Murphy. Yes, almost ten years," said Charlie.

"You have both been busy developing your careers, and doing well, from what I hear," said Mr. Murphy. "Sit down. Do you care for a drink? How was your tour in Europe?"

"Thank you, yes. My tour in Europe was intense. I'm not sure I should schedule so many concerts in such a short span of time. I do it that way to protect my alone time."

"Alone time?" said Mrs. Murphy.

"Yes. I need blocks of time to myself, to evaluate what I've been doing, learn new music for the next season, and restore my soul," said Charlie. "Do you find you need that kind of time as well, Laoise?"

"I do, though I don't schedule myself as intensely as you do," said Laoise. "Tell Mum and Da about your concert in Zurich."

"My mentor, Ignacy Paderewski, surprised me by showing up at my concert in Zurich a week ago," said Charlie. "I hadn't seen him for a long time. He honored me by playing an encore. The audience rose as one to thank him. It was a thrilling moment. I owe him so much."

"We heard Paderewski play during his Irish tour years ago," said Mr. Murphy. "It was magical. He had a young pianist with him—"

"That was you!" exclaimed Mrs. Murphy. "I only now realized that. We were impressed way back then, weren't we, dear?"

"We were indeed," said Mr. Murphy. "I can only imagine how rich your playing must be now, after all these years of experience."

"Mr. Paderewski toured Ireland in February 1895," said Charlie. "I was fifteen. I came to the Academy in Dublin that fall."

"Mum and Da, if you want to hear Charlie play, I have an idea. I told you that the New York Philharmonic has invited both Charlie and me to play in concerts in September featuring Irish classics, yes? That's how we ran into each other again. If Charlie could stay here for this next week, it would facilitate us practicing together. What do you think?"

"If it's in any way inconvenient, I'll be happy to stay with my Dublin cousins where I am now," said Charlie. "It's no problem either way."

Mr. Murphy looked from his daughter's face to Charlie's and back again, then at his wife. "I think that would be grand. Don't you, dear? Ah, there's the bell for dinner."

Laoise walked into the dining room for breakfast ahead of Charlie and bent around her father's newspaper to give him a kiss. "What's the news this morning, Da? I'm still thinking about the Steamboat Ladies you mentioned yesterday. I'm proud of our Trinity College deciding to accept female students before British universities did, and granting degrees to female British scholars who had completed their courses."

Mr. Murphy said, "Not good news today, my dear. Listen to this: 'Danish Ship *SS Norge* Wrecked on Helen's Reef, Over 600 Feared Dead.' Good morning, Charles."

"How terrible!" exclaimed Laoise walking to the sideboard. "Read us the article, please, Da. Helen's Reef is in the North Atlantic, isn't it?"

"Yes, four hundred-some miles northwest of County Donegal," said Mr. Murphy. "Please help yourself, Charles. I'm sorry to say Theresa is not feeling well this morning."

Charlie looked at Laoise.

"I haven't told you, Charlie. Mum suffers from heart problems. She has good days and bad days."

"I'm sorry to hear that," said Charlie.

"I'll go see her after breakfast, Da."

Charlie picked up a plate as Mr. Murphy began reading the article about the shipwreck. *I feel strange. I don't know whether I can eat ...*

"Fog Tuesday, June 28 ... Ship hit a rock and immediately backed away, but a hole torn in the hull ... 727 passengers, 240 of them children ... searching for survivors ... ship sank just twelve minutes after hitting the reef ..."

Charlie heard the crash of his plate on the floor, and everything went black.

"Charlie, Charlie! Wake up!"

That's Laoise's voice. Coming through a tunnel. Charlie struggled to open his eyes and sit up. Laoise and her father bent over him. "I'm sorry. How embarrassing. I'm fine now."

Mr. Murphy helped Charlie to a chair. He buried his face in his arms on the table.

"Charlie, what's wrong? What happened?" asked Laoise.

"Give him a moment, Laoise," said Mr. Murphy. "Here, Charles. Drink this."

Charlie raised his head and accepted a glass of water. "Thank you, sir. I'm so sorry." He gulped half the water, then rubbed his eyes. "I've been terrified of storms at sea since childhood. Sailing is hard for me. I can't seem to get past—" His eyes glazed, and his whole body trembled. He put his head on the table once more. "I'm sorry." His words came out muffled.

"How can we help, Charles?" asked Mr. Murphy.

"I need to lie down for a little while," said Charlie. "But please—don't leave me alone."

"We'll help you to the couch in the sitting room," said Mr. Murphy. "Laoise can stay with you. I, unfortunately, must leave for a business meeting."

"I do apologize, Mr. Murphy," said Charlie.

"We'll talk more after I come home," said Mr. Murphy. "Laoise, don't hesitate to call the doctor if Charles needs care. I'll see you this evening." He bowed and left.

"Rest, Charlie," said Laoise, covering him with a blanket. "Shall I play for you?"

"That would be wonderful," said Charlie. "Thank you, Laoise." *How humiliating! How can I ever get past this? Laoise may lose interest in our relationship after seeing me like this. I wouldn't blame her. And her parents ... I'm mortified.*

Laoise began playing the soothing melody of "Méditation" from *Thaïs. This is the first piece I ever heard her play ...*

Charlie woke to stillness. *Where am I? What happened? Oh, the shipwreck. The Charlie wreck. Laoise—*

He pushed back the blanket and sat up. *What will she think of me after this? She'll be polite, no doubt. But it won't be the same ...*

The door opened and Laoise rushed in. "Charlie, you're awake! I saw through the edges of the curtain on the door. Oh, I'm so glad you're all right! Are you all right? I've been so worried!" She sat beside Charlie and threw her arms around him. "Charlie, tell me what happened when you were a boy, to create this terrible fear in you."

"Are you—I mean, are we—that is—?"

"Am I scared off by what happened to you, is that what you're asking, Charlie? Of course not! I want to know everything about you! The hard and painful things as well as the good things. I have my own challenges, you know."

"You do? To me, you seem perfect. I can't imagine you ever—"

"Well, no. I've never passed out listening to a newspaper article. But I have my own issues, Charlie. You'll have to learn about them sooner or later. I guess with this incident it will be sooner. But you first. Tell me about sailing when you were a child."

"I've never told anyone about this, except Mr. Paderewski," said Charlie.

"Just tell me," said Laoise. "Don't be afraid."

Charlie told her. About the first storm at sea, when he disobeyed his captain-father and could have died as a result. About the second storm when his adopted sister Cally's father did die, leaving her and her brother Teddy orphans. About his fear of thunderstorms, even when on land. About his fear of sailing, necessary as it was for him to tour in both America and Europe.

Along the way, Charlie pulled out his handkerchief and gave it to Laoise, her sapphire eyes spilling tears.

Finally, he stopped. *She listened. She didn't shut down or withdraw. Instead, she moved* to *me.* Charlie pulled Laoise close, and they wept together.

"So, Laoise," said Charlie, as they walked in the Murphys' garden the next day. "You know another one of my deep dark secrets. But I don't know yours. Do you want to tell me?"

"I know I said I would, but I'm afraid of how you will react," said Laoise.

"I understand. I was afraid you would pull away from me when I fell apart at the news of the shipwreck yesterday. And in New York City when I told you about Mr. Barrow. But you didn't. I can't promise how I'll feel, since I don't know what your challenges are. But if you want to take the risk, I'm here."

"Thank you, Charlie. I do want to tell you. I love the idea of having an ally."

"I would like to be that for you."

Laoise stopped to smell a rose. "My mother loves her garden. Isn't it beautiful?"

"It is, one of the loveliest I've seen."

"I'm afraid of losing my mum. Every time I leave home, I worry I won't see her alive again. It's a worry I carry constantly. I can't imagine my life without her. I've considered giving up my career as a musician so I can stay home with her. How can I ever get over it if she dies while I'm on tour?" Laoise burst into tears and buried her face in Charlie's chest.

"Oh, sweetheart, I'm sorry. I didn't realize her condition is so serious," said Charlie, holding her close. "Do your parents know how you feel? What do they say?"

Laoise sniffed. "Mummy doesn't want her illness to interfere with my music. She tries to prepare me for losing her. I don't understand how she can be so cheerful about it."

Tears flowed once more. Charlie guided her to a bench and sat quietly holding her.

"Da says it's a decision I must make for myself. The doctors can't say how long she may have. It could be weeks or months or years. So, it's impossible to plan. If I knew she only has a few weeks left, I would cancel my itinerary and stay with her. But Mum says that would make her sad, as if I'm just marking time, waiting for her to die. I don't know what to do. My brother has moved to Belfast, and we seldom see him."

"I can see how difficult this is, Laoise. Did your parents want more children?"

"Yes. Mummy had a premature birth, a wee boy, too small to live. Delivering him almost cost her life, because of her heart condition. The doctor said she couldn't risk getting pregnant again. I was five, and I remember the birth vividly, Mum screaming, Da yelling. I was terrified. I still am." Laoise stopped, then said so softly Charlie could hardly hear her, "I'm afraid—"

"You're afraid?"

"Yes."

"What are you afraid of?"

Laoise was silent, emotions playing across her face. Finally, she whispered, "I'm afraid of childbirth. I don't want to have children, Charlie. I'm afraid I might die. Because of this, I've never wanted to get married." She glanced at his face and then down again to her lap. "But then I saw you again ... And I'm afraid you won't want me now. Now that you know."

"Laoise, all I think about is you. You are more important to me than any number of potential children. Look at me, sweetheart. I love you. I want to share my life with you. Perhaps we need more time to know each other before we make definite plans, but you fill my heart. I want us to face life together, whatever it may bring. Do you want that too?"

"I do, Charlie. I love you. I have loved you for ten years."

A kiss left them both breathless.

Dublin, Sunday, July 3

"I know you must leave tomorrow, but I don't want you to go, Charlie," said Laoise after church and dinner. Her parents had finally released them from a lively analysis of her concerts Friday and Saturday evenings, colored by complaints about the construction on Merrion Street that doubtless would tangle up downtown Dublin for years to come.

"Must I wait until September in New York City to see you again? I'm trying to be brave, but this is hard," said Laoise.

"I have an idea. But what is that scent?" Charlie stopped walking and sniffed the flowers around them. "I'm sure I've smelled it before, but I can't place it."

Laoise sniffed too. "It's Mum's Cupani, these pretty purple sweet peas. Mum likes them because they grew in her grandmother's garden, a reminder to her of a precious relationship."

Charlie bent, smelled, and said, "Yes! I remember now! They grow around Cally's cousin Micky's home in Youghal. Have I told you about them? Have you been to Youghal?"

"No and no," said Laoise. "Everything you say about Cally and her family has an air of mystique. I look forward to meeting the flesh and blood person."

"So, about that—"

"First, tell me your idea about when we can see each other again."

"When is your next concert?"

"Two weekends from now, June 15 and 16 in Belfast."

"Good, then this might work. You could take the train to Waterford this Friday and play with me Saturday evening in a benefit for the city. Would you like that? We could play a couple of the pieces we've been practicing. It would help us prepare for New York! I can't ask the orchestra to play with us on such late notice, though. It will have to be a duet."

"That sounds delightful, Charlie! Will your mother be there?"

"No, just my sister Margaret and her family. Mum is with Cally and Cora in Idaho."

"Oh, right. The treasure hunt you told me about."

"Yes. It came at just the right time for Cally, when she had to be away from Kansas City."

Laoise shook her head and poked Charlie. "This whole story—the accusation of horse theft, the crazy treasure hunt—it makes me wonder what kind of family you come from!"

Charlie laughed with her. "Just don't make any final judgments until you actually meet them. I think they're pretty special, even if a bit unusual."

"Well, I've been told my life is unusual too. Never boring!"

"I'll let my brother Daniel know you'll be playing in Belfast. And we'll see each other on Friday in Waterford. I already can't wait!"

CHAPTER 23

TREASURE HUNT REVIEW

Stricker Homesite, Friday evening, July 1

CALLY LOOKED AROUND FROM HER PLACE at the outside table, memorizing every detail of the homesite. *I loved my time at the Robison's, but it's nice to be back. I miss baby Isaac already. If we're leaving soon, I want to remember everything about Idaho. Each color, each smell, the way the light holds a unique warmth unrelated to the temperature. Cora captures it so well in her paintings. This place has burrowed itself into my heart.*

"Yes, you may be excused to play for a while before bed," Cora told the children as the adults lingered at the table.

"Your cherry pie was delicious, Cora!" said Cathleen.

"Next I'm going to try an apple pie," said Cora. "Margaret told me these are early-ripening apples so sweet we don't need to add sugar."

"Isn't it wonderful to have fresh fruit from the orchard every day? Apricots, peaches, cherries, apples. Soon, pears. I'm thinking of canning some of this fruit for them to come home to. I found everything we'll need," said Cathleen.

"Sure!" said Cally. "Let's do that next week. The children can help us."

Cora turned to Flora. "You were starting to say something, Flora, before we started talking about fruit."

"I think it's time for you to continue your treasure hunt," said Flora. "You've all seen for yourselves how well I'm doing. Falling Water and Margaret can help me if I need them.

"Will you be able to limit your medical service to a reasonable level, once word gets out that you're well again?" asked Cathleen.

"I think so." Flora looked at Cally. "Though it's clear to me I need an assistant. With the irrigation canals opening soon, more people will settle in this area. My clinic won't be adequate."

Flora's trying to communicate more than she's saying. Cally gave Flora a small nod and a puzzled expression. *I wonder what she's thinking.*

"I had an interesting conversation with Mr. Hansen at his store today," said Cathleen. "Did you know he plans to move?"

"No! I haven't talked to him since before my illness," said Flora. "I'm sorry to hear that. He and Anna have given me strong support since they moved to Rock Creek four years ago." She stood, holding the back of her chair. "Where are they going? They invited me to move back in with them when Herman and Lucy return from Germany this fall."

"It's an amusing story," said Cathleen, putting her hand on Flora's. "Developers are wooing Mr. Hansen to a new town they're planning on the railroad and irrigation line, seven miles north of Rock Creek. They'll name the town after him if he agrees to move! He laughed when he told me. He's in no hurry to move and says he won't be flattered or pressured into anything. But he thinks any town built near the railroad and the irrigation canal will grow, and soon Rock Creek will be left behind."

"I can't imagine Rock Creek without them," said Flora. "John and Anna are a force for good in the school, the court, and the city council. Not to mention their store and my clinic."

"Perhaps I shouldn't have said anything," said Cathleen. "I've no wish to upset you, dear Flora. I didn't know you have such a close relationship with them. As soon as you can, you should talk with them yourself. I think that will allay your fears better than anything I can say."

Flora sat down again, took a deep breath, and smiled at Cathleen. "I will. Don't worry, Cathleen. It was bound to come out soon, if John is talking about this so openly at the store."

"We could invite John and Anna and their family to our Sunday supper!" said Cally.

"Good idea," nodded Flora. "Someone could go to Rock Creek tomorrow to invite them."

"I can," said Cally. "Felicity wants fabric for more doll clothes for Lizzy. I'll take her with me so she can choose."

"Josie will want to go too, then," said Cora.

"Returning to the treasure hunt, isn't it time to open the next clue?" asked Flora.

"Yes. But it would help me to review the first six, after such a long time not thinking about the hunt," said Cally. "I have much of it written down, and Shane can help me remember what happened since he joined us in Soda Springs."

"Falling Water has offered to teach the girls beading," said Flora. "Perhaps she could entertain them tomorrow morning, while we review the clues and read the new one. Do you want to be in on this, Cathleen?"

"I wouldn't miss it," said Cathleen. "Tell me when to be here."

"Ten o'clock tomorrow morning," said Flora. "Can Shane take a message to Falling Water right after breakfast, Cora?"

"Yes. He'll love being part of an important adult conversation," said Cora.

"We can do the essential chores before ten," said Cally. "Do you have paper we can use, Flora? I want to make a chart, to be sure we're not forgetting anything important."

❧

"I'm delighted to be part of this discussion," said Cathleen as the adults gathered around Flora's kitchen table.

"So," said Cally. "On our chart I want to include place, date, person who had the clue, other significant people, contents of the clue, tasks to complete, outcome of those tasks, and what Uncle William told us about himself."

"Interesting," said Cathleen. "You think William trusted whoever embarked on this hunt more than he trusted his family or others while he was alive?"

"It seems that way to me," said Cally. "I'll be interested in your perspective when you hear more. It's almost like he was seeking absolution, or at least forgiveness."

"Curiouser and curiouser," said Flora. "Oh, there come Shane and Falling Water and a couple of her grandchildren. I'll set them up on a blanket in the shade by the river. Don't start without me!"

"I'll start making soup for lunch," said Cora. "This conversation could take a while."

❧

"I'll be the secretary, filling out the chart as you talk, Cally and Shane," offered Cora.

"Thank you, Cora! That lets me peel and cut peaches while we talk, to advance our canning project," said Cally.

"I'll help you!" said Cathleen.

When the conversation reached Soda Springs and Cally recounted Lizzy's revelations, Cathleen jumped to her feet. "Oh! Oh no! I've made a terrible mistake! I had no idea! I thought—I should have paid more attention—I thought—oh, this is awful!"

"What is it, Cathleen? What's wrong?" asked Cora.

"I wonder if this is redeemable somehow," said Cathleen, pacing around the table. "Oh heavenly Father, please forgive me. Give me just a minute, girls." She sat down and covered her face with her hands. Cally, Cora, Shane, and Flora looked at each other, mystified.

Cathleen took a deep breath, wiped her eyes, and said, "All right. I'm ready to tell you. But let me tell it straight through before you ask questions or make comments."

"All right," said the others.

"As you know, I sailed on the *Lion III.* I feel safe under Paudeen's care; he's an excellent captain. I'm proud of Peter for designating Paudeen as captain in his will." Cathleen wiped her eyes once more. "The voyage brought back happy memories of sailing with Peter." She paused a moment, then continued.

"On this crossing, I became quite annoyed with a young sailor. Somehow, he learned that my name is Cathleen Malcomson and came to me with a story so farfetched I was convinced he was an opportunist. I didn't treat him kindly. Oh God, please forgive me."

Cathleen covered her face with her hands. After a moment, she lifted her head and continued. "The sailor told me his name was Billy Malcomson, son of Uncle William."

"You found Billy!" shouted Shane, then covered his mouth and turned red. "I'm sorry, Grandma. I was supposed to stay quiet until you finish. But we've been looking for Billy for *so long.* This isn't terrible. It's wonderful!"

"You may not think so when I tell you everything, Shane. I was sure this sailor knew the *Lion III* is owned by Malcomsons and invented a story to obtain some imagined Malcomson wealth. He told me he hoped to earn enough money as a sailor to search Ireland for his father, who had disappeared when he was small. He asked for an address where he might find William and one day asked me for money so he could begin his search right away.

"I didn't give him an address, of course, because William is long dead. I didn't tell him this, because I didn't believe his story. Nor did I give him money.

"This Billy, as he called himself, couldn't have been more than sixteen years old. God forgive me, I rejected his story in part because he was dark skinned. I couldn't imagine any circumstance in which his story could be true."

Cathleen closed her eyes and raised her hands. "Lord, I confess my uncharitable and prejudicial assumptions. Can you even now cleanse my heart and redeem this situation?"

The group sat silent as Cathleen wept. Finally, she wiped her eyes with her handkerchief and continued. "The sailor kept wanting to talk with me. I avoided him. I considered talking with Paudeen about this irritating sailor, but thank God, I never did. Paudeen would have arrested him on the spot.

"Just before I disembarked, the sailor pressed a paper into my hands. I stuffed it in my pocket without even reading it. Hmm, which dress would that have been?" Cathleen felt in the pockets of her dress. "Not this one. I'll check the others when I'm back at Margaret's."

Cathleen took a deep breath and looked around the table. "That is my sad tale. Can you forgive me? I have wronged our family. And Peter's cousin, hard as that is to believe."

Cally jumped to her feet and hugged Cathleen. "Oh, but don't you see, Cathleen—you've solved a part of this hunt that has seemed unsolvable. As Shane said, you found Billy! Likely he's still a sailor on the *Lion III,* don't you think?"

"More accurately, he found me," said Cathleen. "And I pushed him away. He was so anxious to find his father, he may have left the ship by now. He may be wandering around Ireland asking people whether they know William Malcomson."

"I'm curious what he wrote on that paper he gave you, Cathleen," said Cora.

"It will be easy to find out," said Cathleen.

"Any of us would have responded as you did, Cathleen," said Flora. "You had no context for believing the sailor's story. This discussion gets more interesting by the minute! If Cally hadn't undertaken this review, you might never have remembered the boy on the ship!"

"I'm sure God forgives you," said Cora. "Can you forgive yourself?"

"I'll have to think about that," said Cathleen. "I hope one day I can ask that young man's forgiveness. After I left the ship, I didn't give him another thought. I feel I have failed some divine test."

"I can't say I understand your distress, Cathleen. Self-blame seems to run in this family," said Flora. "It's time for lunch. I need a rest after we eat." She turned to Cally. "I'm thinking of going to check on Eden and her baby, and Freddy's leg tomorrow morning, returning in time for Sunday supper. Would you care to go with me?"

"Yes, unless I'm needed to help prepare for the evening." *Maybe Flora will explain her cryptic comment from earlier.*

"We've had practice doing it without you," said Cora. "Cathleen and I can manage, since everyone who comes brings food."

"Then may I invite Felicity to join us, Flora?" asked Cally. "She may prefer to stay with her cousins, but she seems enchanted with babies these days."

"Of course, if she doesn't mind the long wagon ride."

"Then we'll continue this conversation after Flora rests," said Cora.

"After lunch I'll look for Billy's paper," said Cathleen.

"May I go with you, Grandma?" asked Shane.

"There's nothing I would like better, Shane."

"Here I am, rested and ready to hear more of this fantastical tale," said Flora. "Did you find Billy's paper, Cathleen? Shane, you look like you're about to burst."

Shane looked at his grandmother, who smiled and nodded. He jumped up from his chair.

"Yes! We know how to find Billy!"

Cathleen extended a crumpled bit of paper. Cora read, *"I'm sad you don't believe me, Mrs. Malcomson. But if you change your mind, contact my Uncle Cecil in Fish Haven. I'm in touch with him. I hope you will come to see the truth in what I told you. Billy."*

"Very nice handwriting," said Flora.

"His mother said he was at the top of his class in school," said Cally. "Cora, do you know—has Thomas been communicating with the Fish Haven family?"

"Yes," said Cora. "The last time I talked to him, Thomas told me he had received a telegram from Melody saying all was well between her and her mother and she planned to stay."

"How wonderful!" exclaimed Cally.

"Yes, Thomas felt the same way, like a miracle has taken place. He telegraphed back asking her to write him the details and had just received her letter when we talked. Melody wondered whether he would be back in Idaho any time soon and if so, whether he could help Cecil move her things from Pocatello."

"I remember she took very little with her on the train," said Cally. "I didn't know whether it was all she owned, or whether she didn't want to give Minnie the idea she had come to stay."

"Melody is losing strength," Cora continued. "Thomas knew this would happen, but it's still sad. She told him she's learning not to be so reactive to her mother. She doesn't have much energy, so she's learning to listen and to think before she retorts. Her words. I've not met

Melody, of course, but Thomas has described her so well to me I feel like I know her."

"This is amazing." Cathleen clasped her hands and looked at the sky. "Thank you."

"When do you plan to talk to Thomas again, Cora?" asked Cally.

"Next Saturday. But I could try calling today and see whether I catch him at home."

"Mummy, can I tell him?" asked Shane, bouncing in his seat. "I was there! I met Miss Melody. Please, Mummy?"

"Oh! I had forgotten all about inviting the Hansens to Sunday supper," said Cally. "Shall we go together now, before the store closes?"

"I'll call Felicity," Shane called over his shoulder, already running toward the river.

"We'll have to pick up the treasure hunt review another time," said Flora. "How about Monday after lunch? I think I'll need the morning to rest, after visiting Eden and Sunday supper."

"And Monday morning is catch-up time for chores," said Cora.

"I'll go hitch Cammie to the wagon," said Cally. "I hope the Hansens will come, Flora. I hadn't realized they were such close friends of yours."

"It will be lovely to see them again and catch up with the tale of the new town," said Flora. "I'm ready for another rest."

CHAPTER 24

REVELATIONS

Traveling to the Robison home, Sunday, July 3

"WE WOULD GO AND COME BACK ALL IN THE SAME DAY?" asked Felicity.

"Yes. We'll be back in time for Sunday supper," said Cally.

"Then I don't want to go, Mummy. I'll stay here and see you at supper."

"I thought you might enjoy seeing baby Isaac," said Cally.

Felicity cocked her head. "I like baby Isaac," she said. "But he's too little to play with. I like Brian better. I'll see baby Isaac when he's big enough to come to Sunday supper."

We'll probably be gone by then, Cally decided not to say.

"All right, sweetheart. Give me a hug. Mind Auntie Cora."

"Bye, Mummy. Bye, Miss Flora." Felicity didn't wait for the wagon to pull away. She ran to play with Josie and her new birthday doll.

"The children seem happy here," said Flora. "I'm glad. None of us will be here much longer. Herman and Lucy and their children will be home in September."

"I'm glad the Hansens are coming to supper tonight," said Cally.

"Yes. They are good friends. Their children are charming. A little older than yours."

"I met Johnny yesterday, working in the store. Spitting image of his father."

"Yes, a kind boy. Fourteen now, I think. Speaking of ages, Cally, if I tell you something, will you keep it strictly to yourself?" asked Flora.

"Of course," said Cally.

"Today is my birthday. I am forty years old," said Flora. "I'm having trouble grasping that number. My life is flying by much too fast."

"Happy birthday, Flora! But wouldn't you enjoy sharing this special day with everyone?"

"No, thank you, Cally. Remember—you promised not to tell!"

"I won't, but may I ask why?"

"I keep hearing my father's voice in my head, telling me no man would want me if I became a doctor. That I would be an old maid and live alone and lonely the rest of my life. And here I am, alone, just as my father predicted."

"I think about that too. I can't imagine anyone will want to marry me as a single mother."

"May I ask, Cally, about Felicity's father?"

"A man raped me when I was fourteen," said Cally. "He's in jail, because of other evil things he's done. But Felicity asks me often why she doesn't have a father. I told her to ask God for one. I hope that doesn't make her mistrust God."

"I hear you. I've had enough disappointments to mistrust him myself," said Flora.

"I understand. I've only recently begun to think God cares about me. But is there something you would change in your life if you could? From watching your interactions with Florence, it seemed you've been determined to make your own decisions."

"Funny you should say that, Cally. I've been reviewing my life decisions one by one, wondering whether I would change any of them if I could. There was a man once ..."

Flora's voice trailed off, and she seemed not to be seeing the high desert they drove through. Cally noted the beautiful markings on a kestrel hovering overhead. *I wish I could take a photograph like Benedicte would, so Cora could paint it.* The bird dove suddenly, taking flight again with a small creature in its beak. *I couldn't see whether that was a mouse or a chipmunk or something else.*

When Flora didn't continue, Cally asked, "Do you want to talk about him?"

Flora gave herself a little shake. "He was a fellow student at medical school, more open to welcoming females into the profession than most of our classmates. But he was ambitious in ways I was not, and we parted with some animosity. He said I would be wasting my life here in the wilderness. He probably married well, has lovely children, and is successful in his profession. Is that what I would have wanted? When I think about my patients here, I have to say no. Yet—"

"Yet you wish it could have been both/and, instead of either/or? That's what I wish too," said Cally. "Both Felicity and a man to share my life."

"Well, no use having a pity party," said Flora, straightening, her voice changing tone. "My next decision will be whether to move to the new town once it's established. I do see the advantages of living near the railroad and the canal. And I understand many Rock Creek residents will want to follow the Hansens there. But increased population will require more doctors. It will probably be easier to find one willing to live in the new town than out here, so perhaps I should stay in Rock Creek. I need to discuss this with John and Anna."

"It sounds like a hard decision."

"Yes. We'll be driving directly past the location of the new town of Hansen," said Flora. "Imagine the sense of power the developers must feel, creating something out of nothing, a thriving community in the middle of sage and brush."

"Transformed through irrigation into flourishing farmland," said Cally. "I would love to see the miracle happen."

"Well, you could, you know, Cally," said Flora, looking at her.

"What do you mean?"

"As I mentioned yesterday, I need an assistant. You're the first person I've met who has the qualities I would be looking for."

"What do you mean exactly, an assistant?"

"Well, let's turn that around. Is there anything about my life that appeals to you, Cally? Anything you could see yourself doing?"

"I once dreamed about becoming a doctor. That was before Felicity," said Cally. "I don't see that as possible now. But I have wondered about training as a nurse. Do you know how long that would take?"

"I'm not well informed, but last I knew nursing programs varied from six months to three years in length. There's no standard curriculum. The schools are formed by hospitals to train nurses to work for them. There must be nursing schools in Kansas City, Cally. There are none yet in the states of Idaho or Oregon, as far as I know."

"It's just an idea," said Cally. "Six months to two years sounds manageable, but three seems too long. I'm pretty sure Cora and Thomas would support me."

"Unless things have changed while I've been here, nursing schools do not admit married students nor permit them to marry during their course of study."

Cally laughed. "No worries there! But you said nursing programs train their students to work in hospitals. I would rather do what you're doing, Flora, caring for people in a clinic or in their homes, not in a hospital. What you do is so—so personal. You become part of a community, of people's families. I love that. So, would training in a nursing school make sense? Or would most of it be a waste of time, not relevant to the realities of life in a place like this?"

"I studied at New York Homeopathic Medical College for Women, graduating with the class of 1886. My focus was public health, so I learned from the beginning to care for people in their homes. I worked in a hospital for only one year, the Brooklyn Women's Homeopathic Hospital founded by Dr. Susan McKinney Steward, one of my medical school teachers. She was and is one of my lifelong heroes. She taught me self-respect as a woman in a field dominated by men. Am I boring you, Cally, with all this ancient history?"

"Not at all. I'm fascinated. Please continue."

"Dr. McKinney, as I knew her, pioneered prenatal care and the treatment of childhood diseases, including malnutrition. She was brilliant. She came up with protocols based on holistic medicine long before others in the field gave attention to children. She was the single most important teacher and role model in my life."

"Is she still alive?" asked Cally.

"As far as I know. Her first husband died in 1892, and she remarried in 1896. I haven't kept track of her since because she traveled with her new husband, who was a chaplain in the U.S. Army. I would love to see her again, to say thank you for her impact on my life both personally and professionally. What I've had to face as a female doctor here in Idaho is nothing compared to what she had to deal with in New York City."

"People didn't respect female physicians there either?"

"No. And they particularly didn't respect female doctors with dark skin. Dr. McKinney didn't let that stop her. She treated every patient with equal compassion, no matter their race. In that way too, she gave me an example to follow."

"Your friendship with Falling Water, for example," said Cally.

"Yes. And I'm grateful for my homeopathic training, which is more open to natural treatments than traditional physicians tend to be. Falling Water has taught me so much. When I came here, she befriended me, not the other way around. She found ways to communicate even though she didn't yet know much English."

"Thank you for sharing her with us," said Cally. "Oh look! Is that a hawk?"

"Yes. It's called a red-tailed hawk, though you can't really see the red while it's flying."

"I'm just realizing you couldn't have been here very long when you met Uncle William."

"True. I was still trying to get my feet under me in Twin Falls when he showed up. He had strange ideas about marriage, but a high regard for women's abilities in general. He encouraged me when I felt I would never be accepted here as a female physician."

"Obviously, you meant a lot to him, too."

Flora nodded. "To begin with, I mostly delivered babies. I was grateful for a midwife in New York City who taught me everything practical that I know."

"Including breech delivery, apparently, since that's what happened with Eden."

"Yes. And once a woman has a breech or another complication, it's more likely the same thing or another problem will happen again. I hope to have the opportunity today to talk with Silas and Eden about methods of birth control. She would truly be risking her life if she gets pregnant again. Cally ..."

"Yes?"

"Are you ready to tell me what happened to you during Eden's delivery?

Cally flinched, as if Flora had struck her.

"I'm sorry, Cally. Clearly, it's a painful topic. But maybe it would help to get it out, not leave it trapped inside your head. Don't worry about getting emotional. I won't mind."

"I haven't told anyone about this. Ever," said Cally, her eyes brimming.

"I'm listening."

"My mother and my infant sister died in childbirth. And it was my fault," said Cally.

"How was it your fault?" asked Flora.

"I did something that displeased my mother, and she told me I would be the death of her," said Cally. "And she was right."

"What happened?"

"When she was pregnant, I heard Mammy tell my da she didn't like me and—and hoped the new baby would be everything she always wanted in a daughter." Cally turned her head as sobs erupted. Flora waited.

"I—I was devastated," said Cally after a moment. "Out loud, I said, 'I hope the baby dies.' And she did."

"So, you believe your wish and the words your mother spoke had the power to end her life and the baby's?"

"Yes. I think the bad faeries overheard. They always look for ways to cause mischief or worse," said Cally, blowing her nose.

"I see. Tell me about the delivery."

"The baby came too soon, too small to live. And blood poured out of Mammy's body. My mammy screamed, Da yelled, and then nothing. Silence. Da held the dead baby, and then threw himself over Mammy's body and wailed. And blood was everywhere. Da didn't speak to me for months and months. I could tell he knew Mammy's and the baby's deaths were my fault."

"Eden's bleeding triggered these awful memories," said Flora.

"Yes. I had to get away so I wouldn't cause her to die too," said Cally. "I know it doesn't sound logical, Flora. It's just something I know, as obvious to me as that the sky is blue and grass is green. I cause harm to people I care about. I couldn't bear doing it again."

"Cally, what does it mean to you that Eden and Isaac are fine?"

Cally wept again, sobbing so intensely she could hardly breathe. Flora halted Cammie and turned to face Cally.

"Tell me," said Flora.

"I was so afraid," whispered Cally. "And when Silas appeared carrying Isaac, I was sure he was dead. But he wasn't. He was pink, and warm, and breathing. I haven't felt so grateful for anything since Felicity was born alive and well."

"And Eden—"

"Yes. You were a miracle worker. I couldn't believe it."

"Cally, we're almost to the Robisons' so I won't do it now. But on the way home, when your emotions have calmed, I want to tell you my perspective as a doctor of what happened with your mother and sister. All right?"

Cally gulped and took a deep breath. "I'm sorry, Flora, for dumping all this on you."

Flora placed her hand on Cally's. "I asked, remember? Healing of such difficult experiences requires sharing them with someone. It's too heavy a burden to bear alone. I suspect you've been trying to solve your own problems since you were a small child."

"Yes. I don't want to be a burden to other people."

"I understand. Now, we have about ten minutes. While I drive the rest of the way, I want you to think about the joy of seeing baby Isaac again, healthy and sweet. Have you decided whether to accept their invitation to be his godmother?"

Cally smiled. "He's part of my heart, that's for sure. But we'll be leaving soon to continue the treasure hunt, and then return to Kansas

City. It seems fairer to Isaac to have a godparent who lives here. Also, I'm not Mormon. I'm Catholic. I wouldn't be able to teach him what his parents want him to understand."

"Ah. Perhaps you should ask what the godparent role means to them. It may not be the same as in the Catholic tradition," suggested Flora.

"Good idea. Thank you, Flora."

"Here we are. Ready, Cally?"

Cally took a deep breath and smiled. "Ready."

☙❧

"Cally. I suspect your mother had placenta previa. Do you know what that is?" asked Flora on the way home.

"No."

"There's no way you could have caused that by your thoughts and wishes. And I'm quite sure your mother was simply expressing frustration in what you heard her say."

You weren't there. You don't know how Mammy looked at me, how she treated me, the things she said—not only that day, but most days.

"I'll explain placenta previa using the example of a delivery I helped with a few months ago. Think about it in terms of a woman you don't know, rather than in terms of your mother."

"I'll try," said Cally. As Flora explained, a thought echoed and reechoed in her mind. *Is this true? Is it possible I didn't cause Mammy and the baby's death?*

☙❧

"Are we ready?" asked Cora Monday afternoon. "Where's Flora?"

"She just woke from her nap. She'll be here soon," said Cally.

"I brought water for everyone," said Cathleen, carrying a tray to the outside table. "I suspect there's still a lot to discuss."

"There is, yes. The hardest part is still to come," said Cally. "I wish Thomas were here to tell it. Speaking of Thomas, how was your phone call Saturday, Cora? Oh, here you are, Flora."

"Shane did a great job explaining about Billy," said Cora, smiling at her son. "Tell them what Daddy said, Shane."

"He said he would call Mr. Martin at the bank today to schedule a time to talk with Mr. Cecil, Miz Melody's brother," said Shane. "They don't have telephones yet in Fish Haven, but Mr. Cecil drives to Montpelier to deliver fish. Daddy hopes he has heard from Billy."

"Thomas was excited you had contact with Billy, Cathleen. I'm sure this is all going to work out well." Cora took a drink of water.

"Today is Billy's birthday!" exclaimed Cally. "July 4th, right? He's fourteen."

"May I pray for him?" asked Cathleen. "Lord God, bless Billy on his birthday, and please send your angels to protect him wherever he is. Of your mercy, guide us to him. Amen."

"Amen," said the others.

"So, where are we in the treasure hunt story?" asked Flora.

"We only got as far as Soda Springs and Lizzy's death," said Cally. "Clue number four was the hardest so far, don't you agree, Shane?"

"Daddy went to Old Fort Hall without us. I wanted to go, but Mr. Rainey said no."

"Who is Mr. Rainey?" asked Cathleen.

"He's a man Uncle William knew," said Shane. "But I want Aunt Cally to tell this part. I'll come back later."

"All right. I understand, Shane," said Cally. "Here. One of you read clue #4, and then I'll explain it. I warn you, Cathleen, this won't be easy. Five and six will be more fun."

CHAPTER 25

CLUE #7

Stricker homesite, Tuesday, July 5

"THANK YOU FOR WAITING UNTIL TODAY to read clue number seven," said Cathleen. "I confess I had trouble sleeping last night, trying to absorb the fact of Uncle William being a murderer."

"A repentant murderer," said Flora. "That matters, doesn't it?"

"Yes, and the fact that he made the best restitution he could," said Cally. "You would have been amazed by the attitude of Andy's parents. They even acknowledged their part in raising their son to believe he could treat other people as he did."

"To me that isn't in the same category of wrongdoing," said Cathleen. "Well. Today, I'm focusing on the marvel of Thomas arriving here just when you needed him, Flora. Don't you find that miraculous?"

"I do," nodded Flora. "We wouldn't be sitting here having this conversation if Thomas hadn't shown up when he did. And my gratitude to all of you and Margaret and Falling Water for your care of me is too big for words."

"It's been a privilege for us. Are we ready to open clue number seven?" asked Cora.

"Here's the packet," said Flora.

"You read it, Cally," said Cora. "You're the one who's been in on this from the start."

"All right. Let's see ... Here's another envelope for you, Flora."

"Read the clue first," said Flora.

Cally unfolded the paper. "This time it's not a poem. It says, *You've made a long journey, and I'm deeply grateful for the time you have invested in following the whims of an old man. You've been shocked, no doubt, along the way. But you've also seen God's amazing provision for me through the wonderful people he brought into my life. I hope you can see this as a story of redemption and apply hope to your own life in some way.*

It gives me great satisfaction to think my gifts can express my thanks to my friends and perhaps make a small difference to whatever circumstances they face.

My deepest desire is for my son Billy to find a place in the Malcomson family, to be loved and cared for in ways I can no longer offer him.

I have no way of knowing how this experience may have impacted you, treasure seeker. Please accept my deep gratitude for the time and inconvenience of embracing the challenge. May God richly bless you as he has me.

You have only one more step to complete: a return to Boise, where I left the final packet. If Mr. Eastman is still there, please express to him my thanks for his role in this adventure.

I wish you Godspeed.

William Malcomson."

Cally looked up. "It's not really a clue. It tells us the treasure hunt is over."

"And Billy is the treasure, like we thought!" said Shane.

"We don't know what's in the final packet in Boise, though," said Cora. "What does yours say, Flora?"

Flora opened the envelope, fat with bills. She drew out a small piece of paper. "This one is a poem, of sorts:

A home of your own, Flora. You find the place.

Your treatment of me was nothing but grace.

If by now you are married, your husband provides.

But if not, then imagine that I'm at your side.

Find a place large enough for your clinic to flourish.

A house to grow old in, and children to nourish."

"Children to nourish?" said Cathleen.

"He's referring to my desire to care for malnourished children, as my mentor did in New York City," said Flora. "I told William I wished I had space for a classroom, where I could teach mothers nutrition and other important childcare principles. Including ways to plan for the number of children they wish to have, rather than spreading their resources so thin that everyone suffers. And other radical ideas, like letting girls grow up a little more before they marry. Ryan's Bethany, for example, was only seventeen when she died in childbirth."

"How hard for her family, as well as for Ryan," said Cathleen.

"Sadly, that's not uncommon here on the frontier, where there are more men than women to marry them. But I don't think it's fair to the girls or to their children. I didn't realize William had absorbed so much of my dream."

"Did he give you enough to make your dream possible?" asked Cally.

"I've never reduced my dream to dollars and cents. It is an interesting moment to receive this gift, though. Have I mentioned my conversation with John and Anna Sunday evening?"

"No," said Cora.

"They are thinking seriously about moving to the new town," said Flora. "Though it will be a year before the town is platted and essential buildings constructed. John is quite sure it will largely replace Rock Creek because of the railroad and the irrigation canal. He invited me to draw up a plan for a clinic that can be part of the new settlement from the beginning. Do you see how timely Uncle William's gift is?"

"Will you return to live with the Hansens in the meantime?" asked Cathleen.

"Yes. Perhaps they'll host Sunday suppers, if Herman and Lucy don't prefer to continue them here. The suppers are becoming popular. How many people did we have Sunday?"

"Thirty-one adults and fourteen children, if you count baby Brian," said Shauna, who had walked over and stood by her mother during the conversation. "I counted three times. We didn't have room for everyone to eat at the table."

"It was lovely," said Cathleen. "I'm glad everyone wants to continue the tradition of evening prayer. Doesn't Ryan have a fine reading voice? I bet he's a good singer, too."

"Mummy, we're hungry," said Shauna. "Can we have lunch now?"

"We can if you'll help me bring the food from the kitchen, sweetheart. I baked bread for sandwiches."

"Yum," said Shane. "I want mine with butter and honey. I'll call Josie and Felicity."

"May I walk with you back to Margaret's, Cathleen?" asked Cora. "I have an idea."

"I noticed you've been quiet today," said Cathleen.

"I've been thinking ... This treasure hunt came at a perfect time for Cally, since she had to be away from Kansas City. But we still don't know what will happen with the legal case against her for the horse she borrowed. Do you know about that?"

"Yes. Thomas told me. The trial should take place in August, right?" asked Cathleen.

"That's what we've heard, though Thomas hasn't learned the date yet," said Cora. "If the treasure hunt is almost over, I wonder what Cally should do until the trial. I don't think it will be safe for her to return to Kansas City before then."

"Perhaps she could stay here?" asked Cathleen. "She seems to love helping Flora."

"She does. I confess I'm eager to return home," said Cora. "I didn't imagine we would be here so long, three weeks already. I miss Thomas and all my home comforts and routines. I won't miss sleeping on the floor."

Cathleen laughed. "I'm grateful to Margaret for sparing me that! The children seem to be enjoying the experience. That's a grand blessing."

"It is. I don't think they'll ever forget this. Shane, especially, is absorbing a different perspective on life. He's matured this summer, don't you think?"

"He's a remarkable boy," affirmed Cathleen. "He's developed a profound concern for Billy without ever having met him. He seems delighted that Billy might be the treasure."

"Yes. The time here has been good for Cally, too. She's different. Lighter. Freer. More confident. More expressive. Have you noticed?"

"I have," said Cathleen. "I think the treasure hunt has offered her opportunities to wrestle with some of the pain from her own past. What about you, Cora? Is there anything you have particularly enjoyed?"

"Painting! I never imagined a landscape like this one."

"You capture its beauty and help us appreciate it too," said Cathleen.

"Cathleen, remember how Cally described Lizzy's daughter May Lee's paintings yesterday? And Benedicte Wrensted's photographs?

Wouldn't it be fun to have a grand art show in Kansas City this fall, featuring the work of all three of us? We could call it 'Images of Idaho.' I'd like to include Falling Water's baskets and beadwork too. They are unique and beautiful."

"What a fabulous idea!" said Cathleen.

"Thank you. I would like to travel to Pocatello to meet Benedicte and see her work, and to Soda Springs to meet May Lee and see hers. Would you enjoy going with me, Cathleen? I think Cally would be willing to care for the children for a couple of days."

"I would love that, Cora! What a grand idea!"

"Then I'll call Benedicte Wrensted to introduce myself and my proposal and ask which day in the next week or so would be convenient for us to visit her. And I can call that man who befriended Cally at the Idanha Hotel—Calico, I think?—to find out how I can contact May Lee. If she's still living in the mountain cabin, perhaps she would be willing to come into town with some of her work to show me. Us."

"This sounds very doable, Cora."

"I'll call them tomorrow after I ask Cally about keeping the children. If Benedicte and May Lee are interested, we can set dates for traveling. Meanwhile I can talk to Falling Water."

"I love ending the day with such creative thoughts, Cora. Have I told you what a blessing you are to me?"

"You have, Cathleen. I love you too." Cora gave Cathleen a warm hug, waved to Margaret, and turned back toward the homesite.

Thank you, God, for these ideas. Thank you for caring about my needs too. This idea cheers me immensely. I can't wait to tell Thomas!

CHAPTER 26

WATERFORD

[For a map, see "Waterford and Portlaw" under Historical Links on HorseThief1898.com.]

Margaret's home, Waterford, July 5

"AFTER JUST ONE DAY HERE, kind as Margaret and Percy are to me, I'm once more keenly aware I don't have a home," scribbled Charlie in his journal. "I know Mummy couldn't keep Mayfield after Father died, but I miss it terribly. Seeing Midnight and Rosy here accentuates that sadness. Midnight should be in her stall at Mayfield, waiting for a wild run to the river. Rosy should be sticking her setter-nose into every corner of Mummy's garden, searching for chipmunks to chase. I don't like seeing her getting old and staid. I feel old too. Old and homeless. Strange, isn't it, comparing myself to a raggedy street person? But where is my home? Many people welcome me, here and in the United States. But always as a guest.

"It's time to admit I've had a nagging sense of resentment about Uncle William's treasure hunt, though I tried to maintain a good attitude while I was in Idaho, for Cally's sake. I see now that my resentment is tied up with Mayfield. When Father died, Mummy quickly realized she did not have the resources to maintain Mayfield, even with the school. The person who did have both resources and interest in buying our home was Uncle William's son, William II. Isn't that ironic? If Uncle William hadn't bankrupted Malcomson Brothers by his stupid (forgive me!) mistakes, our inheritance from Grandfather Joseph would have allowed us to keep Mayfield. And with my siblings established elsewhere, it probably would have come to me.

"Thus I'm tangled up in regard to indulging Uncle William's treasure hunt, and I admit I have emotionally withdrawn from it—not just because of my music or because of Laoise. What I don't see is how to reconcile within myself the loss of my beloved home. How can I get past my resentment of a man who has been dead for twelve years? He managed to pass on to his own family significant wealth while depriving us of our 'birthright.' I don't want bitterness to grow in my heart. I don't. Especially with Laoise, I want my soul to be free, at peace, able to embrace joy without complicating factors."

Charlie looked out the window at his nieces chasing each other across the grass, then dipped his pen again. "Perhaps it's this new relationship with Laoise that's making me long for a home of my own. A place where she will be waiting for me, or I for her. A place to come back to together. With all our things in one place, instead of scattered from Dublin to Waterford to New York to Kansas City as they are now. Imagine, having a place that's *ours*. Perhaps that's what would help me heal from the loss of Mayfield."

Putting aside his journal, Charlie took out a sheet of stationery. "My dear Laoise . . . "

"Charlie, what's going on?" asked Margaret. "I've never seen you so distracted."

Charlie blushed. "Is it that obvious? Well, if you have a bit of time, I'll tell you."

"The children are asleep, and Percy is meeting friends at his club, so yes, I have time. Fire away, Chuckles. I'm all yours."

"As you say, Gritty," Charlie laughed. "What memories those nicknames evoke!"

"Yes, but you won't deter me that easily. Did you find buried treasure in Idaho, or have you won some grand music award, or have you found your true love? I suspect the latter."

Charlie blushed again. "Perhaps so. Though there's truth to your other guesses too."

"Tell me, beginning to end, all the wee details. I've waited for this for years and years."

An hour later, Margaret said, "So, when will I get to meet this wondrous woman?"

"How about this weekend? Laoise can come from Dublin on the train Friday and go home Monday. I invited her to play two pieces with me at the Waterford benefit concert. I want to show her Mayfield—maybe Saturday morning? And we'll need some practice time together."

Margaret clapped her hands. "How delightful! I get to be the first one of our family to meet her! Does anyone else know she exists?"

"Mummy does. I wrote her a letter she should have received at Thomas's. So he knows too. And now she's with Cora, and I wrote Cally. But only you know all the wee details."

"And Daniel?"

"Daniel's the one who doesn't know anything at this point. I plan to invite him and Meghan to attend one of Laoise's concerts in Belfast July 15 and 16. I would love to go myself, but I sail for New York, as you know, on July 18." Charlie paused for a sip of port.

"Well then, take the train to Belfast on Thursday, go with Daniel and Meghan to her concert on Friday, and travel back here on Saturday. You'll still have the full day Sunday to rest and prepare to sail on Monday," said Margaret. "How long since you've been to Belfast?"

"Too long. I'll think about that. If I do it, I'd like to surprise Laoise."

"Not all women like surprises," said Margaret.

"I think she does," said Charlie. "There's such a lot to learn about each other."

"If it's like me and Percy, you'll be learning about each other the rest of your life."

"What are you learning about me, dear?" asked Percy, walking into the drawing room.

"Well, just today I learned you don't favor plum pudding," said Margaret. "Why didn't you ever tell me that before?"

"You like it so much I didn't want to spoil your pleasure." Percy kissed his wife and sat next to her on the divan. "What have you two been up to?"

Margaret looked at Charlie. "Do you want to extend your circle of confession?"

"Confession? What does Charlie need to confess?" asked Percy.

"He's in love," said Margaret. "And we get to meet her this weekend."

"Aha," said Percy. "Tell me, Charlie."

"The short version," said Charlie. "Because I've used up my quota of words for the day."

"The short version is perfect," said Percy.

"I miss Mayfield terribly," Charlie told Laoise as they rode to Portlaw Saturday morning. "I was born there, and somehow took it for granted, thinking it would be my home the rest of my life, as it was for my father. But when Father died so unexpectedly, everything changed."

"You've already been through what I fear so much, losing a parent," said Laoise, cradling Charlie's hand between both of hers. "Thank you for sharing this special place with me."

"It won't be the same as when we lived there," said Charlie. "But at least you'll be able to imagine the setting when I talk about my childhood."

"Margaret and Percy have been so kind," said Laoise. "And their children are as charming as you led me to expect. I enjoyed meeting Cook too. She's part of your family, isn't she? How lovely that Margaret invited her into her home when your mother left Mayfield."

"Cook is particularly fond of Thomas," smiled Charlie. "I confess, her food is the standard by which I measure all other cooking."

"Dinner last night was delicious!" said Laoise. "You might as well know now, Charlie, I'm not a good cook. I don't want you to be disappointed when you discover that."

"Perhaps we can learn together," said Charlie, hugging her. "Ah, here we are. I'm glad the baroness is traveling, so we can look around on our own. She's been so gracious, letting our family come here whenever we like. So, Mummy's school was around the other side that way, and the stable is around the side this way, where Midnight used to live. And ..."

"Charlie," Laoise said as they climbed the slope back toward the house from the river. She paused long enough that Charlie stopped walking and looked at her.

"I'm listening, Laoise."

"Charlie, is this—all this—" Laoise gave a wide sweep of her arm. "Is this what you need to be happy? A large estate like this one? There's an intensity about your attachment to Mayfield I need to understand. Because I don't see—"

"You don't see how we could possibly afford something like this, is that it?"

"That's part of it. I can't imagine the costs of maintaining such a place, even if it were owned outright. I don't—" She paused again.

"It's all right. Tell me," said Charlie.

"I don't want to live under financial pressure for the sake of land and buildings, Charlie, charming as they may be. I would rather live in a small, simple place without financial worries than spend my life constantly concerned about money. And I want our life to be *our* life, not our parents' lives. I want to live—how can I say it? I want to live freely, free to be *us*, to create something new together."

Laoise looked at Charlie so anxiously, his heart melted. He started laughing. Laoise's face changed to hurt and bewilderment.

"Oh no, Laoise, I'm not laughing at what you said. I'm laughing at myself. I finally see how I've made this place into an idol of sorts. Bear with me, sweetheart," he chortled. "My laughing is the sound of chains breaking. I can be free, free!"

Charlie ran crazily around Laoise, in a wild dance. After watching him, perplexed, for a moment, she stretched out her hands. Charlie grabbed them and they danced together until Charlie pulled her down with him on the grass in a hug that quickly caught fire. Laoise finally pulled away, putting her hand over Charlie's mouth.

"No, Charlie. We can't. I won't. Not yet. I don't want—"

Charlie pulled Laoise to her feet and knelt before her, his eyes on her face. "Laoise, will you marry me, my darling? Will you live with me in a small, simple place, a place we make beautiful in our own way? Will you walk with me into the future we create together through our love, embracing the complexities of our gifts and callings, figuring out together how to live freely and joyfully? Will you accept my love for you, my passionate desire to be happy together? Laoise, sweetheart, I love you with all my heart."

"Oh my, Charlie. I will. I love you too."

This time, it was Charlie who broke away, took her hand, and walked with her back to the carriage and forward into the new life they would create, together.

"The carriage is here," announced Margaret and Percy's butler Monday morning. "It's raining, sir."

"Thank you, Simpson," said Charlie, handing him Laoise's valise and violin case. "All set, Laoise?"

"Thank you for a wonderful weekend," said Laoise, hugging Margaret and the children. "Please say goodbye to Percy for me."

"You're a beautiful lady," said Sally. "Cate thinks so too."

"Why, thank you, Sally and Cate. I'm glad I met you," said Laoise. "Goodbye, Charlie."

"Uh-uh," said Charlie. "I'm going with you to the station."

"Oh." Laoise put an envelope in her pocket. "Then I won't give this to you yet."

"Now I'm curious," said Charlie as they walked out the door. "Ready to run? Or do you want an umbrella?"

By the time he said this, Laoise was halfway to the carriage. Charlie ran after her, and brushed raindrops from her hat as they settled onto the seat.

"I love rain," said Laoise. "It's so cozy."

"A gentle one like this, me too," said Charlie.

"When will I see you again? This is a repeat of a conversation we've had too many times already. Will it only be in New York City in September?"

"Tell me your schedule for the next few weeks," said Charlie.

"The first week of August, a tour of the British Isles," said Laoise. "Then I have a break until traveling to America mid-August. I'll play in Boston, Baltimore, and Charleston following our concerts with the Philharmonic in September."

"Hmm, we'll have to think more about that. Here we are."

"Until sometime," said Laoise. "I hope sometime will be soon."

"Me too," said Charlie, holding her close. "I'm so glad you could come this weekend. I loved performing with you."

"The audience seemed to like it too," said Laoise, tears shining in her eyes. "Goodbye, my love." She pulled the envelope from her pocket and put it in his hand.

"Goodbye, sweetheart."

Charlie read Laoise's letter as the carriage trundled back to Margaret's house.

My dearest Charlie, how can I say goodbye to you again so soon? I hate this. Is there nothing we can do to be together more often?

As you know, I'm concerned about my mum. I don't know how much time we still have with her, and I desperately want her to be present at our wedding. Do you think that's a good enough reason to consider getting married soon?

If I am shocking you by my forwardness, please forgive me, my love. I know it's been a short time since we reconnected, and we haven't yet spoken of a wedding date. It's complicated, with the commitments we both have and the perplexing question of where we should make our home: Dublin? Waterford? New York? Kansas City? Somewhere else? I am praying God will show us a path forward.

With all my love, until next we meet,

Laoise

Friday morning, July 15

"All set, Charlie?" Margaret brushed a speck from Charlie's suitcoat. "Cook made a lunch for you."

"Always spoiling me. Please tell her thank you."

Charlie hugged his nieces and baby nephew and sister and picked up his bag. "Until Sunday, Gritty." He turned toward the door. A bell chimed.

"A telegram for you, Master Charlie," said Elaine, extending a silver tray.

Charlie set down his bag and opened the telegram. "It's from Mummy," he told Margaret. "There's a special celebration in Idaho next weekend, an art show. Thomas is going. Mummy wonders if I can make it." He pulled out a pocket calendar. "No, I can't. Can you please telegraph back, Margaret, saying sorry, I'll meet them in Boise City."

"Not at the Stricker place?" asked Margaret.

"No. They're going to Boise City after the art show. I'll join them for the ending of the treasure hunt and for a concert on the 30th. I'm afraid I've lost track of some of the details. Cally's been the one who has followed it through, beginning to end."

"It's been wild, that's for sure. And you've been, um, distracted," laughed Margaret. "I'll send the telegram."

"Thank you, sis. You're the best." Charlie kissed her, then picked up his cases and turned toward the door. A bell chimed.

"Another telegram for you, Master Charlie." Elaine once again extended the silver tray.

"This one is from Paudeen," said Charlie. "'Repairs to *Lion III* more extensive than first thought. Ship sailing a day late, July 19.' Perfect timing. Margaret, I can stay an extra day in Belfast and attend both of Laoise's concerts! Perhaps I can meet her brother. Bye!"

This time he made it to the carriage and rode away.

☙❧

"That was spectacular!" said Meghan, as she, Daniel, and Charlie pushed through the crowd toward Laoise Friday evening. "And what fun to surprise her! Oh. . . I see."

Laoise's eyes had locked on Charlie's. *Clearly, Laoise has lost the thread of the current well-wisher's conversation.* Meghan watched the well-wisher track Laoise's gaze as well, back to Charlie. The man smiled.

Meghan poked her husband, whispering, "Daniel, look! Look at the two of them."

"I see," said Daniel. "Well, that answers a lot of questions."

ଔ

"Laoise, is there any way you can come with me?" asked Charlie as they emerged breathless from a kiss on the way to the train station from Daniel and Meghan's on Tuesday. "Any way at all? September in New York feels too far away."

"No way at all," said Laoise. "Maybe after my British Isles tour ends in August—"

"All right. Keep thinking about that. Cally's trial in Kansas City will be in August sometime. We don't know the exact date yet. It's a big event for our family. You could meet my mother, and Thomas and Cora, and—"

Laoise silenced Charlie with another kiss as the carriage slowed and stopped.

"Sir," said the driver.

Charlie started and looked at his watch. "I must hurry, or I'll miss my train. I love you, Laoise. Bye until August!"

"I did say 'maybe,'" said Laoise out loud, staring into the station long after he disappeared. *If Mummy is well ...*

CHAPTER 27

BABY BRIAN

Stricker homesite, Sunday supper, July 10

"WHAT A DELIGHTFUL IDEA, CORA! Could we have an art show here, too?" exclaimed Anna Hansen after Cora described her plan for Kansas City. "John, what do you think? Should we have it at our house? Let's set a date! We can invite everyone in the community."

"How about combining an art show with medical check-ups for the children before they start back to school?" said John. "What do you think, Flora? Are you recovered enough for that? You could note whether any of the adults need attention, too, and schedule appointments for them. You've been out of circulation for a while with this illness."

"I can do it if Cally will help me," said Flora.

"Cally? Do you have medical training too?" asked Anna.

"No, ma'am. That is, not yet. Flora has taught me a few skills, and I hope to be trained as a nurse in Kansas City this next year," said Cally.

"I didn't know that!" said Cora.

"Yes, well, it's a developing idea," said Cally. "I sent away for information from St. Joseph Hospital's training school. Thomas told me about it. It's new—just started in 1901. They've graduated two classes so far."

"I didn't know you've been talking with Thomas about this!" said Cora.

"I sent him a telegram last week asking him to find out whether Kansas City has nurses training schools," said Cally. "He sent me a return telegram just yesterday, and while I was at Hansen's I wrote to St. Joseph's."

"Oh," said Cora, looking hurt.

"I've been watching for a chance to tell you, Cora. Yesterday and this morning you disappeared."

"You're right. I wanted to paint the river, to show that Idaho isn't all desert," said Cora. "I hadn't told you before now about my art show idea either. So, I guess we're even, sis."

"Have you defined dates for visiting Benedicte and May Lee?" asked Cathleen.

"Yes!" said Cora. "We can go on Wednesday and come back Saturday. That is, if you're willing to watch my children, Cally. I'm sorry I haven't asked you before now. I invited Cathleen to go with me to Pocatello and Soda Springs."

"I'll be glad to care for them," said Cally. "I have ideas for projects and adventures."

"What ideas, Mummy?" asked Felicity, walking up to the table.

"We'll talk about it later, when your cousins can be part of the conversation," said Cally, glancing at the rock pile where a group of children played. "I'm surprised you're not playing with your friends."

"I'm sad," said Felicity.

"Why are you sad, sweetheart?"

"Because Mr. Ryan and baby Brian didn't come today," said Felicity. "Miss Priscilla said Brian is sick."

"Oh?" said Flora. "I'll ask Priscilla about it." She walked to the far end of the long table.

Cally pulled Felicity onto her lap. "Shall we say a prayer together for baby Brian?"

"Yes, please, Mummy," said Felicity. "Dear God, please make Brian well." She scrambled down, saying, "I'll go play now, Mummy!"

"The children have a good time together," observed Cathleen.

"Yes, though they scare me with their jumps," said Cora. "One broken leg this summer is enough. I'm trying not to be such a worrier, since all the children do it. I'll feel better if I can't see them." She moved her chair to the other side of the table.

"Cora, John, Flora, when shall we schedule the art show and clinic?" asked Anna. "It's too bad Lucy Stricker isn't back yet from Germany. She would love this."

"If the other two artists could return with Cora, we could have it next Sunday and Monday, right?" said John.

"Umm, I think we need a little more preparation time," said Cora. "How about this: We have the art show and clinic on Friday and Saturday a week later and conclude with a grand supper on Sunday."

"What dates are we talking about?" asked Anna.

"This Friday will be the 15th, right?" said Cora. "So, a week later, July 22nd to 24th. Assuming, of course, that Benedicte and May Lee can come then. And Falling Water."

"Perhaps a grand Sunday supper could double as a farewell to our guests from Kansas City," said Flora. "A way to define the end of their time here."

"I'll ask Thomas if he can come for the weekend before going to Boise City!" said Cora.

"If I understand Charlie's plans correctly, he is scheduled to arrive back here on Tuesday, July 26th," said Cathleen. "Perhaps he could leave

Ireland a few days earlier, to participate in this grand weekend. Perhaps he and Thomas could come together from Kansas City."

"Then will we all travel to Boise City?" asked Cally. "Charlie promised the Eastmans a concert there on July 30th. It would be fun to all be together to receive Uncle William's last packet. You should go with us, Flora! Come to think of it, I bet the Eastmans would enjoy coming for your art show, Cora. I've written Mary Ann about the treasure hunt now and then. She loves feeling part of it."

"I'm not thinking ahead that far yet. We'll see," said Flora.

"I don't know how much time Thomas can take off from work," said Cora. "But I'll certainly ask him! We need to return home for the children to start school the second week of August. Cally, what's wrong?"

"Oh, was I that obvious? I'm sorry. I've started getting worried about the trial. I wish we knew the date," said Cally.

"A trial?" asked Anna.

"It's a long story for another time," said Cora.

"You can stay with me in the meantime," said Flora. "I would love that."

"Thank you, Flora. One thing at a time, isn't that what you've told me, Cathleen?"

"'God's faithfulness is renewed every morning,'" quoted Cathleen.

"It's time for evening prayer," said Cora.

"Flora, what did Priscilla say about Brian?" asked Cally.

"Ryan doesn't think it's serious, but if the baby gets sicker, he'll bring him," said Flora. "Or send a message with Priscilla or Abigail. I gave Priscilla suggestions to pass on to Ryan."

"We can include prayers for Brian in our intercessory time," said Cathleen. "And ask God to direct our plans. John, will you do us the honor of reading this evening?"

"I'll call the children," said Cora. "Did you see where they went, Cally?"

"No. I'll go with you to find them," said Cally.

"Children, where are you?" called Cora, as they rounded the old log store.

Shane's head appeared as he climbed the curving stone steps from the dry cellar, followed by Tucker and Freddy.

"The girls are in jail," said Tucker.

"In jail?" said Cally, running toward the boys. She heard pounding and muted yelling from inside the dry cellar. Todd fiddled with the lock.

"Todd told me the dry cellar used to be a jail," said Shane. "We made a posse and captured the girls and locked them in. We've been trying to let them out, but the lock is stuck."

"I can't get it open," said Todd. "I'm sorry, Miz Cally. We were just playing."

"Let me try," said Cally, carefully descending the steps. "No luck. It's too rusty."

"Keep trying. I'll get help," said Cora, running back to the gathering at the table.

Jerry and John quickly appeared. Cora returned a minute later carrying a small jar of oil. Margaret and Cathleen followed her.

"No more playing in the dry cellar, boys," Jerry said sternly when the girls were finally freed. "As punishment, Todd and Freddy, I'm taking you home now. Sorry not to stay for the prayer time, ladies."

"Shane will miss it as well," said Cora.

"And Tucker," said Margaret. "You'll be a small group tonight, Cathleen."

Monday, July 11

"My mother sent me to fetch Miz Flora," said Abigail, climbing down from her wagon after greeting Shane. "Baby Brian has taken a turn for the worse."

"I'll call her!" yelled Shane, running toward the house. "Mummy, can I go with Miz Flora to Mr. Ryan's house?"

"What's happening, Shane?" asked Cally, wiping her hands as she emerged from the kitchen. "Your mother is out painting somewhere."

"It's baby Brian! He's sicker!" said Shane. "I have to call Miz Flora!"

"I see. Hello, Abigail. Thank you for coming. Do you know anything more about Brian?"

"Only that his fever has gone up and he's crying all the time," said Abigail.

"I heard yelling," said Cora, wiping her paint-stained fingers on a rag as she walked into the homesite through the trees. "What's happening?"

"Baby Brian is worse. Shane has gone to call Flora," said Cally.

"She'll want you to go with her," guessed Cora. "Can the children play by the river so I can finish my painting?"

"Of course. Thank you, Cora. Shane wants to go with us."

"Leave quickly, then, or you'll have all the children wanting to go, especially Felicity. She's in love with that baby. I'll track down the girls and take them to the river after you go. Did anyone offer Abigail a glass of water? Never mind, I'll get it."

"His temperature is elevated, and he's a bit congested, but I don't see a rash," said Flora. "You're right that his neck is swollen. Hold him, Ryan, while I listen to his lungs. ... Clear. Let me feel his throat."

Baby Brian pulled back and cried.

"He has the mumps," said Flora. "Shane, don't come any closer, and don't touch the baby. In fact, you better wait outside. Who was Brian with the last few days, Ryan?"

"Only the Jenners," said Ryan. "Oh, that's not true. Saturday we went to Twin Falls for a new blade for my scythe."

"What day were you with the Jenners?" asked Flora.

"Yesterday. I asked Priscilla for advice about how to care for Brian," said Ryan. "Gabby was there learning baking from Priscilla. She's the only one who held him."

"It's likely the Robison children will get the mumps too, starting with Gabby. It's very contagious," said Flora. "Abigail, can you take us to the Robisons? Eden must keep the baby completely away from the other children, especially Gabby. I don't want Isaac to catch this. It may already be too late."

"Perhaps I could stay with the Robison children at their house while Eden and baby Isaac stay in safety at our house," suggested Abigail. "I'll listen in while you tell Ryan how to care for Brian."

"There's not much to do," said Flora. "The main concern is hydration since it hurts Brian to swallow. If he refuses milk, Ryan, soak a clean rag in honey water and let him suck it. He'll like the sweetness. But keep offering him milk. The worst of the symptoms should disappear on their own in two or three days. If his fever goes up, give him a cool bath and don't bundle him up. This disease is miserable but it's self-limiting and not dangerous for a child as large and healthy as Brian. For infant Isaac it could be another story."

"I remember having the mumps," said Abigail. "My mother gave me applesauce. I liked it."

"That's a good idea. Too bad it's not apple season yet," said Flora.

"Mother might have some jars left over from last year," said Abigail. "If we can stop by my house on the way to the Robisons I can ask her. And ask about Eden and Isaac staying there and pack a few clothes."

"It's generous of you to do this," said Flora. "I would volunteer Cally, but she'll have four children to care for while Cora and Cathleen travel. With luck, we'll prevent the mumps spreading to the homesite. Both of you, watch how I wash my hands, and then copy me while I watch you wash. You too, Ryan."

Cally held out her arms.

"No, just lay the baby down, Ryan. I don't want Cally to hold him today," said Flora.

"Thanks for offering, Cally," said Ryan.

"Has either of you had the mumps, Ryan and Cally?" asked Flora.

"I have," said Ryan.

"Not that I remember," said Cally.

"Then, Cally, stay in the wagon when we reach the Robisons'. It's worse for adults."

"Sorry, Ryan," said Cally.

"I don't want you to get sick," said Ryan.

"You missed a big conversation Sunday," said Cally.

"Tell him about it another time," said Flora. "For baby Isaac's sake, we must hurry. Don't worry about Brian, Ryan. You'll lose some sleep and some work time, but he'll be fine."

"If Gabby gets sick, you can come share the fun at the Robisons' with me," said Abigail.

"Good idea. I don't like doing this alone," said Ryan. "I do worry, Dr. Flora."

"Of course. You're a loving father. But keep telling yourself this will soon pass."

"Ask Priscilla," said Cally to Ryan, walking backward toward the wagon. "We talked about having an art show a week from Friday."

"I'll ask her!" said Ryan. "Don't get sick, Cally. Bye."

I'm not worried about getting sick. I'm disappointed Felicity won't see as much of Ryan or Brian in our short time left here as she hoped. Cally climbed into the back of the wagon with Shane. *Oh, all right, I'll admit it: I'm disappointed for myself too. I liked Ryan calling Flora Doctor Flora. I like him doing so many things considered "women's work." He's not rigid about male and female roles. I like that. Oh, all right, I'll admit it, but only to myself: I like him. I think he likes me a little bit too. Why else would he come over every day I spent at the Robisons'?*

"Aunt Cally!" Shane said loudly.

"Oh, I'm sorry, Shane. What were you saying?"

"I don't remember whether I had the mumps when I was little."

"None of you have had them since I've been with you," said Cally. "That's a good question to ask your mummy. I do know Felicity has not had the mumps."

Jerry was home for lunch when Abigail pulled up at her home. Once he and Priscilla understood the situation, he said, "I'll take Miz Flora and Cally and Shane back to the homesite, Abigail, so you can go to the Robisons and stay. That way Silas can bring Eden and the baby right away. Miz Flora, while Abigail is getting ready, write down for Eden and Silas what you want them to know. Priscilla and I will keep track of the situation at both houses."

"That's sensible, Jerry. Thank you."

"Might as well eat lunch while you're here. We have plenty of leftovers," said Priscilla. "You can write while you eat, Miz Flora. I'll go prepare a room for Eden and Isaac."

"Thank you, Priscilla."

"Potato casserole. Yum!" said Shane, when Jerry brought plates to him and Cally while they waited for Flora in the wagon.

"May I have a piece of paper too, Silas?" requested Cally. *I'll write for Ryan a quick account of our plans, so he won't have to wonder about our conversation on Sunday.*

"Yes, I'll give your note to Ryan," said Jerry when he dropped them off at the homesite. "I've had the mumps. I'll stop in tomorrow to see how Brian is doing."

"Don't touch him!" said Flora. "And wash your hands before you leave Ryan's house. I don't want you bringing germs back to Isaac."

"Yes, ma'am," said Jerry, driving away.

"So, it's reached the letter stage," smiled Flora as they walked into the Stricker house.

Cally blushed. "How else can we get to know each other, with so many people around?"

"Hmm, maybe I can help," said Flora.

Tuesday, July 12

"I have clinic from 1:00 until 4:00 this afternoon," Flora told Cally. "Back to my usual Tuesday rhythm. Can you assist me? If we have time, you could help me go through my supplies. John sends an order for me every two months. I missed one because I was sick."

"I'll confirm it with Cora," said Cally. "I don't think she'll mind watching Felicity, since I'll have her three kids on my own for four days. No word about Brian, right? Or about Gabby?"

"No news is good news," said Flora. "Did Cora breakfast early, or is she sleeping late?"

"She was up when it was still dark. Wanted to paint the sunrise," said Cally. "The art show has lit a fire under her. I expect to see the children tumbling out of the station any minute."

"They were up late last night. But wasn't the campfire fun?" said Flora, petting Fauna. "The singing, the stories, the jokes. That Josie is a stitch!"

"She's a livewire all right, with her own brand of humor," said Cally.

"The one I don't feel I know as well is Shauna," said Flora. "What powers her wheel? I've found that such a useful expression since you taught it to me!"

"I think Shauna will be a philosopher and a poet. She observes everything, writes it all down, and makes interesting connections. I was like her as a child."

"You were? I wouldn't have guessed that."

"I lost my childhood journals. It would be entertaining to read them now," said Cally.

"Did you grow up in Kansas City?" asked Flora.

"Oh no. I moved there shortly before Felicity was born," said Cally. "I spent my first years in Ireland."

"It's interesting how you switch to Irish terms when you think about Ireland."

"Do I?" said Cally. Fauna jumped up and ran toward the station. "Here come the children!" *Good timing. I don't want to think about my childhood right now.*

"Is any breakfast left?" yelled Shane. "What shall we do today, Aunt Cally?"

"I think we should clean out Cammie's stall," said Cally. "Dr. Flora hasn't been able to do that because she's been sick. I think Cammie will be grateful."

"Eeyouuu," said Shauna, wrinkling her nose. "Can I feed and brush Cammie instead?"

"We'll all take a turn with the cleaning," said Cally. "That's fair, don't you think? Focus on how happy Cammie will be when we're finished."

"And how grateful I'll be," said Flora. "Thanks for the wonderful idea, Cally!"

"If we work hard, we'll have time to splash in the river before lunch," said Cally.

"Who's making lunch, Aunt Cally?" asked Shauna. "Maybe I can do that."

"Nice try, sweetheart. I already made it," said Cally, tickling Shauna. "Eat your breakfast and I'll meet you all at Cammie's stall. Who knows—maybe we'll find a treasure under all that muck! No more jam, Felicity. Save some for Josie."

"I don't want jam. I want honey," said Josie. "Shane showed me how good it is."

"All right. I'll see you in a few minutes," said Cally, walking to the kitchen to wash the oatmeal pot. *I wish it weren't so hard to communicate with neighbors. I wonder how Ryan is reacting to what I told him about our plan to leave in two weeks. Oh well. I need to come up with a treasure to hide in the muck for the children to find.*

CHAPTER 28

RYAN

Stricker homesite, Saturday afternoon, July 16

FAUNA LEAPED TO HER FEET AND RAN DOWN THE TRAIL.

"They're back!" shouted Shane, jumping up from the card game he played with Shauna. The twins raced after Fauna, rounding the bend.

"Where's Grandma?" asked Shauna. "Oh, I see Josie and Felicity, so Aunt Cally stopped at Miz Margaret's on the way here, left Grandma, and picked up the girls."

"Welcome back!" said Flora, stepping onto the porch with a tray of glasses as the group trooped toward the house. "I tried my hand at making lemonade!"

"Mmm, delicious!" said Cora. "You're hired, Flora. I won't have to make it anymore."

"I'm sure you told Cally all about your trip," said Flora. "Are the art shows on, both here and in Kansas City?"

"Yes!" said Cora. "I'm so excited. Benedicte's photographs and May Lee's paintings are fabulous. And it was a pleasure to get to know them, too. They will arrive on Thursday."

"I like your paintings the best, Mummy," said Josie.

"Thank you, sweetheart, but wait till you see the other women's work. I'm delighted to showcase their gifts and Falling Water's too. I'm glad she confirmed before we traveled." Cora turned to the twins. "How are you two? I've missed you!"

"They've done a whole lot of work around here," said Flora. "I'm calling them the Dynamic Duo. I wish I had their energy."

"Come see what we did in the barn, Mummy," said Shauna.

"Give me a minute to get out of these travel clothes," said Cora. "Then I'm all yours."

"Are you feeling well, Flora?" asked Cally. "I wasn't happy about leaving you this morning with that headache."

"I'm better, thank you, Cally," said Flora. "I spent the morning mostly resting. I intend to consult Falling Water about these ongoing headaches. I wonder whether they are a long-term effect from the spotted fever."

"I've heard of headaches called migraines," said Cally.

"Yes. But I never had headaches before I got sick. Did you know, Cally, that migraines are the first human malady mentioned in ancient literature? Sorry—I love medical trivia."

"Well, I hope you get over your headache before we leave."

"I do too," said Flora. "There come the twins and Cora. I'm amused by how they take ownership, even though it's you who thought up projects for them."

"They're happy and one way or another, the work gets done," said Cally. "Cora, I forgot to ask—will Cathleen join us for supper, do you think?"

"I doubt it," said Cora. "I don't think we'll see her until tomorrow. What's been going on around here? Any more mumps?"

"It's making the rounds of the children," said Flora. "Eden and Isaac are still at the Jenners. So far so good. Someday when he's older he can get the mumps too without consequence."

"What about baby Brian?" asked Cora.

"Did you say baby Brian?" asked Felicity, running over from her doll house in the rock pile. "He's fine! Mr. Ryan brought him yesterday to show Dr. Flora."

Cora noticed Flora glance at Cally. *Hmm, something is going on here ...*

"Fauna let me give Brian a ride on her back," Felicity continued. "She walked slowly and carefully so Brian didn't get hurt. She did, Mummy!"

"Felicity and I had a small disagreement about whether that was an appropriate activity for Brian," explained Cally. "You're right, sweetheart. No one got hurt. But—"

"Fauna is sensitive to small children," said Flora. "I'm surprised you aren't all in the river, as hot as it is."

"Can we, Mummy?" arose from all four children.

"We can," said Cora and Cally together.

Sunday morning, July 17

"Felicity, would you like to help me take care of baby Brian this afternoon?" asked Flora.

"Yes! Will Mr. Ryan be here too?"

"Mr. Ryan wants to show your Mummy something. He's going to take her for a ride in his wagon before Sunday supper," said Flora.

"I could hold Brian in the wagon," said Felicity.

"I think he'll enjoy his nap more if he's not bouncing around," said Flora. "Come help me make a bed for him on the floor of my bedroom. They will be here soon."

"All right," said Felicity.

"Where there's a will, there's a way!" laughed Ryan. "I had the will and Flora conjured the way."

"Where are we going?" asked Cally.

"I want to show you one of my favorite spots along Rock Creek," said Ryan. "It's a quiet stream, but there's one place where it goes over a waterfall, making a deep pool. I think it's beautiful. I haven't had time lately, but I used to go there often."

"With Bethany?" asked Cally.

"Yes, or by myself," said Ryan. "Don't you love places where you can relax and enjoy God's beauty?"

"I do," said Cally. "I found a spot near the homesite where I like to journal and pray."

"I have so many things I want to ask you," said Ryan. "But I don't want to be nosy. So just tell me if you don't feel comfortable talking about something I bring up. All right?"

Cally nodded. "Same here, Ryan. One thing I've guessed is that there's a story behind naming your son Brian. It can't be accidental that you made your two names rhyme."

"That's unfortunate, perhaps. Bethany and I planned to name him Samuel. But when she died and my world fell apart, I wanted a strong name, and Brian was the strongest I could think of. Do you know the story of Brian Boru?"

"Of course! I'm Irish," said Cally.

"Here we are," said Ryan, pulling over near a shady glen. "Can you hear the waterfall? It's a short walk from here." He jumped down from the wagon seat and offered Cally a hand. "We were talking about Brian Boru. I remember Da telling me stories. Naming my son after him is a way of keeping my Da close. Even though he's been gone so long I hardly remember him."

"Where is your family from in Ireland?" asked Cally.

"County Cork. Priscilla told me. I would love to go there some day to see what my parents left behind when they emigrated. Perhaps I even have relatives there. I have no idea."

"I'm from County Cork too!" exclaimed Cally. "Until I was seven, I lived on a farm near a small town named Killeagh. I still have relatives there. In fact, Cathleen knows them. She brought me a letter when she came from Ireland."

"I've been trying to figure out your relationship with Cathleen," said Ryan. "Felicity calls her grandma but you and Cora both call her Cathleen. Was your husband her son, then?"

"No. It's a bit complicated. Cora and Thomas adopted me as their sister when Felicity was a baby. So, she calls them aunt and uncle and calls Cathleen grandma. But we're not related by blood. Oh, lovely!"

A cascade splashed into a green pool. Trees bent over the water. Cally stood for a moment relishing the coolness of water and shade.

"'The world is full of magical things patiently waiting for our wits to grow sharper,'" murmured Ryan. "William Butler Yeats. I've been reading his poetry, trying to find my Irish roots. And John Woolman, to understand my Quaker parents."

This place reminds me of my magical experience in Glenbower Wood. But I don't know Ryan well enough to tell him about that.

"Where did you get the books?" asked Cally.

"They belonged to my parents. Priscilla saved them and a few other things from my family. I've treasured them for years but only now started reading them."

"Maybe because you're trying to figure yourself out now that Bethany is gone," said Cally. "My father used to quote Yeats too. 'Red rose, proud rose, sad rose of all my days.' Da said it's about the suffering and the beauty of Ireland. Yeats likes to write poems about roses, so lovely despite their thorns. I've always loved them, enough to name my daughter Felicity Rose."

"It's a beautiful name. Shall we sit on this log?" asked Ryan.

"This is so soothing, Ryan. Thank you for sharing your special place with me."

"You're welcome. May I ask, Cally: did Felicity's father die?"

Cally took a deep breath. *I knew this would come up sooner or later.* "No, he's in jail. Felicity was born as a result of assault. She's never met her father, and I don't want her to."

"Oh my, Cally. You've been through a lot. I had no idea," said Ryan. "I'm glad Thomas and Cora adopted you."

"Me too," said Cally. "God has cared for us in amazing ways. Your life hasn't been easy either, Ryan. Like me, you lost your parents. Would you like to tell me more about Bethany?"

"She was young, seven years younger than me, just fifteen when I met her," said Ryan. "This is one of my quarrels with God. How could he take someone so young, so beautiful, so full of life? For what purpose? I don't understand it. I've been angry as well as sad. For months I shut myself up and didn't see anyone except Jerry. I poured my life into Brian. He's the only good thing to come out of this terrible situation."

"Sometimes anger is an easier emotion to feel than grief," said Cally. "That's been my experience, anyway. Anger gives me a feeling of power when my life is unmanageable. But Cathleen has been helping me explore what's underneath the anger. I didn't know I had so much pain hidden away under there. I recommend talking to her if you get the chance."

"Interesting. I hadn't thought about my anger that way, as a defense to hide behind. But I can see it's true."

Cally sat quietly, watching the flow of the water. After a moment, Ryan spoke again.

"Cally, I need to make something clear to you. I don't know how long it may take me to 'get over' Bethany, or whether I ever will. My life turned inside out when she died. But I desperately want a friend, someone near my own age who can understand my struggles because life hasn't always been easy for her either. Can you be my friend? I feel so lonely sometimes. A four-month-old is not the best conversationalist in the world."

"I understand, Ryan. I often feel lonely too. I'll be leaving soon, but if we can write letters and share our joys and griefs, that would be delightful for me," said Cally.

"Flora told me you may go to Boise City and then come back here for two or three weeks before you return to Kansas City," said Ryan.

"Possibly. I'm waiting to find out the date of an event in Kansas City," said Cally.

"May I ask what kind of event?" asked Ryan.

"I've been accused of stealing a horse," said Cally. "No, don't laugh—it's serious."

"I know how valuable horses are around here," said Ryan, sobering immediately. "I laughed because a horse thief is the last label I would ever imagine pinning on you."

"Thanks—I guess. The trial is supposed to take place in August, but we don't yet know the date. Thomas thinks it would be unwise for me to return to Kansas City before the trial because there's a reward out for me."

"With a wanted poster and everything?" said Ryan.

"Yes, a wanted poster and everything. In the newspapers, on the walls of the courthouse, the post office, the police station ... a good likeness, too. I saw it in the *Kansas City Star.*"

"Who'd have guessed, Cally? You *look* harmless!" He poked her and she laughed.

"Thanks for helping me see humor in the situation. Cora tells me I'm too serious."

"Then tell me, what are five of your favorite things? Don't think about it. Just say the first five things that come to your mind."

"Cora's sculptures. Felicity's laughter. Sewing pleats exactly right. My brother Charlie's music. Sitting in a beautiful place like this one talking to a new and interesting friend," said Cally. "Your turn."

"Birthing baby lambs. Bethany's cookies. Sunsets in winter. Brian's soft skin. Diving into cool water on a hot summer day." As he spoke, Ryan pulled off his shirt and shoes and threw himself into the pool formed by the waterfall. "It's refreshing!" he yelled. "I don't suppose you want me to splash you?"

"No, I don't," laughed Cally. "But if you promise not to splash, I'll dip my feet in. I don't want to get my dress wet before Sunday supper. ... Oh, this feels so good!"

"The day will come when women won't have to wear so many clothes," said Ryan.

"Oh, so you're a prophet?" asked Cally.

"No, just practical," said Ryan, treading water. "Don't tell anyone, but when it was just Bethany and me on the farm, she wore pants and a shirt, like me. 'Unbelievable freedom,' she used to say. I can't believe other women won't catch on. I just entrusted you with one of my secrets, Cally! If you want to tell me one of yours, I promise it won't go anywhere else."

"I want to write a book someday," said Cally. "Not a serious book—a fun book. Don't forget—you promised not to tell!"

"As long as you include at least one woman wearing pants, I won't tell," said Ryan, flicking water in Cally's face. "Sadly, I think it's time for us to head back. We don't want to raise eyebrows by arriving late for Sunday supper."

"This has been delightful, Ryan," said Cally, pulling her feet out of the water. "May I drive?"

CHAPTER 29

THE ART SHOW

John and Anna Hansen's home, Rock Creek, early Friday morning, July 22

"I CAN'T BELIEVE THIS!" exclaimed Cally, tears running down her cheeks as she stared at a painting May Lee had leaned against the fireplace.

"Cally, are you all right? What's wrong?" asked Anna, running over to her from Falling Water's display of beautiful baskets.

"This picture," said Cally, waving her hand at the painting. "I saw this. I *saw* it, by Grays Lake, on the way to Caribou Mountain. The old covered wagon. I can't believe it. The painting exactly matches the memory in my head." She looked around. "Where's May Lee?"

"I don't know. She must have stepped out for a moment," said Anna.

"I want this painting," said Cally. "Please don't let anyone else buy it."

"Shall I put a 'Sold' sticker on it?" asked Anna. "I don't know what May Lee will charge. It's gorgeous."

"The price doesn't matter," said Cally. "There's one other painting of May Lee's I want if she brought it to sell. A wolf."

"Over there by the window," said Anna. "A 'Sold' sticker on that one too?"

"Yes, please. For Flora," said Cally. "I can't believe this," she said again, quietly this time. *Thou shalt be a watered garden ... Calico talking about resilient flowers ... You were speaking to me, weren't you, God? This painting will help me never forget.*

"Yesterday went well, don't you think, John?" asked Anna. "I'm pleased Cally bought May Lee's striking wolf painting for Flora. It does look uncannily like Fauna. I'm not sure how much our artists have left to sell."

"Both the art show and the clinic were successful. The whole Rock Creek community turned out, at least a hundred people. Do you think anyone will come back today?" asked John.

"If they don't, we'll have a lot of lemonade to give away!" said Anna, stirring a huge pot. "There's not a single lemon left in the store. And almost no sugar."

"A delivery from California is due on the train Monday. I ordered a surprise for Flora."

"You did? What is it?" asked Anna.

"Have you noticed how worn her shoes are? I don't think Flora pays attention to things like that. Sunday I engaged that Malcomson girl—Shauna, I think her name is—to sneak into Flora's room to find out her shoe size. I ordered two pairs, one sturdy and one a little nicer, though it wouldn't meet your standards for dress shoes, my dear. I think Flora will be pleased."

"John, you are so thoughtful!" said Anna, kissing him. "What did you order for me?"

"You'll have to wait for Monday," John said, his eyes twinkling. "I've enjoyed getting to know Miss Wrensted and Miss May Lee. I'm seeing Idaho with new eyes through their art. And Mary Ann Eastman is remarkable in her own way. A very kind woman."

"I'm glad you built us a house spacious enough for events like this, John. Is it about six weeks until Flora will move back? I intend to give her clinic a good scrub before then."

"I see people gathering. Are you ready to open?"

Anna joined her husband at the front window. "As soon as Cora arrives with the ladies from the hotel. I don't see Flora, though. I hope she knows she can come straight in to set up."

"She was so tired after seeing patients all day yesterday, I suggested she rest this morning, Anna. We'll open the clinic whenever she shows up."

"I need to settle with the artists the things I want to buy, mostly to decorate Flora's clinic. Including a set of Falling Water's pretty baskets to hold supplies."

"All right, my dear. Here are the ladies," said John. "I'll go close the store so Johnny and Annabelle can have fun too."

"They'll love that!" said Anna. "Good morning, Benedicte, May Lee, Mary Ann, Cora. Did you sleep well? Has anyone seen Falling Water? Let's open the doors!"

"Cally and Shane should be here soon with Thomas. I'm glad he'll make it for the afternoon," Cora told Anna late morning. "Thank you for helping all of us with sales."

"It's my pleasure. I expected Falling Water this morning," said Anna.

"I did too. She said she would bring more baskets today."

"Strange. Do you have anything left, Cora?"

"One or two. This one I planned to take home to Kansas City, but I can paint another there." Cora pulled a large canvas from behind a sofa.

"Cora! This is stunning. Let's give it pride of place over the fireplace. Put a high price on it, please, so no one else will buy it. John!" Anna called.

John broke away from his conversation with Silas Robison. "Yes, dear?"

"Can you please take down May Lee's painting, which I already bought for the clinic, and hang this one of Cora's over the fireplace? Cora, I can feel the coolness of the water, with the sun dappling through the branches. And the ducks on the water are charming. Oh my. I do want this one."

"Excuse me, Anna," said Cora. "Someone is looking at my painting of the log cabin."

"Here we are! Remember your first time here, Thomas, finding Flora so sick?" said Cally. "While you and Shane freshen up at the pump, I'll get the sandwiches I made to eat on our way to the art show."

"Mummy will be so happy to see you, Daddy," said Shane. "The girls, too. And Miz Flora. She tells everyone you saved her life."

"Who is that, Shane?" asked Thomas, pointing to a horse galloping around the curve.

"It's Falling Water's son, Walter! Look—I think he's bleeding, Daddy!" said Shane.

Thomas raced after Shane, just in time to break Walter's fall as he pitched forward.

"Attacked," said Walter, and passed out on the ground, blood spurting from his head.

"Cally, help!" shouted Shane, running back toward the house. "Walter's hurt!"

"What happened?" cried Cally. She rushed out, Fauna at her heels. "Oh my. Press your handkerchief on the wound, Thomas. I'll get bandages and water. Shane, take Walter's horse and fetch Flora from the Hansens' as fast as you can."

"His leg is bleeding too," Thomas told Cally when she returned. "Who would do this? And why?" Cally substituted a clean cloth for

Thomas's blood-soaked handkerchief while Thomas ripped Walter's already ruined pants to examine his thigh.

"I hope Flora gets here soon," said Cally. "That gash will need stitches for sure. Take over again with his head and I'll apply a pressure bandage to his thigh. Flora taught me how."

Walter moaned and tried to sit up, lifting his hand toward his head.

"Easy, Walter," said Thomas. "Lie still. Your head is still bleeding. Shane has gone for Dr. Flora. Can you sip some water? Cally will help you as soon as she bandages your leg."

"Attack," said Walter. "My mother. My son." Then he lost consciousness again.

"He must have lost a lot of blood," said Thomas. "And more people were attacked than just Walter. What can we do?"

"Let me think," said Cally. "At the art show, people will miss Falling Water. When Shane tells them about Walter, I expect a group will take off for the Shoshone settlement. I don't think there's anything we can do until Flora gets here."

"Flora can care for Walter better in her clinic," said Thomas. "Can we move him? He's bigger than I am. I don't think I'm strong enough to lift him into the wagon."

"We could try using the cart Walter made when Freddy broke his leg. It's behind the barn." She tied the bandage on Walter's thigh as securely as she could and watched it for a moment to see whether blood continued to seep. "I'll get it."

"This can work, I think," said Thomas when Cally returned hauling the cart. "I'll anchor the wheels with stones. Now, can you hold the pressure on his head, Cally, while I pull Walter up?" Thomas grunted with the effort. "He hasn't regained consciousness. And he's cold as ice, despite the heat of the day. I think he's in shock."

"We should put his head lower than his heart," said Cally. "But that might increase the bleeding from his head. Flora, we need you!"

As Thomas and Cally pulled Walter into the clinic, they heard the beat of hooves. Flora rushed in saying, "I just need to wash my hands. ... Now then. Help me move him to the bed, Thomas."

"Has anyone gone to the Shoshone settlement, Flora?" asked Thomas, covering Walter with a blanket and handing Cally a fresh cloth for his head.

"A group of men took off immediately," nodded Flora. "Falling Water didn't show up for the art show. Did Walter tell you anything?"

"He said, 'Attack. My mother. My child,'" said Cally, watching Flora stitch Walter's thigh wound. "Who would attack, and why?"

"At the art show a man told us the Shoshone had been ordered to move to the Fort Hall Reservation," said Flora. "Walter resisted, saying they were on the land of their people. Perhaps soldiers from Fort Hall attacked Walter so the rest of the People would move to the reservation out of fear. The army is supporting the 'clearing of the Indians' so their land can be sold to settlers attracted by the irrigation canal."

"I can imagine Falling Water reacting to protect her son," said Cally. "I'm terrified she may be dead."

"Maybe his son tried to protect Walter too?" said Thomas. "What a horrible situation!"

"You always show up at a moment of crisis, Thomas," said Flora.

"I'm happy to see you healthier than when I left," said Thomas. "What more can we do for Walter? Isn't it worrisome he hasn't woken up yet?"

"It is. I wish we had a way to get fluids into him," said Flora. "I have no way of knowing how much blood he lost. Has the bleeding eased at all, Cally?"

"Yes," said Cally. "I think we can apply a pressure bandage."

"I'll use his chin to anchor the bandage. Don't touch the wound unless it starts bleeding again, more than seeping. Thomas, fill a pitcher from the pump, and then care for the horses. Cally, when he wakes, help him sip water, as much as he'll take every couple of minutes." While she spoke, Flora filled a bag with supplies.

"Are you leaving?" asked Cally in alarm.

"There may be others injured at the settlement. Cammie is rested enough, I think, for us to take her with the wagon. Set the water here, Thomas."

"One question, Flora. Shane?" asked Thomas.

"Cora insisted he stay with her at the Hansens'."

Thomas nodded and ran out the door to the horses.

"Cally, Walter will be in pain when he wakes. Give him willow bark. I see no evidence of internal bleeding, but ask him what happened in more detail, to help us understand whether he has other injuries. Give him broth from yesterday's soup, too, if he'll take it."

"Flora—I'm sorry. Falling Water and her family are precious to all of us, but especially to you," said Cally.

Flora stood still for a moment, her head down. Then she wiped her eyes, took a deep breath, and said, "If it's as bad as we fear, there will be time for grieving later. Right now, we must do what we can to contain the damages." She picked up her bag and strode out the door.

A small and sober group gathered around the outdoor table that evening. Cathleen had gone home with Margaret. Flora, grieving, shut herself in her room, Fauna keeping guard outside her door. Under Cally's watchful eye, Walter still slept. Felicity insisted she and Lizzy eat supper with her mother.

"Let's go for a walk," suggested Thomas to his family. "We're all so sad about Falling Water and Walter Jr.'s deaths, I haven't had a chance yet to hear about the art show."

"You missed seeing Mummy's beautiful paintings, Daddy," lamented Shauna as they walked toward the river, Josie's hand in Thomas's. "People bought them all."

"But I'll paint more after we go home, Shauna. I have them tucked away right here." Cora tapped her forehead. "I want to paint Falling Water while I still remember her clearly."

"I enjoyed seeing Benedicte and May Lee again," said Thomas. "It seems they did well at the show, too."

"Yes, they must both create more works for Kansas City," said Cora. "I think this event showed May Lee her paintings can matter to other people."

"But now Falling Water can't go to Kansas City," said Josie, starting to cry. "Daddy, I want to go home."

"Let's sit here," said Thomas, noticing a log by the river. He lifted Josie to his lap, and Shauna and Shane pressed into him on both sides. Cora stood behind them, ruffling Thomas's hair, staring at the river. Together, they wept.

❧

"What do you think about Boise City, Cora, with all that's happened?" Thomas asked after their children were asleep. They sat in the clinic, watching still-unconscious Walter so Cally could put Felicity to bed.

"Like Josie, I just want to go home. What about you, Thomas?"

"I have mixed feelings. I want to help you create some normalcy again for our family. And I want to support Cally in concluding this treasure hunt. It will be hard for her to go to Boise City alone. Charlie will arrive there soon, however, for his concert on Saturday."

"The Hansens have planned a big Sunday supper at their house tomorrow evening," said Cora. "I do want to stay for that. It will give the community a chance to mourn Falling Water and Walter Junior's deaths."

"A type of memorial service," said Thomas.

"Yes. John and Anna want everyone to sign letters protesting the aggression of the soldiers, one to send to Washington and one to the commanding officer at Fort Hall. I don't know whether they will make any difference, but it's something we can do." Cora sighed. "I've learned there are people who don't even believe the Shoshone have souls. Can you believe that? They equate killing Indians with killing animals. It makes me want to return to Ireland."

"Where many still view the Catholic Irish in similar terms," said Thomas. "Daniel has written me about the seething unrest. He fears another bloody uprising demanding independence from the British. We know England won't easily give up Ireland. It's too profitable to them."

"The Irish have too long labored and starved to fatten the British," said Cora. "Injustice seems to be everywhere."

"Including in the south of this country," said Thomas. "Cousin Silas wrote me a long letter detailing the laws that have been passed to oppress the former slaves and limit their ability to control their own futures. In some states they can't vote anymore or hold office or respectable jobs. Silas wonders whether I can take any time this fall to join him on his lecture tour."

"I don't have brain space to think about that yet," said Cora. "I hear Cally in the kitchen. She offered to watch over Walter tonight. You can sleep in her bed."

"On the floor, right?" Thomas laughed. "Anywhere will do, as long as I'm with you."

"I can't think anymore tonight about Boise City," said Cora.

"Then let's say goodnight to Cally and go find our floor," said Thomas.

CHAPTER 30

THE TREASURE

Stricker Homesite, Monday morning, July 25

"YOU UNDERSTAND WHY I'M GOING HOME, don't you, Cally?" asked Cora after breakfast.

"Of course," said Cally. "I would love to go home too. Except I can't. Have you heard anything yet about the date of the trial, Thomas?"

"Not yet," said Thomas. "My assistant will send a telegram if he learns anything."

"So, Cora, you, Shauna and Josie will leave for Kansas City Wednesday, while Thomas, Shane, Felicity, and I will travel to Boise City to meet with Mr. Eastman. Charlie will join us there. What about Cathleen?" asked Cally.

"We'll ask her when she comes for lunch," said Cora.

"Say, Cally, who was that handsome young man sitting beside you and Felicity at Sunday supper?" asked Thomas.

"A friend," said Cally. "His name is Ryan Byrne. Felicity is enchanted with his baby son, Brian. His wife Bethany died a few months ago in childbirth."

"I'm sorry to hear that," said Thomas. "Very recently, then."

"Yes. He loved Bethany dearly. It's a terrible loss, for him and for wee Brian."

"If you can be a good friend to Ryan, it will mean a lot. His name sounds Irish."

"Yes. And his family was Quaker, like your father's family. Ryan was orphaned when his parents died from cholera on their way to Oregon when he was four. Flora cared for him until another farm family took him in." *I need to change the subject before Thomas asks more questions.* "Flora sure said nice things about us all at Sunday supper, didn't she? I'm glad Eden and her family could be there, finally mump-free."

"People have treated us so graciously," said Cora. "Flora will miss us, I think, especially with Falling Water gone too. I'm glad she'll move back to the Hansens' in September."

"I'm glad I could be here at the beginning and at the end of your time here," said Thomas. "Charlie missed the Stricker experience entirely."

"When does he expect to arrive in Boise City?" asked Cally.

"Thursday, I believe, assuming no further delays with his ship," said Thomas. "He'll be riding west while you and the girls travel east, Cora."

"You can wave to him out the train window," said Shane, joining the adults. "You don't mind me going to Boise City, do you, Mummy?"

"Of course, I don't mind," said Cora, hugging him. "You've invested so much in the treasure hunt. You must finish it."

"Daddy, Dr. Flora says I have to ask you if I may take a turn sitting with Walter."

"You may, son. Follow Dr. Flora's directions carefully," said Thomas.

"Where are the girls?" asked Cora.

"They're sitting by the river, trying to figure out what they can do for Falling Water's family. They haven't come up with anything yet," said Shane. "No one feels like playing."

"I'll go find them," said Cora.

"I've noticed a few things need repair around here," said Thomas. "When you finish your turn with Walter, you can help me, Shane. First, we'll drive to Rock Creek to call the bank in Boise City for an appointment with Mr. Eastman on Friday."

Shane brightened. "Thank you, Daddy!"

Idanha Hotel, Boise City, Wednesday evening, July 27

"Did we get the same room, Mummy?" asked Felicity.

"I don't know yet, sweetheart," said Cally. "Uncle Thomas is checking us in. I'm looking forward to sleeping in a bed again!"

"I'm glad you came with us, Grandma," said Felicity, swinging Cathleen's hand.

"I wouldn't miss it," said Cathleen.

"Lizzy is excited to be back here. Will we eat that food again, what was it called?"

"Basque. Yes, if you like, Felicity. It's unique, Cathleen. I think you and Thomas will enjoy it. Oh, there he comes," said Cally.

"What took so long, Thomas?" asked Cathleen.

"I received a telegram about the trial," said Thomas, looking at Cally. "It's scheduled for Tuesday, August 23rd."

"Oh," said Cally. She frowned and said nothing more.

Thomas waited a moment, watching Cally. Then he said, "Oh, and I had some work issues to resolve. Now we can go find our rooms!"

"And then eat rice pudding!" said Felicity.

"And *solomo*. And flan!" said Cally.

"There were two messages for you, Cally," said Thomas, handing them to her as they walked to the elevator, followed by three bellboys carrying their luggage.

"This one is from the Eastmans!" said Cally. "They've invited us for dinner Friday evening. We can phone from the desk when we go back downstairs. I would like to accept."

"I enjoyed meeting Mary Ann at the art show," said Cathleen. "Are you all right, Cally? About the trial?"

"It's a relief to know the date, and a bit scary at the same time. But I'll spend three more weeks with Flora! And Felicity will start school!"

"Mummy, when am I going to see Jenny?" asked Felicity.

Cally read the second message. "The Hanovers are inviting you to play Saturday afternoon."

I don't remember the bed being too soft. Cally scrunched her pillow and turned over, but sleep didn't come. *I can't stop worrying about the trial. For all these weeks it felt unreal, like it couldn't possibly be true. I hoped it would be cancelled or disappear somehow.*

Cally slipped out of bed, grabbed her shawl, and tiptoed into the sitting room. Pushing aside a curtain, she looked out at a clear sky and a full moon. *Last time we were here, I had a terrible nightmare. Since Cathleen came, I haven't had any bad dreams!*

"In peace I will lie down and sleep, for you alone will keep me safe." Aisling's prayer again. Thank you, God.

Cally wandered around the room, idly looking at the paintings hanging on the walls.

"Thou shalt be like a watered garden."

Oh. That hasn't crossed my mind for some time. What does it mean? She stopped in front of a garden painting by Abbott Fuller Graves. *Does it mean you have plans for my life? So I don't have to worry about the trial?*

"I will never leave you or forsake you."

Cally felt her eyes grow heavy. She returned to the bedroom and eased back into bed beside Felicity. *Thank you, God. I like talking with you.*

"Charlie won't make it until tomorrow afternoon," said Thomas, joining Cally and Cathleen for a late breakfast Thursday morning. "I was able to change our appointment at the bank to four o'clock. Charlie will go there directly from the station."

"Why the delay?" asked Cathleen.

"The track repair Cora's train encountered on their way home."

"Oh, is everyone all right?" asked Cally.

"They're fine. Cora telegraphed me from Fort Collins. They should arrive home this evening. I have something for you, Cally. I'm sorry I forgot it with all that happened at the Strickers'." Thomas handed Cally an envelope.

"It's from St. Joseph's ... I've been accepted for nurses training! Classes begin August 29th. Unless—" Cally stopped, her smile turning to a frown.

"Unless what? Oh, I know. The trial," said Thomas.

"Yes," said Cally softly. "What if—"

"Not a chance," said Thomas. "It's something you have to do, that's all."

Cathleen gave her hand a warm squeeze.

"What's good for breakfast in Boise City, Idaho?" asked Thomas.

❧

An assistant ushered Cally, Thomas, Cathleen, Shane, and Felicity into the bank's conference room promptly at four o'clock Friday afternoon. As he served them glasses of water, and lollipops for the children, a knock sounded. Charlie entered, panting and sweaty.

"You made it, Uncle Charlie!" exclaimed Shane.

"I ran all the way from the station," said Charlie.

"I surmise there is cause for celebration," said Mr. Eastman, smiling as he opened the door. "A question for all of you. May Mary Ann join us? She's been living and breathing this treasure hunt since you left here in May, Cally."

"Of course, she can join us," said Charlie, glancing at the others for affirmation. "Welcome, Mrs. Eastman. It's lovely to see you again."

"Please, call me Mary Ann, Charlie. Hello, Cally, Felicity, Cathleen, Thomas, Shane. I had such fun at the art show." She frowned. "Until the end, when the Indian woman was killed. But I want to have an art show here in Boise City. Do you think Cora would come?"

"You'll have to ask her," said Thomas.

"Sit down, everyone. Do we have enough chairs?" said Mr. Eastman. "Now then. Thomas or Charles, one of you accompany me to the safe, to fetch the final packet."

"Go ahead, Thomas," said Charlie. "I need to catch my breath."

"Charlie," said Cathleen. "On the *Lion III,* did you see—"

"Billy? No, Mummy, I'm sorry. Paudeen told me he left the ship when they returned to Ireland after your crossing. No one knows where he is."

"I don't want my lollipop anymore," said Shane.

"I am to open the packet," said Mr. Eastman. He withdrew a single sheet of paper, a thick envelope, and a small parcel. "The envelope goes to the eldest male Malcomson pursuing the treasure hunt." He bowed to Thomas. "You will determine dispersal of its contents."

Thomas glanced around the table. "Our family doesn't function quite that way. But I accept being the one to administer what I presume to be money. With full consultation."

Mr. Eastman smiled. "The parcel is meant for any female Malcomson present, or one attached to the eldest male Malcomson," he said. "I believe that is you, Mrs. Malcomson."

"Oh no," said Cathleen. "Cally's the one who persevered through this treasure hunt beginning to end. She should have it."

Mr. Eastman inclined his head and handed the parcel to Cally. "Please open it, Cally."

Everyone watched as Cally undid the string and paper, revealing a jeweler's box. She gasped when she opened it. "How beautiful! I've never seen anything like this. You should have it, Cathleen." Cally placed the box in front of Cathleen.

Mary Ann leaned over for a look. "A star garnet! These are extremely rare. The purple color is extraordinary. Do you know anything about this, Hosea?"

"It's a genuine treasure," said Mr. Eastman. "Uncle William told me a miner sat beside him in a bar in Pocatello one night. He gave your uncle a hard-luck story and asked him whether he would be willing to purchase a gem, so he could get out of debt. William was struck by the stone's beauty but had no idea what it might be worth. He insisted on taking it for appraisal.

"The miner reluctantly let the gem go with some sort of guarantee from William, I don't remember what. They agreed to meet at the same bar twenty-four hours later.

"When William returned the next night, the miner didn't appear. Eventually William learned that the miner's creditors had come after him, and, not trusting him to come up with the money he owed them, they got into a fight and killed him. The creditors then skipped town.

"William was left with the highly valuable star garnet. He told me he considered taking it to his wife. But he didn't want her to think he was bribing her to make amends. Finally, he decided to create a treasure hunt for which the gem would be one of the rewards. The idea grew in his mind until it became what all of you, and Mary Ann and I vicariously, have just experienced. A remarkable achievement, both to design and to decipher."

Mr. Eastman stopped for a drink of water. "My dear, if the Malcomsons had not come along in time, the garnet would have gone to you. But I know you are happy, as I am, that William's wishes have been fulfilled."

Mary Ann smiled. "Cally's letters allowed me to be part of the treasure hunt. For me, that has been treasure enough. The gem is in good hands."

"Cathleen, what you do with the garnet is up to you. You may keep it, give it away, or sell it. You decide," said Mr. Eastman.

Cathleen handed the box back to Cally, folding her own hands over her adopted daughter's. Cally frowned.

"You have persevered through adversity, Cally," said Cathleen. "You've earned this."

I have? I've no idea what to do with a gemstone! I know—I'll give it to Cora.

"Finally, we have the paper," said Mr. Eastman. "You may read it, Charles."

"It's the title to a property in a place called Franklin, Idaho."

"As the crow flies, it's not far from Bear Lake, but there's no road directly between the two," explained Mr. Eastman. "Franklin is less than a mile from the Utah border. Early Mormon settlers believed they were in Utah, until a survey in 1872 established the state boundary. William was amused to learn the oldest European settlement in Idaho has only existed since 1860 and wanted a piece of it. Far different from the ancient settlements of Ireland, I'm told."

The group around the table smiled and nodded.

"The property can be sold, and the proceeds used for whatever purpose you wish."

"What's wrong, Shane?" asked Cathleen.

Tears spilled from Shane's eyes. He scrubbed them furiously, but a sob escaped. "B-Billy is the real tre-treasure. Wh-why can't we find him?"

"That was a delicious dinner," said Charlie as the adults gathered with a bottle of port in a sitting area at the end of their hall at the

Idanha after dinner at the Eastmans' Friday evening. "Mary Ann seems quite fond of us."

"She loved the treasure hunt," said Cally.

"Is Shane all right, Thomas?" asked Cathleen.

"He's brokenhearted about Billy. We committed to pray for him together every night at bedtime until Billy is found. That seemed to comfort him. I think he'll sleep."

"What surprised each of you most about the end of the treasure hunt?" asked Charlie.

"Like Shane, I hoped Billy would somehow show up at the end," said Cathleen.

"After all the revelations about Uncle William along the way, I expected a final disclosure," said Cally. "And Mr. Eastman did tell us the story about the miner and the garnet. I didn't expect more money, property, and a jewel. Billy is the only treasure I care about. For me, the hunt hasn't ended. I still have Billy's envelope."

"I agree. The treasures don't seem to matter much—even the garnet—since we haven't found Billy," said Charlie.

"We must decide what to do with the three treasures, but I guess there's no hurry," said Thomas. "They've been sitting in Mr. Eastman's vault for twelve years."

Charlie took a sip of port. "What if, between now and the trial, each of us makes a list of ideas of what to do with the three treasures? When we're together for the trial, we can share our thoughts and decide."

"Good plan, Charlie," said Thomas. "Everyone agree?"

The others nodded.

"Shane and I must start home Sunday," said Thomas. "What about the rest of you?"

"I'll return to Flora's until time for the trial. Can Felicity go home with you, Thomas, to start school on time?" asked Cally.

"Of course," Thomas responded.

"I'm on a schedule," said Charlie. "I agreed to the Boise City concert because I'll be playing in California the next couple of weeks. My first concert is Wednesday evening in a city called Sacramento. I'll spend next weekend in Oakland and San Francisco, then head south to Los Angeles," said Charlie. "Would you like to see California, Mummy?"

"I'll return to Kansas City with Thomas, Charlie. Someday I'll visit California, but I've had enough adventure for this trip. I'll be happy to take Felicity under my wing, Cally."

"Thank you, Cathleen, for your help with Felicity and for your prayers," said Cally.

"You have them, my dear," said Cathleen. "Every day."

"A violinist named Sean Gregory will arrive from Weiser around noon tomorrow to play with me," said Charlie. "I'll need to spend the afternoon with him. But I'll have the morning with all of you."

"Mr. Gregory! He played with Charlie at the Idanha in Soda Springs," said Cally. "I'm glad we'll have time together tomorrow. Now I must go to bed before I fall asleep right here and have to be carried to my room."

"There's a picture to end the day with, sis!" laughed Charlie. "I get your head."

"I'll take her feet," said Thomas. The brothers tackled Cally, hoisted her between them, and carried her off, cackling like hens.

Chuckling, Cathleen waved at her departing children.

CHAPTER 31

KANSAS CITY

Stricker homesite, Saturday, August 20

CALLY TUCKED HER JOURNAL INTO HER VALISE and took a last look around the station. *I'm quite sure I got everything from the house.* She hefted her suitcase, picked up her valise, and walked outside. A horse and wagon she recognized pulled up, and Ryan climbed down.

"Good morning, Ryan. We already said goodbye, so ..."

"I'm going with you," said Ryan as Flora emerged from the house and waved.

"Oh, that's kind of you. I'm sure Flora will appreciate not having to make the long trip to Twin Falls," said Cally.

"No. I'm going with you to Kansas City. Flora is driving us both to Twin Falls."

"What? Why? Where's Brian?" asked Cally, her brow creasing.

"Brian is with Priscilla and Jerry will care for my sheep while I'm gone. The community decreed we can't send you off by yourself, Cally. Not for something as intimidating as a trial." Ryan extended his hand. "Let me help you with your suitcase. Then I'll put Danny Boy in the barn. Flora will care for him while I'm gone."

"Speaking of the community...," said Flora, who had pulled Cammie up beside Danny Boy. From both directions people converged on the wagons. Cally gasped and put her hand to her mouth as she recognized one face after another.

"You've become part of us, Cally. We love you," said Margaret.

Tucker held up a bunch of wildflowers. "They're for you, Mith Cally," he lisped.

"I made a flower, Miz Cally," said Gabby, running toward her. "From ribbon. See? Can I put it on your hat?"

"Look at me, Miz Cally!" yelled Freddy. "No crutches!"

"I made lunch for you and Ryan," said Anna. John carried a lovely wicker basket. "I think it will take you quite far toward Kansas City."

"Also," said John, "We brought you a surprise to open on the train." He set a wrapped package and the wicker basket in Flora's wagon within reach of the bench.

"Miz Cally," said Walter, walking slowly toward her, an infant in his arms. "This is my wife, Sunrise. She couldn't come to the other events because of our baby's birth."

"Thank you for saving Walter's life," said Sunrise. "I made a gift for you."

"Oh, they're beautiful," breathed Cally, admiring the beaded moccasins Sunrise offered her. "So soft. Thank you. I will treasure them."

"They're to wear, not to treasure," said Sunrise.

"I love them," said Cally. "Walter, what has happened with your people?"

"The community's letter to the captain at Fort Hall gained us a few weeks, until I am strong enough to help with the move," said Walter. "We will leave Falling Water and Walter Junior to keep watch over Dr. Flora."

"We will not stop fighting for justice, in the name of my dear friend and your son," said Flora, wiping her eyes. "I will never get over my broken heart. We must not let evil win."

Walter and Sunrise bowed and moved away. One after another, people Cally could name and some she could not, greeted her and gave her gifts. "I'm overwhelmed," she said in a low voice to Flora when there was a lull.

"We must go now, or you'll miss your train. Ryan, I'll let you drive. Help Cally into the wagon." Flora climbed in beside Cally. As they moved, people ran alongside, handing Cally gifts and yelling goodbye until they drove around the curve in the trail.

"I'm overwhelmed," Cally said again.

"Ryan, give Cammie her head. Hold on, Cally!" said Flora.

Good. I can sit here in the rush of the wind and try to absorb what just happened. Both the community's farewell and the fact that Ryan is going with me to the trial!

"Write to me," said Flora as she hugged Cally goodbye. "I want to know what you're learning. It will help me with designing the training I told you about."

"I will," said Cally.

"We must board, The conductor is beckoning to us," said Ryan.

"Goodbye, Flora!"

"Goodbye, Cally! Until we meet again!"

"Open the Hansens' surprise package!" said Ryan as the train trundled on its way.

"All right," said Cally. "Oh my. It's one of Falling Water's baskets. So beautiful." Cally stopped to wipe tears from her eyes. "With a note from Anna: 'A small gift to remind you of the beauty and the tragedy of Idaho. Come back to us. We love you. John and Anna.'"

"Are you all right, Cally?" asked Ryan.

"That's such a complex question I hardly know how to answer. Like a tangle of different colors of string," said Cally.

"Pick one string and tell me about it," invited Ryan.

"You. The fact that I don't have to make this trip alone," said Cally, and burst into tears.

Ryan pulled his handkerchief from his pocket, put his arm around Cally, and let her weep. When the tempest eased, he offered her a jar of water from Anna's lunch basket.

"Better?" he asked.

"How—how did you learn to do that?" asked Cally.

"Do what?"

"Just be there," said Cally.

"Ah. Bethany taught me that," said Ryan. "She told me the worst thing to do when a woman is crying is try to talk her out of it. And the second worst thing is to pull away or walk away. Eventually, the crying will stop and *that's* the time to talk. On her terms."

"A wise woman, Bethany. What else did she teach you?"

"Her terms are probably not the same as mine. So don't assume I know. Let her tell me."

Cally laughed. "Now that I've had my cry, I feel peaceful. Almost as if I believe everything will work out."

"Almost," said Ryan. "Maybe your 'almost' is why I'm here. So you can bounce your worries off my confidence. I cannot imagine a universe in which a judge or jury would condemn you for something you did as a child, terrified and alone."

"And yet," said Cally, crying again. She choked out through her sobs, "And yet we live in a world where a soldier ca—can kill a woman and a young man, and severely injure that young man's father. Wi—with impunity."

"Terrible things happen," agreed Ryan. "That doesn't mean they will happen this time."

"Terrible things ha—have happened to me," Cally said. "And to you."

"We're not immune. But we have a choice, Cally. I've been thinking about this since Bethany died. I can let fear and anger and bitterness flood me and control me. Or I can give those feelings back to God, as often as I need to, and live in freedom. I have that choice."

"You talk to God?" Cally asked, surprised. "I've never heard you mention God."

"It's a private part of me, one Bethany and I were just beginning to explore," said Ryan. "The wonder of bringing a child into the world impacted us deeply. It humbled us. But we can talk more about this later, Cally. You look like you need a nap."

"You're so thoughtful," said Cally with a huge yawn. "Did Bethany teach you that, too?"

She didn't hear his answer.

Kansas City, Monday afternoon, August 22

"Cally, I'm Mr. Logan, Thomas's lawyer," said the attorney, sitting across from her at Thomas and Cora's dining room table. "He has asked me to represent you in court tomorrow. He told me your story, and I've read the newspaper accounts, but I want you to tell me what happened. Take your time and tell me everything. No detail is too small."

"Some of it is not very—very nice," said Cally. "I haven't even told Cora and Thomas the whole thing."

Mr. Logan raised his eyebrows. "I can handle it. Start at the beginning. Why were you traveling by yourself?"

Telling the Rochester policeman and the Anthonys and then Charlie and Paddy was practice for this. Cally took a deep breath and plunged in. She responded to Mr. Logan's questions as factually as she could.

"I'm impressed," said Mr. Logan. "You told a difficult story calmly. That will stand you in good stead tomorrow. But if you feel emotional when the time comes, don't worry. I will help you through it."

"I have to tell it again, in public?" asked Cally, gripping the edge of the table.

"You were alone most of the time, so the jury must hear it from you, Cally."

"Mr. Logan, what could happen to me?" asked Cally.

"Horse theft is a felony. You could—"

"What is a felony?" asked Cally.

"A felony is a serious crime, for which the minimum penalty is one year in prison."

"I didn't know I was doing wrong," whispered Cally. "I only knew I must find my brother, and I was too sick to walk."

"You don't fit the profile of a horse thief, Cally. And I will argue that a fourteen-year-old girl ought not be charged as a felon. The maximum penalty for horse theft is ten years in prison, plus a fine double the value of the animal. Since Felicity was returned promptly and no harm came to her, I will argue against the fine."

"Felicity saved my life," said Cally.

"That will not be lost on the jury," said Mr. Logan. "But should they conclude you must be punished with a jail term, I will insist on the lightest possible sentence, given your age when you committed the theft and your responsibility as a mother."

"I didn't steal Felicity," said Cally. "I only borrowed her. I left a note saying I would take her back as soon as possible."

"According to the law, anything taken without consent of the owner is theft," said Mr. Logan. "Public opinion is in your favor, Cally, but horse theft is serious. My greatest concern is vigilante justice, should the jury's conclusion not please everyone."

"That's why I had to leave home for all these months," said Cally. "But I thought the trial would resolve it."

"I hope it will," said Mr. Logan. "Now, Cally, we must consider what questions the prosecutor may ask. This can be hard, but the more prepared you are, the easier it will be. Who will attend court tomorrow who can give you courage?"

"So many kind people," said Cally. "My brother Charlie. My adopted mother Cathleen. Cora. Thomas. Ryan."

"Ryan. Who is he?" asked Mr. Logan.

"He is a new friend from Idaho," said Cally. "He understands grief because he recently lost his wife in childbirth. The community there asked him to come with me from Idaho so I wouldn't be alone on the train.'"

"What were you doing in Idaho?"

"I worked as an informal assistant to the local doctor. I've been accepted to St. Joseph's nurses training school, to start next Monday. That is—"

"If we win the trial. I understand, Cally. Our task is simple. It is simply to tell the truth. If we do that, I believe we will win."

"Thank you for your confidence, Mr. Logan."

"Could Ryan testify to the work you did in Idaho? As a character witness who is not part of your family?"

"You would have to ask him, sir. He's caring for my daughter while I'm with you."

"Please introduce me when we finish. Several more witnesses are due to arrive, I believe. A Dr. Tann and Mr. and Mrs. Williams."

"They are coming too? I didn't know that!" exclaimed Cally.

"Cora told me they were deeply involved with you after the horse theft—pardon me, horse borrowing," said Mr. Logan. "So they are essential witnesses. Now, Cally, imagine the prosecutor asks you difficult questions, and you begin to feel upset. What will you do?"

"I will try to remain calm, sir."

"If you start feeling emotional, look for a member of your family in the gallery, so you know you are not alone. Remember, no matter what the prosecutor says, he is simply doing his job, trying to win the case on behalf of his client."

"I understand," said Cally, taking another deep breath.

"How will you respond if the prosecutor says, 'The law is the law, ma'am. You stole a horse and escaped without punishment. You tell a good story, but are you above the law?'"

Cally thought for a moment. "I will say, he is right. I borrowed Felicity without the permission of her owner. The question is whether the law has any space for mercy for a child. A child who was desperately ill, desperately wounded, and desperately alone."

"That's good!" said the lawyer. "Now say it again, looking me straight in the eye as if I am the prosecutor. Speak as calmly and clearly as you just did."

"Yes, sir," said Cally, wiping her sweaty palms while she repeated her statement.

"Now, how will you answer if the prosecutor asks, 'Are you saying, then, Miss Malcomson, that it is appropriate for crimes to go unpunished?'"

"I will say, 'No, sir. Mercy is not the same as absolution. Now that I understand the law, I realize I was wrong to take Felicity without permission, even though I fully intended to take her back to her owner as soon as I could. But in disciplining my daughter, I have found there are times when mercy should triumph over justice, because she is just learning right and wrong. When I took the horse Felicity, I had no intention of bringing harm to her or to her owner."

"Are you Catholic, by any chance, Cally? I don't think many people use the word absolution in everyday conversation." Mr. Logan smiled.

"Yes, sir. I'm sorry, sir. I could say—"

"No, no. What you said was fine. One more question and then I'll ask your friend Ryan to speak with me. What if the prosecutor says, "Miss Malcomson, you are an orphan and an immigrant. Why should a United States court grant you any favors?"

"I was an orphan and an immigrant when I took Felicity, that's true. But I have been adopted, both by my family and by my country, with documents to prove both of those facts." Cally started to cry. "My—my family is here with me. I am a sister, a daughter, and a citizen. I am the mother of a citizen. I have served my family and my country as well as I know how."

Cally buried her face in her arms and sobbed. A knock came at the door. "Cally? Are you all right?" asked Cora, opening the door.

"She is free to go, Cora. I'm sorry I was hard on her. I take no joy in it. I need her to be ready for whatever may happen tomorrow, that's all," said Mr. Logan.

"Thank you for that," said Cora. "Come, Cally. Mr. Logan says you may leave."

Cally blew her nose, wiped her cheeks, stood, and said "Thank you, Mr. Logan."

Felicity and Lizzy sat with Ryan on the couch, looking at a book. Felicity leaped to her feet and ran to Cally, throwing herself into her mother's arms.

"Mummy, are you all right? Lizzy was worried because you were in there so long. She thought you were crying. Mr. Ryan wouldn't let me knock on the door."

"Yes, sweetheart, I'm fine," said Cally. "Tell Lizzy there's nothing to worry about."

"Mr. Ryan and I were finding all the G's," said Felicity. "It's my homework. I already know ABCDEF. Shane and Shauna and Josie are doing their homework upstairs. Aunt Cora and Grandma are making food for lots of people. Uncle Charlie went with Mr. Max to pick up Dr. Tann and the Williams. I wish Mr. Ryan brought baby Brian."

"Had brought," said Cally. "You wish Mr. Ryan had brought baby Brian."

"Yes, I do," said Felicity. "I miss him."

Charlie went to the station? I wonder why. There was no need for him to go.

Mr. Logan cleared his throat. "Cally, may I meet your friend Ryan?"

"I'm sorry, sir. This is Ryan Byrne. Ryan, Mr. Logan will represent me tomorrow."

"Would you be willing to speak with me, Mr. Byrne? I need a witness who isn't part of Cally's family."

"I'll be glad to," said Ryan. Mr. Logan shut the dining room door behind them.

"I hear horses! Maybe Uncle Charlie and Mr. Max are back!" Felicity ran to the door.

Two carriages pulled up. Max jumped down from the first one to assist Athena and Richard Williams and Dr. Tann. As they hugged Cally and exclaimed over how much Felicity had grown, Cally kept her eye on the other carriage. Charlie opened the door from inside, stepped out, and extended his hand to a beautiful young woman with dark hair and bright blue eyes. *Laoise! She must be Laoise!*

Behind Laoise exited a young man, also with bright blue eyes. "Teddy!" Cally screamed. She threw herself into his arms. "How did you—"

"Dr. Tann sent me a telegram," said Teddy. "He told me which train to catch so we could come together. The woman with Charlie is—"

"Laoise!" exclaimed Cally. Laoise turned from Felicity and smiled. *No wonder Charlie loves her. Oh, I am so happy. I don't think I can hold any more happiness. I know now why Cathleen and Cora are making so much food.*

"Mr. Ryan!" shouted Felicity as he and Mr. Logan appeared in the doorway. "This bee-yoo-tiful lady is Uncle Charlie's friend! Her name is Laoise!"

Ryan looks relaxed, so it must be all right. Oh, here's Thomas.

"Did I come to the right house? I could hear talking and laughing a block away."

"Daddy! Daddy! Teddy came!" shouted Shane, who had appeared along with Shauna and Josie. "And Mr. Williams and Mrs. Williams! And Laoise!"

Shauna and Josie can't keep their eyes off Laoise. I don't blame them. She's stunning.

Cora beckoned to Thomas from the doorway.

"Shall we go inside?" said Thomas. "Supper is ready."

Cally took a deep breath and guided Teddy into the house. "I need to help serve, Teddy. I can't believe you're here!"

"I'll help too," said Teddy. "I came to be with you."

"How is your sweet Starlight?"

"We're going to have a baby, Cally!" said Teddy.

"Oh, that's wonderful! When?"

"Around the new year," said Teddy. "Will you come?"

"Of course!" said Cally. "That is, if—"

"If the trial goes well, right? I'm not worried. We've come through bigger challenges than this," said Teddy. "Mrs. Malcomson, it's good to see you. Let me carry that tureen."

After Thomas offered the blessing, Charlie tapped his goblet. "I want to introduce Laoise to you all at the same time. Laoise has been my friend since we studied together at the Dublin Academy of Music. I am thrilled to tell you that I have asked, and she has said yes!"

Everyone cheered and clapped. Laoise lifted her left hand to display a sapphire circled by tiny diamonds. "Your ring matches your eyes," observed Josie.

"Have you set a date?" asked Cora.

"Not yet. We're working on it," said Charlie. "We don't want to wait long, but we're both committed to several months of touring."

"We've agreed neither of us will schedule anything beyond our present obligations," said Laoise. "We're tired of goodbyes."

"Do you play the piano too, like Uncle Charlie?" asked Shauna.

"No. I play the violin," said Laoise.

"Then you can play together!" said Shane.

"Yes, we can. And we will, with the Philharmonic in September in New York City. That's what brought us back together. You're all welcome to come!" said Charlie.

"I plan to attend your concerts before returning to Waterford," said Cathleen, smiling at Laoise. "Congratulations, Charlie and Laoise! I'm delighted for you!"

"Will you favor us with after-dinner music?" asked Thomas.

Charlie and Laoise looked at each other. "We would be happy to," said Laoise.

Charlie tapped his goblet again. "Not all of you know Cally's brother Teddy. He's a musician too. Did you bring your harmonica, Teddy?"

"Yes, but—" began Teddy.

"Excuse me, sir," Max said to Thomas, walking into the dining room. "A telegram has arrived. That is, two telegrams."

"Thank you, Max. They're for you, Cally," said Thomas.

"One from Margaret and one from Daniel. Both wishing me well tomorrow," said Cally. "How very thoughtful."

"I confess this is a bit overwhelming. I only have one brother," said Laoise.

"I'll draw you a family tree!" said Shane.

"One, two, three ..." counted Shauna under her breath.

"It may be best if I interview Dr. Tann and the Williams at their hotel," said Mr. Logan. "I'm not sure we'll be able to hear each other above a piano and a violin and a harmonica."

"There are sixteen people at this table!" announced Shauna.

"It's the first time we've used all the leaves. I thought it was too big, but Thomas was right. We did need this huge table. Let me introduce Nora to you all," Cora said, smiling at a young woman who was clearing away dishes. "Nora is helping us with this supper."

"Can we stay up for the music, Mummy? Please?" asked Josie. "And can Felicity sleep with me and Shauna tonight?"

Cora looked at Thomas. "All right. But no fussing when I tell you it's time for bed. You have school tomorrow. All right if Felicity sleeps with the girls tonight, Cally?"

"Yes," said Cally, looking at Felicity's hopeful face.

"The young man with the harmonica is the brother you were trying to find?" Mr. Logan asked Cally.

"Yes. He lives in the Oklahoma Territory with the Oneida. Please don't make him testify, Mr. Logan. He wasn't with me at the time I took Felicity."

"All right. I'll think more about this, but for now I'll let it go."

"Will you have dessert before you leave, Mr. Logan?" asked Cora. "I tried a dish I learned in Idaho—rice pudding. Nora will serve it right now."

"I'll help," said Cally, pushing back her chair.

Mr. Logan looked at his watch. "We do have a trial tomorrow. And I for one have not finished preparing."'

"Just a few bites of rice pudding," said Thomas. "You won't be sorry, Mr. Logan. It's delicious. Then Max can take you, Dr. Tann, Richard, and Athena to The Eldridge."

"I thought we'd discuss what to do with the treasures this evening," Charlie said quietly to Thomas after the foursome departed for the hotel. "But that's not how it's turning out."

"We'll find another time," said Thomas. "There's no hurry, right?"

"I guess not," said Charlie. "If Cally has what she needs to pay for her nurses training."

"I'll make sure of that," said Thomas.

"How are you, sis?" asked Cora, walking into Cally's room after saying good night to the last guest. "Felicity is enjoying her sleepover with her cousins. 'Like in Idaho,' she said."

"I can't figure out what to wear tomorrow," said Cally. "What do you think?"

"Your green dress," said Cora without hesitation. "It's beautiful but not ostentatious. Really, Cally, whatever you wear will be fine. You carry yourself well, and your natural kindness shines through. That's what will be your best defense tomorrow."

"I hope you're right," said Cally. "Green it is."

"Cally, I have a question. I don't want to hurt anyone's feelings." Cora sat on Cally's bed. Cally sat down next to her.

"So, ask."

"It's about Teddy. Do you think Thomas should offer him some, um, ordinary clothes for the trial tomorrow? Won't it be awkward for him to go in his Oneida dress?"

"He is Oneida now, Cora. Has been for eight years. He's married to an Oneida woman. I think it would feel more awkward to him to dress in our clothes. He's used to people staring and pointing. I don't think that will bother him."

"All right. But if you want to give him the option—"

"Dressing him like Thomas would make you and maybe others feel more comfortable. But not Teddy," said Cally firmly. "Cora, thank you for your hospitality to all these people. And your unfailing steadiness and generosity to me. I can't imagine where I would be without you."

"And I can't imagine life without you, Cally. I love you." Cora hugged her. "Tonight was a trial run for Nora. What do you think? Thomas and I realized we need to hire someone, since you'll be in nursing school. Your absence the last three weeks made me realize how much I've counted on your help. Thank you, Cally, for all you've invested in our family, with such grace and skill. You are amazing, and we haven't properly recognized that."

"You took me in off the streets and gave Felicity and me a family," said Cally. "All the thanks go from me to you."

Cora smiled. "We can agree to disagree about that." She stood. "I do have one other question. Shane is begging to go to the trial. What do you think?"

"Hmm," said Cally, smoothing her green dress. "He has walked through so much with me this summer. And it would be educational for him. But what about the other children? If Shane can go, they'll want to also. I don't think I can handle having Felicity there."

"Perhaps just Shane and Shauna, if she wants to go? We can tell Josie and Felicity it's just for older children and adults," said Cora.

"They'll pout, but I think they'll get over it. Felicity plans to take Lizzy to school with her tomorrow to 'meet' her classmates. I think she'll be fine," said Cally.

"All right. I'll talk about it once more with Thomas, and we'll decide about Shane and Shauna. I hope you'll sleep tonight, Cally."

"Thank you. I believe I will. Cathleen prayed that for me as well. Good night."

"Good night, sweet sister."

CHAPTER 32

THE TRIAL

Kansas City Courthouse, Tuesday, August 23

"WHO ARE ALL THOSE PEOPLE?" Cally asked Thomas as their carriage approached the courthouse Tuesday morning.

"Hmm, let's see if we can read their signs as we drive by. That one says, 'Change our laws!'" said Thomas.

"'She's no thief!'" read Shane. "And that one says, 'Mercy triumphs over justice.'"

"Look at that group over there on the left—they're chanting something," said Cally. "Can you hear what they're saying?"

"The law is the law," said Teddy. "'The law is the law,' over and over again."

"Now they've switched," said Shauna. "Now it's 'We want justice!'"

Cally gripped her stomach. *I feel sick. This is bad already.*

Cora touched Cally's hand. "The decision will be made in the court room, not out here."

"Their signs say, 'Anti-Horse Thief Association.'" said Thomas. "I'm going to ask Mr. Logan about them."

"Most people support Cally," said Teddy. "See that sign? 'She's a mother, not a thief!'"

"And there's another: 'The horse was borrowed, not stolen. Be kind, Judge Jones!'"

"Listen!" said Thomas.

"Cally! Cally! Cally!" mimicked Teddy.

"How do they know my name?" whispered Cally.

"It was in the papers. I'm glad Mr. Logan suggested we use the back door," said Cora. "It would be unnerving to have to push through that crowd."

"He'll be waiting for us," said Thomas. "Good man."

"Do you know in what order he plans to call you?" asked Teddy.

"I think it will be me, then Mummy, Charlie, Ryan, and Cally, then Dr. Tann and the Williams, and Cora," said Thomas. "Something like that."

଼

"Oh my," said Charlie, guiding Laoise and Cathleen to seats midway down the gallery. "I'm glad we decided to come early!"

"I've not been to court before," said Laoise. "Is this unusual?"

"I haven't either, except when Thomas and Cora adopted Cally and Felicity," said Cathleen.

"Nor I," said Charlie. "Horse thievery is not unusual. But this case has received a great deal of attention from the press. Look, there's a man from the *Kansas City Star.*"

"I can't imagine how awful this must be for Cally," said Laoise, gripping Charlie's arm.

"True, but also a relief. It's been hanging over Cally's head since April," said Charlie.

"I'm glad Cally's seated at an angle, so we can see her face," said Cathleen. "Will you pray with me for her while we await the judge?"

"Certainly," said Laoise, and bowed her head.

"Here we go," Mr. Logan told Cally as a door at the side of the bar opened to admit Judge Jones. "Remember, the prosecution presents Mr. Finelli's case first. When it's our turn, I'll start with your family, and then Ryan."

"Then me. I feel sick," said Cally.

"Take a deep breath and a drink of water. Better?"

"Cou—could I ask Cathleen to pray for me before we start?"

"It will have to be quick," said Mr. Logan, glancing at the judge, who was polishing his glasses.

Cally turned around, found Cathleen, and gestured. Cathleen rose and walked to the row behind Cally, squeezing in beside the Williams, Dr. Tann, and Teddy.

"Please pray for me," said Cally, her voice trembling.

"I will," said Cathleen, placing her hand on Cally's shoulder. The others followed suit.

"God our loving Father, you know how Cally feels facing this trial and its uncertain outcome. Please ease the worries of her mind and heart, and give her your peace."

Judge Jones cleared his throat.

"Amen," said Cathleen. She touched Cally's cheek, smiled, and returned to her seat.

"Better now?" asked Mr. Logan.

"Much better." *Amazing. I do feel peace, God. Thank you.*

"Mr. Fischer, you may open for the prosecution," said Judge Jones.

Mr. Finelli's attorney stood. "Thank you, your honor. Our case is straightforward. The defendant committed a crime. With the aid of her doctor, her crime was covered up and never brought to justice. We are here to remedy that. I call Mr. Joel Kauffman to the stand."

Mr. Kauffman took the oath and sat, identifying his name when asked.

"Occupation?"

"I am a farmer."

"Then you are keenly aware of the importance of horses in our society, both for transportation and for labor."

"Yes, sir. The horse is the single most important asset most people possess."

"Do you have any other skills or commitments of interest to the court today?"

"Yes, sir. I am a long-time member of the Anti-Horse Thief Association."

"Describe for the court the implications of this membership."

"I am committed to defending the community from thievery of all kinds, and especially of its horses. When a theft occurs, I can be called upon to pursue and capture the thief and turn him or her over to be judged by our laws. We are not a vigilante group, taking justice into our own hands. We serve as an extension of the law, assisting where needed."

"Were you involved in any way with the theft of the horse Felicity on April 7, 1898?"

"Yes, sir. Since Felicity is unusually valuable, I was appointed to one of four posses organized to apprehend the thief," said Mr. Kauffman.

"Was your posse or any of the others successful?" asked Mr. Fischer.

"No, sir."

"Were there extenuating circumstances?"

"Yes, sir. Felicity's owner, Mr. Finelli, attempted to pursue the thief by himself. Unused to riding bareback, he fell from his galloping horse and suffered a fractured leg. This occurred early in the morning, and it took some time for Mr. Finelli and the horse he was riding to be found, transported back to his home, and his injury cared for. Thus, the thief had a significant head start, and we did not know which direction he—or should I say, she—had fled."

"Is it unusual in your experience to have this outcome when pursuing a thief?"

"Yes, sir. We are skilled in what we do. In most cases, we locate horse thieves and turn them over to the authorities within twenty-four hours," said Mr. Kauffman.

"What was the Anti-Horse Thief's conclusion when Felicity was returned to Mr. Finelli?"

"As you know, sir, Felicity was accompanied by a coffin purporting to contain the remains of the thief. With the coffin buried, and Felicity safely home, we considered the matter resolved. The fine each of us had paid was returned to us."

"You paid a fine, Mr. Kauffman?"

"Yes, sir. If we fail to return a horse stolen from one of our members, each of us pays a fine to help the owner purchase a replacement of his lost property. This is one of the benefits of membership in our society."

"How did the case return to the attention of the AHTA?"

"Mr. Graham Abernathy, custodian of the New Santa Fe Cemetery, claimed to have seen the thief visiting the grave. When he dug up the coffin, it contained rocks rather than the remains of a human body. Therefore, the thief was still at large. The pursuit was taken up again by the AHTA. We encouraged Mr. Finelli to seek legal redress, for although Felicity was returned to him without harm, Mr. Finelli suffered a fractured leg. He still walks with a slight limp."

"Did the AHTA appoint you to testify today?" asked Mr. Fischer.

"No, sir. I volunteered. The law is the law. I want to do my part to keep us all safe."

"Is there anything else you wish to say to the court, Mr. Kauffman?"

"Yes, sir. I believe the court cannot be lenient in a matter so grave as horse theft. It would set a precedent that might embolden other horse thieves. I therefore advocate for the strictest penalty the law allows. Not only did a theft take place, but deception was practiced, by the defendant's physician. I hope he too will be brought to justice."

How awful! Please, God, don't let Dr. Tann suffer on my behalf.

"Thank you, Mr. Kauffman. Your witness, Mr. Logan."

Cally's attorney rose. "Mr. Kauffman, are you aware that the defendant left a note for Mr. Finelli when she took Felicity, explaining she had borrowed the horse and would return her as soon as possible?"

"I became aware of that much later, when I read it in the newspaper," said Mr. Kauffman.

"Does the defendant's belief that she was simply borrowing Felicity alter your assessment of the case?" asked Mr. Logan.

"No, sir. Horse thieves are notorious con artists. There is no end to their, shall we say, 'creativity' in getting away with their crimes. The defendant took Felicity from her owner without his permission. That, sir, is the definition of theft."

"Mr. Kauffman, you stated that the Anti-Horse Thief Association is not a vigilante group, but rather assists the inadequately staffed official law enforcement in Kansas and other states. Have I accurately restated what you told us?"

"Yes, sir."

"Yet, Mr. Kauffman, with some frequency, stories circulate of vigilante justice, including whipping, lynching, and hanging of horse thieves. Some of those stories have been connected to the Anti-Horse Thief Association. Can you explain this to me?"

"It's true, sir, that at times in their zeal members act outside of our mandate. We are quick to discipline and sometimes remove said persons from our association. The AHTA cannot be held responsible for the actions of other organizations or individuals."

"Would it be fair to think, Mr. Kauffman, that fear of vigilante justice could influence a person like Dr. Tann in the choices he made for his patient, Callandra Donnelly Malcomson?"

"I am aware, sir, of extreme cases in Missouri. Our discipline here in Kansas is much tighter, but I understand our citizens may be influenced by what they hear from across the border," said Mr. Kauffman.

"Thank you, sir. No further questions," said Mr. Logan.

"He's right," Cally whispered to Mr. Logan. "By his definition, I did steal Felicity."

"I call Mr. Graham Abernathy," said Mr. Fischer.

"He's the one who figured out the coffin was fake," someone in the gallery said.

Strange. I so enjoyed the outing to the cemetery with Felicity. I had no idea it would lead to trouble! Replaying her memories, Cally missed most of the graveyard tender's testimony.

"No questions," said Mr. Logan.

"I call Mr. Anthony Finelli," said Mr. Fischer.

Cally looked with interest at the man who had once tried to shoot her. He explained in detail how valuable Felicity was and how outraged he felt when the defendant stole her. He described the anguish he endured for hours after falling off his horse, helpless and in terrible pain until the milkman found him while making his morning deliveries. He reiterated that the law was the law, Cally had stolen his horse, and had escaped justice. He repeated Mr. Kauffman's assertion that her note promising return of Felicity meant nothing to him.

"This case is crystal clear," Mr. Finelli concluded. "I ask the court for justice heretofore denied me. What kind of society will we be if we allow wrongdoing without consequences?"

"No questions," said Mr. Logan.

"No questions?" whispered Cally.

"We want as little attention on them as possible," Mr. Logan whispered back.

Mr. Fischer turned to the judge. "The prosecution rests its case."

The spectators murmured and stretched, while newsmen wrote furiously on their pads.

"We will ask the court for mercy on the merits of the case, Cally," Mr. Logan continued quietly. "Take a deep breath. There is much in your favor. Do you want me to request a recess before we begin our defense?"

Cally shook her head and crossed her arms to control her trembling. "Let's just do it."

Mr. Logan rose and addressed the jury. "You have heard the prosecution's case. The defense does not dispute the facts. The defendant, Miss Callandra Donnelly Malcomson, did take the prize horse Felicity from Mr. Finelli's barn without his permission on April 7, 1898.

"Our witnesses will tell you why she did so, the condition they found fourteen-year-old Miss Malcomson in that fateful morning, and what kind of person she is. You will quickly realize she does not fit the profile of a horse thief.

"The question before you is this: Does the law have any room for mercy? Please keep this question in mind as you hear the testimony of Miss Malcomson's family and friends, and those who were directly involved with her on the day Felicity was taken. You will also hear Miss Malcomson testify on her own behalf. I believe you will see, as I do, the need for interpretation of the law as it relates to this case. I call Mr. Thomas Malcomson."

"I'm glad my part is over," Charlie whispered to Laoise as he found his seat.

"You did well," Laoise whispered back. "It was clear how much you love Cally."

Mr. Logan stood and said, "I call Mr. Ryan Byrne."

Ryan side-stepped his way to the aisle past Shane, Thomas, Cora, Shauna, and Max.

"Mr. Byrne, are you romantically involved with the defendant?" asked Mr. Logan after Ryan confirmed his name, address, and occupation.

"No sir," said Ryan. "Cally has been a good friend to me as I grieve my beloved wife Bethany, who died in childbirth five months ago."

"Ryan has invested a lot in Cally, coming all this way," Laoise whispered to Charlie.

"He has. Perhaps he doesn't realize it himself yet, but I suspect he cares more about her than he's telling us," Charlie whispered back.

"How long have you known the defendant?" asked Mr. Logan.

"Only a few weeks, sir. This summer Cally assisted our local doctor. She helped care for my infant son when he had the mumps. Before that, she assisted with the complicated labor of a close friend of mine, staying a week after the birth to ensure the tiny baby got off to a good start while his mother recovered. The parents asked Cally to be their baby's godmother. I helped the family in various ways that week, and Cally and I became friends."

"Is it common for neighbors to assist each other like this?" asked the attorney.

"Yes, sir. It's essential to our survival," said Ryan. "We have no services available to us as you do here in the city. We help each other."

"You described for me a community farewell to the defendant," said Mr. Logan. "Can you explain to the court what made it unusual?"

"Sir, if you will indulge me, I would like to use an analogy to explain this. Our community lives in a high desert, where the most prolific vegetation is sagebrush. But the land is fertile, and whenever water is present, the desert blooms. This has been our experience of Cally. She was like living water among us. Wherever she went, hope, healing, and beauty blossomed."

Cally stared at Ryan, her mouth open, eyes wide and bright with tears.

Mr. Logan spoke. "That is lovely, Mr. Byrne, but could you be more specific?"

"Cally assisted our country doctor for only a few weeks. But the morning she was to depart, many people from our farm community gathered to say goodbye. One after another, they expressed to Cally what her care had meant to them. Many gave her handmade gifts. I heard several beg her to come back. It was extraordinary in that she had been with us such a short time. Dr. Flora and I had to take her away or we would have missed our train."

"What did you conclude from observing this farewell?" asked Mr. Logan.

"Evidently others felt as I did, that Cally was kind, generous, and skilled in caring for families dealing with illness. From my conversations with her on the train, I realized her own struggles and losses have made her sympathetic to the challenges of other people."

"Ryan has a good grasp of Cally's character," Charlie whispered to Laoise.

"How did you come to accompany her from Idaho to Kansas City?" asked Mr. Logan.

"Members of our community asked me to do so, sir. Someone—I suspect the doctor—leaked the news that Cally faced a trial. Some of my neighbors imagined that if she made the long trip by herself, her understandable fears in relation to the trial might become exaggerated." Ryan smiled at Cally. "I was tasked with keeping her safe, calm, and hopeful. One neighbor offered to care for my son so I could travel."

"You have a close-knit community, Mr. Byrne. Tell me, did you at any time observe or hear about the defendant doing or saying anything you would judge inappropriate?"

"No, sir," said Ryan.

"So, you believe the defendant is a person of integrity?"

"Yes, sir," said Ryan. "Our community would be delighted to have her back among us."

"Thank you," said Mr. Logan. He turned to the prosecutor. "Your witness."

Judge Jones looked at the prosecutor, who shook his head. "No questions, your honor."

"You may stand down, Mr. Byrne," said the judge.

"I call the defendant, Miss Callandra Donnelly Malcomson, to testify on her own behalf," said Mr. Logan.

Cally wiped her suddenly sweaty palms on her handkerchief, looked behind her at Teddy, who gripped her shoulder, and stood. She took the oath and sat, found Cathleen's smile, then turned to her attorney.

"Miss Malcomson, tell the court what happened to you when you were fourteen that led you to take the prize horse Felicity for a ride without the owner's permission."

"Sir, before I tell my story, may I speak to Mr. Finelli?" asked Cally.

Mr. Logan raised his eyebrows and looked across to Mr. Finelli and his attorney, and then to the judge, who nodded.

"Mr. Finelli, I am so sorry you broke your leg. I only found out about that in April, from an article in the *Kansas City Star.* Whatever the outcome of this trial, c—could you forgive me for taking Felicity without your permission and for being the cause of your injury? Only now, hearing Mr. Kauffman, have I realized how severely I wronged you. I don't deserve your forgiveness, but will you please think about it?"

The gallery rustled. Mr. Finelli inclined his head. Cally wiped her eyes, looked up, and said, "I am ready, Mr. Logan."

Laoise gripped Charlie's hand.

"Please explain to the court what happened on April 7, 1898."

Cally straightened, looked up at the gallery, and told her story.

"Look at her," whispered Laoise to Charlie, tracking Cally's gaze to Ryan, who sat two rows in front of them. "I believe she's talking to Ryan. It's like she's blocked out everyone else."

"You're right," Charlie whispered back. "There is definitely a bond between those two."

When she finished, Ryan smiled and gave Cally a thumbs up. The gallery collectively breathed a sigh. Cally wiped her hands on her handkerchief once more, then looked at Mr. Logan for the next question.

"Miss Malcomson, you were headed to the Oklahoma Territory to find your brother at the time you 'borrowed' the horse Felicity," said Mr. Logan. "Is your brother present today?"

"Yes, sir," said Cally. "He joined the Oneida Nation as a child."

Teddy stood and bowed. People in the gallery whispered and pointed.

"Thank you, Mr. Donnelly," said Mr. Logan. Teddy sat.

"Now, Miss Malcomson, on that fateful day, why were you dressed as a boy? Do you not like the gender God gave you?"

Mr. Logan asked question after question, and finally said to Mr. Fischer, "Your witness."

The prosecutor's words were almost identical to what she had practiced with Mr. Logan. Cally responded with her question about whether the law had any room for mercy to a sick child. A child who had been attacked and violated and felt desperately alone. Who was with child herself as a result of that attack, though she didn't yet know it.

"If you were alone, how can we know you are telling the truth? Is there anyone here who can vouch for your story?" asked the prosecutor.

"Yes, sir," said Cally. "Dr. George Tann and Mr. Richard Williams and Mrs. Athena Williams. Also Mrs. Cora Malcomson, and Mr. Max Judson. Each of them played a role in saving my life, as I have described to you. So did the mare Felicity, but she couldn't be with us today." A ripple of laughter spread through the room. Charlie looked at Laoise and chuckled.

"I will want to hear from each of your witnesses," said the prosecutor. "No more questions, your honor."

"You may return to your table, Miss Malcomson," said Judge Jones.

As she sat again beside Mr. Logan, he smiled at her before standing to call Dr. Tann. Suddenly exhausted, Cally folded her arms on the table and rested her forehead.

"She looks completely spent," Charlie whispered to Laoise.

"I would be too," Laoise whispered back. "But wasn't she magnificent?"

"Truth is always beautiful," Charlie whispered. "I hope the jury recognizes it."

Cathleen touched Charlie and with a smile, put her finger to her lips. Charlie nodded and settled back in his seat.

Mr. Logan turned to the jury. "Dr. Tann has been accused of deception. He will explain to us his reasoning in taking the actions he did, both in returning Felicity to her owner and in sending a coffin purporting to contain the remains of the horse thief. As you listen to him, consider what you would have done in his position."

Mr. Logan turned to the witness. "Now, Dr. Tann, explain to us your experience with the defendant and why you chose to act as you did."

The jury returned after only forty minutes. "Is that good?" Cally whispered to Mr. Logan.

"We'll soon find out," he whispered back.

"The defendant will rise," said the bailiff. Cally stood, holding the back of her chair.

"Gentlemen of the jury, how do you find?" asked Judge Jones.

The foreman stood. "Your honor, the jury unanimously believes it would be unjust to punish an ill and fevered child for a crime she did not know she was committing. It is evident to us that the defendant has used well the six years since April 7, 1898. We commend her for dedicating her life to serving others. We recommend she pay her debt to society by completing her nurse's training and returning to serve on the Idaho frontier for at least three months. Further, we urge the court to require reparation from the plaintiffs for the mental and emotional suffering they have needlessly caused an upstanding citizen, since no harm came to them or to the horse Felicity apart from Mr. Finelli's broken leg. Thank you for allowing us to serve."

The gallery erupted in cheers and applause. Judge Jones banged his gavel. "Thank you," he said to the jury, then looked at Cally. "Miss Malcomson, the court accepts the verdict of the jury. The charges considered here today will be stricken from your record."

He turned to the plaintiffs. "Mr. Anthony Finelli, the court orders you to donate the money you offered as a reward for capture of the horse thief to St. Joseph's Nurses Training School, where Miss Malcomson plans to train. With that this case is closed. Bailiff, you may clear the courtroom." The judge banged his gavel, smiled at Cally, and left the bench.

"Cally, you are free to leave with your family," said Mr. Logan.

Cally, sat down, trembling, as journalists raced from the courtroom and her family and friends gathered around her, talking excitedly.

"Thank you for defending me, Mr. Logan," said Cally. "You've been wonderful."

"You are quite wonderful yourself, young lady," said Mr. Logan.

"This calls for a celebration!" said Cathleen. "Thomas, is there a place we can go nearby? Can you join us, Mr. Logan?"

"We'll find a place," said Thomas.

"Come on, sis," said Charlie. "Let's get out of here."

EPILOGUE

St. Joseph Hospital lecture hall, Kansas City, Missouri, August 29

A NUN TUCKED A NOTE INTO CALLY'S HAND as she walked into the lecture hall at St. Joseph Hospital for the opening exercises of the fall 1904 term of the Nurses Training School. Cally joined her class, wearing a blue pinafore identical to theirs. She smiled at the girl sitting next to her and glanced at the note.

"Miss Malcomson, come to my office after opening exercises. Superintendent Sister Irmena."

Oh no! Am I in trouble already? How did the nun who gave me the note know who I am? Cally looked around, but everyone else was focused on the stage, where a nun rose to face the audience.

"My name is Sister Irmena. I am the superintendent of this nurses training school. Most of you have met our matron, Sister Frances. She is here to serve your personal needs, not only in the nurses' residence but in matters of the heart and soul. We believe strong and healthy nurses are best prepared to care for their patients."

Sister Frances stood and inclined her head.

"It is my privilege to introduce our graduates, and then release them to their work in the hospital. As you know, St. Joseph Nurses Training School opened in 1901, so we have graduated two classes. Graduates of 1903, please rise."

Some fifteen women in nursing whites and stiffly starched caps rose.

"I commend you, class of 1903, for the exceptional service you have rendered to the patients of St. Thomas Hospital. I appeal to you to invest generously in your role as mentors to our new students, helping them learn through your knowledge and experience. As you are aware, we will soon be pairing each of you with one of our trainees. Please treat them kindly. You may return to your work." Sister Irmena smiled at the group.

The nurses bowed and exited the lecture hall.

"Graduates of 1904, please rise." Another group of nurses rose.

"Nurses, you well remember your fears and feelings as you sat two years ago where our new students sit now. I ask you to recall the process you have undergone to arrive where you are today and extend compassion more often than criticism to these courageous young women. May I count on you for that?" Sister Irmena looked expectantly at the nurses she addressed.

"Yes, Sister Irmena," they replied in chorus.

"Thank you. You may return to your patients and your tasks."

The nurses bowed and exited.

"Now I will introduce our faculty for this term, before our hospital director, Father Bernard Donnelly, speaks to us ..."

Donnelly! Could he be related to my family somehow?

Sometime later, Cally pinched herself. *God, forgive me, I have no idea what Father Donnelly's been saying. All I can think about is the stream of goodbyes since the trial: Dr. Tann. Mr. and Mrs. Williams. Teddy. Ryan. Cathleen with Charlie and Laoise to New York for their concerts. Oh no! I never showed Charlie May Lee's Grays Lake painting!*

Tears pooled in Cally's eyes. She took out her handkerchief and blotted them away.

If Charlie and Laoise get married in Dublin, I might have to go back to Ireland. Which is worse, my fear of going back, or the disappointment I will feel if I miss their wedding?

The audience laughed. Cally startled. *I must try to pay attention. ... Ryan left such a sweet letter for me. I haven't had time to respond, even with Nora taking my place in Cora's home. I'm surprised how hard that feels. And Billy is always in the back of my mind, the treasure we never found, his envelope tucked away in my desk. Thomas says Cecil hasn't heard from him. Imagine him wandering around Ireland trying to find the father he doesn't know is dead. Only fourteen years old—*

The student next to Cally sneezed. Cally offered her handkerchief. The young woman frowned and shook her head. Cally heard Father Donnelly say, "mission of our school." He inclined his head and turned away from the podium. The students around Cally began clapping, so Cally did also. *How will I ever make it through this training if I can't pay attention?*

The students around her rose, so Cally did too. The hospital chaplain offered a prayer. The students murmured "Amen," and crossed themselves, then settled back in their seats for their first lecture. Cally followed suit. *I must focus!*

From the aisle beside Cally's row, a nun beckoned Cally. Apologizing, Cally edged past the students who had entered after her. The nun took her arm and hurried her out, saying "Sister Irmena must not be kept waiting." She knocked on a door labeled "Superintendent."

"Miss Malcomson? Thank you for coming. Please, have a seat," said Sister Irmena. "Sister Martha, we would enjoy tea, please."

Tea? I'm not in trouble? What is this about, then?

"Miss Malcomson, we have followed with great interest the newspapers' accounts of your story and your trial," said Sister Irmena.

Will this haunt me the rest of my life? Will I ever live it down?

"We are honored that you selected St. Joseph's for your nurse's training. The day after your trial, the school received a generous gift from Mr. Finelli. With it came a stipulation, however, from Judge Jones."

"A stipulation, Sister Irmena?"

"Yes. Tell me, what has motivated you to begin training as a nurse, Miss Malcomson. What do you hope to accomplish through a nursing career?"

"I hope to return to Idaho, to assist a doctor who cares for farm families," said Cally. "They live scattered across a large area, with almost no medical care available apart from Dr. Flora. I saw her need for assistance and found joy in helping care for the courageous frontier families I was privileged to meet."

Sister Irmena nodded. "I expected you to say something like that, given the conditions Judge Jones attached to the gift. But we are a hospital training school, Miss Malcomson. Our nurses work in hospitals, not in homes. Our training would be of questionable value for you."

"Does that mean you will not be able to accept Mr. Finelli's gift, Sister Irmena?"

"We don't know yet. It would require us to develop a different type of training, alongside our hospital training. I am thinking this through, evaluating possible resources, including the Visiting Nurse Association. I need time to work out a proposal for our faculty to consider."

I'm causing extra work for this woman I never met before! "May I know the stipulation Judge Jones attached to the gift?" asked Cally.

"He requires us to prepare you for service as a frontier nurse. As far as I am aware, there is no such nurses training program in Kansas City, or perhaps anywhere."

Sister Irmena sipped her tea. "Miss Malcomson, Kansas City once equipped pioneers to venture west along the Oregon Trail. I'm intrigued by the thought of following in that tradition by preparing nurses for the western frontier. It's clear to me that your training with us should not be longer than a year. For your second year, I believe we should apprentice you to your Dr. Flora. I must learn whether she would be willing to take on that role with you."

"You can reach her at Rock Creek, Idaho, Sister Irmena. Dr. Flora Spencer. She trained in New York City under Dr. McKinney."

"Dr. Susan McKinney, now Dr. Steward? I admire her tremendously. Hmm, I wonder whether Dr. Steward could help us ..."

"I don't know, ma'am."

"Miss Malcomson, would you be willing to go home, and return to see me a week from today? I must formulate quite a different training program for you."

"I feel honored that you are taking this so seriously, Sister Irmena."

"I hope to identify other young women motivated to serve on the frontier, Miss Malcomson, perhaps even among the nurses we have already trained. We must work together to understand the skills you will need. Now allow me to bless you as you go home for what is, I suspect, a much-needed week of rest before we see each other again."

"Thank you, Sister." *How can she know how much I need a week of rest?*

"Lord God, bless thy daughter, restore her body and her soul from the immense pressures she has recently sustained, and guide us into thy will for her life and for our school. Amen."

Historical Notes

Susan B. Anthony, 1820-1906, grew up in a Quaker family, and from age 17 dedicated her life at great personal sacrifice to causes of justice, particularly for slaves and for women. She is most well known for her role in obtaining the vote for women, which finally occurred at a national level in 1920, fourteen years after her death. Her loyal sister, Rochester, NY school teacher and principal **Mary Stafford Anthony**, 1827-1907, actively supported her more famous sister's endeavors. There is no historical record of the sisters taking in children like Cally and Teddy (see *Horse Thief 1898*), but it would have been consistent with their characters for them to do so.

The **Anti-Horse Thief Association** was one of many societies organized in the 19th century to apprehend and punish horse thieves. A fascinating book detailing this history is John Burchill's *Bullets, Bridles, and Badges: Horse Thieves and the Societies that Pursued Them,* published by Pelican in 2013. *Treasure Hunt 1904* focuses on Kansas and Missouri, but other states had even more severe penalties for horse theft. A Pennsylvania law, repealed in 1860, called for 39 lashes and cutting off the ears on first offense and branding with HT on the forehead for a second offense. In Ohio, horse thieves could be hanged without a trial. Common penalties elsewhere were flogging, shaving the thief's head and beard, and fines of up to three times the value of the horse. Missouri's law requiring not less than fifty and not more than one hundred stripes was not repealed until 1923, though it had not been applied for many years, giving preference to fines and imprisonment.

Brian Boru, 941-1014, former high king of Ireland, revered for his courage and integrity and for breaking the Viking hold on Ireland. Boru is the subject of extensive literature, music, and at least two operas.

Mary Cassatt, 1844-1926, was born in Allegheny, PA (now part of Pittsburgh), but lived most of her life in France. She was one of four female Impressionist artists who exhibited their works along with men. She was a close friend of Edgar Degas. She received the Order of Chevalier of the Legion d'honneur from the French government in 1904 in recognition of her contributions.

Butch Cassidy's Wild Bunch robbed Montpelier's bank on August 13, 1896. It is the only bank still standing robbed by Butch Cassidy. Since this is such a colorful part of Montpelier's history, I invented the "copycat" robbery in chapter 7.

The **Great Baltimore Fire** in February 1904 destroyed more than 1500 buildings in thirty hours. The **Great Toronto Fire** in April 1904 destroyed most of that city's downtown.

Hosea B. Eastman, 1835-1920, founded the Boise City National Bank in 1886 and served as its director until his death, providing an economic anchor to the rapidly growing city. He married Mary Ann Blackinger and had three children. The fourth floor of the bank building was constructed in 1904. All other details in the book about his and Mary Ann's life and relationships are fictional.

Abbott Fuller Graves, 1859-1936, loved to paint gardens and flowers. Though American, he was influenced by French Impressionism.

John F. Hansen, originally from Denmark, and his wife **Anna** were important civic leaders in Rock Creek, ID and Hansen, ID (named after John) in the late 1800s and early 1900s. They owned a grocery store in Rock Creek which functioned as a community center, and John was superintendent of schools as well as playing many other roles. Their attitudes and actions in *Treasure Hunt 1904,* while fictional, are true to all I could find out about them.

Joseph Rainey ?-1928 (a young adult in 1864), born in Pocatello, son of a French Canadian and Sorrell half-blooded mother, worked with J. N. Ireland for the Ben Holladay Stage Line and later as an interpreter and scout for the U.S. Army and the Fort Hall Indian Reservation established in 1868 for Shoshone, Bannock, and Lemhi tribes. He later moved to Malad, Idaho. Toward the end of his life, he identified for the authorities the site of Old Fort Hall, 25 miles southwest of the new Fort Hall. Rainey had a reputation for kindness. He was trusted by both Indians and whites.

William Malcomson I, 1813-1892, was a younger brother of **Joseph,** sons of Quaker **David Malcomson** who founded a business and shipping empire in Ireland in the 19th century. Upon Joseph's early death, William became head of Malcomson Brothers, one of the most prosperous enterprises in Ireland. Through a series of disastrous decisions, William bankrupted the company. William disappeared from Ireland in 1890 after a rupture with his wife and sons and reconnected with them in 1892, shortly before his death in London. I invented this story of where he was and what he did during those missing years, with apologies to his living descendants.

The **Milner Dam and irrigation project** was named after Stanley B. Milner, a Salt Lake City banker who along with easterners Frank H. Buhl and Peter L. Kimberly financed the project envisioned by rancher Ira Burton Perrine. Perrine's dream became reality when on March 1, 1905, the dam was opened to fill a thousand miles of canal and laterals, irrigating 262,000 acres of desert. Farmers had already helped each other clear their 160-acre holdings of sagebrush and were able to plant and harvest a bumper crop that same year. Pioneers from across the country heard about the miracle of water which transformed the desert into the "Magic Valley" of south-central Idaho, soon producing fruits and vegetables as well as grains. New towns were organized along the canals, named for the financiers who had believed in Mr. Perrine's dream. In this book, the transformation effected by water serves as a metaphor for the growth and change God brings to Cally's life in southern Idaho: *Thou shalt be like a watered garden.*

The Oregon Trail conjures huge caravans of covered wagons laboring through the wilderness, part of an extraordinary migration of people to the frontier west in the latter half of the 19th century. Dozens of books have been written about the half million intrepid individuals and families who risked everything to travel over two thousand miles in hope of better lives. I've read a fair number of these books, both fiction and nonfiction. But what became of the pioneers who through fate, fortune, or fatigue didn't travel to the end of the trail? This novel represents a small glimpse into that rich, variegated, and neglected history.

Rock Creek, Idaho, two miles upstream of the Rock Creek Stage station and the Stricker ranch and homesite, established a post office in 1871 and a school in 1878. The 1900 census counted 146 people in the greater Rock Creek area, including the Stricker Ranch, mostly cattle ranchers and farmers. John F. Hansen opened his store there in 1900. By then the town also boasted a pool hall, hotel, and candy store. The town of Hansen was platted in 1905 on the irrigation and railroad line seven miles north, upon John Hansen's promise to move his store there. In the years following, the town of Rock Creek all but disappeared.

Rock Creek Stage Station, built of lava rock with a sod roof in 1864 by the Ben Holladay Stage and Freight Line, was a desert oasis on the Oregon Trail for forty years, functioning as a saloon, dance hall, post office, and polling place. James Bascom built a trading post close by in 1865; at that time the only one between Fort Hall and Fort Boise. It served Oregon Trail pioneers, miners, and ranchers. Bascom sold the store to rancher Herman Stricker in 1880, who closed it in 1897. The station itself burned in 1907.

Susan Maria Smith McKinney Steward, 1847-1918, was the third African American woman to earn a medical degree in the United States and the first in New York state. In 1881 she co-founded the Brooklyn Women's Homeopathic Hospital and Dispensary where she focused on childhood diseases and malnutrition and prenatal care. She pioneered treatments recognized later by traditional medicine, caring for pregnant women and pediatric patients of all races. She advocated for the civil and social rights of women in medicine and in society. Her husband Reverend William G. McKinney died in 1892. Four years later, she married army chaplain Theophilus Gould Steward.

Rancher **Herman Stricker**, born in Germany, bought the Rock Creek Station trading post in 1876 and managed it until he closed it in 1897. Herman married **Lucy** Walgamott in 1882; they had seven children and ranched a thousand acres along Rock Creek. After their log home burned, they built a large house in 1900-1901 near the former Rock Creek Station. Some of its seven bedrooms (five upstairs and two down) were used to house cowboys. The house has been preserved by the Idaho Historical Society and can be viewed with its 1916 addition and summer kitchen, along with the old trading post and other buildings. The log trading post is the oldest known building still standing in Idaho. See https://history.idaho.gov/stricker/ and more information on

HorseThief1898.blog, including photos. I invented the Strickers' trip to Germany to accommodate my story but tried to be faithful to the fascinating setting.

The **Visiting Nurse Association of Kansas City** was organized in 1892 to provide skilled nursing to the sick in their homes and to teach health and the prevention of disease.

Wolves as pets: Could Flora have domesticated Fauna to the extent indicated in this book? Here is an article suggesting the answer could be yes: https://gizmodo.com/what-happens-to-wolves-when-theyre-raised-like-dogs-1796458238. In the book, Fauna lives both dependently (by her choice) and independently of Flora. Fauna's strong bond to Flora keeps her close, while her wolf-needs and instincts require she be able to run free, for exercise and for hunting. Flora does not try to keep Fauna confined, nor does she carry the responsibility of feeding Fauna. This is possible because she lives in such an isolated place. Most of my research indicates it would not be possible to maintain a pet wolf in an urban setting.

John Woolman, 1720-1772, American Quaker merchant and preacher whose abolitionist writings influenced the Society of Friends to abandon slave ownership, the first organized group in the United States to do so.

Benedicte Wrensted, 1859-1949, emigrated from Denmark in 1894 after running a photography studio there. She is most remembered for her photographs of the Northern Shoshone, Lemhi, and Bannock tribes of Idaho from 1895-1912, but she also photographed the development of Pocatello, Idaho during those years. She chose to live in Pocatello to be near her brother **Peter Wrensted**. In 1912 she moved to Los Angeles and lived there until her death. Many (170) of her photographs are preserved at the Smithsonian Institution, the National Archives, and the Idaho Museum of Natural History. In the 1980s, Smithsonian anthropologist Joanna Cohan Scherer succeeded in identifying 84% of Wrensted's subjects.

The Year 1904 in the United States: The flag had 45 stars. Average life expectancy was 47 years (infant and maternal mortality rates were high). There were 8,000 cars in the country with 144 miles of paved roads and maximum speed limit 10 mph. Motorized ambulances were not added to the fleet of horse-drawn ambulances in New York City until 1910. 14% of homes had bathtubs. 8% had a telephone. Alabama, Mississippi, Iowa, and Tennessee were more populated than California. The population of Las Vegas was 30. The average wage was 22 cents/hour. More than 95% of births took place at home. 90% of practicing physicians had no college degree. Leading causes of death were pneumonia, influenza, tuberculosis, diarrhea, heart disease, and stroke. 20% of adults couldn't read or write; 6% graduated high school. Marijuana, heroin, and morphine were available over the counter. Laudanum, an opiate containing morphine, was used for pain relief. 18% of households had at least one fulltime servant. Only about 230 murders were reported in the whole country; many murders were avenged extra-officially.

William Butler Yeats, 1865-1939, Irish poet and senator of the Irish Free State. He received the Nobel Prize for literature in 1923.

Route of the Treasure Hunt, East to West

For more information and maps, see HorseThief1898.blog.

Montpelier, Bear Lake County, originally Clover Creek, then Belmont; Brigham Young renamed it Montpelier after his hometown in New Jersey. Settled by Mormon pioneers. Elevation 5,981 feet. Population: 1900 1,444; 2010 2,597. Rail line reached Montpelier in 1882.

Characters: *Ezra Martin, Connie O'Brien, Miz Minnie, Ebony, Cecil*

Soda Springs, Caribou County (Oneida County in 1904). Named for hundreds of natural carbonated springs; a landmark on the Oregon Trail. Elevation 5,774 feet. Population: 1900 428; 2010 3,058. The luxury Idanha Hotel, built by Union Pacific Railroad in 1887, was considered one of the finest in the world. The name came from Idanha Mineral Water, bottled locally and shipped all over the country, a million bottles a year at its height. Mineral springs were claimed to effect remarkable cures.

Characters: *Calico, the Hanover family from Boise, the Chens, Sean Gregory from Weiser, ID*

Caribou Mountain (not to be confused with Mt. Caribou in Maine, in Alaska, and in British Columbia) near Soda Springs is part of a mountain range extending from the Rocky Mountains named for prospector Jesse "Cariboo" Jack Fairchild, who participated in the Cariboo gold rush in British Columbia and in 1870 discovered gold in (present day) Idaho. Chinese miners outnumbered whites five to one. At the time, Chinese men were referred to as Chinamen, a term now considered derogatory. The peak is still called "China Hat." At 9,803 feet, Caribou Mountain is the tallest in the Caribou range and the second highest peak in southeastern Idaho.

Characters: *Lizzy, May Lee*

Old Fort Hall, 1834-1856, was originally built on the Snake River as a fur trading station. It became an important stop on the Oregon Trail for 270,000 emigrants on their way west. Soon after Fort Hall, the Oregon and California Trails diverged. The town of Fort Hall developed eleven miles east. Both were included in the Fort Hall Indian Reservation for the Shoshone-Bannock under the treaty of 1867. The first Fort Hall was torn down to build a new one, and in 1870 yet another Fort Hall was constructed 25 miles northeast. No buildings at any of the three Fort Hall sites remain standing. A reconstruction of the original Fort Hall can be seen at Pocatello.

Joe Rainey, *Mack and Eileen and children*, Peter Wrensted

Pocatello, established in 1889 as the county seat of Bannock County, was named after Shoshone Chief Pocatello. The 1870 gold rush brought settlers in large numbers, and Pocatello became an important railroad junction for both north-south and east-west Union Pacific lines. Irrigation from the nearby Snake River and the Portneuf River turned the city into an important agricultural center. All of these factors attracted a diverse population, segregated in the late 1800s into two parts, as described in the book. Elevation 4,462 feet. Population: 1900 4,046; 2010 54,255. Over half of Pocatello's residents are Mormon.

Mrs. Brady, boarders, Benedicte Wrensted, *Melody*

Rock Creek town developed upstream from the Rock Creek Stage Station, built in 1863 by the Ben Holladay Stage and Freight Line. In 1865, James Bascom built the Rock Creek store next to the station. It became an important stop on the Oregon Trail. German immigrant **Herman Stricker** bought the store in 1876 and operated it until 1897, while ranching 1000 acres on Rock Creek. The town of Rock Creek had a post office by 1871 and a school by 1878. By 1900, 146 people lived in the Rock Creek area, including the Stricker Ranch, mostly ranchers and farmers. Danish immigrant **John F. Hansen** opened a store in the town, which also boasted a hotel, a pool hall, and a candy store. The town lost population after the town of Hansen was established seven miles north on the irrigation and railroad line, and is today almost a forgotten memory, though the **Rock Creek Station and Stricker Homesite** has become a tourist attraction.

Donny, Flora, her pet wolf Fauna, Margaret, her son George and Betsy and grandson Tucker; Jerry, Priscilla, and Abigail Jenner; Falling Water, her sons Walter and Raymond and their children, Walter's wife Sunrise; Silas, Eden, Todd, Gabby, Freddy, Dinah, and Isaac Robison; Ryan and Brian Byrne; Florence Gardner, her driver; John and Anna Hansen

Twin Falls, county seat of Twin Falls County, was settled much later than Rock Creek, but with the advantage of the railroad and in 1905, irrigation, soon outgrew the older settlement. It soon became the most important city in the "Magic Valley," so called because of the transformation of the desert through irrigation, a scheme of Twin Falls' founder, Ira Burton Perrine. Perrine founded the Twin Falls Land and Water Company in 1900. The dam and over a thousand miles of irrigation canals were financed chiefly by Stanley Milner of Salt Lake City. The Milner Dam was completed in 1905. Elevation: 3,734 ft. There is no census data for 1900, but in 1910 the population was 5,258; 2010 44,125.

Boise City (now simply called Boise), state capital of Idaho, county seat of Ada county. Elevation 2,704 feet downtown. Population: 1900 5,957; 2020 235,684. Settlement of the Boise Valley was achieved at great cost to the native Shoshone Bannock tribes, who were finally driven out by the U.S. military to Fort Hall Reservation in 1869, in Idaho's "Trail of Tears." Idaho Territory became a state in 1890. Discriminatory laws against non-white people in late 19th-century Idaho restricted the freedoms of people of color across Idaho (see *Idaho Ebony: The African*

American Presence in Idaho State History by Dr. Mamie O. Oliver, 1996). The 2020 census lists 88% white, 3.1% Asian, 1.6% African American, and 0.7% American Indian, a 1% shift across categories in Boise since 2010. This book does not attempt to address the Hispanic/Latino presence in Idaho's history.

Discussion Guide

Horse Thief, Chapters 1-5

1. Have you ever found yourself on the run, either literally or emotionally?
2. What's one of the most frightening or traumatic experiences you've had?
3. In Chapter 2, Cally thinks, *You have no idea, my precious child,* when Felicity complains that the trip is long. What differences do you see between how Felicity is growing up compared to the challenges Cally faced when she was five? (You'll be able to respond better to this question if you've read *Horse Thief 1898.*)
4. What do you notice about the relationship between Cally and Charlie in these chapters?
5. After telling parts of her story to Nathanael and Sarah, to the Rochester policeman, to Miss Anthony and Aunt Mary, and then to Paddy and Charlie, Cally thinks, *"I can't handle talking any more about my story. It's been too many people, too much."* Can you describe a time you felt exposed like that? How did the situation turn out?

The Treasure Hunt Begins, Chapters 6-13

1. The "treasure hunters" visit Boise City, Montpelier, Soda Springs, Old Fort Hall, and Pocatello. What "treasure" did you find for yourself as you traveled with them?
2. Which character would you most like to meet in person: Mr. Eastman, Mary Ann Eastman, Mr. Martin, Connie O'Brien, Minnie, Calico, Lizzy, May Lee, Joe Rainey, Mack, Benedicte Wrensted, Mrs. Brady, or Melody? What would you like to ask or tell the person you chose?
3. Charlie, Thomas, and Cally had no idea William would be telling them his story through the treasure hunt, or that it would include such difficult information. Both Charlie and Thomas consider stopping. What motivates Cally to continue?
4. The phrase *Thou shalt be like a watered garden* keeps popping into Cally's mind. What do you think it means?

5. Thinking of your own life, how do you evaluate Lizzy's "no regrets, no grudges," philosophy?

At the Stricker Homesite, Chapters 14-29

1. In what ways could the huge irrigation project be seen as a metaphor for what's happening in Cally's life? See more information about Milner Dam in the Historical Notes on HorseThief1898.blog.
2. In Chapter 13, Melody said, "I'm worn out, like a desert inside, all dry and dusty. I want to find some peace before I die." In what ways might she be experiencing the gift of "irrigation" of her heart with her family in Fish Haven?
3. How do you think Billy might have been impacted by the way he grew up?
4. In Chapter 15, Felicity observes that her mother has many old friends. Do you have "old" friends? Describe one positive experience with an "old" friend.
5. What unexpected treasures does Cally discover during her weeks at the Stricker Homesite? How might they relate to the persistent phrase, *Thou shalt be like a watered garden*?
6. What treasures did Cora find in Idaho?
7. How did you react to Cathleen's confession about Billy?
8. What do you see happening between Cally and Ryan?
9. What are five of your favorite things?
10. How did you respond to Flora's sister Florence?
11. Did you see Flora changing in any way?
12. The Art Show ends with unspeakable tragedy. How do you feel about that?

Charlie and Laoise, Chapters 11, 18, 22, 26

1. Charlie receives less attention than Cally in *Treasure Hunt 1904,* yet he discovers treasures as well. Describe his relationship with Cally in the first eight chapters. Did you think or hope they might get involved with each other romantically?
2. How did you respond to Charlie's reconnection with Laoise in chapter 11? What did you like or not like? Did anything surprise you?
3. In chapter 18 we get a feel for what Charlie and Laoise naturally share as well as how little they know about each

other; how new this relationship is, despite their strong attraction. How do you feel about their friendship at this point?

4. What might help Charlie heal from his sailing and storm traumas? What about Laoise's fear of childbirth?
5. As each honors their professional commitments, Charlie and Laoise become tired of goodbyes. What challenges do they face in nurturing their relationship that would be easier in today's world?
6. Her mother's health is a huge pressure on Laoise. How do you think she and Charlie can navigate that?
7. In chapter 26, we're brought into Charlie's deep desire for a home of his own. This parallels Cally's desire to feel more fully a part of her adopted family. How do the events of this book contribute to healing of their wounds and fulfillment of their needs and desires? What is still unfulfilled by the end of the book?
8. Were you surprised by the events in chapter 26? How do you feel about Charlie proposing only a month after he and Laoise reconnected?
9. Given Laoise's and Charlie's relationships and commitments, where do you think they might choose to live when they marry? What type of community do you think they need?

The Treasure, the Trial, and St. Joseph Hospital, Chapters 30-32 and the Epilogue

1. How do you feel about the way the treasure hunt ended?
2. How do you evaluate what the treasure hunt revealed about Uncle William?
3. What surprised you about the trial?
4. How would you describe Cally and Ryan's relationship at the end of the book?
5. What would you do in Sister Irmena's place regarding the judge's stipulation?
6. How do you envision *Thou shalt be like a watered garden* coming true in Cally's life?

With Appreciation

Community is important in *Treasure Hunt 1904,* as it was to me in researching and writing the book. I am profoundly grateful to each person who contributed, many of whom gave significant time to this project. My sister Marsha and her husband Vance of Meridian, Idaho hosted me, drove me around, helped me research, and gave me great ideas. Billy as the treasure was born from one of our discussions. It's been a delight to learn with them about southern Idaho and come to appreciate its particular beauty.

An amazing group of friends read the manuscript and helped me shape it into a much better book than I could have produced by myself. You each know the generous contribution you made, and I hope you are pleased with the result. A thousand thanks to Dave and Bonnie Liefer, Elaine Elliott, Rita Friesen, Karen Johnson, Elisabet Hogstrom, Janice Griswell, Meredith Dobson, and my husband David Kornfield for the many hours you invested to enrich this work.

My friends Timmy Podnar and Rhonda Herman were my very first readers, encouraging me that this story was worth pursuing. Thank you for your support and kindness. I look forward to reconnecting to my wider community, after burying myself in this project for many weeks. I believe my husband will be happy when I can think about other topics and begin to get our house and our life together back in order. Thanks, Dave, for your cheerfulness through it all, and for the discussions we're already having about Book Three of the Cally and Charlie Series! I look forward to traveling to Ireland with you!

I am grateful for the help of the Idaho Historical Society, particularly Angie K. Davis, who helped me understand Pocatello's history. I "met" Curtis W. Johnson, fifth-generation descendant of the Stricker family, through the Friends of Stricker, a volunteer organization whose mission is to support the Rock Creek Station and Stricker Homesite legacy, in cooperation with the Idaho Historical Society. Though we have not met in person, Curtis generously gave his approval of my fictional account in name of his family. I appreciate the support of various members of the Friends of Stricker and hope my story will encourage visitors to seek out the significant historical site they nurture and that I came to love through the eyes of the characters in my book.

I hope "Uncle William's" living descendants will enjoy and where necessary forgive my imaginative filling in of his historically missing years. Thank you, Will, for "loaning" your family's history to me! I hope in some way this book will help you value your family even more.

I am happy that the same talented team from EA Books who did such a beautiful job with *Horse Thief 1898* will again put together *Treasure Hunt 1904.* Marsha, Rebecca, Robin, Ardythe, and all of you: I love working with you wonderful and gifted people.

Finally, a shout out to my nephew Joel Griswell, who invested his artistic talents once again to create the cover image for this book. He quickly caught on to what I wanted and meticulously cut out the decrepit covered wagon to make it fit into beautiful southeast Idaho scenery. See more of Joel's work at TheSoundtrackGallery.com. If you want to hire Joel, contact him at joel.a.griswell@gmail.com.

Coming next . . .

FACING THE FAERIES, 1906

Book Three of the Cally and Charlie Series

Where is Billy?
What trouble is he getting into?
Will Cally finally be able to give him his inheritance from his father?

Will Laoise's mother be well enough to attend their wedding?

Where will Charlie and Laoise make their home? How will she handle the advent of a child?

How will Cally deal with her fear that the faeries are just waiting for her to return to Ireland to bring harm to the people she loves?

What will happen to Cally's relationship with Ryan and her growing love for frontier nursing as he becomes increasingly drawn to the dangerous cause of Irish liberation?

Where do Felicity and Brian fit into all this?

And what happens to Thomas when he gets more involved with Cousin Silas in the American South?

Book Three, ***Facing the Faeries 1906***

It's coming

Made in the USA
Middletown, DE
06 November 2022

14129143R00243